T0301148

# RED MENACE

**Joe Thomas** was born in Hackney in 1977. *Red Menace* follows *White Riot* as the second in a trilogy of novels set in East London, which will conclude with *True Blue.*

### Also by Joe Thomas

**THE UNITED KINGDOM TRILOGY**
*White Riot*

**THE SÃO PAULO QUARTET**
*Paradise City*
*Gringa*
*Playboy*
*Brazilian Psycho*

**STAND-ALONE**
*Bent*

# RED MENACE

## JOE THOMAS

First published in the United Kingdom in 2024 by Arcadia Books

Arcadia Books
An imprint of Quercus Editions Limited
Carmelite House
50 Victoria Embankment
London EC4Y 0DZ

An Hachette UK company

A CIP catalogue record for this book is available
from the British Library.

ISBN (HB) 978 1 52942 340 2
ISBN (Ebook) 978 1 52942 341 9

1 3 5 7 9 10 8 6 4 2

Typeset in Minion by MacGuru Ltd
Printed and bound in Great Britain by Clays Ltd, Elcograf S.p.A.

## Author's Note

Though set during certain factual events of 1985–1987, *Red Menace* is a work of fiction. Where possible, and in the context of a work of fiction, I have used the recorded words of real-life figures, in some instances weaving these into my own dialogues, though the interactions and situations these figures share with my characters are imagined. Acknowledgements follow the main text and include a comprehensive bibliography of all sources consulted and notes referencing all quoted material.

The Acknowledgements itemise instances where fact and fiction meet, what happened and what I have imagined; I provide information as to which is which – as far as that is possible in the context of a work of fiction – as well as where further information can be found. A guiding principle: the scenes in which real-life figures appear are fictionalised versions of real-life events, or fictional situations created to deliver factual information based on their testimony and footage. Where fictional characters appear in scenes set at recognisably historical events, these are fictionalised and used fictitiously. The police officers in the novel and their actions are entirely fictional. Whilst the bands, the music and the magazines in the text are real, my characters Suzi and Keith are fictional and therefore the portrayal of their work and their interactions with those real people and groups is wholly imagined. There was also no Jon Davies character in real life nor any Merv Michaels, nor anyone holding the roles those two characters have. Compliance Ltd, Excalibur Financial Solutions and the haulage company East London Logistics are invented companies, and whilst the LDDG is based on the LDDC, all of the interactions and behaviours of the fictional companies are invented by me and do not reflect any real-life actions or property transactions. In real life, Ron Bishop's role in the Docklands regeneration was carried out by Reg Ward, who did none of the things Ron does and is widely credited with the success of the real-life Docklands regeneration. Other principal and minor characters and their associates are fictional or used fictitiously.

Throughout the text, factual quotations are attributed and referenced in the notes. Quotations from the speeches and writings of well-known and less well-known figures, and from other texts pertaining to them, are a matter of the historical record and also cited in the notes; any conversations or interactions they have with my characters are entirely invented.

This novel is dedicated to the memory of Cynthia Jarrett.

'We had to fight the enemy without in the Falklands. We always have to be aware of the enemy within, which is much more difficult to fight and more dangerous to liberty'

**Mrs Thatcher**, speech to the 1922 Committee

# The Gift

## Christmas Eve 1973, Wapping –

*It's dark out, and cold –*

*But you're sitting in a parked car next to the river, the heating's roaring and it's prickly hot inside.*

*'Have a gander,' Alf says, gesturing at the water, the wasteland. 'Drink it in.'*

*'Not sure what I'm looking at, Alf.'*

*'All this land,' he declares, 'it's no one's.'*

*'Property is theft,' you suggest. 'All that?'*

*Alf laughs. 'Good one.' He grins. 'Anyway, it's land, not property,' he says, 'and with land, it ain't theft if you just take it.'*

*'Not sure I follow your logic there, Alf.'*

*'Adverse possession.'*

*'I don't know what adverse possession is, Alf.'*

*'You will.'*

*Alf points with one hand then points with the other hand. 'Tower Bridge. Greenwich.' He brings his hands together. 'Ours, now.'*

*'Once upon a time in the east,' you say.*

*Alf approves of that, nods. 'This is your patch.' He starts the engine. 'Happy Christmas.'*

*Wapping, you think: it's got a ring to it.*

# The Gab

## Late June, 1985, Stoke Newington, Hackney –

Parker examines Trevor and says –

'Tell me what happened.'

Trevor's pulling hard on a cigarette, jittery. Black eyes and broken nose –

'I was down The Line like I am a lot, you know,' Trevor says. 'I go down the Roots Pool Community Centre, you know that, play dominoes, have a drink, see people. Anyway, I was sitting on a wall on Sandringham Road, talking to a couple of friends.'

'They can vouch for this, can they, these friends?'

Trevor nods. He blows smoke through his broken nose. 'A dirty white hire van comes screeching to a stop and a handful of them pile out, Regional Crime Squad, easy to spot, leather jackets, jeans and trainers.'

'And they go straight for you, do they?'

Trevor nods. He grinds his cigarette out between thumb and forefinger, flicks it into the road –

'They take me by my arms and drag me into the back of the van and they take off all my clothes.'

'They mention your name at all, did they?'

Trevor shakes his head. 'They put a blanket over my head and pushed me into the nick and when I asked them why me they said someone had tipped them off that I was selling drugs.'

'Then what?'

'I told them I don't sell drugs and after a few hours they gave me back my clothes and told me I could go.'

'What did they say exactly?'

Trevor thinks about this. 'You can go, but we're going to get you.'

'We're going to get you?'

Trevor nods. 'That's what they said.'

'And you didn't recognise any of them?'

'New faces, all.'

'You're sure about that?'

'You remember who was there before, yeah?'

Parker nods. 'Course I do.'

'Well, so do I.'

'Fair point,' Parker concedes.

Parker offers Trevor another cigarette, lights it for him, gestures at his nose, his eyes –

'Do that, did they?'

Trevor makes a face. 'What do you think?'

'And since?'

Trevor shakes his head. 'Nothing.'

Parker nods, considers what Trevor's told him. 'This might be a good result, all told.'

Trevor laughs, incredulous. 'A good result?' Trevor indicates his nose, his eyes – 'How is this a good result?'

Parker smiles. 'Trust me, son. You'll see.'

# PART ONE
## *Dancing in the street*

July 1985

# *1*

## *Pigs*

13 July 1985, Live Aid Benefit Concert

Suzi Scialfa skipping up the steps on Wembley Way, helicopters buzzing, stalls setting up knick-knacks and flags flanking the tight corridor to the stadium, the sun fattening, the tower blocks shimmering, the smell of coffee and bacon –

*Live Aid.*

She fingers the pass she's got under her shirt. It's early, very early, but she's here on assignment and she wants to get the full flavour of the day. Her camera bag hangs casual off her shoulder; her boots click.

Besides, she's been told by some PR chancer that if she's not in by six thirty with her 'laminate', she might as well forget it, that's how busy it's going to be.

'Noel Edmonds is sorting the helicopters,' he laughed on the phone a few days before. 'Biggest airlift since the Falklands.'

Suzi raised her eyebrows at that.

'Elton and Spandau in their fatigues, giving it the conquering heroes.'

Suzi waited –

'I don't know if your mob will be on one, but if you can have a word with Weller, they'll need to be up early, all right?'

So just past six and Suzi's at the backstage entrance flashing her laminate, flashing a smile, inside now, circling the cavernous hallways, equipment piled up, black cases stacked, lighting rigs with blokes halfway up adjusting, fiddling, not a lot of noise, the odd clang of a spanner, the occasional shout, and she's round and following the signs to the artists' area, and it's empty but for a few caterers setting a breakfast table with coffee and tea and bacon sandwiches –

'You want one, love?'

Suzi nods, smiles, thanks the old dear, adds a spoonful of sugar to her tea, finds a plastic chair and a plastic table, opens her bag and pulls out her notebook, checks her watch, thinks – Keith will be here in about an hour with her mob:

The Style Council.

They've been part of it for a while already, The Style Council, even abroad with them, not too long ago.

She smiles now at how that all came about.

'We are not going to bloody Poland, Keith,' she'd laughed.

'We bloody are!' Keith insisted. 'Weller's asked for us personally.'

'To go to Poland?'

Keith's head in the fridge.

'They're shooting the video there for the new single. Socialism, love.'

'I know about Poland, Keith.'

Keith, triumphant, holding aloft two cans of lager. 'Well then.'

'I don't know if I want to go to Poland with The Style Council is my point.'

'It's a great song,' Keith added solemnly.

'I don't doubt it.'

'Come on, Suze, imagine – the Iron Curtain.'

Suzi sighed.

'It's a statement. Don't you want to be involved?'

On his hands and knees then, Keith crawled with the lagers towards the kitchen table where Suzi sat.

She smiled. 'You wally.'

Keith opened the cans, handed her one. 'Let's drink to it.'

'We'll see,' Suzi said. 'But I'm not promising anything.'

Keith grinned. 'You're a heartbreaker, girl.'

'I know exactly what I am,' Suzi winked.

And here she is, again –

Live Aid.


Parker's propped up in bed with a cup of tea and a spliff, his new bird Carolyn cooking them breakfast in her knickers, singing along to his favourite Ann Peebles LP *Straight From the Heart* about how she's ninety-nine pounds of goodness, of soul, and he smiles and yells –

'Get in here, brown sugar!'

And she appears in the doorway, a plastic Lea & Perrins apron loose from her neck, a wooden spoon in her hand and she says –

'Like a black girl should.'

Parker laughs. 'Jagger's not on for ages, darling.'

He turns on the portable in the bedroom and there's some bequiffed ponce in braces and T-shirt interviewing Paul Young.

He yells, 'This new telly your mate sorted is perfect.'

'I'll tell him!'

Parker sips his tea, has a toke. Yeah, perfect, he thinks.

Apparently, this geezer Rodney, he's been flogging them for weeks, specially to watch the big concert in bed.

Ann Peebles quietens down, and Parker's breakfast appears.

'Lose the apron, gorgeous,' he instructs.

He's handed a tray, and Carolyn climbs in after it, lifts a piece of toast –

'What's all this?'

She grins. 'You share your bed, you share your breakfast, big boy.'

'To be fair,' Parker says, 'there's a lot of it.'

He forks sausage, dips toast in beans.

Carolyn nods at the TV set. 'Who's this?'

'Paul Young.'

'Who's Paul Young?'

'It's a good question,' Parker says. 'I'm not convinced Paul Young himself really knows who Paul Young is.'

'You're funny.'

Parker grinning: 'I'm here all week.'

They eat, her legs warm on his, her skin soft, a prelude, he's thinking, he's thinking all morning in bed watching telly –

He's also thinking about the meeting he had the day before, with his runner, Noble.

Parker looking on as Detective Constable Patrick Noble read the transcript of Parker's most recent conversation with Trevor from a week or so before.

They've been using Trevor for a couple of years now, since Noble got those photos of him muling drugs and cash for DCs Rice and Cole at Stoke Newington nick, and Parker – Trevor's mate, or so Trevor thought – laid out to Trevor quite what was what and that Trevor was now working for them.

Trevor's situation was simple: Rice and Cole picked him up on a stop-and-search, took him in, left him in a cell for a few hours, threatened him with possession and intent, then showed him two bags, one big, one small.

Trevor told them he didn't deal drugs.

They told him that if he wanted to pursue that line of defence, they'd put the bigger bag on him.

And if Trevor could be a little more cooperative, then they'll make the little bag go away and Trevor will work for them.

And if Trevor didn't fancy that, they'd put another bag on his little sister and get her working one of their other lines.

Trevor's been treading pretty carefully last couple of years, so what Parker tells Noble happened to him is a bit of a surprise.

Noble jabbing at the bottom of the page –

'You can go now, but we're going to get you.'

Noble adding, 'Those exact words don't half ring a bell.'

Parker nodded. Colin Roach. Death by shotgun wound in the foyer of Stoke Newington nick –

Noble said, 'So Rice and Cole have been moved on? He didn't know any of these faces?'

Parker shook his head. 'No one he recognised, and no one recognised him.'

Noble nodding. 'I'll see what I can find out.'

Parker personally reckons it's a merry-go-round to protect the firm within a firm – in other words, you don't stay too long in one place, and nothing sticks.

There's a word for what Parker is now: spycop.

And sometimes it's difficult to know if he's spying on the cops or the robbers. Noble's got him chasing about all over the gaff.

Undercover, Special Demonstration Squad, Special Branch – no one but Noble knowing what he does –

Parker reads the annual reports, knows the party line:

The Special Demonstration Squad provides intelligence, unavailable from other sources, concerning groups whose main overt actions are demonstrated, peacefully or otherwise, at street level in pursuance of particular aims or extreme political ideologies.

He's part of the covert activities inspired, it's been said – and Parker's laughed whenever he's heard this – by the Chinese philosopher Sun Tzu writing in the 4th century BC:

What is called foreknowledge cannot be elicited from spirits nor from Gods, nor by analogy with past events, nor from calculations. It must be obtained from men who know the 'enemy' situation.

Noble nodded, no doubt wondering if he could find anything out, said, 'Keep Trevor sweet, and I'll get you some context when I can.'

Parker nodded. 'I think I've got another in, guv.'

'You on the level?'

'It's perfect,' Parker told him. 'She's on the committee. It's a way in.'

'You be careful, son.'

'Aren't I always?'

'What's her name?'

'Carolyn.'

'Carolyn?'

'Like Aretha's sister.'

'That what she told you, is it?'

'Pure class, guv.'

And she is, Parker thinks, she's pure class.

Sometimes, he reflects, living a lie ain't too much trouble at all.

He surveys the scene: the fried breakfast, the classy girlfriend, the cosy portable, the sweet tea –

*Where did it all go wrong, eh?* He smiles.

*Fleet Street. The pub empty, must be a first. You nod at the barman and point at one of the pumps.*

'Coming right up.'

*You hear the door, and your man comes through it, gestures at a table and sits down.*

'Make it two, will you?'

*You hand over a note and take the drinks over.*

'This is a joke, is it, meeting here?' *you ask.*

'He wants to see you.'

'He as in him.'

*Your man nods.*

'And we're meeting here?'

'It's empty. All the hacks are up at Wembley, or at home in bed. No one's doing nothing else today, mate, you know that.'

'Drink up,' *you say.*

*Your man shakes his head.* 'No, you sit tight here, and I'll give you the nod when he's ready.'

'In here?'

'There'll be a car, outside.'

*Your man stands.* 'You sit tight, all right?'

*You nod. You go back to the bar. The TV is on. You wave your glass for another.*

'It's just starting now.' *The barman points at the screen.* 'Here we go.'

*You lean on the bar and study the picture and you hear the words:*

IT'S TWELVE NOON IN LONDON, SEVEN A.M. IN PHILADEL-PHIA, AND AROUND THE WORLD IT'S TIME FOR LIVE AID.

*You take your pint. Walking away you say,* 'Turn it down, will you.'

Jon Davies pushes a heaving shopping trolley across the small car park in the Safeway at Stamford Hill. His boy, Joe, dragging his feet alongside, eight years old in a few months, dressed in full West Ham away kit, socks pulled up, nose deep in his copy of *Shoot!*. Jon's daughter, Lizzie, not far off her second birthday, sitting in the trolley's kids' seat and saying something about the trees and the birds, and Jon thinking –

There aren't any here.

Jon loads the boot with the shopping, encourages the boy to get in.

He wrestles his little girl into her car seat as she hums and sings, the clip's stuck, always bloody stuck, never quite long enough, or she's never quite small enough, and then the click and the relief, and the boy's in, and Jon breathes out, slowly, opens the driver's door and puts on the radio and –

IT'S TWELVE NOON IN LONDON, SEVEN A.M. IN PHILADEL-PHIA, AND AROUND THE WORLD IT'S TIME FOR LIVE AID.

'If we're quick,' he tells the boy, 'you won't miss Status Quo.'

'Dad.' The boy shaking his head.

Jon smiles. Good lad.


Suzi snapping backstage.

Paul Young sitting in a cabin, receiving guests. Paula Yates fluttering about, beautiful, looking wry as Phil Collins asks Paul Young to sign something for his kids.

Phil Collins is going, 'One to Simon saying something like your dad's great.'

Laughing, Paula Yates says, 'I love all these instructions.'

'To Simon,' Phil Collins repeats, 'anything you want.'

Paul Young gets a pen out.

Phil saying, 'Can you sign my trousers?' and laughing, on his heels, awkward.

Paul Young in a Byron shirt, billowing cuffs and a V-neck almost at his belly button.

'How old are they now?'

'He's eight and she's twelve.' Phil handing Paul something else to sign. 'Joely.' Phil scratching his head, fiddling with his hair. 'J-O-E-L-Y.'

Someone pointing a camera at the pair of them, filming. Suzi stands back.

'What's this then?' Paul Young asks.

The pair of them pose. Phil Collins says, 'This is happiness backstage.'

Raising their eyebrows, mock flirting, winking at the camera.

The Hard Rock Cafe has recreated its London restaurant as a tent, and this is where everyone seems to be. There's a lot of refreshment, Suzi notes, and it's not yet eleven o'clock, buckets on the bar filling with cash donations. A brisk trade at the toilet doors.

Suzi feels a warmth on her neck. 'What's a nice girl like you doing in a place like this?'

She turns and kisses Keith. 'Bloody hell, love, you pace yourself, OK?'

'It's not my fault.' Keith grinning. 'I've palled up with the Quo's sound guy.'

'Course you have.'

'They're on before us, so I have to.' Keith still grinning, he can barely contain himself. 'Coordinate,' he says, cracking up.

'What's so funny?'

'They missed the line-up, you know, Charlie and Di.'

'Who did?'

'The Quo.'

Suzi's laughing too now.

She saw the royal couple shaking hands with the haircuts and the costumes, the jackets and the trousers, the cigarettes and the deference, in an orderly queue, Brian May towering above, a pale blue suit and bird's nest hair –

'They wanted to go,' Keith says, 'but Francis has to get through his warm-up, his scales, his breathing, tunings and whatnot. They're on at twelve, so there wasn't time.'

Keith now red and bent double.

'Punchline, love, come on.'

'Well, let's just say this.' Keith's tapping his nose. 'They're all definitely feeding the world today, if you know what I mean. It's a white one, Suze, snow all over the gaff. Do they know it's Christmas?'

'It looks like *you* know.'

Keith nodding, seriously. 'A man's got to do, love.'

'Well, take it easy.' Tapping her watch. 'Don't let Weller catch you.'

Keith nodding, leaning in, conspiratorial. 'Everyone's wired, Suze,' he says. 'Nervous as anything. Weller's jittery as fuck.' He pauses. 'You know who's not nervous?'

'Francis Rossi.'

'Yeah!' Keith delighted. 'The Quo don't give a fuck, they're cool as you like. Honestly, love, they are the only ones who aren't nervous.'

Suzi laughs. She looks at her watch. 'What time are you on?'

'Twelve nineteen.' He sniffs. 'They're saying they don't care what time you go on, but you go off when you bloody should. They'll pull the plug.'

'I'll be there, love, you know I will.'

Keith smiles. He takes a step back from Suzi and windmills an arm, ushering Nik Kershaw past, who smiles and winks. The fake pot plants are sweating in the heat, no breeze, lots of big shirts sticking to skinny bodies.

'Look around,' Keith offers. 'It's like punk never happened. It's all very cordial. Even George is being nice.'

'That's a turn-up,' Suzi says.

'Yeah –' Keith laughing again – 'he said to Weller, "Don't be a wanker all your life, have a day off."'

'I love you,' Suzi says. 'Now be good.'

Keith bouncing away; Suzi snapping.


Parker pops out to get the papers.

'Blink of an eye!' he shouts as he leaves, Carolyn soaking in a fragrant bath, radio tuned to the build-up –

He's into his preferred newsagent on Stoke Newington Church Street in moments.

'All right, Sanjay?' He addresses the proprietor from the entrance. 'How's tricks?'

'Can't complain!'

'These prices, mate.' Parker grins. 'You bloody can't.'

He selects a tabloid and a broadsheet.

At the counter, Sanjay hands him his usual – rolling tobacco and Rizla paper.

Parker hands Sanjay a tenner. Sanjay hands Parker a fistful of coins.

The radio's on, quietly, and Parker nods at it. 'Cricket?'

'Of course!'

'Good man,' Parker says. 'Gower's a hero.'

Outside, he walks towards Clissold Park for a hundred yards or so and enters a phone box. He feeds ten-pence pieces and dials Detective Constable Noble's home number for their daily briefing.

'Hello?'

'All right, Lea, darling?' Parker says. 'Your fella about, is he?'

Parker listens as Lea yells for Noble.

She doesn't know what their relationship is; far as she's concerned Parker is an irritant to her domestic bliss and a bad influence on her newly domesticated life partner.

Noble says, 'All right, son?'

'Yes, guv. You?'

'Can't complain.'

'It's a popular sentiment.'

'Listen, nothing new?'

'Nothing.'

Noble clears his throat. 'I've got something on what we talked about last time, all right?'

'You mean young Trevor's predicament?'

'I do. The new faces at Stoke Newington you mentioned. Trevor's right for once. Rice and Cole have been moved on, and there's a whole gang of debutants in situ.'

'Right. Makes sense.'

'Hard to know why exactly, but it seems there were a few rumours and misgivings about the integrity of the unit doing the rounds and the simplest way of kyboshing them was a change of personnel.'

Parker thinks: exactly what I said.

He says, 'What about Williams?'

DI Williams who headed up Stoke Newington but no word for a while. Before that, worked with Noble back in the late seventies on the Race Crime Initiative –

'Unclear,' Noble says. 'You might want to look into that. Or not.'

Parker nods. 'Anything else?'

'Take the day off, enjoy the music.'

'What a line manager.'

'One thing though,' Noble says. 'Wapping.'

'Wapping?'

'Keep your ears open.'

Parker nods. 'This part of the official job description?'

'Nah, the other one.'

'Right,' Parker says. 'Will do. Wapping. Can't give me any more than that?'

'It's all I got.'

'Little way from the manor, isn't it?'

Noble breathes. 'That, son, is the point.'

'Got it. You got the telly on then?'

Noble laughs. 'It's a bit different to Victoria Park.'

Meaning Rock Against Racism, 1978 and all that, Parker knows all about Noble's little counterculture dalliance –

He was there himself, just a big kid –

Parker smiles. 'Have a good one.'

Back down to Church Street and he considers all this.

Parker has been treading a very fine line for a few years now.

Officially, he's a spycop, part of the Special Demonstration Squad, headed up by 'Old Bill' Stewart and run by Noble who's got himself a cushy number as a team of one reporting only to Chief Inspector Young.

Parker is, officially, aggressively infiltrating activist groups in Hackney, including the Roach Family Support Committee, which he has been a part of since 1983, the year Colin Roach died in the foyer of Stoke Newington police station and it was called suicide when it appeared plain as day that it was not.

Officially, Parker's job is to provide information on activities pertaining to the RFSC – and any other activist groups in the area.

*Unofficially*, Parker is on the sniff for anything dodgy out of Stoke Newington nick. And now there's been an all change, it might well be back to square one.

Noble's been building a case against Stoke Newington for a couple of years now, but the timing's never quite right. And Parker doesn't know if anyone's listening, Noble keeps that part to himself – for Parker's own good, so he says – but it does mean Parker can't do much except what he's told.

He's been involved with some low-level dealers, helped out here and there, facilitated, not quite crossing any irrevocable lines –

Trevor, of course, but really, Parker's only been steering him, not getting involved *per se* –

That's the detail: don't do too much. Deniability.

This new thing that's happened to Trevor does feel like a step up, an intensification of what they're doing in Stoke Newington.

Parker wonders what the best move is, Trevor-wise. If they're scooping up people off the streets and fitting them up in the station, it suggests to Parker that it might be about arrest numbers, showing the world they're doing their jobs, massaging the figures and whatnot, simple stuff.

Which, Parker thinks, means they're colluding with the *actual* dealers, or, to use a phrase, robbing Peter to pay Paul, or, more succinct: you don't nick your business partner.

Either way, he wonders about young Trevor, wonders what his responsibility to him, or anyone else, really is –

As he jumps the stairs back up to his front door, he also wonders if Wapping, whatever it is, might speed things along a bit, and it's about time.

Truth is, this lovely new bird of his is pure neighbourhood, friends and family all over the shop, and this is not unhelpful for either of his roles, in an official, or otherwise, capacity.

Though it doesn't stop him thinking:

*Hang about, I really like this one.*

He turns his key, pushes open the door and hears:

IT'S TWELVE NOON IN LONDON, SEVEN A.M. IN PHILADEL-PHIA, AND AROUND THE WORLD IT'S TIME FOR LIVE AID.

Carolyn perched on the sofa in dressing gown and head towel, rubbing cream into legs stretched out on the coffee table.

Parker drops the papers down next to her.

She hands him a freshly poured glass of lager.

Parker nods at the telly. 'I didn't know you liked Status Quo.'

*The pub isn't any busier since your man left –*

*And no sign of him coming back any time soon.*

*You pick up a newspaper that's been left on the bar, study the cricket reports.*

*Halfway through the third test at Trent Bridge. England with a very decent first innings score. Gooch got a few, then Gower made a magnificent 166. Australia have started well, and the pitch looks sound, so you think, a draw then, and not a great deal of point putting any money on it.*

*You admire David Gower. Elegant, makes it all look so easy, that thing about time, about how the best players of any sport have a bit more of it.*

*You signal the barman; he pours another.*

*He brings it over to the table, shrugging. 'It's not as if there's anyone else here to serve.'*

*Like David Gower, you've got a bit more time yourself.*

*Status Quo droning on and on about some Caroline.*

*You shake your head, focus on your tabloid –*

*On this day, you read, in 1881, Pat Garrett shoots Billy the Kid.*

*On this day, in 1960, the US Democratic Party nominates John F. Kennedy for presidential candidate.*

*In 1967, on this day, twenty-seven people die in the Newark race riots.*

*In 1935, Emperor Haile Selassie rejects the claim that Abyssinia falls under the Italian sphere of influence.*

*Twenty years later, on this day, 13 July, Ruth Ellis is the last woman in England to be executed.*

*Full of interesting facts, your tabloid.*

*You look out at Fleet Street in the sun and think:*

How many of these facts were written in this very saloon bar?

*You fold the paper, return it. One thing he won't need, is another tabloid.*


*Mildenhall Road, Lower Clapton.*

Jackie's in the front garden nattering with next door when Jon and the kids pile out of the car.

Jackie shooing the kids through the door and down the stairs –

Jon, weighed down with shopping bags, smiling at Mrs Singh, kissing Jackie, saying, 'You got the telly on today, Mrs Singh?'

'We've got them all on, Jon,' she laughs. 'All three of them!'

She throws her hands in the air as if to say, Jon thinks, *we're all doing our bit.*

Jackie smiles. 'It's all ready for you, love.'

'Great.'

'You better get a wriggle on, Jon, that group you like are next.'

Jon lifts the shopping bags and shrugs at Mrs Singh. 'See you out the back later, then.'

'Save me a sausage,' Mrs Singh replies, laughing.

Jon's in the door and down the stairs and into the kitchen and he hears Status Quo on the portable TV that is propped in the window, screen facing out into the garden, where Jon's children now stand and gawp.

He dumps the bags on their – fairly new – round white dining table, pulls charcoal from one of them, opens the freezer, removes a can of – now very cold – Special Brew, pops the tab, pours a significant measure into a small glass and goes, Ahh.

Outside, on the small patch of grass that is circled by concrete, a rusty barbecue awaits Jon's expertise.

'Give me a hand, would you, son?'

The boy's hand is rummaging in a large bag of crisps, and he is, Jon notes, transfixed by Status Quo.

'Never mind,' Jon says.

He pours the charcoal into the drum, he squirts some sort of fluid all over it, fluid recommended by the man in Safeway – 'Idiot-proof,' the man told Jon, nodding at the boy. 'A child could manage it.' – and he drops a lit match.

It catches and takes, there are flames and smoke, and he's got fifteen minutes or so now for the charcoal to grey and the embers to settle.

He polishes off his measure of Special Brew, pours himself another, and he lowers himself onto his deckchair just as Paul Weller bounces on to the stage in red sweatshirt and white trousers, and the boy punches Jon's shoulder and goes, 'Yes, Dad!'

Jon grins.

The weekend before, Jon and his son cycled across Millfields Park and then down the canal towards Hackney Wick.

Football matches on the marshes to the left, graffiti on the towpath, wasteland and abandoned barges, rubbish thickening the scum on the water, bubbling, foaming like a foul casserole, shapes in the darkness under the bridges scurrying about, past the turning to Victoria Park, and down past Stratford, alongside the A12, under the Bow Road roundabout on the High Street, right onto Limehouse Cut and down towards the Basin, narrow path and tower blocks, wheels crunching through the gravel, youngsters sprawled on the banks, the air thick with smoke, walkers in determined poses, knapsacks and boots, and they reached the Basin, and they stopped, and Jon pointed east.

'Look over there,' he told his son.

'I can't see anything, Dad. There's nothing there.'

He was right, of course, there isn't really anything there.

*Jon* could see the buildings at Greenwich, the park stretching up and south. *Jon* realised the Thames Barrier wasn't much further along – they went to have a peer at it only the summer before. Jon, scanning west-east, located Wapping, Heron Quays, Surrey Quays, the Isle of Dogs and Millwall dock – but he *knows* they're there, is the point, and he knows what's come of them.

And what's next.

'There soon will be.'

'What do you mean, Dad?'

'What can you see? Look carefully.'

'A lot of space. A lot of concrete. Some cranes?'

Jon smiled.

'So they're building something?'

'They're going to.'

'It's a bit ugly, isn't it?'

Jon laughed. 'Your grandad wouldn't like to hear that, son.'

'Why not?'

'He worked not far away, most of his life, his dad too.'

'Grandad Ray?'

Jon nodded. Jackie's old man.

You always know when someone's worked on the docks their whole life, Jon thought, it's obvious.

They bloody tell you.

'Why are you showing me this, Dad?'

Jon considered the question. 'One day, you'll remember this place as it is now, and you'll see it as it will be, and you'll think, crikey, that's changed.'

The boy nodded, unconvinced.

'Your grandad Ray and his dad – and his dad, more than likely – all made their living working the docks, but it all fell apart a few years ago and it's not a job you can do anymore.'

'Why not?'

'There are machines, son, great big shipping containers.'

'Doesn't that mean you'd need *more* men?'

Jon laughed, kicked his pedal into place. 'Come on, let's do the circle.' He pointed down another tributary out the Basin. 'That'll take us right up to Victoria Park. I'll get you an ice cream.'

'Race you, Dad!'

And the boy was off.

The real reason they were there is Jon's latest work project:

The London Docklands Development Group and the changes to the lives of the people of Tower Hamlets, Newham and Hackney that will occur as the area is regenerated.

A call for a borough solicitor from one of several councils, and Jon seconded out to Tower Hamlets on account of his faultless handling of the National Front planning dispute in Hackney, which began in 1978 and was resolved in 1980.

Jon's job, ostensibly, is to protect council residents' interests, to work *with* the LDDG and ensure that the development as a whole – and planning applications more specifically – are transparent and have a social benefit for the long-term council residents –

As he watched his son weaving and bobbing ahead, through Mile End and back up to Bow, he thought about his brief, which in summary amounts to:

Monitor the London Docklands Development Group and directly and indirectly associated land and property investment in Hackney, Tower Hamlets and Newham.

To ensure fair practice.

It's a big lot of nothing, of nowhere, he thought, scanning the wasteland, the empty basins, the dried-up canals, the rotting warehouses, the docks –

A big lot of nothing now, the docks.

Regardless of all this, the Victoria Park ice creams were a lovely result.

Now, The Style Council on the telly, the boy resting his arm on Jon's shoulder, Jon Special Brew-buzzing, and Monday morning – his first day in this new legal team – feels a very long way away indeed.

Jackie through the kitchen and out the back door, wafting at her nose, pointing at the barbecue.

'That under control?'

Jon indicates the screen, mouths the words to the song: 'You're the best thing ever happened to me.'

Jackie shaking her head, smiling.

'Dad,' says the boy.

'Fair point,' Jon smiles.

Keith singing along to Weller and Dee, winking at Suzi standing to the right of the sound desk, stage left: 'You're the best thing ever happened to me.'

Doing all the gestures, giving her the eye, mooning.

She's loving it.

Dee looks amazing in her white top and white trousers, black belt and white headband.

The sunglasses, cool as anything, and only wearing them as she was so nervous, she botched her make-up.

'I threw up a minute ago,' she laughed, Suzi trying to keep Dee's head still and concentrate with the eyeliner, up the ramp to the stage. 'When Quo came off, Geldof told them they'd just played to two billion people. Rossi said, "I'm glad you didn't tell me that before." That's when I threw up.'

Suzi's not sure about Mick Talbot's boating jacket. Aside from the Henley regatta look, it's bloody roasting hot up there.

A sea of faces, sweating in the sun, it's the only way she can describe it; pink and white skin, melting.

She edges closer and snaps:

Weller's back – sharp red top, white trousers, tight hair – out into the crowd and up into the seats, up, up –

Just framing a helicopter's descent.

The song's going well, it sounds great, and though it might not be the most obvious opening number, the crowd that Suzi can see are swaying and smiling, doing that seaweed-in-the-stream, eyes-closed lovers' dance –

It's fair to say that Paul Weller has changed Suzi and Keith's lives.

Keith's regular gig, Suzi as unofficial band journalist and photographer to go alongside her staff job at *The Face*.

Respectable, they are now.

After her dad passed away, at the end of 1983, she did what she promised him she'd do with her inheritance:

Bought them a flat.

A flat in the Leopold Buildings on Columbia Road.

Keith likes the style and the facade:

'Historic tenement chic, love,' he said. 'Good old Maggie.'

'If you have been a council tenant for at least three years,' Mrs Thatcher told the country in 1980, 'you will have the right, by law, to buy your house.'

Of course, she and Keith hadn't lived there three weeks, but it didn't impede the sale.

'We're in danger of becoming yuppies,' Keith is wont to remark.

It's a change from Stoke Newington; they're not in Hackney anymore, technically, but Tower Hamlets, with its forbidding association with the docks and its flirtatious proximity with the unsavoury City of London –

The song goes on, Paul Weller teasing out that lovely guitar line, Dee dancing, harmonising: she does the heavy vocal lifting live, Keith always says. Suzi can see why: she's talented.

Camelle Hinds playing bass with his shirt unbuttoned and flapping about, which, tacky as it looks, is sensible given the heat.

The security team in front of the stage spraying the audience with water. The audience, cheering, signalling for more.

Gary Wallis shaking and tapping congas and tambourines. He's wearing, Suzi notes, a pair of shorts that don't look much roomier than Speedos. White socks pulled up; pastel squares above white on his high-buttoned polo shirt –

What Paul Weller has done for Suzi, too, is show her how to channel activism, make music political. The video for 'Shout to the Top' all about the miners' strike.

The packaging of the single. A photo of Stacey Smith, Paul Young's model girlfriend, on the front, and on the back:

NO! TO ABOLITION OF THE GLC & THE LOCAL COUNCILS

YES! TO THE THRILL OF THE ROMP

YES! TO THE BENGALI WORKERS ASSOCIATION

YES! TO A NUCLEAR-FREE WORLD

YES! TO ALL INVOLVED IN ANIMAL RIGHTS

YES! TO FANZINES

YES! TO BELIEF

Suzi feels engaged and involved, active.

It nags at her that she no longer is, at a grassroots level.

Looking at the 72,000 people in front of her, all of them parting with twenty-five quid to be here, she thinks: how many of you could have helped the Roach Family Support Committee?

And then: the guilt that she stopped helping them herself.

How many of the bands backstage would have played a benefit for Colin Roach?

No one even bothered finding out.

Suzi snapping –

Paul Weller saying, 'This shows what can happen when people get together, and this song is dedicated to that spirit,' and off they go into 'Internationalists'.

Suzi skirts the stage, aims her lens at the crowd.

Someone waving a solitary red balloon.

Yellow-shirted security keeping up with the water.

Fists in the air, a lot of jumping up and down.

A small island of photographers who don't have the right laminate.

Coming off the crowd: a white heat.

A couple of Union Jack flags, TV monitors, and the main sound desk halfway back, in what looks like a bunker –

The turning point, Suzi thinks, was Poland, that was when they became an integral part of the Councillors.

There to shoot the video for 'Walls Come Tumbling Down!'

The alcoholism they saw there was terrifying. Everyone drank anything they could.

In the hotel at breakfast, Steve White told her, 'They might have cornflakes and milk but no sugar. Then the next morning, there'll be milk and sugar but no cornflakes. Something is missing all the time.'

It was supposed to be about socialism, but there were troops on the street.

Back home, Paul Weller told Suzi: 'People always hold up the Eastern Bloc as examples that socialism doesn't work, but it wasn't socialism, so that argument is redundant. Socialism doesn't mean everyone should have nothing, it means everyone should have something.'

A very good video, though.

Miming on stage in a club playing to grim-faced working men, frolicking about on trams, adverts for communist factory production cars, statues of soldiers, the Councillors in their long European coats and their haircuts, a full-colour contrast –

And now, on the hottest day of the year, playing the song at the biggest concert in history.

Steve White on the drums, in shorts and white, high-buttoned polo shirt, tongue hanging out, grinning wildly.

'"Walls Come Tumbling Down!" has that unashamed message of optimism,' Steve White told Suzi in an interview for a feature in *The Face*. 'Unity is powerful. I thought, "Yes!" When we did the demo, Paul said, "It's got to be a balls-out soul tune. I want it to be very on-beat like a Motown thing. When you do the drum fills, think of Keith Moon."'

Suzi smiles, her Keith waves, taps his watch –

Suzi thinking about something Bob Geldof said: 'If I have a choice between Steel Pulse or Wham! on this show, I'll take Wham!'

Parker and Carolyn saunter to Clissold Park, arm in arm, nice little buzz going, passing a can of cold lager back and forth, listening to the concert through the open windows of every car and every home they pass –

Loved up.

'This "Global Jukebox" they're all on about,' Carolyn says, 'not exactly very *global*, is it?'

There's a white heat hanging above the cars, throbbing above the street, spreading through the estates –

'I was there in Victoria Park, nineteen seventy-eight,' Parker says. 'Those Rock Against Racism blokes might have been smug, earnest cunts, but they had one thing right.'

Carolyn smiling, Parker notes, as they pass the fire station, dead leaves rolling on the concrete, browning in the sun, cracking –

'And that was?'

'Every gig they did, it was a black band that headlined, that went on last.'

'I know what headlined means.'

'Top of the bill, too, I mean.' Parker stops. He's grinning. 'On the posters and whatnot. Everyone remembers The Clash headlining Victoria Park. But Steel Pulse went on after them.'

'I wasn't there.'

'A lot of people who were there *weren't* there, darling, if you get my drift.'

She takes his hand, nudges her fingers between his. He lets her. With his thumb, he teases the gold ring she wears, the soft flesh of her palm –

'Steel Pulse in their outfits doing "Ku Klux Klan". That was something.'

'I'd have thought you'd be sniffing glue at the back.'

'Charming,' Parker laughs. 'Point is, a black band on last in principle, that's activism in its own way. There's a message in that.' Parker points at an open window, The Style Council falling out of it. 'What's the message in this?'

'White Jesus.'

Parker swoons, laughs. 'Good one.'

They pass the library, the town hall, reach the edge of the park.

The sound of tennis balls being hit, kids tearing about the place, dogs yapping and growling, chatter and corks, radios echoing –

Carolyn points at the off-licence over the road. 'I'll pop in and get something, shall I?'

'What are they expecting exactly, your family?'

Carolyn smiles, digs Parker in the ribs. 'White Jesus,' she says.

Parker watches her cross the road and go into the shop.

He follows. He's smiling as he sits down on the low wall that fringes the churchyard on the corner. In the park, beyond the gates, the tallest trees sway reluctantly.

There's a lull in the traffic, a quiet.

He can hear birds and splashing, the thud of heavy bass in a slow-moving car. He looks up at the – what's the word? The spire? The steeple? – up and up, dizzying it is, spiralling up and away from him.

He shuts his eyes –

When he opens them, two teenagers – gawky-looking black lads in wide lapels and flared corduroys, drinking cheap cider from a plastic bottle – are ambling past.

Parker's giving them a nod and a wink when an unmarked van pulls up alongside.

The back door opens and three white men in leather jackets and jeans, white trainers, jump out.

Regional Crime Squad, Parker thinks. Then he thinks: these lads?

In moments, the plain clothes have them lined up against the wall next to where Parker is sitting.

'Top of the morning to you all,' Parker decides.

One of the leather jackets turns. 'You best fuck off, mate.'

Parker nodding, standing, weighing this up. 'I think I'm all right here, mate, thanks.'

The two lads shaking, terrified. The leather jackets patting them down –

'You two ain't from round here.'

The lads shaking their heads.

'Where then?'

'Tottenham,' one of the boys says.

'Tottenham where?'

'The Farm.' The same boy, shaking, looking down.

The plain clothes laughing, shaking their heads –

'Course you are.'

Parker calls out, 'Don't let their hands anywhere near your pockets, boys.'

'What did you say?'

Parker smiles. 'Plant is what I said. Want me to spell it for you?'

First leather jacket steps towards Parker. 'You're lucky I don't nick you for loitering.'

'I am lucky.'

The other two have, by now, stopped their frisking.

Parker hears, 'Nothing, guv.'

The black lads shrugging, watching as well.

The hiss of a bus, the rattle of a motorcycle, the whine of a car alarm –

A breeze in the trees, whistling.

Parker puts his face close to the face of this plain-clothes officer of the law.

He speaks, quietly. 'And who's your guvnor, son? That fat Welsh bastard Williams still about? Or now Rice and Cole have done one it's someone new entirely?'

Nothing happens for a moment.

Then: Carolyn's voice – surprised, panicked – shouting, 'Shaun!' and again, 'Shaun!'

One of the black lads turns, eyes wide –

Parker hears a bottle smash, Carolyn running up the road –

He leans in closer. 'Leave it, all right? Just jog on.'

In his eyes, Parker notes the plain-clothes officer's uncertainty, and it's enough.

'Easy does it,' Parker adds, thinking: was it you lot that pulled young Trevor –

Then: the plain clothes back in the van, pulling away, exhaust belching. The black lads laughing, open-mouthed, jostling each other, pointing at Parker.

Carolyn hugging one of the lads, asking him if he's all right, his face in her hands, asking him, 'Are you all right, are you all right?'

'Thanks to him, yeah.'

Parker puts his arm around Carolyn. 'I think he's all right.'

Carolyn looks up. 'You did this? You helped them?'

'All in a day's work.'

Then: Carolyn slaps the lad round the back of the head. 'Pussyhole,' she says. 'What have I told you? I ought to beat you.'

'We didn't do nothing,' the lad protests.

'They didn't do, darling.' Parker nods up the road. 'You know what this lot are like.'

Carolyn's nodding now, furiously nodding, biting at her nails –

She hits the lad again. 'You scared me.' Then to Parker, hand on his arm. 'Thank you.'

The lad says, 'You know this hero then, do you?'

Carolyn sighs. 'This is my cousin, Shaun.'

Parker extends a hand. 'Delighted to make your acquaintance, young man.'

Shaun bows, his pal giggling, whooping.

Parker pulls a folded wad of notes from his pocket, hands it to Shaun. 'Now you take yourself and your mate to the offie and buy whatever it was your lovely cousin dropped as she raced up the road to save you.'

Shaun grins.

Parker taking Carolyn by the hand, walking away –

'And there's a bottle of Strongbow on me in that,' he calls out over his shoulder.

The two lads crack up laughing.

Parker thinking, *nobody knows what I'm doing, nobody knows a thing about what I'm doing.*

Nobody knows. Nobody knows but Noble and Old Bill Stewart.

Her arm around him, Carolyn says, 'Fucking pigs.'

'Yeah,' Parker says, squeezing her hand. 'Pigs.'


*Your contact pops his head round the door of the pub.*

*'About time.' You nod at the telly. 'I've had enough of this long-haired Mick telling the world and his wife how he doesn't like Mondays.'*

*'Free the Wembley One.'*

*He holds the door and ushers you through.*

*The street is all bright light and white heat.*

*'Hottest day of the year then,' your man says. 'Don't worry, there's air conditioning in the car, all mod cons.'*

*You consider Fleet Street. It was never going to last, you think, tight spot like this in central London. And after what her ladyship did to those northern Ernie pickets last year, no way they're going to keep the chapels running.*

*Closed-shop union culture is a dead duck.*

*Fifteen thousand and fifty pounds a year for the clever clogs who write the stories; eighteen thousand for the production worker who runs the presses.*

*Print halls filled with white males from east London. Males from east London you know very well.*

*Tony Benn banging on about the miners' strike being a radicalisation and there's never been so many socialists about the place.*

*Her ladyship is clearing that right up: conventional wisdom being that the government needs union consent – she's turning this on its head.*

*About bloody time.*

*Your man points up Chancery Lane and you walk in silence towards High Holborn and the Gray's Inn Road, where the presses run.*

*For now.*

*'What does he want exactly?' you ask.*

*'To look you in the eye.'*

*'And?'*

*'He wants to look you in the eye and tell you he loves you.'*

*'I'm flattered.'*

*'If it wasn't for the way you're organising things,'* your man tells you, seriously now, *'this would never work.'*

Thank you very much and here's your cut.

*Which is growing –*

*'If he takes me out for a meal,'* you say, *'he's paying.'*

*Your man laughs. Ahead, a black limo.*

*'Nearly there.'*


*99 Mildenhall Road, Lower Clapton.*

The barbecue is sizzling with Safeway's finest sausages and burgers. Jon's doling out lager and white wine, and his guests are pouring it down their throats quicker than Jon can keep up.

'Very lucky with the weather,' says Jackie's cousin, Kate, gulping wine and mopping her brow.

Jon smiles. 'We could do with a gazebo.'

Kate and her husband live down the road at number 125. 'The kids are in the cellar, Jon. It's the only place they can cool off!'

Jon laughs.

'They're not in the cellar, Jon!' Kate says.

'I know, Kate.' Jon points. 'They're in my kitchen.'

'They are!' Kate shaking now with laughter, she is.

'Have a top-up,' Jon offers.

'Well, I'm not driving!'

Mrs Singh leans over the fence and hands Jackie a tray of samosas. Jon hands Mrs Singh a bottle of Guinness. 'Enjoying the show, Jon?'

'All for a good cause, Mrs Singh.'

Mrs Singh looks grave for a moment. 'I understand, Jon.'

Jon smiles, thinks, I didn't mean *that* exactly. I'm enjoying the *day*.

Doc and Sandra who run the corner shop on Millfields Road offer

Jon a glass of the champagne they've brought with them, and Jon says, 'When in Rome, eh?', tips it down and hands back the glass.

Doc laughs. 'It's your glass, Jon.'

'Possession is nine-tenths of the law.'

Doc, a handsome, nattily dressed Jamaican, puts his arm around Sandra, his tall, blonde wife. 'Finders keepers,' he grins.

Sandra raises an eyebrow and shakes her head.

Jon stumbles past to the television set, pops the sound back on, and Spandau Ballet –

*Ayeleen*. 'Why's Tony Hadley wearing a big leather coat, Leenie, on the hottest day of the century, or whatever it is, I'm telling you, he must be sweating buckets.'

I look at Lauren, my best and oldest friend, and think: no one makes me laugh like you do.

The TV is on in my uncle Ahmet's cafe where I've worked weekends and evenings for a few years now. He's across the road at the old porno cinema he and his business mates have bought to do up into a flash Turkish mosque. It looks great from the outside already, I'll give him that. It might take a while longer on the inside.

'I thought you fancied him, Lauren?'

'It's what I'm saying, Leen, think about it.'

I smile. The cafe is empty. Not a sausage. Not that we serve sausages anymore. My uncle has turned the place into a sort of cafe-bar, is what he calls it, giving the new arrivals the glitz of the West End at a third of the prices. Welcome to the neighbourhood. 'This is patter,' he says. 'Ayeleen, you'll learn it. We're very proud of you.'

Truthfully, he bought a dimmer switch, painted the walls velvet, put up a few mirrors, and filled a fridge with wine and bottles of Turkish lager.

'I mean, it's the hair, isn't it?' Lauren's saying. 'It just looks more *natural* on Tony Hadley.'

'Hair in general?'

'What I'm saying, Leen.'

We're lying across a banquette, I believe is my uncle's word for the seating, feet up, doing each other's nails, looking at Spandau Ballet's hair.

'That saxophone player,' I say, 'doing the solo. I mean that can't be natural, can it?'

'Like a hat it is. Or a parrot. A cockatoo.'

'You know what they say about you, Lauren?'

She's laughing. 'That I like a cockatoo?'

'Oh, we're very clever, now, aren't we?'

'We are.'

'What I'm saying, Laur.'

The bell above the door rings and in walks my cousin Mesut.

Lauren explodes in laughter. 'State of it,' she's saying. 'Look at the state of it.'

Mesut looks genuinely upset. 'What is it? State of what?'

Lauren looks at me. 'I think it's the clothes, don't you, Leenie?'

'I think it is.'

'All of the clothes. You get dressed in the dark this morning, Mesut?'

Mesut blinks. '*My* clothes?'

Lauren points across the room. 'There's the mirror. Use it.'

'I know quite well what it is that I'm wearing, Lauren.' He turns to the television. 'I love this one,' he says. 'I love it.'

Lauren says, 'Shall I tell him, Leen, or do you want to?'

Mesut, looking up at Spandau Ballet, says, 'Tell me what?'

'Do you think you're *in* Spandau Ballet, is that it, Mesut?'

He doesn't take his eyes off the screen. 'I was there, Lauren,' he says, 'in the early days, that club in Soho. I'm a Blitz Kid.'

Lauren, straight face, and I'm biting my lip.

Thing is, Mesut's a good cousin, and he's helped me out before, and it's because of him that I never have to deal with the weekly handovers that mean we keep our licence.

'What year is it, Mesut?'

'Nineteen eighty-five.'

'Correct. And, Mesut, in nineteen eighty-five, you are how old exactly?'

'I'm twenty-one, Lauren.' He turns, looks at her. 'A man, now.'

'Well,' Lauren says, 'you certainly took your time about it.'

Mesut tuts and turns back to the telly.

'Spandau Ballet started out playing those Soho clubs when exactly, Mesut?'

'A couple of years ago.'

'It was nineteen seventy-nine, Mesut.'

He shrugs.

'You used to wear those clothes, did you, when you were there?'

He looks at Lauren. 'You don't know anything, Lauren.'

'When you were fifteen, you wore those clothes out to the Blitz club?'

'So?'

'So, Mesut, when you were fifteen, you were playing football in Clissold Park and in bed by nine o'clock!'

'You don't know anything, Lauren, all right?'

'As you've previously informed me.'

'Stop teasing him, eh, Laur. Here.' I hand Mesut a Turkish lager. 'Now that you're a man and everything.'

'Cheers, Leenie.'

Tony Hadley's charging about the stage and sweating, crooning 'True', Lauren singing along.

The bell goes again, and my uncle appears, grinning.

'Girls,' he says. 'Tell me what you're doing this afternoon.'

'Wotcha, Mr Ahmet. How's the porno palace?'

'Don't be cheeky, Lauren.' He shrugs off his coat, folds it neatly over a chair. 'I ask again: what are you girls doing this afternoon?'

'Nothing, Uncle.'

He's grinning even more now, and I know what that look in his eye means.

'You're wrong, Ayeleen.' He taps his shirt pocket. 'Come and see what's in here,' he says.

'Creep.'

'I told you not to be cheeky, Lauren. Come on, Ayeleen.'

'Good song that,' Mesut says. 'Come on, Ayeleen.'

'Oh my goodness, Mesut, the state of you.'

I go over to my uncle – this is an old routine of his – and just as I reach out my hand, he grabs it and shakes it wildly.

He's laughing and I'm laughing and then he whips out two tickets and –

'Are those what I think they are, Uncle?'

He points at the street where there's a black car parked right in front of the cafe.

'You girls,' he says, 'are on your way to Wembley.'

Lauren's jaw drops –

'What?'

Mesut drained of colour –

'*What*?'

'Go on.' He hands me the tickets. 'If you leave now, you'll still see most of it.'

'But how?'

He's smiling. 'Someone owed me a favour. If you hurry up, you'll not miss much. And you're taking the car. He'll be waiting nearby to bring you back.'

We're shaking and laughing –

'Be good, girls.'

We're shrieking and jumping about –

Mesut's furious.

Uncle looks at him and says, 'I think you can take that trench coat off now, Mesut.'


Suzi circling with her camera. Gary Kemp mopping his brow, talking to Phil Collins –

'It's so hot, I mean three numbers, I feel like I've done an entire gig. Really, just incredibly hot.'

Phil Collins saying, 'Yeah, I saw Parfitt and he said it was really hot, it was white, reflective, off the crowd.'

'Yeah,' Gary Kemp agrees. 'The audience is just really hot. They're all squashed in, sweating.' Phil laughs at that. 'Absolutely amazing, you won't believe it. I didn't want to go off, you know.' Pointing at the film crew. 'You're not still making this film, are you?'

Phil Collins laughing, 'Nah.' He shakes his head, smiles. 'No.'

Gary Kemp thumbing at the camera. 'Every time we have a conversation there's one of these!'

Gary Kemp wanders off.

Phil Collins, asking no one in particular, 'Where's the dressing room?'

Status Quo sit on plastic chairs at a plastic table, drinking.

There's a camera rolling and an interview.

'How did it feel to be on?'

Francis Rossi leans forward. 'Eh?'

'How did it feel to be on?'

Bob Geldof giving him bunny ears behind, grinning.

'When we were there, great.' A pause. Quo look wry, Suzi thinks, like they're not sharing something. Francis Rossi nods. 'I wanted to stay there.'

Geldof rears up. 'You can fuck off home now, you're finished.'

'No need to swear, Bob!'

That's Rick Parfitt, Quo rhythm guitarist, billowing pink shirt, shaggy-haired, impish, a plastic tumbler of red wine on the go.

Parfitt, with his thumb, gestures over his shoulder as Bob Geldof retreats. 'These bloody hippies.'

Suzi spots Elton John in a Cossack hat.

He's talking to Nils Lofgren, one of Bruce Springsteen's guitar players.

Springsteen's touring Born in the USA and he left the stage set up at Wembley so that Live Aid could borrow it, Suzi gathers.

That was nice of him.

Not here though, is he, she thinks, The Boss.

Apparently Bob Geldof told Freddie Mercury that 'the entire stage was built for you, practically. Darling, the world.'

Suzi thinking: I thought the stage was built for Bruce Springsteen.

Elton offering Nils his services as a piano player.

Nils smiling.

A rumour Suzi's heard is that Gary Kemp has been in intensive physical training as he's been challenged by Nils to a back-flip competition while playing the guitar riff to Spandau Ballet's hit 'True'.

Suzi thinks it might be one of the more outlandish of the rumours going around.

Nils and Elton drift off, pleased with their exchange.

Elton, asking no one in particular, 'Any more of that red wine?'


She's got a family then, Parker notes, that's for sure.

They're in a picnic circle, about a dozen blankets spread out, a couple of cast-iron pots bubbling away on camping stoves, three coolers spilling ice, Red Stripe bottles bobbing about, kids chasing each other, dogs chasing the kids, teenagers mooning and mooching, and Carolyn's grandmother with her arm around Parker saying –

'I gather you're the man of the hour, sir.'

'Well,' Parker begins, 'I don't use the term hero lightly, but it does feel apt this morning.'

Carolyn's grandmother likes that one.

She slaps him hard across the back. 'You seem like a good boy.'

She pauses, gives him a sharp look, then smiles –

'Welcome,' she says.

She's hooting with laughter, hand on his shoulder, bent double now, wheezing. 'I'm going to mind my rice and peas, young man.'

She moves away, smiling. 'You be welcome, hero.'

Carolyn hands Parker a bottle. 'She likes you.'

'I think it's *you* that she likes, darling.'

'She loves me, hero. But she's only got to like you.'

'And how do I accomplish that exactly?'

Carolyn nods at the bubbling pots –

'Go and offer to assist, graciously step away when you're admonished

41

for offering, make sure you eat at least three helpings, serve me before yourself.'

'This is excellent advice.'

Parker pulls at his Red Stripe and scopes the group.

He recognises one or two of the cousins about Carolyn's age from the Roach Family Support Committee, knows at least one of the boyfriends to nod at, if not yet by name. He's moved on a little since he hung around with the draw smokers and the wannabe rude boys. To be fair, most of them have moved on too; you reach an age when you either are or you aren't rude, everyone knows it and things settle the way the chips have fallen.

Parker's little friends, it turns out, have not all graduated from slinging ten-bags to their friends. They're working in garages now, or stacking shelves, or on the make down the market, or signing on, or not working at all, or –

Well, one of them, Marlon, has moved up in the world, as evidenced by his flash car and prime piece of council real estate.

Marlon, Parker believes, once had certain designs on Carolyn, designs that were, while never wholly discredited, never in fact reciprocated.

Marlon, Parker sees, is currently loping across the common towards them, grinning gold teeth. He's carrying a bottle of champagne and a smart transistor, which blasts Sade singing 'Your Love is King'.

Marlon points at Carolyn and mouths the words.

Carolyn ignores him, kisses Parker, nods at the radio, Sade getting louder.

She says, 'Global.'

'Yeah,' Parker laughs. 'Global as in council estate in Islington.'

They watch Marlon slap hands and bump fists. 'Marlon,' Carolyn nods. 'The Don.'

Parker raises an eyebrow. 'That right?'

'That's what I've heard.' She smiles. 'He's certainly in better threads, at least.'

'Top ranking.'

'Quite.'

'Oi, Marlon,' Parker shouts. 'Be a good boy and bring us a lager.'

He's smiling, Marlon, but he doesn't much like the instruction. He brings over two bottles of Red Stripe and twists off the caps.

'I just been down the line,' Marlon says. He hands Parker one of the bottles. 'Police talking to the locals. Bobbylon bwoy got one serious tump. Pig had his helmet knocked off.' Marlon laughing. 'Playing football with it in the street, they were.'

Carolyn rolls her eyes and drifts off.

'What were you doing down the line, Marlon?'

Marlon smiles. 'Keeping an eye on our younger bredren, you know.'

'I do know.' Parker takes a pull of his beer. 'What was the Old Bill doing there?'

Marlon nods over at Carolyn's cousin Shaun and his mate. 'Same ting.'

'Right.'

'Bit of community outreach, what they call it. Conversation. Diplomacy.'

'Who with?'

Marlon grins. 'Our younger bredren.'

'Work out, did it?'

'Put it this way,' Marlon reasons. 'The pig with no helmet had his trotters up.' He flicks his fingers, which snap, crack. 'He took a one-two, man serious with his combination. Didn't go down, fight back.'

'Sounds tasty.'

'Bacon burned,' Marlon laughs. 'Crisp.'

'They didn't want a word with you?'

'I'm like a whistle, boss, you know me.'

'Oh yeah?'

'Oh yeah. Clean as.'

'I thought you meant something else.'

'Don't be cheeky.'

Parker smiles. 'Wouldn't dream of it, old son.'

Marlon turns, slightly, so that they are both angled away from the family.

He says, gesturing again towards Shaun. 'They weren't in uniform.'

'They weren't.' Parker shakes his head. 'Well,' he says, 'they were in the Regional Crime Squad uniform, if you know what I mean.'

Marlon nodding. 'It feel like more than coincidence to you, bobbies out making nice on Sandringham Road, same time the detectives stop and search?'

'Nothing surprises me anymore, Marlon.'

'I'll have a word with the man now.'

'Like your mind, pal.'

Marlon nodding.

They bump fists. 'Be lucky,' Parker tells him.

Marlon grins, ambles away. '*Born* lucky.'

Parker stands alone for a long moment. The picnic-party bubbling, the heat –

Carolyn, her arm linked with another smiling cousin, rescues him. 'Our granny wants to know what it is your family do, hero. You best go tell her.'

'She wants to know that my old man, my uncles, their old man, and his, are all printworkers down the Gray's Inn Road. You couldn't tell her that yourself?'

Carolyn's cousin, mock-serious, kissing her teeth. 'She want to know about the *unions*, Parker.'

Parker shaking his head, resigned. 'Come on then, darling.' He puts his arm around her, Phil Collins bawling take a look at me now. 'You are about to see a very sexy side of mine.'

*In the limo there's a small television, which is tuned to the concert.*

*Course it bloody is. The volume's down, thank God, and you're wedged between your contact and a middleman –*

*The limo ghosts along the Gray's Inn, his son pointing out the local buildings they own and what goes on where.*

*On Bouvier Street, the limo pulls over. Your contact hops out and beckons you to do the same. He points at a nondescript building.*

*'What can you hear?' he asks.*

*You smile. 'Very good.'*

*'Nothing,' he says, nodding. He flicks his fingers out from his hand. 'Puff,' he says. 'Vanished into thin air.'*

*'What's this performance all about, eh?'*

*'It's a kind of magic.'*

*'You're funny. They on today, then, Queen?'*

*With his hand on the small of your back, he guides you to the limo again. 'In you get,' he instructs.*

*And there the man sits, smiling.*

*'Shall we go for a drive?' he asks, this man, who's relying on you to do a job for his man.*

Jon Davies is, by now, quite drunk.

Not long ago he argued the toss with Doc over the relative qualities of Sting and Phil Collins.

'See, it's about the *talent*, man,' Jon offers. 'Sting was White Jesus up there, blessing us. More of it in his little finger, he's got, talent. He glows.'

Doc laughs. 'The boy *floated*, it's a hard fact.' He snaps his fingers. 'He sure mek it look easy.'

'What I'm saying, Doc, talent.'

'But take a look at Phil Collins.'

'Good one.'

'Man *need* talent, looking the way he does.' Doc's laughing again.

Jon says, 'It's craft, what Phil's got, craft and graft. He's earned it, these songs. Earned it through his *labour*. Which, given his politics, is ironic.'

'Hard to disagree, Jon, very hard to disagree.'

Jon remembers watching U2 for what felt like a very long time.

'They've been playing this song for ten minutes,' he said, incredulous, but no one listening.

Now, one of Jackie's cousins has cornered Jon and is educating him on his latest venture, or 'enterprise'. Jon's looking for the boy – where *is* he? – but he doesn't want to be rude so he's nodding at whatever it is that Jackie's cousin is talking about. Jackie's cousin Mitchell, this is, or 'Chick' to his pals and everyone else.

'Why Chick you may ask?' Chick will enquire of new acquaintances, though few people do ask, the size of him. 'I'm chirpy, that's why, always was. Even as a nipper. Even as a *baby*.'

He's wont to wink then, Chick, the implication being *me*? *A baby*?

That's right, once upon a time, believe it or not, the size of me now.

'Cheep, cheep.'

Chick is Jackie's old man's side of the family, the docker side.

Kate – the other cousin in attendance, still here, still laughing, still sucking white wine into her mouth – is Jackie's mum's side, south coast, originally, near Bournemouth.

Chick is an affable man but fancies himself a bit wide, and Jon likes to keep him – at family gatherings at least – well oiled, chugging along in the slow lane, smiling.

He's a man who, should anything not be quite in order, would certainly have a word, keep everyone kosher, nothing too heavy, mind.

'The enterprise,' Chick is saying, 'is a syndicate. That's my new game.'

'What's your new game, Chick, sorry?'

'The syndicate, Jon, is my new game. Property investment.'

'Wasn't that your old game?' Jon is, still, feeling really quite drunk.

'Jon, you've had a few, I grant you, but keep up.'

Jon nods. 'You're right, sorry. The syndicate.'

Chick grins, leans forward. 'So the syndicate, Jon, is an opportunity.'

Dire Straits kick in with the riff and then the chorus.

Chick winks. 'Money for nothing, Jon, is what it is.'

'Chick's for free?' Jon manages and Chick laughs.

'Yeah, but no, not quite.'

Jon's got an eye on the portable, enjoying Mark Knopfler's clobber, his sweatbands and headband, his pumps.

In the garden, the guests adopt air-guitar poses, laughing.

Mrs Singh waving a Guinness, the boy's appeared too, right in front of the television, serious. And, oh look, there's Sting again, floating about in white –

Chick's telling Jon about the property portfolio in which he is investor, co-signatory and interested party. The syndicate.

'We've got a gym which we're turning into a sauna and massage parlour, a snooker club that's going to become a nightclub, a nightclub that'll be a restaurant, and a pub.'

'What plans have you got for the pub, Chick?'

'The pub's going to be a pub, Jon, just better.'

'Right.'

'Point is your clientele in the area is set to change, what with the new airport and all that palaver. Yuppies don't want worn carpets and stale beer-stink, tear-ups in piss-smelling car parks outside. It's an emerging market.'

Jon nods.

'But until the golden egg hatches, we got to keep who's there now happy, savvy?'

'Very clever.'

'It's an opportunity.' Chick slaps Jon on the shoulder. 'My old man and his mob would be pissing themselves if they clocked a Canning Town goon like me in charge of a property portfolio in the up-and-coming West India Docks, Jon.'

'That where they worked?'

'You're spot on.'

'What about your brothers?'

'Between you and me, they didn't fancy it.'

'No?'

'No. They don't have the cash.'

Jon looks up. A plane, silent, inching across the blue screen of the late-afternoon sky.

Chick raises his chin. 'There'll be a lot more where that came from when they open the airport.'

'How much cash,' Jon asks, 'did your brothers not have?'

Chick smiles. 'What they ain't got could fill a very large space, Jon.'

On the television, the crowd cheers.

Jon watches Jackie line bottles against the wall.

Onto the barbecue, Doc sprays water. It smokes and fizzes.

The boy leads Lizzie in circles, dancing round a campfire –

Hands in buckets, rummaging in melting ice.

'We'll powwow, Jon,' Chick says, enigmatically.

Bull-necked, he turns to address the gathering.

'You wanna have a word, Jacks!' Chick calls out to his cousin, nodding at Jon. 'The face on him! Like a wet weekend, I'm telling you!'

'Worry not, Chick,' Jon smiles. 'She will.'

Chick roars, points at the television. 'Queen are on,' he says. 'I wanna watch this, even if he is a poofter!'

Over the back fence, dogs bark.


*Ayeleen*: Lauren's face is all pink and she's jumping up and down, her hair stuck to her forehead with sweat.

I love you, Lauren, I think, you're my best friend in the whole world and here we are together, and everyone around us is smiling, and the sun is still shining, and this is the best day ever –

And the music stops for a moment, and I can see Freddie's about to say something, and Lauren says, 'Look, Leenie, he's dressed just like we are.'

And he is, I think, those Adidas and that tank top and the jeans with the high waist, and Lauren says, 'We need to get ourselves a matching belt and armband too!'

And she's delighted, and I'm grinning at her, and the sound of the cheering is a bit much, but then we can hear Freddie saying, 'This next song is only dedicated to beautiful people here tonight – which means all of you. Thank you for coming along, you are making this a great occasion.'

And Lauren's squealing, 'That's us, Leenie, that's us!'

And for a moment, I think, yes, that's true, that's us, and it's a beautiful moment, and the crowd is silent just for that moment and then the band starts again and I –

'I love this one, Leen,' Lauren yells. 'And I love you, too!'

And then everyone is singing along about love being a crazy little thing and I'm thinking, it's not really, is it, it's simple – it's love.

Suzi, sitting alone, the backstage area reeking of stale smoke, stale booze, stale sweat –

Keith nowhere to be seen.

Suzi smiles and fiddles with her camera. She looks over her notes and thinks:

*What* exactly *have I got here?*

Rock stars, pop stars, drunk and high, competing –

But for what, exactly?

And that's where they all are now, jostling for position on the ramp before the big singalong at the end. Who can get closest to Geldof and Mercury and Elton and McCartney, where the cameras will all be, zooming in on their cherry noses and tired eyes, doing their bit, letting everyone know that today we're all a part of it, feeding the world –

Suzi lets this thought pass. It's not entirely fair, after all.

They're not all bad, and in her notebook there must be something worth sharing, something to celebrate. She flips pages, she scans scribbled thoughts. She licks her forefinger, she licks her pencil –

An insight from an 'insider':

'Sting played solo only as his band had demanded to be paid before they went on. Sting told them to fuck off and promptly walked on stage with just a guitar and started with "Roxanne".'

'Smug cunt,' Keith had declared. 'But he's pretty fucking good.'

He was very good, Suzi thinks, made it look so easy. He had all the time in the world up there, it looked like.

She jots thoughts, soundbites.

Something is troubling Suzi, and it might be the heat, it might be the drinks, it might be this proximity she's had all day to quote unquote *greatness*, but she also knows that it's something else –

She's a part of it; she used to be a part of something else. It can't really be so simple, can it, that you're either doing good or you're not. This, she thinks, is what it means to grow up, not buying a bloody council flat, getting on the property *ladder*.

This being thinking.

Suzi hears a scuffed step, a slip, looks up –

Paul Weller lowers himself into the plastic chair beside her. He nods at her camera, her notepad, raises an eyebrow –

Suzi smiles, nods. 'All done, I think. You?'

Paul Weller shrugs.

The Style Council had hopped off after their slot to film a performance for national television. Back now, for the finale.

Suzi gestures at the disarray, the plastic cups, the ashtrays and fag ends, the bottles. She nods at the noise from the stage, the crowd within the stadium. 'What do you make of it all, this?' she asks Paul Weller.

Paul Weller pouts, narrows eyes, does a little cringe. He shuffles in his seat and nods at Suzi, nods at her notepad.

Suzi leafs through to a blank page, pencil raised, on the record –

'When I was a kid,' Paul Weller begins, 'I remember asking my dad how long a mile was. He took me out into our street, Stanley Road, and pointed down to the far end, towards the heat haze in the distance. To me there was a magical kingdom through that shimmering haze, the rest of the world, all life's possibilities. I always return to where I came from, to get a sense of my journey and where I'm heading next.'

Suzi, nodding, asks, 'And what's next?'

Paul Weller smiles, winks. 'You asking for me, or yourself, girl?'

Suzi thinks: it's a very good question.

Parker on Carolyn's sofa blissed out; Carolyn in the kitchen frying up a late, late tea.

After the park, the pub.

Marlon back early doors, looking flash, Parker noted, all that black geezer lingo to the fore, and Parker thinking, *Him*, really?

He's not sure, so no judgement, but Noble was on about a recycling scheme at Stoke Newington, which might corroborate Parker's thinking on what happened to Trevor, and it does look like young Marlon's business interests have widened, excuse the pun, it does look like Marlon is on a considerably more decent screw than he was when Parker first met him and they became friends.

Because they *are* friends.

Parker knows the boy and he wouldn't make him for a turncoat, no sirree.

'Didn't know your bredren was all in the printworks,' Marlon had said. 'Why you never join them? What is it you really *do*, Parker?'

Parker has an answer to this. A lie that is true is a lot easier to maintain. 'This and that, you know.'

Marlon, grinning, goes, 'Yeah man.'

'One of my uncles,' Parker continues, 'he moves jewellery down at Hatton Garden, just down the road from the presses. He started off in the same chapel as my old man and the rest of them, but he didn't fancy it, walked out on day one, five minutes later he was in a pawnshop and the rest is history, as they say.'

Carolyn listening now. Marlon, leaning across the table, says, 'And?'

'I help him out, you know.' Parker winks. 'Muscle.'

Marlon likes this, smiling very broadly. 'You a *big* man, big man.'

''Nuff respect, yeah?'

Marlon whoops. 'I thought you were a clever fella too, though. Too clever for muscle work exclusively, you know?'

Carolyn, by now, has turned to her cousin, her hand in Parker's, her eyes, her smile, directed elsewhere.

'There's a book, Marlon, which I help to look after.'

'All jewellery?'

'Pure gold, son.' Parker winks, grins. 'More gold than you've got in your big gob.'

Yeah, Marlon liked that, Parker thinks.

And no judgement, he reminds himself. It was a good night, end of, and here he is now, exactly where he wants to be, Chez Carolyn –

Though he *had* ducked out to honour a prior engagement to meet Trevor, give him an update.

'I fancy cigarettes,' he said to Carolyn. 'For a change up. Once in a while you can't beat a Woodbine, girl.'

She laughs at that and off he trots, Green Lanes to a Turkish deli where Trevor's waiting. Skulking in the piss-stinking alley round the side, he's rattled, Trevor –

'You were right, old son,' Parker says. 'New faces.'

'You remember the first time I saw Rice and Cole, yeah, I told you?'

Parker nods.

'I was in the dumplings cafe, Sandringham Road, downstairs having a drink.'

'I remember.'

'They did a bust there, everyone stock-still, and it's me they come to with a baggie with fifty quid in it.'

'You know I remember.'

'They took me in, done me with possession.'

'But they dropped the charge.'

'I don't deal drugs.'

'Not then you didn't.'

'What I'm saying. Next time, a month after that, and I'm attacked by a geezer with a knife, and who gets pulled in for questioning?'

Parker nods.

'Yeah, me.'

'What's your point, Trevor?'

'I don't need this to start all over.'

Parker sniffs. 'Everywhere's got that urine tang to it, don't you find, Trevor? Basically smells of piss, London.'

Parker looks up and down. Crates of vegetables, rotting. Empty bottles of Efes, their tasty local lager. A bike with no wheels –

Dustbins overflowing, bowls of water and food for the local moggies, a tyre and a broken stereo –

The back door of the deli opens and a hairy bloke with a spattered apron and a meat cleaver lights up, nods.

Parker returns the nod.

He knows what this lot are about.

All sorts of rumours regarding the crates of rotting vegetables for a kick-off – what they put inside them, import export etcetera, poppies and opium and whatnot – and Parker knows it's heavy enough to give them a swerve, old country dirt, proper mafia.

There was that bar on the High Street that Rice and Cole collected from, same owner as used to have The New Country Off-Licence and Foodstore across the road from it, before he sold it and then some kid was popped on the doorstep by a sniper or something like that. Old country, new problems. Crime and politics go hand in hand, which complicates the business side of the crime, the *business* –

Question on Parker's mind is who runs the book *now*, who collects?

Trevor's shaking his head, he spits and hacks, coughs, holding back the tears, Parker thinks.

Trevor sucking his teeth, spits again, says, 'I hear you playing house with a lickle black girl.'

Parker raises an eyebrow.

And Trevor goes on. 'She know what it is you do?'

'Do *you* know?'

'I know with who it is you're in cahoots. That's quite enough for your blackbird to done fly away, I'd have thought.'

Parker softens, smiles. 'Listen, I don't want all this to start over for you neither. I told you it might be a good result and I believe that it might.'

'How?'

'Well, for a start, you're off the hook with old Rice and Cole. They're out the picture, it seems, for good.'

Trevor shrugs.

'And the new lot don't appear to know you by face or name, that fair?'

Trevor nods.

'So it's clean slate, give or take.'

'Which means what for us?'

Parker nodding now –

'Which means keep your nose clean and if they pick you up again, you use your phone call wisely.'

'That number you gave me?'

'Bingo.'

'So do nothing?'

'There's word about a recycling scheme, I want to know anything you hear about that.'

Trevor nodding, pulling tobacco from his teeth –

Parker says, 'You know Marlon, yeah?'

'Everyone knows Marlon.'

Parker grins. 'He's not exactly the shy and retiring type, I'll give you that.'

'What about him?'

Parker's not sure –

'Just keep him in mind, all right?'

Trevor nods.

'Now, on your bike,' Parker says. 'I need to make a purchase here and get back to my woman.'

Trevor smiling now –

'Yeah man,' he says, and Parker shakes his head, grins and winks –

Back in the pub with a swagger, a cheer, the returning hero, but Parker's thinking about Noble on the telephone. As well as his concerns over the recycling, Noble also mentioned something about that ginger bird they'd used in the Colin Roach business. And wondered what she was up to now. Parker insinuated that Noble might be on the sniff – she was all right, the bird – and was haughtily reminded of Noble's ongoing domestic bliss with the lovely Lea. Not that this was any deterrent, mind, and there was no call for Noble to have come on all mardy, boys will be boys and all that.

Parker's buzzing mind never turns off, he sometimes reflects, trying to keep things distinct, to *compartmentalise* –

What he'd said, Noble – what he'd *asked* – was what about the redhead's involvement with music, which group was it her fella knocked about with?

Parker got fairly close to her when they both turned out for the Roach Family Support Committee, but he hadn't thought about her for a good while. And her fella wasn't exactly a person of interest.

Now, back Chez Carolyn, watching the highlights reel of the big day in the middle of the night, he remembers.

It was The Style Council.

Parker smiles to himself. She might well have been there, lucky tart.

He makes a mental note to tell Noble when he rings for their daily tomorrow afternoon.

*Then*: here they are, Jagger and Bowie pratting about to 'Dancing in the Street' –

From the kitchen, Carolyn yells, 'I prefer the Laura Nyro and LaBelle version.'

'Course you do, sweetheart,' Parker yells back, knowing she means the almost-medley with 'Monkey Time' on that album they did together.

He levers himself out of the cushions, digs out the LP from the pile on the floor – she really must organise these better, he thinks – thumbs the record from its sleeve –

He calls, 'Let's do the monkey, shall we, darling?'

From the kitchen, a whoop, laughter –

Parker sashaying towards it.


*You're looking out over the Thames from your Wapping flat cradling a mug of tea and thinking –*

What have I just been told?

*The drive was a half-hour east to The Facility, as it's being called by those in the know. Those who are really in the know call it:*

Operation X

*'As in X marks the spot, or x-tra, x-tra, read all about it?' you asked.*

'Very good,' your man said.

'I'm here all week.'

'You bloody won't be.' He didn't look amused at this, your man. 'Now,' he went on, 'that thing you did with those electricians, from Portsmouth. I want you to do the same with your security.'

You said nothing.

He added:

'There's a reason, it's important, and I'm going to trust you.'

You nodded. You said, 'I'm flattered, but given what I know, not surprised.'

He smiled at that. 'You'll have heard that they're going to be using The Facility to print The London Herald.'

You nodded. 'I had heard that.'

'That's what everyone was told. That's how they've kept a lid on the project. It's reasonable that they've moved a small team of employees over from Gray's Inn Road and Bouvier Street for that purpose.'

All from the same chapel, of course, all from the same union, you think, now.

'But The London Herald doesn't exist.'

'I suppose it doesn't, no.'

'And it won't ever exist.'

You nodded.

'What they need from your organisation is assurances of complicity and silence.'

You thought: heavy work.

'That The London Herald will not ever exist will slowly become ever more apparent to anyone involved at The Facility.'

'And you want me to make sure that no one else finds that out.'

He nodded. 'What I like about you is you're quick on the uptake.'

You thought, monkey see, monkey do.

Now, you're thinking, Bobbins here might have just sussed this out –

'The other thing I like about you,' he said, 'is that you don't seem too interested in what will come out of The Facility.'

*'I'm not,' you said.*

*Now you think, I know exactly what's coming out.*

*The mini television played the video of Jagger and Bowie miming away in a warehouse to 'Dancing in the Street', part of the big day.*

*'Know where that is?' you asked.*

*'I do not.'*

*You pointed out of the window, south-east. 'Down the road. A warehouse in which my organisation has interests.'*

*'Doing your bit for charity.'*

*'They needed somewhere to film the video for this fiasco of a record.'*

*He smiled then. 'Mick's an ambitious boy. He wouldn't miss all this.'*

*'It didn't come cheap.'*

*'And why's that?'*

*'Supply and demand. There was nowhere else for them to go at the notice.'*

*'You made sure of that.'*

*'Shell company, a landlord's title. Good business.'*

*Being ironic, 'And you donated the fee to Live Aid, of course.'*

*'If any African kid sees more than a couple of bacon sandwiches a week for a month or two thanks to these millions of quid that are pouring in, I'll donate more than that.'*

*'That's the spirit.'*

*'What do you get out of all this?' you asked.*

*He looked at you then, made a gesture to the driver and the door opened. 'I've never heard you speak so much. I like it.'*

*Now, you think, that was what is known as obfuscation, a MacGuffin. It's a good story, the Jagger-Bowie one, memorable.*

*You get on the blower and ring Terry.*

*'Hello?'*

*You can hear him rubbing sleep from his eyes –*

*'You awake, Terry?'*

*You hear a cough, a scratch, a retch –*

*'I am, yes.'*

*'Good. Come and pick me up. We've got some visits to make.'*

*'Now?'*

*'Yes, now, Terry, you're awake, aren't you?'*

*'Yeah, but I don't know if anyone else is.'*

*'Surprise, Terry, is half the battle.'*

*'If you say so.'*

*'I do say so. And Terry?'*

*'Yes?'*

*'Remember the electricians a month or so ago?'*

*'I do.'*

*'Good.'*

*You hang up.*

*In your hand is a piece of paper with a list of names of security personnel currently working at The Facility. Your security. Which is why you're going out now.*

*They won't be waiting up –*

*A guard who's been shooting his gob off about a Canning Town lock-up. Two of your boys with wrenches and pliers, seeing to him.*

*Nil by mouth.*

*Midday tomorrow, everyone will know to keep shtum.*


Mrs Thatcher is in what Denis calls her 'Chequers snug'.

She's watching the television with her cup of Ovaltine and preparing herself for her four hours in bed.

On the television, a recap of the events of the day, an extraordinary one, she gathers. She's already had word that it was the worst day in history for retail trading. It must take quite something, she reflects, to put the British off shopping.

She's watching as the great and the good take their seats in the stadium. She recognises many more of them than she'd ever admit in public. She smiles at this, sips her warm drink, narrows her eyes –

There's Diana, Princess of Wales, like a giddy schoolgirl.

Denis shuffles past in open dressing gown and briefs. He nods at the television as Prince Charles heaves into view, his face one of feigned composure, confused, his bride giggling.

'He'll need to watch that one,' Denis mutters. 'They'll be lining up for her, the rock and rollers.'

Mrs Thatcher ignores him. They will, of course, have already lined up for her, she thinks, as they should, paying the royals their due. They'd have lined up for *her* too, Mrs Thatcher, had she chosen to attend. Had she even acknowledged the event at all.

The camera settles on another blonde woman, another beautiful blonde woman, tending to her children as her husband plays the great man –

Mrs Thatcher knows that this woman's name is Paula Yates.

'They're all at it, then,' Denis says. 'The *girls*.'

Denis drags himself on down the corridor.

She, Mrs Thatcher, sighs.

It's funny, she thinks, *money*.

Her government is currently negotiating an arms deal with Saudi Arabia, for example, which should be worth around £43 billion, which has to be at least a thousand Live Aid concerts, judging by what they're saying on the television.

Christ, she thinks, the cash for commissions, bribes, middlemen and so on sitting in Swiss banks is about three times what they've managed to squeeze out of the public today.

It's the naivety of it all that she admires, oddly.

The belief they have that they might actually be making a difference. Must be nice, that sort of innocence.

Events like Live Aid are just a day off from reality, she thinks, for a country like ours, exactly when the organisers claim reality is what they're all about.

# PART TWO
# *Uprising*

1 October–6 October 1985

# 1

## *Grime*

October 1985

*Shaun.* Every day it's the same question. It's always the same question –

'Where we going, man?'

Every day the same answer:

'I dunno, man. Home?'

So that's where we go, home, slowly, slowly home.

Me and my boy Anton in the same class now, out the door at the same time, same football practice cancelled again, same no pitch to use, so we drag our feet through the same Tottenham streets back to the Farm.

'Youth club, yeah?'

And the same answer to that, too: where else we gonna go, bruv?

'Chips first though, yeah?'

'Yeah, but you're buying, yeah, your round, bruv.'

'My round?'

'Your round, what you deaf?'

'I can hear you chatting something about my round, but I think I must be hearing wrong.'

'What, you got that grease, that wax is it, all up there in that earhole you can't hear what I'm telling you?'

I'm laughing now. 'Nothing to do with no wax, it's more the words ain't making no sense, is what I mean to say.'

'So it's that you don't *understand*, bruv, not that you can't hear me clearly saying it's your round on the grub?'

'Anton, every day the same.'

'No need to get too philosophical, yeah? It is your round. I bought them chips yesterday. *Therefore.* Yeah?'

I laugh. 'I understand *that.*'

Anton stops, his bag falls to his feet, he claps. 'You paying attention, boy, in English now, yeah? Therefore. Conclusively. *Rhetorically.*'

I smile, a big grin. 'Yeah, Miss Wilson worth paying attention *to*, you know.'

Anton shaking his head. 'Mate, it's wrong, man. She's white and she's old.'

'Nah, man, she's well nice.'

'Seriously wrong,' Anton says, pushes the caff door open, the steam in the windows, the elders with their hands warming round thick white mugs of tea, workmen eating beans and bacon, sausage and toast –

The smell is always welcome, even if the proprietor pretends to himself that we're not.

'You two again?' he addresses us, his arms crossed.

The underarms of his blue shirt are swampy dark. His vest underneath – you don't wanna know.

'Here.' He hands Anton a tinfoil tray of chips. 'Salt and vinegar over there.' He nods. 'Takeaway,' he smiles, not meaning it. 'Come again!'

Anton holds two coins in the air. 'Tip's included, Stav,' he says. He places the coins carefully in the dish on the counter. 'Treat yourself.'

I stand by the door examining the pictures of Tottenham players all over the walls, think about what's going to happen to them this season, maybe I should make the switch to Liverpool, everyone else at school seems to be into them.

'Come on, you Spurs,' Anton says, cheerily –

As if he can hear what I'm thinking, nah, it ain't on, is it, changing –

Outside, it's getting darker earlier, and there's a cold to it, the wind, and the chips are hot and salty, and the vinegar stings where I've chewed the inside of my cheek trying to eat school dinner, these chips really cleansing the palate, is the word, Anton says.

We share the tray, our fingers full, our mouths full, our bellies warmer, I lick grease from my hands, lick salt from the tinfoil –

'That's disgusting,' Anton says.

'It's natural, is what it is.'

'You're an animal.'

'Proud.'

Anton screws the foil into a ball, tosses it in the air, kicks it at an overflowing bin.

'Goal!' he shouts.

'Pick that up,' I tell him. 'Respect, yeah.'

'Yes, Uncle,' he says, but he bends down, picks it up –

The lights on the streets are coming on, the market stalls are coming down, there's a trickle of people on and off the buses, into and out of the estate.

Damp in the air, chilly.

We pass the sign that welcomes you to the Farm, the little blocks of colour given to each tower, looks like Lego, like a toy town, something for kids to play with, the list of services, of things to do, sort of the truth:

Neighbourhood Office, Youth Association, Social Club, Community Day Care, Play Centre & Park –

DRIVE SLOWLY – CHILDREN

Anton turns to me. 'You think that lot'll be here again?'

'Who?'

'Hackney, you know.'

I nod. 'Yeah. I don't know. Why not, I s'pose.'

'That's what I mean, bruv.'

I point ahead. 'For the grub, innit, that's why.'

'You reckon? All this way for a free plate of beans?'

'You wouldn't?'

Anton slaps my shoulder with the back of his hand. 'Why do you think I'm going, man? Beans.'

I'm smiling but I ain't sure it's all about the beans, good as they are.

I seen some of these faces, and one or two, you know, they ain't too nice, ain't very friendly, not exactly *community-minded*, as they say in the Youth Association, so I don't know.

I live here, so here I am.

Jon Davies' office is small.

But it's his and his alone.

He's got a tinny portable radio on:

'Breaking news: an Israeli air raid on the PLO headquarters at Tunis has left an estimated sixty-eight dead.'

'In yesterday's press conference, Deputy Assistant Commissioner Richard Wells described the shooting of Mrs Groce in Brixton as tragic. He acknowledged that there were "genuine feelings, particularly those of the relatives and friends of Mrs Groce", but blamed the riots themselves, in which over fifty people were injured and over two hundred arrested, on "an unruly criminal element".'

'Yesterday in Peckham, south London, black youths threw petrol bombs at police and set fire to buildings in echoes of the disorder.'

He flips the dial, the scratch and buzz, and then:

Prince jazzing on in his little red corvette and a segue into Bonnie Tyler yelling about how she's in need of a hero.

Jon smiles.

He doesn't have to debate which station he listens to with anybody, one advantage of the office being his and his alone.

And the reason that it's his and his alone is that, over several months, it has become quite apparent that the cross-council initiative to monitor the London Docklands Development Group and associated land and property investment in Hackney, Tower Hamlets and Newham, is a department of one.

Jon has met members of the council planning committees several times; it was never at the same time, always individually. Jon initiated further contact and scheduled meetings; at these meetings, Jon was the only attendee, council planning committee members being of the opinion that Jon has it all under control and there is little for them to do. Jon wrote progress reports and calendared debriefs; said reports remained unread, the debrief sessions involved Jon debriefing himself.

It was a puzzler.

The goal of the cross-borough, cross-council initiative is to ensure transparency in planning and land management, to avoid planning disputes, to avoid – significantly – conflict of interest and/or favouritism/nepotism in the distribution of contracts associated with land development projects, and to avoid preferential treatment regarding what was called, with a lovely sense of breadth in Jon's opinion, 'lucrative opportunities'.

Jon goes to his office in Bethnal Green Town Hall on Cambridge Heath Road every day.

It's only up the road from his previous home in Hackney Town Hall, literally up the road, but it feels different, bigger, emptier, very much a different council, a different borough –

Building's nice, though, to be fair.

Jon's office is tucked away at what they're calling 'lower ground level' but which feels to him like the basement, if not quite the cellar.

In his first week, he was left alone a good deal of the time and he did a bit of exploring, noting the baroque exterior and art deco stylings inside.

He enjoys the Henry Poole sculptures very much:

Charity above the main entrance, Justice above the side door on Patriot Square, Truth and Happiness adorning the council chamber –

Not a bad quartet of principles, of goals.

In his work, he wonders how often the four intersect.

When the town hall was extended east on the Patriot Square side, they put a sculpture of the Blind Beggar of Bethnal Green above the entrance to the new wing.

Jon thinks: that's more like it.

He reports to his tri-council superiors on a fortnightly basis; they give Jon the bravo and keep up the good work, old man, and Jon does.

What Jon does is he logs and checks all land and property deals, claims and possessions, that take place in the tri-borough area of Hackney, Tower Hamlets and Newham.

It's dry work, daily basis-wise.

But it does throw up the odd conundrum.

While he is working to monitor the London Docklands Development Group and associated land and property investment in Hackney, Tower Hamlets and Newham, it does appear to him that he is in fact working *for* the London Docklands Development Group.

It does, sometimes, feel like he is chasing his own tail.

(The name of that snake that eats itself, *Ouroboros*, is Jon's unofficial motto for his department of one.)

First thing Jon did was a bit of straightforward research, lay-of-the-land stuff, in a memo to himself that's pinned above his desk, the framework, is how he thinks of it, of what he's supposed to be doing:

i.   The London Docklands Development Group was established by the Secretary of State for the Environment, under section 135 of the Local Government, Planning and Land Act 1980 (which, of course, is one particular area of Jon's expertise).

ii.  The London Docklands Development Group was financed by a grant from central government and from the proceeds from the disposal of land for development (which might smack of conflict of interest straight off the bat, Jon suspects, but he has kept this to himself for now).

iii. The corporation will act as a catalyst and will benefit from the full range of planning authority powers (principally those of development control). (Which is another particular area of Jon's legal proficiency, and one certain councillors are sure will be of significant assistance as this full range of planning powers is tantamount to an authority to bypass standard council prerogative in any planning decisions.)

iv.  The London Docklands Development Group is 'insulated' from the local democratically elected councils. The Deputy Chief Executive explains that it is an 'extraordinary arrangement for an extraordinary situation'.

v.   Some bloke called Ron Bishop is Chief Executive.

In other words, Jon sometimes thinks, it does what it wants.

Jon's role: to rubber-stamp legal due process.

It means that the corporation and its governmental connections can confirm that all disposal of land in the Docklands and associated areas have been through pre-approved, all-party, council-vetted procedures, and that council residents are treated with fairness and respect.

Jon Davies' office, then, is small.

But there are certain themes and contexts that feel quite big –

And he's stopped exploring these in his fortnightly reports.

One of the first meetings Jon attended highlighted these certain themes and contexts.

Chaired by Tower Hamlets Planning Committee Chair, Merv Michaels, the meeting concerned the ratification of a proposed development partnership between the Tower Hamlets and Newham councils and a private developer with American financial backing to regenerate the Avalon Housing Estate in Poplar, situated east of Limehouse, west of Canning Town and a little north of the old docks by the Blackwall Tunnel.

Michaels begins it by saying, 'Bit of context: a piece of land in Wapping bought in nineteen seventy-seven, the knocking down of Georgian warehouses and the building of a factory at a cost of just shy of one hundred million quid. That's just down the road from where we're talking.'

Jon notices that no one else is surprised by this information, this amount of money and this rather nebulous statement.

He says, 'Forgive me, Mervyn, bit more on that, if you can?'

Merv smiles, then nods.

The other councillors sitting around the table look down at their notes at this point, busy themselves adding sugar to their cups of tea –

'Not much more, actually, Jon,' Merv says. 'It was a private sale, and the new owner of the property is currently completing the work as set out in the planning application.'

'Private sale to who?' Jon asks.

'To *whom*.' Merv smiles.

'All right,' Jon sighs. 'Private sale to whom?'

'It's all in the planning application, you know your way around by now, I'm sure.'

'What's the factory going to be doing?'

'Planning application, Jon, all you need to know is there.'

'I'm just,' Jon begins, 'thinking of resident interests, that's all, as per my remit, you understand.'

'You were employed this year to exactly that end,' Merv says.

Meaning: the past is a foreign country, son.

The meeting goes on, and it becomes clear that the proposed development of the Avalon Estate is not simply a renovation of existing sub-quality accommodation, but rather the creation of a new urban village, which would contain upwards of a thousand new homes, retail units, an energy centre, community and health amenities, leisure facilities, parks and playgrounds, greenery –

'In Poplar?' Jon says. 'What's the social housing provision of these new homes?'

And Jon's told that that's a detail for when the proposal is drawn up and ratified, and that they're only there today to green-light the drawing up of this proposal going ahead at all.

'So we're voting on a development partnership without knowing what the development itself will actually look like?' Jon says.

'That's what proposal means, Jon,' Merv says.

Jon keeps quiet after this, but he notes a surprising number of buildings in the area close to the Avalon New Village, as they're already calling it, licensed to a company called Compliance Ltd, from *whom* they need certain permissions.

Jon's is the only hand in the air against the proposition.

The meeting wraps up quickly, and over the weeks that follow, it becomes clear to Jon why:

There's a lot of them.

After Avalon, there's the South Quay Estate by St Katharine Docks.

This estate was previously owned by the GLC, which prevented the government's Right to Buy scheme from going ahead there given the resident demographic – relatively wealthy, young, childless, no pets – but since the GLC bit the dust, Tower Hamlets Council are in charge, and now they're saying, very loudly, Right to Buy.

And after the South Quay Estate, there's the Cranbrook Estate, one of the big ones round the corner, and here it's all about community centres and playgrounds and youth associations, so it's very hard to say no to any of that, especially when everything is still a 'proposal' –

Jon's hand in the air again and again, but it counts for nothing, unlike his borough solicitor signature on the planning applications, which certifies that the provision of social housing, of social *benefit*, is in hand –

When Jon finally locates the planning application for the Wapping factory site, he doesn't find a great deal more detail than he got from old Merv.

It's a bright autumn morning, early October, and Jon thinks:

*Why not go and have a gander at one of these Compliance licensed buildings?*

Jon studies his A-Z. He decides on a walking distance criterion from the 277 bus stop near Limehouse, chooses –

Wapping.


Suzi sits in Solid Bond Studios as Paul Weller and Annajoy David outline their mission.

Annajoy David says, 'We've got to help to get rid of this government; we can't just sit on the sidelines.'

Paul Weller says, 'There are only two alternatives as far as I see it.'

He raises an eyebrow in Suzi's direction.

Suzi points at her notepad, filled with scribbles, and the Dictaphone, turning.

There's been a fair bit of lunch wine drunk, and the air is thick with smoke, but Suzi's spent plenty of time in Keith's Sonic Bunker and she knows the score.

'One,' Paul Weller continues, 'armed revolution and the other one, the ballot box.'

Suzi notes that Annajoy David does not smirk or cringe at this.

'An armed revolution isn't that easy to organise, is it?' Paul Weller adds. 'Not in this country, anyway. So I guess you have to try it the other way: the supposed democratic way.'

Annajoy David says, 'We want to broadly create a cultural platform for Labour to be able to speak to young people through and they will have to accept criticism.'

'You get to a point,' Paul Weller says, 'where you think, "Where's it all leading to?" Benefits and raising money are obviously good things, but you're still only dealing with the symptoms; you're not getting to the core. There is the constant dialectic thing: Marxism, Leninism and Trotsky. That is irrelevant. It was a different era. You have to stop talking in those funny antiquated ways and bring the whole up to date and make it more stylised and streamlined. I want to see us put over socialist ideas and ideals in a very accessible way to young people. I just think of my experience, it took me years to ever get any kind of bearing on my own political train of thought, with a lot of unnecessary confusion. So it is very positive. The media is constantly bombarded by right-wing ideas so there's got to be something to redress the balance.'

Annajoy David says, 'We need to inject people with a new enthusiasm for socialism and the Labour Party must be seen to present real alternatives and accept direct input into youth policies. To do that, we need to grasp the imagination of young people and show them that they can effect change and demand a say in the future, using all the art mediums.

'It's not a time to be non-partisan. You have to care and if you don't you have your head in the sand or don't give a fuck about anyone but yourself. You can't sit on the fence. It is very black and white. Thatcher is a tyrant, a dictator. I think she should be lined up against a wall and shot.'

Suzi flips pages and notes a comment from Billy Bragg: 'We are *for* the Labour Party, not *of* the Labour Party.'

'You should talk to Billy Bragg,' Suzi says. 'There's a common cause.'

Paul Weller and Annajoy David exchange a look. Suzi thinks she might not be the first person to have suggested that they do exactly that. She presses the point.

'He's funny, too, you know,' she says. 'Songs about heartbreak as well as politics, little raps between them. He's doing something.'

Paul Weller's nodding now. He looks at Annajoy David with a sort of panting enthusiasm, Suzi thinks, it's sweet.

'For people in popular culture,' Annajoy David says, 'from music to comedy to film-making to fanzines, to come together with the trade union movement will bring a completely different dimension of young people into broad left politics. NUPE and the Transport and General Workers' Union will help with funding and events and venues on the ground. The infrastructure will be paid for by the artists, a self-funding organisation.'

'What brought you two together?' Suzi asks.

Paul Weller lets Annajoy David answer the question, and she tells Suzi that he heard her on LBC giving a speech at a CND rally and he got in touch.

'He said, "My name's Paul Weller and I want to support what you're doing." I said, "Who are you?" And he said, "I'm in a group called the Jam." I didn't know who he was. We met and he said, "I want to help you. I think you're great. Let's do something." So the Jam got on the back of a big truck and played for CND. That's how it kind of started.'

Then there was the Festival for Peace – Brockwell Park again, Suzi remembers – fonder memories than the Rock Against Racism day out down there, when the National Front took back the East End for an afternoon with everyone in south London, blood spilled, and largely by the Special Patrol Group, it was claimed –

The Style Council recording 'Money Go Round' for Youth CND.

This Suzi knows.

Annajoy David is very cool, Suzi thinks, half an hour later in a pub near the studio transcribing the tape. The big scarf, the loose white trouser suit, sleeves rolled halfway up her arms, the rainbow hairband, bouncy hair –

The eyes, Suzi thinks. It's all there, in her eyes. Passion and whatnot –

Wherewithal, that's what it is.

Wherewithal/oomph.

She's capable, Annajoy David, extremely capable.

The pub bell rings time.

Weary, sour-faced old men in oversized, starchy suits hanging off their scrawny shoulders, skin flapping around their brittle jawlines –

They check their watches and sigh, resigned to one more half of brown ale, tipping dirty glasses at the landlord, who rolls his eyes and takes their coins.

Almost three o'clock and time to find somewhere else to sit for a few hours, the bookies, park bench, laundrette beckon.

South end of the Edgware Road –

Pensioner-shuffle.

Suzi spots the pale blue art deco stripe of the ABC cinema on the corner with Harrow Road. The familiar advertising:

A CHOICE OF FOUR PROGRAMMES
IN FOUR CINEMAS
THE BEST IN ENTERTAINMENT
LONDON'S LATE SHOW THEATRE
EVERY FRI + SAT
AT 11.15 PM

She's got to know the area a lot more since spending time at Paul Weller's Solid Bond.

She packs her things, slips her bag over her shoulder and heads down to Marble Arch.

Onto Oxford Street, past the tube and the money exchange, Benetton and Wimpy, HMV and Cerex Souvenirs, Selfridges and C&A, DH Evans –

A man in glasses and combat cap, a grey shopkeeper's coat and grey shirt and grey tie, dark grey trousers and shiny black shoes, a bag strapped around his shoulder has the label:

EIGHT
PASSION
PROTEINS

A placard he carries bears the message:

LESS LUST
FROM LESS PROTEIN:
LESS FISH
BIRD, MEAT
CHEESE
EGG; BEANS
PEAS NUTS
AND SITTING
PROTEIN WISDOM

Hanging just below:

DONATION
7P
BOOKLET
FREE

Beside it, another sign:

WITH CARE
EIGHT
PASSION
PROTEINS

And Suzi thinks, The Protein Man, of *Sunday Times* fame, interviewed earlier in the year, *A life in the day of,* her editor at *The Face* thinking about one of those ironic profiles –

His slogans already picked up by the fashion house Red or Dead:

So it was too late; someone else got there first.

Suzi donates her 7p. She stuffs the booklet in her bag, spots the Number 55 bus and runs for it.

On the bus, an evening paper. Suzi scans headlines:

'Neil Kinnock makes a speech at the Labour Party Conference in Bourne-mouth attacking the entryist Militant group in Liverpool'

'Lord Scarman's report on the riots in Toxteth and Peckham blames economic deprivation and racial discrimination'

'Economists predict that unemployment will remain above the 3,000,000 mark for the rest of the decade'

Happy days, she thinks.

Parker leaves his local newsagent – 'Cheerio, Sanjay' – and examines his tabloid.

Front page screaming:

HURRICANE: MY LOVE BUST-UP

Parker glances at the story, thinks, old Alex Higgins doesn't half fancy a tear.

'Stormy snooker star Alex "Hurricane" Higgins has split with his wife following a bust-up that ended in his arrest.'

A photo of his toothy grin and the long-suffering Lynn with her fringe and a red pout.

It's been, what, three years since his second – and probably last – world title?

Higgins holding his baby, arm round Lynn, blubbing on the televi-sion –

Night of, sloshed in a cheap brothel, head in a Lancashire whore's lap.

Parker tucks his paper under his arm, looks over both shoulders, ducks into a phone box that smells of piss, gathers his ten-pence pieces, dials, waits, punches in his codes –

Says, 'Checking in, October first, aitch-en-eight-eight,' and is put through to Detective Constable Patrick Noble.

'You keeping up with the news?'

'I know a good story about Alex, the Hurricane, Higgins.'

'You're not the only one. He must have the hump this morning.'

'Water off a duck's back.'

'Soppy Mick who can't hold his drink.'

'There's plenty about.'

Noble laughs. 'Go on then.'

'What?'

'This Alex Higgins story. Let's have it.'

Parker nods. 'A lad I knew at Hendon was born up north, not far from Manchester. His old man was a plod in Blackburn. When Higgins won his first world title, he was living up there but didn't exactly have a place of his own.'

'No?'

'No. He was living in a row of abandoned houses awaiting demolition.'

'Explosive talent.'

'Very good.' Parker spits on the floor of the phone box, sniffs. 'Point is, in one week, he lived in five of them, moving each day as they knocked the previous one over.'

Noble, laughing, 'That's a good story.'

'That's not the story.'

'Well, hurry up then, son, I don't have all morning.'

'He likes a drink, as we know, and he likes a flutter, and he likes a fight.'

'Stone me, Parker, this sounds like a real turn-up.'

'No need for sarcasm, guv. Anyway, one night – this is before he's world champ – he's nicked for drunk and disorderly at some snooker hall and they take him in and it's a slow night, so my mate's old man says to Alex Higgins, the Hurricane, not knowing who he is, why don't we play a frame as there's a table in the station?'

'And Higgins says how much for?'

'Spot on, guv. See, they've got him in overnight, so a handful of them – CID, plod, even the janitor, who's apparently quite tasty – take him on, this pissed Mick youth, and he's giving them fifty points and first go and hammering them all and pocketing their hard-earned Queen's penny.'

'Bingo.'

'The luck of the Irish.'

'I should know, son, given my family heritage.'

'No offence, guv.'

'None taken.'

More and more, Parker wonders what it is exactly that he's doing.

'Were you there on Saturday then?' Noble asks.

'In Brixton?' Meaning the riots.

'No, you wally, at Upton Park.'

'I was not, guv.'

'Terrific game,' Noble assures Parker. 'They're all right, Forest.'

'Not good enough though.'

'Frank McAvennie scored twice, Tony Cottee the once, and Alan Dickens made it four.'

'Who scored theirs?'

'No idea.'

Parker listens to Noble breathe and sniff, sirens and horns –

Noble, pointedly, 'And you weren't at Brixton?'

'No. We decided to give it a swerve.'

'I don't blame them for wanting a row.'

Parker nods, sniffs.

Noble adding, 'They never learn, the boys in blue.'

Cherry Groce shot in her home by armed CID, her son Michael wanted for armed robbery, nowhere to be found –

'They should have sent in a plonk,' Noble says. 'The poor cow was in bed.'

Parker thinks, *Pigs*.

'They're saying here' – meaning Scotland Yard – 'Wood Green's next.'

'Wood Green.'

'Yeah, Tottenham.'

'How do they know?'

'Word's been going around a month or two, is what I'm hearing. Stockpiling.'

'Stockpiling what?'

'Petrol.'

'Give over.'

'Lakes of it, apparently, on an estate in west Tottenham.'

'Which one?'

'Broadwater Farm.'

Parker thinks: Carolyn's cousin –

'You hearing anything like that, son?'

'Not a sausage.'

'Well, it's coming from somewhere.'

'Everything does, guv.'

'Very clever.'

'What you can't see is me bowing.'

'At the usual spot,' Noble interrupts, 'there's an envelope, a video.'

'Sounds fruity.'

'It's a news report. You'll note the content and know the context.'

'OK.'

'What I want to know if there's anyone in this news report that you recognise.'

'Crystal.'

'Good lad. You remember our friend I mentioned a few months back, her boyfriend a part of Paul Weller's new outfit?'

'I do.'

'Find out if she's anything to do with this, and either way I want an address, contact details, all right?'

'Shouldn't be a problem.'

'You're right, it shouldn't.'

'One thing, guv.'

'Fire away.'

'This stockpiling in Tottenham.'

'That you've heard nothing about.'

'I might know a bloke who knows a bloke.'

'Authorised?'

'It's not really my patch, is it?'

Noble breathes out hard. 'No one knows what you do but me.'

'I'll take that as you giving me permission.'

Noble laughs. 'Anything new on young Trevor?'

'Nothing new, no.'

Noble considers this. 'See you around.'

Parker hangs up.

There's been nothing new for quite a while, Parker thinks, which might be good news for Trevor, but it's not helping Parker's progress in his unofficial capacity.

Back home, Parker pops the VHS of a recent news report into his video player.

After the killings of Colin Roach and Blair Peach, who lived in the borough, the Hackney Teachers' Association called for the exclusion of police from its schools and about a third – eighteen – took up the proposal.

A ginger newsreader appears on the screen:

'Juvenile crime in Hackney is no higher than the national average and the police are determined to keep it that way.

'The Hackney Teachers' Association doesn't like the way the police are operating in an area where anti-police feeling is high.

'Now the police have responded with a "Good Neighbour" offensive.'

Parker watches a black policeman dancing to Chaka Khan's 'I feel for you' at a school disco, a fairly pathetic attempt to engage with the youth, or whatever the correct policy terminology is.

PC Eddie Thomas patrolling the streets on foot, visiting Burbage Junior School, sure of a warm welcome, banned from the Infants School, however, in the same building.

The headmaster saying:

'The police would come in and say, well, those things don't happen or we're not all bad. The reaction of the children was, well, you know, all right, you may have been specially trained to come and soft-soap us, you're not the ones kicking the life out of us down the station.'

He's got a point, Parker thinks. Now, a black kid saying:

'I mean they can come in and act benign and friendly and say, well, we're your local copper on the beat, give you a pat on the head and that's it, but, I mean, next time they see you on the street, they catch you and there'll still be the same hostile reaction to you.'

Well put. Then, Colin Roach and Blair Peach –

'Bad memories go back a long way.'

Says the reporter.

Back to the disco and coppers clapping with the kids to 'Agadoo' by Black Lace –

Pushing pineapple, shaking the tree.

Parker stops the tape and hits eject. Point is he helped print the pamphlet explaining the Hackney Teachers' Association's decision at 50 Rectory Road, same place as was HQ for the Roach Family Support Committee. Same place the ginger bird Noble was on about used to volunteer –

Parker asks himself if he recognised any of the faces.

He didn't.

He scoops himself up from the sofa and gathers his thoughts.

He re-sleeves the VHS cassette and takes it into his bedroom. He opens his wardrobe and feels for the latch at the back. He flips it open and feeds the VHS cassette into the space behind, re-latches.

He pockets wallet, keys, loose cash.

Sets off for 50 Rectory Road.

There, he finds Carolyn standing behind a desk thumbing through some file or other.

'Babe,' he nods, unsmiling, from across the room, his big frame in the doorway.

Carolyn looks up, goes back to her papers. 'Babe,' she says.

They both wait for the other to crack first –

'Sod it,' Parker says.

Two of his lengthy strides and he's whipped her into his arms and off her feet –

'I'm extremely excited to see you,' he informs her.

'I can tell.'

'Anyone about, is there?'

'Randy bastard.'

Parker kisses Carolyn with a fair amount of urgency –

'There is.' She breaks off, nods towards the door. 'Kitchen.'

'I'll make us a cuppa, shall I?'

'Please.'

A mug in each hand, Parker returns and sits.

'I've been thinking about the Hackney Teachers' Association,' he says.

'Dark horse.'

'Something Marlon said, about the younger brethren.'

'Marlon.'

'Yeah, you know –' being ironic – 'like he's after becoming some sort of guidance counsellor.'

Carolyn, reading again now, looks up. 'What, Marlon? *What*?'

'I'm joking.'

'Which bit?'

'Marlon the parish wiseman bit.'

'But you have been thinking about the Hackney Teachers' Association?'

'I have.'

'And?'

'Well, your cousin, in the summer, Live Aid.'

'They all live in Tottenham.'

'My point, darling.'

Carolyn shakes her head. 'I'm afraid to ask, babe. Getting a straight answer out of you today is like, well, you know, it's hard.'

'He's at school, right, and he's out of school, too. Where does he go? They doing the same thing up there is what I'm asking.'

'The teachers?'

'The teachers, the kids, the Old Bill. The lot.'

Carolyn examines Parker and speaks slowly to him now, as if he were a child, he thinks – or slow. 'Do you want to talk to my cousin Shaun, darling?'

'That'd be sweet, yeah, cheers, babe.'

Carolyn smiling, 'Well, we took the scenic route getting there –'

'No need to be sniffy.'

Carolyn takes a pencil and scribbles something on a scrap of paper, hands it to Parker.

'Address and phone number,' she tells him. 'And if you've any sense, you'll ring ahead.'

'Nice one.'

Carolyn sits down. Indicating the file she's been perusing, she says, 'We've had more statements.'

'How many now?'

'Well over a dozen. And they're all the same, really.'

Parker nods. 'Pigs, yeah?'

'Regional Crime Squad.'

The patterns, Parker's noticing with these statements regarding police malpractice in Stoke Newington and Hackney, follow several models.

The first is that young black men are assaulted by the police as part of a daily campaign of harassment against them – and then they themselves are charged with assaulting the police officers.

If they aren't charged with assault, they're slapped with some other indictable offence, which means, effectively, that they're remanded in custody when their only crime is to have been assaulted by police officers.

What they're charged with and indicted for is never the reason they were picked up.

In other words, these sentences are handed out at the station, presumably decided by some committee, the arresting officers back out on the beat to find someone else –

Then there's the 'reoffenders', who might have previously done a three-month stretch for possession, for example – they're arrested again, beaten up and planted, a longer sentence given if it pans out, which more or less follows Trevor's experience.

Revenge and control are what it seems to be about, Parker thinks. What else?

Parker reckons there's something else going on, the sort of thing that likely wouldn't go into one of these statements given it could well be somewhat incriminating for the chap *making* the statement – *if* Parker's right about something else going on, that is, and, of course, he's not sure exactly what it is that he thinks *is* going on, which is why he needs Trevor.

As a basic principle, 'recycling' is a broad sort of a church: drugs confiscated, seized and sold on through a plod-sanctioned dealer, money kicked back into the firm within a firm. Generally speaking; Parker wonders if there are specifics of which he needs to be aware.

Parker doesn't really believe Marlon's involved in this, does he?

If these things are really happening at all.

That's the problem with evidence gathered from a drug dealer: they'll say anything.

He shakes his head, not even thinking about the protection game Rice and Cole were running, the old slot machine tax –

He nods at Carolyn. 'There a file for volunteers? Here, I mean? Anyone from Tottenham way, is my point.'

'Photocopier room, top shelf. That's not a bad idea, for you.'

'Back in my youth –' Parker grins – 'photocopier room, top shelf would have meant something quite different.'

'I said you were a randy old bastard.'

Parker unfolds his limbs from his own chair now. 'Less of the old.'

'Just one thing – about my cousin, yeah?'

Parker stops, nods. 'Yeah?'

'He's got a lot of aunties and uncles, cousins, you know, but he doesn't have parents, not really.'

Parker thinks what does that mean exactly?

'His mum,' Carolyn goes on. 'Well, she passed when he was very young. And his dad—'

'Ain't around?'

'Jamaica. He couldn't really handle it.'

'Right.'

'What I mean is, he's always looking for a substitute, you know, not that he'd ever say that, or even *realise* it, to be honest.'

Parker nods.

'I just mean be nice, that's all.'

'Course, darling. When am I anything but?'

Carolyn smiles at that, shaking her head.

In the photocopier room, Parker retrieves the file from the top shelf and flips through the pages, the pages of names, the pages of addresses, the pages of photos, the pages of passport photos, a photo for each volunteer, a way of documenting their involvement, a way of keeping track and making sure that each volunteer is on the level, and there she is, *active*, it claims, Suzi Scialfa, living a little further afield now, a Stoke Newington address crossed out and a new one inked in:

Leopold Buildings, off Columbia Road.

But Noble won't be calling ahead in this scenario, Parker thinks.

*The look on the lug's face gives him away –*

*No idea what he's doing.*

*Terry says to him, 'You do know who you're talking to, don't you?'*

*The lug nodding, 'Course I do, yeah.'*

*Terry, arms spread and grinning, raising his eyebrows, shrugging. His meaning:* Well, then.

*You know that look.*

*'I mean, yeah, I've heard of your firm, course I have.'*

*'Firm?' Terry says.*

*'Corporation, I mean, your outfit, you know.'*

*The lug's a quick talker. Big lad, local boy, wide, he shifts in his seat –*

*'I mean, reputation as a business, know what I mean.'*

*Terry smiles. He eases himself off your desk where he's been sitting. He edges around the office, stands behind the lug, who tries not to notice. Terry looks over. You nod. Terry plants his hands on the lug's shoulders –*

*'You're in our office, son, of course you know who we fucking are.'*

*'You invited me to your office, didn't you?'*

*From behind your desk, you speak. 'We did. We appreciate your coming.'*

*Terry says, 'We know all about your outfit, too.'*

*'Yeah?'*

*You nod at Terry, who retires to a chair near the door. You stand. You indicate that the lug should do the same. 'Come with me,' you say. 'I want to show you something.'*

*Terry opens the door. Out you all step onto the forecourt –*

*Relaxed again, the lug says, 'It's a nice place you've got here.'*

*You smile. 'No, it ain't. But that's beside the point.'*

*Across the forecourt, vastness.*

*Ahead, the Portakabins. To your left, the garage. To your right, the storage containers. You indicate the lot with a long sweep of your hand.*

*'It's something.'*

*You lead the way towards the storage containers.*

*'Those shipping?' the lug asks.*

*You nod.*

*'My old man and his old man and his old man all worked the docks.'*

*You sniff.*

*The lug, pointing, 'It's the future, know what I mean. There's no sense in hanging on to the past when it's dead and buried.'*

*'Bygones.'*

*He turns to you. 'My thoughts exactly.'*

*'Your old man,' you say. 'He dead and buried, is he?'*

*A look you note: concern.*

*'No, he's still alive. Unemployed and angry, but he ain't passed yet.'*

*You nod. 'You're probably wanting to know why we invited you.'*

*The lug says nothing.*

*'We invited you,' you go on, 'to talk about your outfit. Your firm.'*

*'I wouldn't call it that.'*

*'You just did.'*

*'Turn of phrase, know what I mean.'*

*'Your firm,' you say, 'is growing.'*

*'It's a syndicate, you know, a few of us, a handful, that's all.'*

*'I don't mean numbers. I mean it's growing physically. Land. Property.'*

*The lug is nodding now.*

*'And it's growing in an area that interests me.'*

*'OK.'*

*'This' – you gesture, again – 'is mine. This place runs thanks to me.'*

*The lug is now nodding furiously. 'It does.'*

*'And that's why you're here.'*

*You look at Terry, smile.*

*The lug spins around. Terry hands him an envelope, a pen.*

*'You'll be wanting to sign what's in there,' you say. 'Terry, lead the way.'*

*You think: it does run thanks to me, this place.*

*You remember how it happened, too. You, a boy, entering the family trade, doing what was asked of you, making the firm good money, running the books, keeping the chaps happy –*

*Keeping things stable and taking no risks, that was something you learned from your uncle, and it was appreciated, in the climate.*

*Don't break the law while you're breaking the law, was how he put it, your uncle.*

*Don't be flash, another favourite of his.*

*Don't be a mug when it comes to business or pleasure. Don't be a silly billy.*

*Don't be a cunt –*

*It held you in decent stead, your uncle's advice.*

*After The Twins, what was desirable was peace and quiet, live and let live, and you were at the forefront of the new business approach:*

*Business first. Divide and rule –*

*The families worked it out quietly and sensibly and you got Wapping for Christmas 1973.*

*Peace and prosperity, a very merry time.*


Jon Davies' riverside walk west to Wapping is an agreeable one.

The sun is out and the air crisp, that cold blue snap of autumn, no wind to speak of, the Thames at low tide, waders nodding about in the mud, gulls shrieking, the clanging of a bell on an orange rescue boat that's moored to a buoy and half-turned in its empty channel, the water drained as if from a bath, and Jon thinks of plastic toys and Johnson's Baby Shampoo, no one about now, the pubs not open, the cranes and the building work silent behind him, and Jon's wondering how much this job of his is really something of an escape.

This morning, like every morning, he left the family home in Mildenhall Road, Lower Clapton, and bicycled to Bethnal Green Town Hall, aware of the good fortune he has to make this very pleasant journey his commute.

The family home: there's very often a certain level of generalised chaos at the precise time Jon chooses to leave for work.

What family home isn't a little chaotic, he thinks now.

It's not really his fault, not *really*, he does have to get to work after all, there's no argument there, but only he knows that when he does arrive at work, there's no one to check on this arrival, no clock to punch, no supervisor keeping an eye on his time management, no meeting first thing for which he needs to prepare –

It's easier, though, to walk out the door than it is to close one inside.

There's no peace to be had, no way to get the old mindset right when the boy's dragging his feet and the little girl's reminding everyone of her needs at top volume.

They made a decision, together, that Jackie wouldn't look for work until Lizzie was old enough to be in a nursery for most of the week, and she likes to take the boy to school and have Lizzie drop him off with her, and there's a logic to that, it's nice, after all, for the family dynamic and whatnot, and Jon agreed to this arrangement, but, as he does now, he sometimes wonders if he *too readily* agreed on the basis that he would no longer be taking the boy to school on the back of his bike and so could push off a bit earlier and get that peace he needs on his very pleasant commute to his empty place of work.

'It suits us all, trust me, love,' Jackie told him a month or so in.

Jon was sitting on his bike while Jackie, bent over, clipped Lizzie into her pram and the boy kicked a ball against the wall beneath the hedge outside the house next door.

'I just feel guilty.'

'Well don't.'

'That's easier said than done, Jacks.'

At this Jackie sighed. She smiled. 'It's not about you, Jon, all right?'

Jon wasn't sure why she'd said that, if he was honest.

*He* said, 'It is if I feel guilty.'

Jackie kissed their little girl and stood. 'I told you, Jon, don't.'

She nodded a come on at the boy, winked at Jon –

'Now, piss off,' she said.

And so Jon, as every day, and without ceremony, pissed off.

Turning it over in his mind now, he wonders what exactly it is he feels guilty *about*. It might be, he considers, the simple fact that it's harder, in his mind, to look after children, even a single child, than it is to carry out the duties of his current position. Childcare is hard work. When's Jon's actually *at* work, it's a holiday. And that in no way denigrates his family life, which is exceptional and makes him very, very happy. It's just a fact: work is easier than looking after your own children.

It's simply less work.

Now, as he passes the Wapping Stairs, he heads away from the river, north, to look at this Compliance Ltd facility and it doesn't take him too long to locate it –

There's fuck all else about, he thinks.

Derelict wharf buildings, empty warehouses, rotting timber and rusted iron –

And there, rising up behind it, a factory and an office block, it looks like.

Jon pauses to appreciate the grandeur of the facility, its gesture –

He looks up, examines the skyline, thinks: what's next?

He remembers Jackie's cousin Chick harping on about his syndicate and its property portfolio, and the new airport, and he wonders, Jon does, if he shouldn't get old Chick on the blower. He also wonders if the London Docklands Development Group includes Wapping in its remit.

This, he thinks, is something he really should know by now. The fact he doesn't is representative of the murkiness around the corporation, Jon tells himself, and not down to incompetence or lack of foresight on his part.

As he approaches the facility, the perspective changes, and he sees that it is ring-fenced at ground level, high steel fences, barricades and razor wire, impenetrable. Closed-circuit TV cameras visible. What Jon thinks must be electronically controlled gates.

There is an entrance, and at the entrance is a barrier, and behind the barrier is a security detail, and the detail – consisting of two large men in suits – is currently sharing what looks like cups of tea and bacon rolls with two police officers in uniform.

They look well acquainted, Jon thinks as he approaches:

They're certainly laughing about something.

Jon delivers himself to the entrance barrier with a smile.

'I've got an appointment,' he says, 'but I'm a bit early. That OK?'

The laughter stops. The police officers, on the same side of the barrier as Jon, take a step back and Jon feels somewhat surrounded as a result.

He looks over his shoulder and gives the officers a thumbs up.

The larger of the security thugs, indicating a lanyard hugging his thick neck, says, 'You got a pass?'

Jon shakes his head.

'Then I don't think you have an appointment, son.'

Jon nods. Jon points, upwards. 'It's for a job,' he says. 'An interview.'

The two thugs exchange looks.

One look seems to say, could be?

The other, clearer: no fucking way.

'There's no interviews today, OK, so piss off.'

Jon smiles, scratches his head. 'I could have sworn –'

'Interviews were last week,' the smaller of the thugs offers.

This smaller thug gets another look: you soppy sod.

First thug nods at the police officers. 'You're not going to need persuading, are you?'

'Of course not!' Jon says, cheerfully. 'I'm just a complete wally, aren't I, turning up on the wrong day!'

'Wrong week,' says the smaller of the thugs.

Another look: turn it in.

The police officers take a further step back.

The larger thug steps around the barrier and towards Jon and leans close to Jon's face. He says, 'My job is nothing to do with what goes on inside this building, you understand?'

'I'm not sure I do, no.'

'My boss' – the thug smiling now, evil with it – 'is nothing to do with the building. We are simply security for the *land*, you understand?'

'As in this is your patch?' Jon suggests.

'As in they look the other way' – pointing at the police officers – 'and we see that you don't forget your visit in a hurry, yeah?'

Jon nods. 'That I understand,' he says.

'Triffic. You have a good day then.'

Jon nods and turns. The police officers wink.

As Jon walks back towards the river, he hears laughter again.

He doesn't turn around –

In the backstreets of Wapping, in the October air, the now grey, damp sky whitening, Jon thinks:

*What was that all about?*

He hopes he doesn't get a similar reception at all the other buildings on his list, those two blokes could do some serious damage and not think too hard about it.

The air damp, the sky freezing, Jon shakes his head.

He feels, from behind him, a hand on his shoulder.

He flinches. He braces himself. He doesn't turn around.

His eyes half-shut, a heart-jumping fear –

'Can I have a word?'

His legs heavy –

'A quick word, I'm on your side!'

His head spinning, his head light –

'I'm not going to hurt you!'

He feels faint, sees stars –

'Wait!'

Bent double now, his hands on his heavy legs, and he's retching –

'Woah! You OK?'

Nodding and retching, the acrid burn, the stomach churn –

'Here, drink this.'

And it's over.

Jon gulps at a water bottle, breathes deeply, heavily, and looks up at the face of a man brandishing a press card with the words 'Socialist Worker' prominent.

Jon spits and laughs. 'You . . .' He points at a man in Lenin cap and corduroy dungarees. 'I thought you were going to beat me up.'

Offended a touch, the man says, 'All right, no need to be funny.'

Jon's laughing hard now. 'Socialist Worker.' He points towards the facility. 'That your new office, is it? Your circulation must be through the roof!'

And this makes Jon laugh so hard that he belches, he belches and he spits, and he straightens up and calms down and asks, 'What can I do you for?'

'You can give me my water back for a start.'

Jon smiles, looks at the bottle. 'You sure?'

'I was only joking.'

'Good man.'

'I'd like a word.'

'I'm all ears.'

'You know somewhere we can go?'

Jon nods. 'I do, as it happens. You fancy stretching your legs?'

As they walk off, Jon says, 'What were you doing there anyway?'

'Those security guards.'

'Lovely fellas.'

'I was talking to one a while back, but he doesn't seem to work there anymore.'

'You didn't get his number?' Jon laughs.

'It wasn't that kind of a relationship.'

'Well,' Jon says, 'I hope he's as cut up about it as you are.'

On the train back from Saffron Walden, Suzi thinks that it was a good day, overall, that her mum seemed OK, and that she wished she did it – visited her mum – a little more often.

Not that it had started perfectly.

'He would have been so pleased for you, love.'

Suzi didn't doubt that her late father would have enjoyed her recent homeowner status – he paid for the flat. Well, his inheritance did. An inheritance that came with one condition – buy a flat.

But Suzi didn't need her mum's first words to her in almost a year to be a reminder.

'It's good to see you, Mum.'

'Come inside, both of you, get out of the cold.'

Suzi resisted the urge to tell her mother that they were only still in the cold thanks to her, that they could have had this conversation in the warm. She resisted the urge to say it, but not to communicate it to Keith in a look.

'Now, now, sweetheart,' Keith reminded her. 'Behave.'

Sweetheart. That was a clever way of mollifying her.

Her old nickname: Suzi Sweetheart.

When she first got on the scene in the late seventies, so many people – so many men – called her sweetheart that she took it on as a moniker, reverse appropriation.

'Can I get you something, Keith?' Suzi's mum flapped. 'A sherry or a lager?'

'Love a lager, Mrs S.,' Keith agreed. 'I know where they are, thank you.'

'You'll help yourself.'

The fridge, Suzi thought, always stocked for someone else.

She wondered what was in there for her and whether it was put there precisely for *her*.

'I'll have one too, Keith,' Suzi called, Keith's head already in the fridge.

'Oh, there's only a few of them,' Suzi's mum warned, a hand on Suzi's arm. 'Have a sherry with me.'

Suzi decided on a sherry, to begin with.

It was, Suzi thinks now, a standard opening gambit. It's not her mum's intention to make Suzi feel the way she does, but it's how Suzi feels.

The train is quiet, and the night dark enough that she can barely make out what's immediately beyond the window. Satellite towns flash by, the commuter belt. How long might it be before they live in one of these, she thinks, for the space, for the kids. There must be a lot of it, space, out here in the commuter belt. All the greenery and the no-mark towns, Shitsville, as her dad put it. Do you need all that space for the kids? Is space a requisite? I mean, she thinks, kids are only small, aren't they?

'Tick tock,' her mum winked as they climbed out the car at Audley End station for the train home.

'Oh, we've got loads of time, Mrs S.,' Keith said, tapping his watch. He dug his hand in his pocket. 'Tickets all present and correct!'

Suzi muttered, 'That's not quite what she meant, love.'

'Sorry, love?'

'Nothing.'

It's the obvious question, though, isn't it? *When*?

Say 'when', was what her mum used to tell her, filling a glass or bowl of cereal with milk. Say *when*.

Everywhere she looks in their neighbourhood there are prams doggedly circuiting the backstreets and parks, one or two sprogs in the prams, and quite often two or three older ones hanging off the sides.

Where's all the space for that?

Suzi is beginning to think that class signifiers are the only guiding principle in Thatcher's Britain. Space, and its acquisition, marking quite clearly the difference between the upwardly mobile and the plebs. Like dogs pissing on trees, new housing developments leak outwards from the city, claiming land, claiming space.

This line of thought, Suzi thinks, is as close to broody as she ever gets at the moment. She drinks from her lager, stares at the blackness through the window, the lights inside reflected like decorations on a Christmas tree, strung across the cold glass, shimmering.

She rolls a cigarette and lights it.

Keith, sprawled across two seats, feet up, brandishes his copy of the *NME* at Suzi. 'Have a gander at this, love.'

Suzi takes it and reads.

A full-page advert for The Style Council, listing the singles and albums that they have so far released, with the strapline:

FOR YOUR LISTENING PLEASURE FROM PROBABLY
THE BEST POP GROUP IN THE WORLD

Suzi smiles. 'Very good.'

'I mean, it's not far from the truth, Suze, looking at that list.'

Suzi doesn't deny it. Paul Weller's made some interesting choices regarding the tracklisting of the two albums. He's hardly front and centre, she thinks, another phrase of her old man's.

But the singles! Not long ago, someone told Suzi that the Jam were the quintessential British singles band – and that The Style Council were going to be even better!

'They're becoming the quintessential British singles band, love,' Keith says.

'European, love,' Suzi replies. 'I think that's more what Weller's after, don't you?'

'As ever, my darling –' Keith stretches and groans, pleasantly – 'I find it very hard to disagree with you.'

'I love you, Keith, you know.'

'As I said, very hard to disagree.'

Suzi smiles. Keith opens another pair of lagers.

She looks at the date in the *NME*: Saturday 5 October, tomorrow, and realises Keith must have picked it up first thing. She checks her watch: the train should arrive in Liverpool Street in fifteen minutes or so. As they skirt Enfield and north Tottenham and cross Hackney Marshes, she wonders how the meeting she helped set up between Weller, Annajoy David and Billy Bragg went.

Soon, they'll be at a party: Friday night and all that will entail. She's looking forward to the boost of more booze, of drugs and talk –

In the night sky, through the blackness of the window, she imagines the line from where she is sitting, across Springfield Park, into Stoke Newington, down, down, down into Tottenham, and oblivion.

Space, she thinks.


*Shaun.* There's a bit of a buzz about the Youth Association, but it's outside, this buzz, all the people knocking about, and me and Anton are tucked in a corner with a few girls from school, so we're looking on.

My cousin's here and she's doing the rounds, which is funny, she's Hackney, really, I mean where she lives, and she comes over and Anton goes, 'All right, Shaun's cousin?'

He gives her a big smile and a wink, and I shake my head.

'All right, Shaun's friend?' Carolyn says.

I give her a look. 'What you doing here?'

'Seeing Gran.'

'I mean *here*.'

'I've been coming here years, longer than you, cuz.'

Anton raises his fork. 'Is this a family dispute that requires some form of mediation? If so, I'm here, I offer my services—'

'Mediation?' Carolyn makes a face.

'General studies,' I say. 'We're doing conflict.'

'Doing conflict? That what they call it?'

'Diplomacy and escalation, Shaun's cousin.' Anton points outside. 'Intimidation and withdrawal. Bluff and countermove. You know.'

We all look out the window. There's a lot more police than normal. A line of them, though friendly, sort of, which is weird.

'What I mean,' I say, 'is there's a lot of Hackney here, and then here's you.'

'I came to see you, stupid.'

'Yeah?'

'Yeah. A favour.'

'Course it's a favour.'

'Hey, respect your elders.'

'Yeah,' puts in Anton. 'Me for a start.'

He's a month older. I shake my head, kiss my teeth, give Anton a look.

'But you can see what I can see,' I say.

'What's the problem with some new faces, Shaun?'

I shake my head. 'Why *they* here?' Meaning the police.

Carolyn looks serious now, leans down between us. 'You know what happened at the weekend down in Brixton.'

Anton examines his plate. I shrug.

'Yeah, well,' Carolyn says.

The girls are chatting something about nails or whatever girls chat about, homework.

I stick out my lip. 'What about this favour, then?'

'My man, you remember him?'

Anton flick-snaps his fingers. 'Hero! Course we remember! Boy really showed those pigs that time, nuff respect.'

I look at Anton. Carolyn looks at Anton. We crack up laughing.

'Nuff respect, yeah, Anton?' Carolyn says.

Anton sucks his teeth, mumbles something about leave it out, eats his beans.

'So,' Carolyn says, 'Parker's coming over, have a look at what goes on here, and I thought you could show him around a bit, bit of hospitality, yeah?'

I pretend that I'm busy, come on, what you think I don't have a life of my own, all that, Anton laughing, going, life of your own, bruv! Carolyn smiling –

'Yeah, OK, OK,' I say. 'When?'

'He'll call at Gran's, all right?'

I nod. 'Why though?'

'Does it even matter?'

I pull a face like, so tell me anyway.

'Community project,' Carolyn says. 'You know, schools, all that, what you do after. No big thing, yeah?'

I shrug. 'Whatever, yeah.'

Carolyn's hands are still on the table, her head down and I watch as she looks outside for a long moment, sees groups of youths sort of shuffling near to this line of police, and everyone's chatting and smiling, like they must be taking the piss, I don't know.

'I'm going to go see Gran now, yeah, see you up there?'

I nod. 'Yeah, see you up there.'

Anton watches Carolyn leave, watches for too long, man, and I cuff him up the head and tell him, 'Respect, man!'

And he gives me this sick little smile and says, 'Yeah man, respect, respect is right! Nuff respect, your cousin, yeah,' and he's laughing and laughing and laughing –

I'm shaking my head. 'No, man,' I tell him. 'That's wrong, yeah.'

And he says, 'Yeah, no, you're right, how's that fine ting your cousin, man, something wrong there, man, something definitely wrong.'

And he's laughing, his mouth full, beans flying –

And I keep looking at the police and, yeah, it all looks friendly and that, but ever since that day when that Parker helped us out, I just been waiting for another day like that, me and Anton, we're big enough now, been for a while –

And when's it gonna happen again, 'cos it's gonna.

There's a bit of movement outside, and the girls next to us shut up for once, they're staring at the door, and a few older man come in, and there's one there I seen about, where though I don't know, and I'm looking at him, and he sees me looking and he grins, and I look down, and he goes, All right?, nods, and I nod, but I don't remember his name and he ain't from round here, where do I know him from anyway, I better ask around, yeah –

Mrs Thatcher dials the number of her favourite senior officer.

'It would be prudent to find proof in some form or other of stockpiling at the location we discussed earlier this week.'

Her favourite senior officer is not surprised to hear her voice, she, Mrs Thatcher, thinks.

Her favourite senior officer says, 'Yes, ma'am, all is in hand.'

'Proof, I hope,' Mrs Thatcher continues, 'whose provenance will be impossible to *officially* disclose and yet incontestable in its origin.'

'Exactly what we have in mind, ma'am.'

'And, I shouldn't need to add, *before* any event.'

'It's all in hand, ma'am.'

'Very good,' Mrs Thatcher says.

She turns back to the papers on her desk, the draft of her speech to the Conservative Party Conference in not even a week, 11 October 1985, the Winter Gardens, Blackpool, ten years, she thinks, since she first addressed the conference as leader.

She picks up her pen. To a section in the middle, she adds the word 'Tottenham'. It now reads:

In Tottenham and Handsworth, the police suffered a hail of bricks and petrol bombs, apparently ready to hand.

It isn't the police who create threats to public order. Nor is it social conditions that generate violence. Yes, unemployment breeds frustration. But it's an insult to the unemployed to suggest that a man who doesn't have a job is likely to break the law.

She looks again at the beginning, is satisfied, she thinks:

When we Conservatives said, 'This is the way,' they said, 'Forget it.'

We were told you can't reform trade union leaders, you can't reform

101

the trade unions – their leaders won't let you. But we did.

We were told you can't abolish price and wage controls – inflation will go up. But we did – and it came down.

We were told you can't give council tenants the right to buy. But we did – and the houses sold like hot cakes.

They said you can't denationalise – the unions won't wear it. But we did – and the workforce positively snapped up the shares.

And we were told you'll never stand a major industrial strike, let alone a coal strike. Mr President, it lasted a whole year. But we did just that – and won.

Next, she examines the end, the climax. She's happy with it, she thinks.

Come with us then towards the next decade. Let us together set our sights on a Britain: where three out of four families own their home; where owning shares is as common as having a car; where families have a degree of independence their forefathers could only dream about.

A Britain where there is a resurgence of enterprise, with more people self-employed, more businesses and therefore more jobs.

A Britain where there is a standard of health care far better than anything we have ever known. Where savings keep their value; and where people can look forward to their retirement, certain of their pension, confident of its buying power.

A Britain where standards in our schools are a source of pride; and where law-abiding men and women go their way in tranquillity with their children, knowing that their neighbourhood is safe and their country secure.

Mr President, step by step we are rolling back the frontiers of socialism and returning power to the people. Yes, we have set our sights high. But these goals are within our reach. Let us ensure that we bring them within our grasp.

# 2

## *Uptown top ranking*

5 October 1985

Saturday morning, first thing, 5 October: Parker finds himself in Tottenham on the Broadwater Farm Estate.

Day before, the Friday morning, and he meets Dolly Kiffin, the estate's matriarch and leader of the Youth Association. She's pretty cool, Dolly Kiffin. Earlier in the year, documented in photos dotted around the modest Youth Association premises, the Princess of Wales made a 'direct approach' to Dolly Kiffin and subsequently visited. There was disco dancing and a pensioners' dinner. It all went swimmingly, Parker gathers.

She gets about, he thinks, the Princess of Wales, remembering Live Aid. Likes a disco dance, that's clear. Must have been quite a party. Old big lugs Charlie wasn't in any of the photos, but perhaps he didn't fancy it: he didn't look too chuffed at Wembley, neither.

Dolly Kiffin was buzzing, too, having only very recently returned from Clarendon, Jamaica, on a two-month trip for the borough council, to facilitate a twinning link with the district where she grew up.

Working closely with council leader Bernie Grant, she tells him, and it's clear to Parker that attempts are being made to provide something resembling security and opportunity for the area's younger population, especially the young men.

Parker reports this to Noble on the Friday afternoon.

'She's on the level,' he says, of Dolly Kiffin.

'Not sure how helpful her being in Jamaica has been in terms of youth guidance, however.'

'I'm not sure how helpful that comment is, guv.'

Noble laughs. 'You seem smitten.'

'Force for good, guv. End of.'

'Fair enough.'

'There's a report, from eighty-one. She sorted it. Listen to this: "The estate ... offered nothing to young black people except a home. They were effectively excluded from the social club. They had no other facilities on the estate. The young men, many of them unemployed, had nothing to do. The old people were afraid of them, the police suspected them. The young women with children were isolated and lonely. The teenagers had the use of a flat in Hawkinge block which operated on three evenings a week, but nothing more. The physical appearance of the estate was run-down and ill maintained."'

'What's your point?'

'Jesus, guv, you had a sense of humour bypass?'

'Hey, don't forget who you're talking to, son.'

Parker breathes, sighs, apologises. 'This isn't easy, guv. I know precisely one person on the ground here. I'm well out of my depth.'

'Don't worry, son, I know it's tough. Stay stylish, you know you're good at that.' Noble pauses. 'Look, I apologise too. I'm being … I think the word is cynical. And there's a reason for that.'

'Any reason you're going to tell me?'

'I've had word from on high.'

'What about?'

'You'll remember the official reason you're nosing about up there?'

'Official meaning unofficial meaning official.'

'OK, clever clogs, spot on.'

'Lakes of petrol, something like that?'

'Bingo.'

'What about it?'

Noble breathes out. Parker's not sure he needs to hear whatever it is that Noble's about to tell him.

'It's what the French call a fait accompli.'

Parker says nothing.

Noble goes on. 'A done deal.'

'You mean this petrol is here?'

'I mean you're the proof that it is.'

'You're having me on.'

'I wish I were, son, believe me.'

'So I don't even need to find it?'

Noble sniffs. 'There's been a spate, last few weeks, of robberies of garages, all sorts, forecourts, private, mechanics, all north London, all within shooting distance of the Farm.'

'That doesn't mean anything.'

'No, it doesn't. But it *is* circumstantial.'

'And I'm the clown that confirms it, am I?'

Noble says nothing.

'Guv?'

'Point is, son, you don't need to spend too much more time there.'

'OK.'

'Have another nose about in the morning, knock off for the afternoon.'

'What a line manager.'

'You've said that before.'

'Why the morning?'

'Good to be seen about the place.'

Parker nods. 'My contact, it's her cousin I'm with.'

'Right.'

'I'm meeting him in a minute. Got something to tell me, something he wants me to see.'

'You best get on then.'

'Yeah.'

'Parker, son, you're doing a grand number, all right? I've told you too much, but for your own good, you understand. There ain't nothing for it, OK?'

Parker nods again. He knows this, and he knows Noble's looking out for him. He knows that all he has to do is *be*.

He says, 'Thanks, guv,' and he means it.

Off the blower and down the street, round the corner, across the road, the estate rearing up around him, graffiti and rats, his big man boots and jacket a two-tone remnant, his eyes skinned, his nous lit up, senses sharp, that bounce, that look, friendly but alert, only a bob or a weave from shaping up, a bit of face, a grin for the local brethren, and then –

'All right, hero.'

Parker grins. Parker mock bows. 'Shaun.'

They slap hands.

'Come on then, big man,' Parker says. 'Lead the way.'

Shaun nods into the estate and Parker zips up his maroon bomber jacket and turns up the collar of his Fred Perry polo shirt. They navigate walkways and alleys, nooks and crannies stinking of piss, groups of youths nodding and calling out to Shaun, who is, Parker notes, extremely popular. One or two catcalls about the white man and Shaun deflects these deftly with some patter about Parker giving his cousin one and it seems to do the trick, so Parker thinks, fair play, on you go, and they're up a level, across a courtyard, it's a maze, he'll give it that, then down again and back, Parker now sees, in front of the Youth Association premises.

Though not actually at the *front* of the premises, but across another corridor and with a clear view –

'We going in again, are we, big man?'

Shaun shakes his head. 'Just watch, yeah?'

'You're the boss.' Parker pauses. 'What am I watching *for*?'

Shaun turns to Parker and makes a gesture meaning all in good time, my friend.

Parker regards the estate.

It's not markedly different from those he's known in Hackney: the same scent of failure, the same disrepair, the same browns and greys and beige – the endless corridors and walkways, a mugger's paradise.

There's a difference here though: it feels like a fortress or a castle with a fucking moat, and why? It feels like it's surrounded despite it spreading out like a stain into the maisonettes and one-up and one-downs on the fringes, creeping into the markets and among the bookies and the pubs, the caffs and the schools, the post offices and the pound shops –

Parker is reminded of highbrow reading from his after-school club: *Utopia*.

There's another difference: there's a lot of boys and young men kicking about; there's not a lot to do, neither, and it doesn't take a commissioned report to work that out.

Shaun points at a group of the young men, the boys. 'See them youths, they ain't from the Farm.'

'No?'

Shaun shaking his head. 'Nah, they ain't even Tottenham. They're from your ends, hero.'

'Hackney?'

Shaun nodding.

'And your mob don't mind?'

'Teaming up.'

'My enemy's enemy is my friend sort of thing?'

Shaun looks amused, Parker thinks, dry.

'If you say so, hero.'

'They're going inside,' Parker notes.

'Cheap dinners in the association.'

'They're here for the grub?'

Shaun laughs. Shaun points beyond the premises, where there stands a group of uniformed police officers.

'That's for show.'

'Right.'

'Reason I've heard is one that's more financially driven.'

'You doing well in school, young man?'

'I am.'

'You mean pushers.'

'Yeah.'

'From Hackney, Stoke Newington?'

'Yeah.'

'I think I can join the dots.'

'Yeah?'

'To extend your financial analogy, I'd say there are likely more free market opportunities in this neck of the woods. Less interference from the old pigs over here.'

'Pigs? How old are you?'

Parker laughs. 'So that's what you wanted to show me?'

'Calm yourself, hero, calm yourself.'

They stand. Parker rolls a cigarette.

'Can I have one of them?' Shaun asks.

Parker groans. 'Here.'

He rolls another and they light them, blow into their hands, stamp their feet –

Then Parker realises why he's here.

Walking around the corner, not a dozen steps away, is Marlon.

'Marlon,' Parker says. 'Well fuck me.'

Shaun grins. 'I thought you'd say that.'

Straight after, Parker gets on the blower to arrange a meet with Trevor, which he sets for Saturday afternoon –

So here he is, Saturday morning, first thing, 5 October: delivering himself again to the Youth Association on the Broadwater Farm Estate.

He's rung ahead.

*Four in the morning and Terry's warming up the car and you're set to do the rounds –*

*'It's fucking Baltic,' you say as you climb into the back seat.*

*Terry hands you a mug of tea.*

*'Get your laughing gear round that, guv,' he says.*

*'You're a gentleman, Terrence.'*

*'Just doing my job, sir.'*

*'As you were.'*

*Your mug of tea steams pleasantly. Terry guides the car softly – you can't abide an unnecessarily fast or jerky driver, and certainly not first thing in the morning. It's not elegant; it doesn't communicate the correct message.*

*You sit back in your seat and study the cityscape, east London a construction site.*

*Cranes dominating emptiness. Steel and concrete. High-rise buildings creeping upwards like some giant animal herd.*

*You think of pods and extraterrestrials. You think of invasion and insurrection. You think of –*

'I've been reading, Terry,' you tell him.

'What for?'

'Says the non-reader.'

'It's a fair cop.'

'Reading, Terry, is a way of sharpening the imagination.'

'You mean it gives you ideas?'

'You could say that, Terry, yes.'

'Any good ones, guv?'

'Ideas? Plenty.'

'Books.'

'Oh, I see. You after a recommendation?'

'Just making conversation, guv.'

'That's another thing about books, they don't half help with the art of conversation.'

'That sounds like a criticism, guv.'

'Terrence, your arts are deployed elsewhere, and more effectively than any conversationalist.'

'Thanks, I think.'

'When I'm reading, Terry, I like to write down my favourite lines. Food for thought, you see.'

Terry says nothing.

'I am currently reading a novel by J.G. Ballard, published in nineteen seventy-five, called High-Rise.'

'Sounds good.'

'They say, Terry, that one shouldn't judge a book by its cover. I'd suggest the same is true regarding its title.'

'Sensible.'

'It is good, however.' You withdraw a slim address book from your inside pocket and open it at B, for Ballard. 'Have a listen to this, Terry.'

You read the words you jotted down only a handful of hours earlier.

All the evidence over several decades casts a critical light on the high-rise as a viable social structure, but cost-effectiveness in the area of public housing and the profitability in the private sector kept pushing these vertical townships into the sky, against the real needs of their occupants.

'What do you make of that?' you say.

'It's very well written, guv.'

You laugh at this. 'Very good.'

'Thank you.'

'Point is, it has given me an idea, one we'll be thinking about today at work.'

'Right, strategy.'

'Luxury, right? That's what's needed round here.'

You indicate the east London area with a sweep of your arm –

'We've been generating capital and profit and acquiring land and property to the extent that this' – another sweep of the arm – 'will be transformed. But proper transformation will need an influx of residents, Terry.'

'Rich cunts.'

'Rich cunts. And what we'll do, Terry, is offer within these luxury highrises a number of social housing units.'

'Why would we do that?'

'We'd do that, Terry, as it means our friends on the council, our friends in Whitehall, and our friends in Downing Street will green-light the construction all the quicker. We'd do that as it means we will disperse certain income through the auspices of the London Docklands Development Group.'

'Clever.'

'Reading, Terry, it sharpens the imagination, as I said.'

'We still going to Canning Town first though?'

'We are.'

'We'll be another five minutes or so, guv.'

The city slips by, cool blue, greying. Street lights on low power, fading. Terry stops the car and you climb out under the Silvertown flyover.

'They know we're coming, Terry, I hope?'

'They do.'

A lock-up and a van parked outside, on its side proclaims: *News Inc. Delivery.*

Inside the lock-up, two men wait, standing. Two white men, two brothers. Two white men of a breed you know very well: violent.

At a table, you see a map is spread out. Good, you think. Terry nods at the two men and a chair is placed at the table and you sit down.

'Morning, boys,' you say. 'Is the kettle on?'

The two men exchange a look.

Terry says, nodding at the office in the back, 'It only takes one of you. Jog on.'

The junior of the men duly jogs on to make the tea.

'You be sure to warm the pot,' you call after him.

'Right then,' Terry says, 'let's hear it.'

Not long after four a.m. and here you are sitting in an amphetamine sulphate factory in Canning Town, plotting.

'We've had word the drug squad know about this place and plan to do us.'

'When?'

'Before Christmas.'

'And where from, this word?' Terry asks.

The man looks worried. 'It came from the other end.'

'The other end?' Terry repeats.

'Sales, I mean, not distribution or manufacture.'

'Well done,' you say. 'You're learning.'

He looks a little less worried now –

'One of the, um, couriers heard from one of the bent – I mean, payroll plods in Stoke Newington.'

'Drug squad where?' Terry says.

'The Yard.'

You nod. You look at Terry and nod again.

Terry says, 'Right.'

He points at the map. With his finger, he circles an address in Wapping, his finger hovering just above the map. Then he brings it down, firmly.

'Here,' he says, 'is a warehouse. Really a complex of warehouses. You're moving there, today.'

'OK.'

'We're using one of the other warehouses in the complex. Our security is there already, and much slicker than here, you understand?'

'Yes.'

'The other warehouse, you keep the fuck away from, you understand?'

'Yes.'

'One of the team will be waiting. How long will you need?'

The other man returns carrying, unsteadily, a tray. He says, 'Three hours, tops.'

'It better be tops,' Terry says.

You nod. You point at the tray. 'I'll have that to go, as our American brethren would say.'

'There's one thing, guv.'

You exchange a look of mock horror with Terry.

'Is there?'

You look at Terry. 'Did you know about this?'

'I did.'

'That's reassuring.' You look again at your man. 'Let's have it then.'

'Well, guv, we're making speed here, right?'

'I believe so, yes.'

'Well, we reckon there's a better market in a new drug.'

'Which new drug?'

'Crack cocaine.'

'I've heard of it. Wasn't interested.'

'No, I understand, but in the last couple of years, up in Hackney, it's exploded. The payroll we have are not really interested in anything else.'

You nod. You consider this. You look at Terry.

Terry says, 'It checks out.'

You nod again.

'What does it mean logistics-wise?'

*Your man's nodding, too, now. 'The product comes in as it does, pure form, OK?'*

*You nod. You've long had a finger in the pure form game, money kicked up, at least, premises rented for storage, distribution and so on.*

*The idea was always that you stayed in the drug game at least indirectly so as to avoid the trouble that goes along with others doing it and not you.*

*Principle being you can manage it alongside the legitimate interests, and if ever a day comes that it looks all over, you can walk away from it in seconds flat.*

*Nothing ties you to it –*

*But if someone else muscles in, then suddenly it's not just the drug game they're wanting, so you keep it tidy and you keep it clear,* indirectly *–*

*But nothing you won't walk away from in seconds flat.*

*It's not a moral question; you're not your old man, his brothers, you know it's a clear, pragmatic decision to* avoid *trouble.*

*There are two bluebottles at Scotland Yard, both high ranking, who are pleased by this decision, and you show gratitude, regularly, without spelling it out, of course.*

*And so far it's working beautifully –*

*Those foreign gangs keep well away from Wapping.*

*A word with one of these high-ranking detectives, and the drug squad whispers will go away –*

*Still, it's not worth taking any chances.*

*Your man goes on. 'We've got the contacts and the network to take that product and then turn it into the new drug in the factory what we're moving to.'*

*You nod again. You look at Terry again.*

*Terry says, 'You know you'll be held responsible.'*

*Your two men, both of them, nod.*

*'You and your brothers will oversee, will you?' you suggest.*

*Your men, two of the six or seven brothers, you forget how many, both nod.*

*'My last question,' you begin, 'is this.'*

*You gesture at the space in which you sit, under the arches at the Silverton flyover.*

*'What do you need to move from here, exactly?'*

*The two brothers look at each other, weigh the question, you see them doing maths in their heads, counting –*

*'We could be done in an hour.'*

*You stand. 'You're on,' you say. You nod at the door. 'Terrence.'*

*As you reach the door, you turn.*

*'A nice touch would be to leave a Christmas card for Scotland Yard Drug Squad, don't you think?'*

*Your two men, your two brothers, smile.*

*'Something like "Good Luck" inside?'*

*As you exit the premises, laughter.*


Mrs Thatcher is on the telephone to the editor of a favoured tabloid newspaper.

She, Mrs Thatcher, says, 'I realise it's early, but I've had my four hours, so—'

'A woman after my own heart, ma'am.'

'Very glad to hear it.'

'What can I do for you?'

'When the time comes, you understand, in north London, there's something you need to know.'

'When the time comes.'

'Brixton, Peckham, Toxteth.'

'I understand.'

'When the time comes, it's important that the papers have the story from a government source.'

'I understand.'

'That source will demonstrate that a certain housing estate in north London has been accumulating and storing stocks of petrol, among other things, acquired illegally across the capital from a number of outlets.'

'I understand.'

'Details to follow.'

Mrs Thatcher replaces the telephone.

Denis stands in the doorway, hands inside his dressing gown, scratching.

'You're up earlier and earlier.'

Mrs Thatcher nods at Denis's busy hands, smiles. 'You can't think why?' she asks.

'That, you know, what's-his-name?' Pointing at the telephone.

Mrs Thatcher nods.

'Gotcha,' Denis says, winking.


*Bethnal Green Town Hall.*

Jon Davies in his office, pondering.

It's Saturday morning, but he's there, pondering away. He checks his wristwatch: not quite eleven. He told Jackie he'd be back by twelve to take Lizzie to Saturday playgroup, toddler gymnastics, so he needs to get a wriggle on.

At least at the weekend he has the car.

It's not an uncommon occurrence, Jon sitting in his office and pondering. But this time he has something very specific to ponder – Big Chick.

The *Socialist Worker* journalist who Jon thought was a paid thug about to beat him up – embarrassing – had, in fact, some very interesting information for Jon.

The journalist's first question was: how did you know there were job interviews going on, or had been going on?

Jon told him that it was the oldest trick in the book to get inside somewhere.

The journalist's look told Jon that he, Jon, had him intrigued.

His next question: who exactly are you?

At this Jon had smiled.

He outlined his role with regard to the London Docklands Development Group and its relationship to the people of Tower Hamlets,

Newham and Hackney – the reason for having a cross-council borough solicitor in place being the monitoring of the award of building and development contracts by the London Docklands Development Group and related parties.

'You're on our side then,' the journalist said.

Jon said that perhaps they might be able to work a quid pro quo, but first he'd need the journalist's name.

The journalist told Jon that his name was Geraint Thomas.

Jon remarked that they were everywhere, the Welsh.

'London Welsh,' Geraint replied.

'So, quid pro quo?'

'Do they like a sing-song in Swansea?'

They both laughed at that.

Jon said that Geraint should go first.

Geraint spoke of collusion between the news organisation currently engaging in works on new premises in Wapping, and the Electrical Production Union. According to Geraint, recruitment for the new premises was conducted in Portsmouth.

'Portsmouth?'

'At the EPU's office in Portsmouth,' Geraint said. 'In fact, the office is essentially a recruitment centre for Wapping, and more than five hundred men interviewed and prepared for a second interview at the Wapping premises itself.'

'I was right then, with that approach,' Jon congratulated himself, quietly.

Geraint told Jon that he was.

Surprised, Jon asked if he had actually said that out loud.

Geraint nodded. He then told Jon the first question the recruits were asked at their second interview in London:

'Are you prepared to cross picket lines?'

Jon asked Geraint about *The London Herald*, the newspaper that the organisation was officially due to print in Wapping. 'Surely the EPU involvement might be for that?'

'Then why Portsmouth?'

'Good point.'

'No,' Geraint told Jon. '*The London Herald* is a front. In fact, they're going to print *all* their newspapers at Wapping – but without the print unions.'

'How are they going to do that?'

Geraint told Jon that he was hoping that's where he, Jon, might come in.

'*Socialist Worker* has not been able to print all this, as a good deal of it is as yet unsubstantiated and *Socialist Worker* has neither the funds nor legal access to even think about angering this particular news organisation.'

Jon nodded at this. Jon shared all he knew about the London Docklands Development Group and the dispersal of land and property and construction contracts, certain overlaps, speculations –

Jon implied he had more concrete and verifiable details to come. Geraint left believing in their quid pro quo and a certain comradeship.

Which is why Jon is pondering his wife's cousin, Chick. It strikes Jon that Chick might be a man who knows a man who knows a little more about what's going on.

The problem is that Chick is family. Jackie would never forgive him. Well, she might, but she wouldn't like it.

Jon needs another way in, non-work. After all, Jon's never actually telephoned Chick, let alone spent any solo time with him.

But what does Jon have that Chick needs?

Jon remembers, opens his desk drawer and thinks that's just the ticket! And then he laughs.

Two tickets, in fact, to see West Ham play against Arsenal at home the following weekend, 12 October.

He feels sudden guilt, heavily. It weighs down on him this guilt: he had meant to take the boy.

No, he thinks, it's not right –

Then he has an idea and telephones the box office at Upton Park, speaks to a very helpful lady –

Now, she tells him, he has two tickets, but by Tuesday morning, he'll have three.

He hangs up happy, and heads home.

Time to take Lizzie to playgroup.

Jon lifts her into the child seat and gives her a fruit juice for the journey.

Up Mildenhall Road, left onto Chailey Street, right on Millfields Road, up to the top then left onto Rushmore Road and down they go, Lizzie gurgling, singing 'weeeee!', right onto Powerscroft and up to the end.

It'd be quicker, Jon thinks, to simply cycle up to Lower Clapton Road – the main road – and turn left. It's more fun this way, though, quieter, and she likes it, Lizzie does, the left and right and up and down of it.

Lower Clapton Road is getting itself a nickname, Jon thinks: Murder Mile.

He was born on it, in Hackney Mothers' Hospital, Jackie, Lizzie and the boy, too. He looks at the hospital entrance now, the white archway set back, leading through to Mothers' Square.

To the left of the arch in white capital letters:

THE MOTHERS' HOSPITAL
(SALVATION ARMY)

He's heard the council plan to demolish and turn it into flats.

It's a piece of his family, he thinks, really.

A real shame.

But Jon is well aware of council needs and budgets and he's not surprised.

Let's hope they keep the facade, at least, he thinks. It's a beautiful front.

Murder Mile, though, doesn't look like much, Jon reckons.

White goods, takeaways, a Turkish barber, furniture wrapped in plastic, and a dirty garage, is what he can see now. Doesn't really look worth fighting over.

He parks his bike against a sad-looking tree and lifts Lizzie out of the child seat. They head in, into the dome of the United Reformed Church. Jon smiles at one of the hippies who runs the place – Prue? Severin? – and she grimaces at him. Jon smiles and turns to go, but Prue or Severin places a bangled wrist on his arm.

'Before you go, Jon,' Prue or Severin says, 'a word?'

'Sure,' Jon says. 'Shoot.'

Prue or Severin – it's Prue, now, Jon realises – Prue says to Jon: 'We've got a slight problem here, at playgroup.'

Jon nods. Jon watches Lizzie with the other children. He watches as older kids circle each other, giggling, watches as they form a square and start a game, start touching each other and then run away, form the square again. Jon doesn't love the playgroup, to be fair. There's a smell to it: sour milk. He wonders why Prue is talking to him.

'OK,' Jon says.

Prue the hippie puts her hands together. She puts on the sort of earnest look that Jon equates with her bangles and her headband, her cropped hair and her hairy jumper. Jon starts to feel uncomfortable. He thinks, uncharitably, that Prue is dressed in a good number of the clothes he himself saw on tables at the jumble sale that the playgroup organised only the week before.

'Thing is, Jon,' Prue says, 'there's an issue here that we're dealing with.'

'Right,' Jon says.

'Yes, an issue. About the kids.'

Jon, he quickly understands, is pleased to hear that this issue is about the kids.

'Well,' Prue goes on, 'it's about a joke.'

'A joke?'

'A joke.'

There's a pause.

'A joke,' Jon says again.

Prue's hands come together.

Jon leans in, trying to communicate, in earnest, a serious countenance.

'It must have been an older sibling,' Prue says. 'The joke, I mean.'

Jon nods. 'An older sibling,' he says.

Prue nods – quite vigorously. 'Yes,' she says.

They look at each other. Jon expectant; Prue appreciative.

'The joke?' Jon says.

Prue nods – regretfully. 'Irish,' she says.

Jon, unsure, waits.

'What do you say to a thief in Hackney?' Prue asks.

Jon doesn't have an answer.

Prue frowns. She says, 'Irish stew in the name of the law.'

There is a silence that Jon feels may never end.

'We can't have this kind of thing in here,' Prue says.

Jon nods.

'If the kids are already thinking these things—'

'I understand.'

Prue nods. 'You understand.'

She touches his arm again, her hand weighed down by her heavily bangled wrist. 'Thank you,' she says.

Jon doesn't know what to make of this.

The kids turn circles, frantically.


Before Suzi wakes, she hears herself groaning.

It's faint, but it's there, distant, but *there*, just there.

She lies still, very still.

She groans. She moans.

She turns her neck towards the sound – a stiff click.

Her eyes closed. Her head tight, her head clamped, her head *pinched* –

She doesn't so much wake up as come round.

It's a relief, when she does, to feel that spin in the semi-dark, that shudder in the gut, that throb deep in the skull, that belief, that certainty, that if she could just drink some water –

Keith, she realises, has thoughtfully left a pint glass full of it next to her side of the bed and she gulps it down, dribbling it from the corners of her mouth, all over her chin and neck.

God, she loves Keith. Good old Keith.

And then she *hears* him, snoring.

Their duvet is riding up between his legs, his Y-fronts askance, his yellowing vest snug around his middle.

Suzi smiles.

Their bedside alarm clock reads 11.17.

She's been asleep for just over four hours. Keith, she thinks, may have been asleep a good deal less than that. Their hangovers manifest in quite different ways: Suzi can't sleep, Keith can, is the essential difference. It means – and she enjoys this thought even now, her head shrieking at her to lie back down – a few hours to herself, a few hours to do whatever she wants. Keith will be out until early afternoon, earliest.

Tentatively, she rolls from their bed.

As a precaution, she wraps a dressing gown around her, nudges the door to the living room –

No one there. And that really *is* a relief.

An empty living room, just a handful of hours since the last of the last of the drugs were inhaled, the final cans of Red Stripe handed round – still quite full now, Suzi notes – is a true blessing.

She makes a cup of tea and drinks it sitting cross-legged on the sofa, looking through the wrought-iron balcony railings over the top end of Columbia Road and the buses heading west along Hackney Road.

It was a good night, another good night.

There's been a lot of good nights these last few years.

Good nights that have stretched urgently into early mornings; good nights that have aspired to becoming great nights, but, instead, have ended with one or more of Keith's friends snoring on their sofa, Saturday or Sunday morning lost to a patchy few hours of sleep and a hangover that takes an afternoon in the pub to shift.

She wonders if it's their lifestyle, meaning, the independent hours they keep, that they work for themselves, essentially – how is that compatible with *not* getting carried away on a Friday or Saturday night?

It's too easy, chasing fun.

And the thrill really is, as they say, in the chase, because once you've caught whatever it is you're after, you're already on to the next thing, the next tail.

She wonders if they might like to slow down a touch, what that might look like.

She does wonder, Suzi, about things like this.

She rinses her mug, dresses in a tracksuit and thick socks, an old donkey jacket of Keith's, gathers her camera and bag and heads out to walk and take photographs.

One thing about all these good nights: she's taken a lot of photographs.

Weekend mornings in Hackney have become her canvas, hundreds of black-and-white images of every corner of the borough. Technically, of course, she now lives in Tower Hamlets, but it's not called Tower Hamlets' Road, and she invariably heads just far enough east and north that the moniker works.

Hackney Road – scene of the crime. She retraces her steps from the night before.

Crossing to the north side, looking back, she frames a shot of her flat in the Leopold Buildings, the NatWest skyscraper behind, rearing up aggressively, and to the west, the Barbican towers.

She thinks of Keith and feels a flood of warmth, a shudder of love, a counterpoint to her buzzing headache and gnawing stomach.

They ended the first part of the night just across the road from where she now stands: the Flying Scud pub.

She angles her camera to capture the rhomboid thrust of its corner, the name on the top floor, number – 137 – halfway down, TRUMAN FINE ALES, across the Hackney Road facade.

Snap.

Funny place, a regular after-hours haunt for them now, a rock pub, a *hair* pub, men and women in denim and leather drinking bitter, pulling guitar poses to Bon Jovi's 'Runaway' and Iron Maiden.

Not very glamorous.

She'd fallen into talking to a friend of a friend who was with them, Wendy, Wendy with her short blonde crop and shoulder pads, drainpipe jeans and big earrings.

'What are you doing *here*?' Suzi yelled.

Pointing towards Shoreditch, Wendy yelled back, 'I work in the town hall, job-share project.'

Suzi nodded, leaned closer. 'What's that then?'

'Advocacy is the fancy name for it. Encouraging employers to offer job shares, basically, helping people work part-time.'

'Sounds very progressive.'

'I used to work for Hackney Council,' Wendy told her. 'Tenants' association, helping build adventure playgrounds, that sort of thing.'

'OK.'

'Then Grapevine, you know?'

Suzi knew. Sexual health information: I heard it on the grapevine, very clever.

'Anyway,' Wendy said, 'after my first child was born, the council offered me twelve hours a week of clerical work.'

'That's outrageous.'

'It is outrageous.'

'So you're helping mothers, then?'

'Not only, but yeah, that's the idea.'

'Any inroads?'

'The council itself, actually, the fire brigade—'

'You get a lot of mothers there, do you?'

'Now, now.'

'I'm joking.'

They both smiled, drank.

'We're out celebrating as we've just persuaded one of the big trade unions.'

'Which one?'

Wendy laughed at that. 'Printworkers, I forget the acronym!'

'And where are your kids tonight, Wendy?'

'At home with their father!'

You can do that then, Suzi thought.

'Drink?'

Suzi can smell the stale beer, taste the sourness, the smoke –

The words 'trade unions' had loosened a memory, 1978 and Moss Evans and the vote that did for Callaghan's government, paving the way for Maggie, the unions acting as inadvertent accomplices in their own demise –

Suzi's role: honeytrap, union man called Dai Wyn, Suzi chasing – always chasing – a story, a lead, used by an unscrupulous detective, very murky.

Then collusion in the Roach Family Support Committee, used as an inside source, persuaded she was doing the right thing, which she thinks she probably was.

The past, she thinks, is never really too far behind you.

She shakes her head, dismisses the thought, walks on, stopping opposite their first port of call the previous evening:

TOP RANK BINGO

It was Keith's idea.

And not an ironic one.

'Honestly, babe, it's a laugh. You're going to love it.'

The building's impressive, Suzi thinks now, another thrusting corner, thick, flat white tiles, like a big white box with horizontal lines drawn evenly across it, simple, a faux chimney running up the Hackney Road side, the word CLUB running down it.

Five of them piling in, deep into the auditorium, cavernous, curved cream ceilings with purple trim, wine-red floral carpets and blue seating around laminate tables, more seats above, empty, in the circle –

'This place, my friends –' Keith with a flourish of his hand – 'used to be an Odeon cinema, hence the design.'

Finding a table and marking cards, Keith handing out pencils –

'Note the art deco look of the place –' giving it the tour guide – 'I'd date this particular building at some point in the late nineteen thirties.'

'Nineteen thirty-seven.' Suzi daring to interrupt, waving a leaflet, everyone giggling. 'You may have read this somewhere before, babe.'

It *was* a good laugh, Suzi thinks.

A few winners, mainly losers, but fun, a buzz about it all, the *social*, Keith keeping the group in line, no misbehaviour, making sure they were all courteous.

'It's the seriousness of the clientele that I admire,' he told them in a whisper. 'This is a place of devotion, of worship. You've got to respect that.'

She smiles now at this, Suzi.

She thinks of Keith asleep, grunting and farting, coughing and scratching and she longs, for a moment, to be in bed with him, to feel the heat from his body is to feel safe, to feel home, and she smiles, Suzi, raises her camera and snaps –

It's been years now, years that they've been together, lived together.

A very good number of years, the sort of number that often leads to weddings and families and other celebrations.

Or doesn't.

Suzi's never sure what it means that she can't help but think like that.

They don't talk about it, is perhaps the point.

She steps out of the way as a tired-looking woman muscles past with pram and toddler, dragging his heels, mum shouting at him to hurry up or we'll miss the bus. A hunchbacked pensioner in brown suit and tie shuffling, hacking into a handkerchief, his wife a few steps behind, thick pink cardigan, hair in curlers, a cigarette in her free hand, milk-bottle glasses, tugging on a shopping caddy, which, Suzi sees, has at least one broken wheel. They stop outside the bingo hall, examine the door, which is locked by a chain.

The woman beckons Suzi with a yellowing finger.

'Dear,' she says, 'can you read what time it opens?'

Suzi smiles. 'Twelve, midday.' She checks her watch. 'You've got a little wait.'

'What's that, love?'

Suzi, louder, 'It opens at twelve o'clock. You'll have to wait.'

'Have to what?' This is the man now speaking.

'She says we'll have to wait.'

'Wait for what?'

Suzi smiling, 'It's not open yet. You've got about twenty minutes until it does.'

'Twenty minutes? To do what?'

The woman's worked it out, Suzi thinks, as she's already setting off down the road, her caddy swerving and bumping, her face set in grim persistence, gums knotted.

'Come on,' she shouts. 'We'll go and see the animals.'

'What bloody animals?' The man sighs, breathes heavily. 'Bloody animals, I don't know.'

Suzi watches them hobble and bump along the pavement, frames the shot, their backs bent, their legs buckling –

Snap, snap.

She follows, slowly, towards Hackney City Farm, the only place with any bloody animals anywhere close.

A short row of terraced houses, the first boarded up, graffiti and rubbish, a tarpaulin and a plastic sheet covering the space where the front door used to be. Suzi hears music, very low, repetitive.

Next door, scaffolding and cement, men in dusty jeans and boots, luminous yellow vests, Irish accents.

She hears, 'They'll be wanting to see about these fucking off,' a builder nodding at the squat. 'His lordship won't be liking all this noise and dirt.' Someone else quips, 'And that's just the fucking dogs.'

Laughter.

Down the road a little further east, an abandoned brewery transforming slowly into this city farm.

She sees the old couple, noses against the gates, watching a horse being led in a wide arc, chickens flapping and squawking, rabbits nibbling on leaves, donkeys chewing hay, shitting on the new patches of grass –

Snap, snap.

A street cleaner pushes a broom in the gutter, not watching where he's going.

A rusted blood-orange Beetle pumps reggae through its blacked-out windows.

In the Turkish restaurant across the road, a man carves meat from a sweating heft of it turning in the window.

A woman pushes a young girl in a wheelchair with tubes hanging from her nose towards the Queen Elizabeth Hospital for Children.

Suzi crosses the road to photograph the frontage, the tall green door flanked by stone pillars and arches, yellowing brick around high rectangular windows on the upper floors, the hospital's name in white script on blue, mounted on the railings on the street either side of the entrance, trainee nurses drifting in and out.

Snap, snap.

She watches leaves fall from spindly branches. She looks up into the white October sky, sun bustling behind, not quite getting through.

She walks west now, turns left onto Columbia Road, a neat triangular route.

Tomorrow, Sunday, and the flower market will heave with stalls and people.

Today, though, it's quiet.

She snaps shopfronts: GENERAL WOOD TURNER, HEAD OF HAIR, LEE'S SEA FOODS, SKY BLUE FISH BAR.

Further along, the road narrows as it curves, the council estates forbidding in the cold morning, greys and browns and concrete pubs, distant sounds of children.

A house in disrepair across the road, the rubble of a building site, a collapsed wall, the front garden boarded up, messy, handwritten graffiti next to a builder's logo:

EXPLOITATION – DISPLACEMENT

DISTRUCTION

DO YOU HAVE NO MERCY?

$$$$$$

Snap.

Near home she ducks into the corner shop and buys eggs and bacon, milk and orange juice, white bread, the *Guardian*.

As she juggles her shopping and purse and keys, she hears a voice saying, You know a place is gentrifying when they start selling *that* newspaper.

She looks up. It's him, Noble –

Again.

'Nice to see you, Suzi,' he says.

'What do *you* want?'

'Come on, be nice, it's only been a couple of years.'

Suzi sighs. 'What do you know about gentrification, anyway, detective?'

He points back the way Suzi's come. 'I call that shithole home, darling.'

'Do you?'

'Straight off the boat and into a Mick slum, my parents.'

'You've got a way with words.'

A pause.

'You're not paying a nostalgic visit, by any chance?' Suzi asks.

Noble shakes his head. 'Your old fella up, is he?'

Suzi shakes her head.

Noble nods, gestures with his chin. 'Let's go and have a cup of tea.'

'You're buying.'

'Well,' Noble winks, 'I'll certainly be paying for it.'

Saturday, early afternoon, 5 October, and Parker's still in Tottenham on the Broadwater Farm Estate.

He and Shaun are having a late dinner at Shaun's: rice and peas, spiced chicken.

'Just like Granny's in Clapton does it,' Parker decides.

'Don't say that to my grandma, hero,' Shaun says. 'You'll be out on your ear.'

The morning's been more of the same: hanging around.

The Youth Association on a weekend is a hotspot.

Parker's noted the presence of youths from Hackney, Stoke Newington, but no sign yet of Marlon. He's looking at his watch, thinking about Trevor and their rendezvous, keen to make some progress here too, though –

'How often you reckon he's up here?' he asks Shaun.

Shaun considers this. 'Few times a week, I hear.'

'You see him a few times a week, or he's here a few times a week?'

'That's a good point.'

'I am duty-bound to instruct, young man.'

'I reckon he's here a few times a week, and I seen him just the once. But, you know, I've heard it, yeah?'

Parker nods. 'Why would your old dear not like the Granny's comparison?'

Shaun smiles. 'It's not just Granny's, hero, it's anyone at all.'

'Fair enough.' With his forehead, Parker indicates the kitchen. 'Any more grub, is there? It's only polite, seconds.'

Mouth full, Shaun nods.

Parker stands with his clean plate. He glides through the saloon doors into the small, steaming kitchen where Shaun's – and Carolyn's – grandmother sits.

She smiles at him. 'Help yourself,' she says. She nods at the stove. 'It's all over there.'

'Much obliged.' Parker winks. 'It's delicious, I'll say that.'

He spoons first rice and peas and then chicken onto his plate.

'I were you there,' the grandmother says, 'tilt the pan like so and pour the liquid over your chicken.'

Parker lifts the pan, raises his eyebrows in a question.

'Don't be shy,' he's told. 'It's where the flavour sits to rest.'

'It's an education, coming here.'

'We're all learning, young man.'

'I'm a very lucky boy.'

The grandmother smiles. 'Don't let Carolyn hear you say that, we don't need it going to her head, you know.'

Parker grins. 'She's an angel, and I can see where she gets it from.'

Kissing her teeth, 'Now, now, you'll have the neighbours talking.'

Parker stands by the window with his plate of food.

The neighbours are above, below, left, right –

He surveys the view:

The northern edge of the estate, facing outwards.

A road between the lower-rise block they're in and a row of council houses.

A first-floor walkway runs around the outside and bends back.

Dirty green grass stretching up towards Edmonton, beating a hasty retreat, Parker thinks, crawling back to whence it came, scarpering.

It's all yellow and mud, the grass.

Kids chucking stones, dogs shitting –

Back in the front room, sat at the table, wolfing his second helping, Parker remarks upon the Tottenham Hotspur pendant that adorns the wall above the electric fire.

'That's not yours, I hope.'

Shaun nods. ''Fraid so, hero. You not a supporter of the mighty Spurs then?'

'I am not.'

Shaun makes a face: *well, who then?*

'I'm forever blowing bubbles, mate.'

Shaun shakes his head. 'Don't mention that round here.'

'I fucking will mention that.'

'Come on, hero.'

Parker grins. 'Only joking. Far as anyone you know is concerned, I'm like Ossie Ardiles in my appreciation for the club.'

'Oh yeah?'

'Yeah. My knees are all trembly just thinking about it.'

'Good one, hero.'

Parker agrees.

Chas & Dave and 'Ossie's Dream', a cup final anthem if there ever was one.

Come on, you Spurs. A bit of a sing-song round the old Joanna –

Course old Ossie had to do one a couple of years ago, off on loan to Paris St Germain while Her Majesty's armed forces gave his countrymen a walloping out in the Falklands. Ricky Villa was moved on, too.

Parker knows a Spurs fan who served, went with him to the Lane once.

A lot of noise about what happened on Goose Green, all that palaver, a lot of noise about the Argies, what they're like, what lessons they learned.

And there he was in the Paxton Road end cheering Ossie with the rest of the faithful, week before singing songs about sinking the *Belgrano* no doubt.

'I ain't gonna lie,' Parker says, 'I do enjoy watching young Glenn Hoddle when he's playing, I'll give your mob that, at least.'

Shaun grunts.

'That thing he's got, time,' Parker says. 'He's like Gower at the crease in that regard, time. It slows down with lads like them, with talent. Talent is time, young man, having it when no one else does and taking it away from them when they do.'

'Not sure I follow.'

'You watch Glenn Hoddle more closely, son, you will.'

Shaun forks more rice and peas into his mouth, thoughtfully.

'It's not something you can learn,' Parker continues. 'It's innate, you know? Inherent. Comes from within, you only have to channel it, tease it out.'

'You're born with it, you mean?'

'Born with it, exactly, it's a gift.'

'From God, yeah?'

'God?' Parker weighs this. 'I mean, I couldn't tell you, son, but there is certainly something of the divine present when Gower's in full, effort-less flow.'

'And Hoddle?'

'It's harder to attribute those qualities to a Spurs man, I'd contend, but yes, perhaps he may have been blessed with some superior vision, awareness, skill, that sort of thing.'

Then Shaun's laughing.

A voice, Carolyn's, saying, 'You really are full of it, aren't you?'

Parker grinning. 'Where did you come from?'

'Door was open. Did you honestly think I wouldn't be checking up on you?'

'Fair play.'

Shaun nods at the saloon doors. 'She's in there.'

'I'll go and say hello.'

'This grub,' Parker says, 'is world class.'

'Like David Gower.'

'You said it, darling.'

Parker's up now and kissing her hello –

Carolyn puts her handbag down on an armchair, shrugs off her coat, which Parker gallantly eases from her shoulders and folds over his arm.

'You heard about anything today?' she says to Shaun. 'Something's going on, you know, downstairs.'

'What do you mean?'

'I mean something's happened but I don't know what.'

Parker's eyes dart from cousin to cousin.

Shaun says, 'We were at the youth centre this morning, been here since midday.'

'Doing what?'

'Talking.' Shaun pointing at Parker. 'Mainly him.'

'Easy on,' Parker laughs, mock offended.

'So you haven't heard about anything then?'

Shaun shakes his head.

Parker says, 'What's the matter, babe?'

Carolyn shakes her head. 'Probably nothing. There's been an arrest, I think. That's all.'

'Right. It happens.'

Carolyn gives him a tired-looking smile. 'It does happen, yeah. Brixton last week?'

'I know, babe.'

'That poor woman, it's no wonder they reacted.'

Parker nodding.

'That poor woman,' Carolyn says. 'She was in bed when they went in looking for her son and she was shot. *Shot.* Just some black boy's mum, that's all she is.'

Carolyn looks at the kitchen door. 'That's all she is.'

Parker says, 'We'll have a nose about later.'

'Yeah, good idea.'

'Pigs, eh? Tell me about it.'

'Yeah.' Carolyn squeezes Parker's arm. She steps away. She says, 'I'll go and say hello.'

*You're looking at the paperwork that's been coming in since that lug signed off on the deal, and it's extensive, the paperwork, and it's clear and simple, too –*

*A portfolio of landed and business interests managed by the consortium, the syndicate your lug represents – they seem to have given it any number of titles – but your own significant and controlling share means that you are handily placed to benefit from any and all profit made by these business interests, or other business interests that take place on the land you now effectively own.*

*That was easy, you think.*

*Adverse possession. Or the threat of it.*

*The gist of the deal was: either you cut us in or we'll take the land and then prove adverse possession.*

*It's not hard to prove, adverse possession, it turns out.*

*Anyway, the syndicate weren't going to argue.*

*Why would they?*

*They'll still make some money themselves. And if they knew what you know about what's setting up in the manor, who's setting up his newspaper group, then they'd be even happier.*

*Money brings money and all that.*

*Which reminds you –*

'Terry, old chum, you reckon those Silvertown thugs will be about ready yet?'

*Terry studies his watch, he shrugs, nods.* 'Should be about now, yeah.'

'Get the car, we'll go and have a butcher's.'

'And the other place?'

*You smile.* 'Two birds scenario, old son.'

*You point at the paperwork.* 'May as well keep track of our latest investments, he who dares and all that.'

'Five minutes?'

'And not a moment longer, Terrence.'


Jon asks Jackie for Chick's phone number and Jackie gives him a look and Jon goes, 'I know, I thought I'd reach out. For the match next Saturday.'

'What match?'

'Arsenal at home.'

'I thought you were taking Joe?'

'I am, I got another ticket,' Jon explains. 'I thought the boy might benefit from a day out at the football with his uncle Chick.'

'He's not his bloody uncle.'

'Well, you know, family.'

Jackie shakes her head. Jackie smiles. 'What are you up to, Jon Davies?'

Jon grins. 'It's all in good faith, Jacks. It's football, that's all.'

'Football.'

'West Ham, you know, family.'

Jackie's laughing. 'I don't know what my cousin has told you, Jon, but he won't be taking you into the players' lounge after the match.'

'He might,' Jon says.

'So that's it!'

'No,' Jon pouts.

Jackie points. Jackie laughs. 'That *is* it! You've swallowed his codswallop and you reckon you'll get to meet Billy Bonds! You wally.'

'No, I don't reckon that.'

'You're sweet, Jon, but you're transparent—'

'It'll be a good afternoon out.'

'Here.' Jackie scribbles a number on the pad they keep next to the telephone. 'He'll be made up to hear from you.'

'We're forever blowing bubbles.'

'Just make sure that's all you're bloody doing, Jon Davies.'

'Dib-dob,' Jon says. 'Scout's honour.'

Jackie eye-rolls. 'Men,' she says.


Suzi then tells Noble that seeing as it's already afternoon they might as well carry this conversation on in the pub given her hangover and its definite need for a recovery drink or two, and Noble says, Yeah, go on then.

'You'll have to lead the way, though,' he adds. 'Only pub I know nearby is a strip joint.'

'Classy.'

'It was for work.'

'Course it was.'

'Ye Olde Axe, Hackney Road.'

'It's well known.'

'Well, let's give it a swerve anyway.'

Suzi nods. She points back down the way she came. 'Royal Oak on Columbia Road is all right.'

They walk in silence, Suzi happy to keep it that way. She finds Noble's lack of small talk refreshing. She thinks why make the effort now, for chit-chat.

In five minutes or so they arrive at the pub.

Suzi points at the signage:

1923

T

R

U

M

A

N

HANBURY

BUXTON

& CO LTD

THE

ROYAL

OAK

Noble says, 'Nice tiling,' and pushes open the saloon door.

Inside, a horseshoe bar and a few old blokes sat at it sucking on their false teeth.

Noble signals for two pints of best and he and Suzi sit down.

Suzi gulps down a few mouthfuls and she immediately feels better.

She worries, sometimes, about that, about how quickly and easily the recovery drink actually works, the efficiency of it, the *undeniability* of it.

The very fact of it can't end well, the physiological aspect, she thinks, surely.

Noble nods at Suzi's drink. 'The cure, is it?'

'The what?'

'Irish for hair of the dog.'

'Right.'

'You know, "Going for a cure?" That kind of thing.'

'Funny people.'

'That we are.'

Suzi nods. 'Hair of the dog it is.'

'"If this dog do you bite, soon as out of your bed, take a hair of the tail the next day."'

'I'm a bit late then.'

Noble smiles. 'Good night, was it?'

'We went to the bingo, among other places.'

Noble nods in the direction of Hackney Road. 'The one up there? My old dear used to go. Your lot do that now, do you?'

'Your lot?'

'Newcomers.'

Suzi decides to let this one slide.

'What is it you want, detective? It's always something.'

'Straight to the chase, then, is it?'

'Yes.'

'Understandable.'

'Whenever I see you again after a couple of years with no word, it's not normally good news.'

'No.'

'Not normally, no. Normally it's not far off blackmail.'

'To be fair, it's not.'

'There must one day be a point,' Suzi says, her cure now really livening her up, 'when it'll stop – you turning up to call in a favour.'

Noble nods. He drinks off the rest of his pint of best. He says, 'We'll have something alongside the next one, will we?'

Suzi raises an eyebrow. 'Really playing the Irish charm card today.'

'I'll take that as a yes.'

Suzi watches him step up to the bar and remembers the very first time she met him, backstage, Rock against Racism, 1978.

She photographed him walking away from her then.

Now, his back again to her, leaning slightly forward over the bar.

She focuses her camera, frames the shot, angles for lights and mirrors and leathery pensioners –

Snap.

She's fiddling with her camera when Noble deposits a tray of drinks.

'Trying to get me drunk?'

'Doesn't look like you need my help on that front, darling.'

Suzi thins her lips. 'Cheers, then,' she says, picking up a whiskey and taking a sip. 'Irish, is it?'

Noble winks. 'A connoisseur.'

Suzi eye-rolls.

'What time you expecting your fella to wake up?'

'Does it matter?'

'Not really, no, just making conversation.'

'Right.'

Suzi shrugs off her coat, sinks back into her carpeted seat. She nods at the bar. 'Your old man drink in here, did he?'

And then: 'Good relationship, was it, with your father?'

Suzi watches Noble chew this over.

'Yours is dead, isn't he?'

Suzi nods.

'Then you'll know all about it.'

Noble sniffs, rearranges his jacket, puts a hand through his hair.

'I want you to do something for me, Suzi.'

'Why?'

Noble makes a face: *leave it out.*

Suzi smiles.

'I think you likely know *why*, Suzi.'

'Have I got any choice?'

'Not really.'

Suzi nods, understanding.

There's a record of what she did, an acknowledgment of her involvement in that undercover operation. That acknowledgement is more about proof than recognition: she's not getting a medal and a slap on the back; it exists to make sure she'll do it again.

'You know, Suzi, that what I'm doing is part of something bigger.'

'OK.'

'I mean, you know that there are certain things I need to be seen to be doing in order to carry out what I really am in fact doing.'

'If that's what helps you sleep at night.'

Noble coughs. 'I have no trouble sleeping, Suzi.'

'Lucky boy.'

'I'm not like some of the other handlers. I don't encourage anything, it's pure observation.'

'OK.'

'There are some who demand their UCOs foment, you know, carry out actual criminal acts.'

'OK.'

'They're in activist groups, like you were, like you might well still be, but some of the UCOs aren't just keeping tabs, they're setting up arson attacks, that kind of thing.'

'Your lad, he's not like that?'

'He's not.' Noble sighs, finishes his whiskey. 'He understands the bigger picture.'

'Does he now?'

'Well, he understands that there is one, which is a start.'

'Thing is, I'm not a UCO, am I?'

'Not officially, no.'

'Not unofficially, either.'

Noble's nodding. Suzi thinks he looks a little wired, tense.

He says, 'Budgets, you know? My lad's stretched as it is, I can't justify it.'

'Cuts, eh?'

'Yeah, cuts.'

Noble knocks back the rest of his pint. 'One more, then,' he says.

Suzi shrugs. She's feeling better, that's true. But there's another feeling now, too – resignation.

She looks up at the clock on the wall and thinks Keith will still be in bed.

After this one, she should go and rejoin him in it herself.

Noble brings back two halves. 'We should probably take it a bit easy.'

'What is it you want me to do?'

Noble puts his hand inside his jacket. He takes out an envelope. He places the envelope on the table. He pushes it across to Suzi.

'Mind the spillage,' Suzi says.

She weighs it and sticks it in her bag. She says, 'There's no point in doing it for free.'

Noble shakes his head. 'Wouldn't be allowed.'

'You need a receipt?'

'Very funny.'

The chatter at the bar is louder for a moment, a raspy laugh, a cheer –

Then, the thick crack of a pint mug breaking on the floor, a groan, a You idiot from the barmaid, another cheer, more laughter, coughing.

The sound of a match being struck. Fresh cigarette smoke. Bar stools scraping on tiles. The toilet door squeaking then slamming.

'You've got an in with the music crowd,' Noble says.

'In a manner of speaking.'

'We hear there's a collective, or something, being formed.'

Suzi shrugs.

'Billy Bragg. Paul Weller. Ring any bells?'

'Maybe.'

'You know what I'm talking about though.'

'Close enough.'

Noble nods. 'Good. It's just a question of observing, Suzi.' He nods at the camera on the table. 'You're good at that.'

Noble stands. 'I need to use the telephone. Shan't be long.'

'Take your time.'

Noble turns, turns back. 'I preferred him in the Jam.'

'What?'

'Weller. He's gone soft in that new pop group of his.'

Suzi shakes her head. She sighs.

She watches Noble swagger across the pub, smiling at the barmaid, who hands him the telephone.

His back's to her, but this time Suzi leaves the camera on the table.

Mid-afternoon. Parker saying to Shaun outside the Youth Association: 'I'm going to check what her indoors was on about earlier, yeah?'

Meaning: see what the Old Bill are up to.

Meaning: you're a young lad, so leave me to it.

Shaun nodding. 'You've been seen, you're all right, hero.'

Meaning: the brothers know your face.

'Take care though, yeah?'

Meaning: I'm a young lad so it's not all gravy.

They slap hands and Shaun mooches off back to his grandmother's flat where Carolyn waits.

The chatter round the Youth Association is about an arrest.

A routine pull on a dodgy plate, a stolen car, an assault on an officer –

Parker thinks: get down Tottenham nick and have a shufty round there.

It's not a long walk and it gets him off the estate, which isn't a bad thing.

He may well have shown his mug about the place last couple of days, but it ain't a given he'll be left alone. Big boy like Parker isn't always inconspicuous. Though, funnily enough, he thinks now, it's not been unhelpful in his line of work.

Hiding in plain sight they call it.

There's the usual mix of hawkers and gawkers, layabouts and hustlers knocking about near the nick. The sort of crowd who look like they should be inside, not circling it. It's pretty standard practice for your desperate snout, Parker knows this. Scavenging for scraps at one nick to pass on up the food chain at another.

Making yourself useful they call it.

Or grazing. Or chewing the cud. Grass-work is the point.

Parker scans faces and gaits.

He's looking for a drug-ravaged countenance that precludes discretion. He does a couple of circuits and bingo.

A pinched-face rodent with dirty hair and gaps in his mouth sidles over.

Parker delivers a cigarette. Three cigarettes. One in the mouth and one behind each ear. They slide in, slow-slick.

Parker points at a caff down the road. Parker says, 'There's more where that came from.'

The rodent shuffles behind him, just about dressed, just about two shoes on – just about.

In the caff, Parker signals for two cups of tea, gives it the benevolent gentleman.

'Cheers, darling,' he offers the bird who brings it over.

She rolls her eyes.

'He'll be needing some sugar,' meaning the rodent, who nods.

'Coming right up,' she says.

Parker nods at the rodent. 'Word is?'

The rodent does a little ratty cough. Parker pushes a tenner across the table.

'Rosebury Road, number plate on a BMW looked off.'

'OK,' Parker says. 'Go on.'

'Beat officer called it in and the plate didn't match the licence.'

'Then what?'

'The driver ran off when they told him he was being pulled.'

'Then what?'

The bird dumps the sugar bowl. A teaspoon clatters.

The rodent spoons in four helpings.

'A scuffle, the driver lashed out. He's been in holding for a couple of hours.'

'What's his name?'

'He gave a fake one at first.'

'How do you know?'

'Beat officer put it about.'

'Why?'

'He's supposed to be a handler.'

Stolen goods, then. All right, Parker thinks.

'And?'

'They're going over to where he lives.'

'Which is where?'

'Twenty-five Thorpe Road. Going end of the afternoon.'

'You're very well informed, know the lingo.'

The rodent shrugs.

Parker adds, 'Why did the beat officer put this about?'

'You tell me.'

Parker nods. 'Fair enough.'

He pulls a fiver from his pocket, pushes it across the table.

Bacon sizzles. Kettles steam. Chips gurgle in fat.

'Get yourself some breakfast.'

The rodent nods.

Parker's up and bouncing out the caff and back onto the streets surrounding Tottenham nick, thinking it'd likely be a good thing to get a little corroboration, when he sees Marlon leaving the police station from a side entrance.

Well, well, Parker thinks. Hello.

Marlon heads for the main road and south.

It's a straight shot, Parker thinks.

The High Road takes you right down to Stamford Hill, then it's only a hop, a skip and a jump to Stoke Newington High Street and the nick there.

Parker follows at a safe enough distance.

He thinks: be casual; if he makes me, I'm just chasing after him to say hello, mates, innit?

Marlon's got his chin tucked deep into his Yank flying jacket, hands buried in its high pockets, box-fresh trainers and a spring in his step.

He's looking up the road behind him, flicking his head quickly back as if checking he ain't being followed.

Back and front, back and front, he looks well paranoid.

It's too much, in fact. Parker pauses in a shop doorway, observes –

He sees Marlon look back and up, back and up, arrowing between Saturday shoppers, swerving kids and grannies, back and up he looks.

And Parker thinks, hang about, he's not worried about a tail, he's looking for a bus.

Which makes sense given where they are and given where Marlon lives.

Be a bit difficult to follow him on a double-decker and remain incognito, though, Parker thinks.

So he makes a decision, runs down the road, claps Marlon on the back and goes, 'What you doing up here then, eh,' and Marlon, quick-grinning, goes, 'I could ask you the same thing,' and Parker tells him he's been knocking about with Carolyn's cousin, Shaun, and Marlon says, 'Youth programme, innit, I'm bringing boys over from Hackney for the free meals and that,' and Parker points, 'You going south? There's my bus.'

And Marlon checks his fat gold watch and nods.

'Come on then,' Parker says.

And they hop on and they bounce up the stairs –

Top deck, front row. Roller-coaster seats.

Marlon unzips his flying jacket, pulls a gold lighter from an inside pocket, a pack of Dunhill, offers Parker one, who shakes his head, indicates his body with a flourish of his hand. 'I'm pure, mate.'

Marlon smiles, lights up.

Then: 'How you been, wide boy?'

Parker thinks about this a moment, weighs it, lips pursed, head tilted one way then the other. 'I'm all right,' he decides.

'Good for you, hero.'

'You calling me that now too, Marlon?'

'It's a nickname.' Marlon's grinning. 'I like a nickname, you know?'

'Well earned.'

Marlon laughs. 'It precedes us, yeah, our reputations.'

'That why you're up Tottenham way, then is it? Your reputation?'

'Opens doors, man, I'll say that.'

Parker laughing too now. 'We are a fine pair of men, are we not?'

The bus stops.

Parker eyes the mirror at the back, seeing who is getting on and off.

Pensioners wrestle with their shopping caddies.

Mums wrangling kids.

Kids chomping on crisps, dribbling fizzy drinks, salt-lipped and sticky-chinned –

Saturday.

Parker also keeping a careful eye on where they are.

His plan: get off the stop before the nick and see if he can discover where Marlon's going – and why.

He still trusts him, to be fair, just about. Parker doesn't want to find out old Marlon here is a snout, or worse. Cahoots is the word Noble's been using.

They've got nothing on the recycling; it's what's got Parker busying about all over the place, Tottenham for fuck's sake, not somewhere he enjoys visiting.

Marlon lights another Dunhill.

'You wanna go easy on those, mate,' Parker says. 'They'll be the death of you.'

Marlon brandishes the relative class of the Dunhill packaging. 'Not these, wide boy, these good for you. Royal treatment,' he laughs.

Parker smiles.

'Look at that colour,' Marlon adds, 'its depth, signifies something.'

'Yeah, lung cancer.'

'I didn't know you was such a pussy.'

'What, too tough for it, are you?'

'Me, I just a rebel soul.'

'I think the song you're after is "Uptown Top Ranking", mate.'

Marlon turns to Parker, snug, tight in their seat, his leather flying jacket squeaking round his shoulders, laughing, he says, 'Just like the bingo.'

And Parker thinks, nah, this bloke's all right, take it easy, it's all in good time.

He slaps Marlon on the back, stands. 'This is me.'

Marlon ushers him past. The bus lurches, Parker catches himself, pulls the cord to ring the bell.

'Toodle-pip,' he says.

On the street, he watches the bus belch and cough its way down towards Stoke Newington police station.

Clear traffic; no way he's catching up now.

He walks and he waits. He watches and he walks.

The bus stops.

Marlon doesn't get off.

*At the warehouse, you survey the scene, consider the history.*

*Then:*

*Bussing in electricians from Portsmouth to wire the place on the sly.*

*First, here, then over at the big building after.*

*A word on their way out, a visit to the south coast, a few envelopes and a bit of muscle and they kept shtum.*

*Now:*

*Atex computer mainframes purchased from Boston, US of A, to the tune of ten million quid, shipped to Paris in unmarked boxes, then put together in London by Yanks in a building in Wapping, in which you now stand, licensed to a cover company called Compliance Ltd.*

*You can hear the accents as they gripe and groan.*

*You tip an imaginary ten-gallon hat at the foreman.*

*'Have a nice day, partner,' you tell him.*

*He looks confused.*

*Terry gives him a pat on the back and he's quickly back to work, shrugging, sweating buckets in his overalls.*

*Visitors from the EPU sneaking in and nosing around every month or so, working out exactly how many employees they'd need to staff and operate the printing equipment when it's installed in the big building in Wapping.*

*You gather they're looking for a bottom-line number, a minimum level and nothing more.*

*You only need the one union for the number they're talking about, you think.*

*Either way, you keep out the way, control security and take the rent and licence money from his representatives.*

*Compliance Ltd: your company.*

*At least, it's yours in profit, if not name.*

*In name, it belongs to a whole number of people, lots of names, though in actual fact it doesn't really bear any names at all, not really, no way, Pedro –*

*It's what's called a shell company.*

*Meaning: that lug and his syndicate have handed it over, the land and the warehouses, all intents and purposes.*

*Of course, you had access, it was yours before they even came along and tried to claim it, to buy it.*

*One of a number that was.*

*The last time the place was used for anything was Jagger and Bowie arsing about, that video for the big concert, filmed 'on location' in Docklands.*

*Where does it all come from, the money, people ask.*

*You know the answer to that.*

*Something old lug and his syndicate don't know, couldn't know:*

*Docklands has become a gold mine,* literally.

*November 1983: a gang of south-east London villains knock off the Brink's-Mat warehouse, Unit 7, Heathrow International Trading Estate, for some £26 million in gold bullion, diamonds and cash.*

*Crime of the century.*

*They went in with petrol and poured it over the staff, threatened them with a match. They were after a few million from the vault, no idea what was inside.*

*There's such a thing, you think, as too big a score.*

*What the fuck is one supposed to do with all that?*

*Well, the first thing one needs is leadership, organisers, enablers, smelters, fencers, lawyers, bankers and accountants to launder the money. A specific series of services you were uniquely placed to provide in the local area.*

*Not forgetting your political connections on the local councils, and, more pertinently, your developing working relationship with the* London Docklands Development Group, *which provides a certain amount of wriggle room regarding land purchases and licensed investment opportunities.*

*Shell companies, offshore financial intermediaries, a firm in Panama –*

*Built on fool's gold is Docklands. Thank you very much indeed.*

*Now, you're doing the wiring and the IT work for* The London Herald *on the quiet, making sure the other unionised technicians don't get a sniff.*

*And how do you do that?*

*You employ yourself to look after security.*

*And what opportunities does that bring?*

*Tell them, Terry:*

*'This way, to the factory.'*

*Terry ushers you across the shop floor, past the electrics and the soldering irons, across the patch of concrete that separates the units, into the smaller of the two, behind, inside of which your Silvertown chancers are making serious quantities of crack-cocaine to sell all over London and beyond.*

*And at the same time, acting on a particular request, with the UK subsidiary of East London Logistics, you have facilitated a £7 million order for 1,000 vehicles and a five-year distribution contract worth something like a million quid a week.*

*Why, you ask?*

*Tell them, Terry:*

*'Well, guv, the distribution deal means sidestepping the railways and wholesale distributers which have one hundred per cent SOGAT union membership.'*

*Go on.*

*'One of our companies is making the trade happen, thereby swerving any accusations of impropriety, God forbid.'*

*Well quite.*

*Very good, Terry.*

*I think what you're saying is that the unions – with the one exception of EPU – are out.*

*'That's exactly what I'm saying, boss.'*

*You're enjoying this coalescing of your somewhat diverse portfolio of business interests.*

*That transport company contract, for a start, will come in very useful.*

*Above, white clouds throb and separate, leak out into the grey sky like spilt milk –*

# 3

## *Violence*

5 October 1985

*Ayeleen*: It's after lunch in my uncle's cafe and the place is empty except, of course, for Lauren, who's got her feet up and reading the paper quite noisily, to be fair, a lot of guffawing.

'What's so funny, Laur?' I ask her.

She's spluttering now. 'It's all funny, Leenie, all of it.'

'Is it.'

Without looking up, she reads, 'Bookish, owlish type, GSOH, into jazz and classical, looking for like-minded lady to attend readings and concerts and orgies.'

'You're making that up.'

'I'm not!' Lauren smooths out the newspaper on the table and points. 'Your *Hackney Gazette* classifieds, Leen, have really come on since the borough got a bit posher, you know.'

I say nothing, smile.

'I'll bet half of them eat in here of an evening.'

I shake my head.

'Come on, Leen, where's *your* sense of humour, eh?'

'I think you're laughing at them, Laur.'

'I'm really not, it ain't like that. It's affection, really, is what it is. Besides,' she pouts, 'maybe I'm looking for a boyfriend.'

'Maybe there's a boyfriend out there looking for you.'

'You're very clever.'

'I know I am, but what are you.'

'We could do this all day, Leenie, you know that.'

I look around the cafe and gesture. 'It doesn't look much like my time is being taken up elsewhere, Lauren, does it?'

'I agree, it does not.'

It's always slow this time of day, but on a weekend, it feels a little sadder, like there should be a kids' birthday party or something, balloons and cake, or long family lunches carrying on through the day, that sort of thing, I always thought.

It's really about our clientele: they come for lunch and then leave.

My uncle Ahmet hasn't quite yet attracted the posh crowd, though you get the odd one or two each day.

I told him: it's too Turkish, the cafe, that's our problem, it's just a bit too Turkish, the decor, the menu, the vibe, and they're a bit nervous, these newcomers, that's all it is, they're intimidated, let's make it friendlier.

'Vibe?' my uncle said to that. 'Who's been teaching you words like that, Ayeleen? Vibe, really.'

All I mean is that we're in a part of the world where, round the corner, there's an eel and pie shop with a handwritten sign on the front on a chopping board covered in blood that says:

LARGER LIVE EELS IN STOCK. PLEASE ENQUIRE.

'Is it going to be a busy night, Leen?' Lauren asks.

'I'll have a look.'

I open the ledger we use as our booking system and under 5 October there are about a dozen names, numbers and times.

Most of the names are Turkish, so, in fact, no, it's not going to be that busy: they know what they want, what we serve and how, and they take their time, our regulars. It's less work for me, and the kitchen staff, too, which is what my uncle doesn't seem to understand: me wanting us to be livelier and all that, it's going to mean a harder job.

'Not really,' I say. 'The usual.'

'You want me to hang around, help out?'

'Course.' I smile. 'Well, I mean there won't be much to help out with, but yeah, course.'

Lauren stands up. 'I better get my uniform on then, hadn't I?'

She goes behind the counter and down the little corridor where the aprons are hanging up outside my uncle's office.

I pick up the newspaper from the table and shuffle it a bit then flick through it.

In the news pages there's the report I'm looking for: a shooting at

The New Country Off-Licence and Foodstore, just down the road, a shop my uncle used to own, only sold it a year or so ago, a shop he used to threaten me with, as in, you don't work hard at school, you'll be in The New Country Off-Licence and Foodstore quicker than you can say O Levels, my girl. They're saying that the victim was killed by a hitman, over here from Ankara, sent by the secret police. What they're saying is that it wasn't this victim who was supposed to be killed, but the owner of the shop, who is 'a vigorous campaigner on trade union rights' and a big man down at the Halkevi Turkish Centre round the corner.

Lauren comes back wearing an apron. 'You reading that again for why exactly, Leen?'

I shrug.

'You know this dead boy, do you? Is he someone you know?'

I shake my head. 'Mesut says he does, the family at least.'

'I bet Mesut says he does.'

'Come on, Laur.'

'Sorry.'

'My uncle knows the owner.'

'Well, yeah.'

'I mean, it feels close, that's all.'

'It's only across the road.'

'Not what I meant.'

'I know, I'm teasing, I'm sorry, Leenie.'

She's only trying to cheer me up, I know that, distract me.

It's a strange feeling, that's all, this kind of thing happening on the doorstep, and no one seems to know what it was about, or at least no one's telling me.

I expect it's all that's being talked about in the football club pool-rooms, the Turkish men's clubs, really, with their smell of sweat and beer and smoke. When my cousin Mesut comes into the cafe, you can always tell when he's been in one. He always tells you, too, that's another way you know. There's always some gossip or news he's got to share, and he always needs to share it. Stories about protection rackets and extortion, prostitutes, who's given whose wife venereal disease, and that's the English word he used, venereal, very formal, and it makes you wonder what Mesut really thinks about it all and is he just happy to be a member of one of these places.

It's all smut for Mesut now, he's obsessed, though he's left Lauren alone since the summer, same time he left his Spandau Ballet fandom behind and became a men's-club man. The other day he came in with a few cards he'd pinched from the newsagent next door.

'I'm telling you, Leenie,' he said. 'It's a dirty world, you've got to get involved.'

I didn't really understand what the cards were on about.

Lauren took one look, gave Mesut the evils.

'The brain on it, Leen,' shaking her head.

We kept the cards under the counter for a while for a laugh and then threw them away, embarrassed. I still remember what it said on them:

TIE AND TEASE MASSAGE.

MAGIC MOMENTS, DISCREET SERVICE.

TONY GETS A BUZZ FROM DEAD BEES.

We never worked out who Tony was.

'You are cheering me up, Lauren,' I say, smiling. 'You always do.'

'Leave it out.'

She knows I mean it, and I know she's happy to hear it. I can see her smiling too.

We start to get the cafe ready for the evening, tidying up and laying the tables, writing up the menu on the blackboard where it's smudged or the specials have changed, setting the lights using my uncle's prized dimmer switch, 'Getting the vibe right, Uncle,' I say, and Lauren laughs.

At five o'clock we sit down with a cup of tea and some baklava that my mother makes for the cafe and which we should be saving for the regulars as a little thank you on the house to have with their coffees or glasses of raki. We eat too many, and I get that sickly, sweet buzz, but we won't eat again until the end of the night, so it's all right. I check the ledger: the first party is due at seven, so we have a little time yet. There aren't many walk-ins at the weekends, maybe as people have their plans made already, I don't know.

I think again about the news report and wonder if it really might have been a hitman sent from Ankara and what it means if it was.

I say this to Lauren who rolls her eyes.

'There's enough violence round here already without someone importing it too,' she says. 'Enough of this, Leen, it's silly.'

'I'm just—'

'Look, round here anything like this is gangs or police or both,' Lauren says, sharply.

I nod. 'I know, Lauren, I'm not an idiot.'

'Never said you was, Leen, only, think about. Your uncle still has those envelopes ready, it's the way it is.'

'I don't know.'

Lauren makes a face. 'You do know.'

I look down. 'Let's finish up, eh, get the place looking right.'

Lauren nods, her eyes narrow, but she doesn't say anything.

The kitchen team have arrived, and the smell of food is strong, mouth-watering.

'My mouth is literally watering,' Lauren says. 'Shall we have a quick kebab?'

And we both laugh at that, but I tell her yes, course, and the chefs make one lamb, one chicken with sauces on the side for us and we eat them quickly, they're delicious, and I think Lauren's right, really, I should stop thinking about that news story.

Pushing five o'clock and Jon Davies is sitting in the car listening to the football results coming in on the radio.

'It's better for everyone if this weekly ritual happens in the car,' Jackie says, and Jon finds watching Final Score on Grandstand more frustrating anyway, cameras showing clips of players clapping, the crowd on their feet, that kind of thing, but never any actual football, of course, and he always thinks, why not, why not just show us a goal or two?

It's distracting, too, the need to look *and* listen, the worry that you're not quite noticing the key graphic or bit of information that has told you whether West Ham have bloody won or not.

In the car, Jon can sit back in the driver's seat and close his eyes and let the information come to him.

He understands Jackie's policy, it does make sense: he's a nightmare if he's inside between a quarter to and a quarter past five on a Saturday afternoon between mid-August and mid-May.

So far, the radio is buzzing with the news that, by drawing 1-1 away at Luton Town, Manchester United have fallen one game short of Tottenham Hotspur's record eleven-match winning start, set in the halcyon days of way back when in 1960.

Jon smiles at this: they'll be enjoying this 'victory' up in Tottenham tonight; they'll celebrate anything.

It's been a lovely afternoon, Jon thinks, local, kids had a good time, what more is there, really?

There they stood outside the Prince of Wales with their drinks, the boy trying to teach Lizzie how to skim a stone across the murky water of the canal, skim one right into the foaming scum on the other side, and Jon said, smiling, 'Here we are again then.'

Jackie didn't love that remark.

'I just mean we're here a lot,' Jon said. 'I mean we *live* here. I love coming here, I always do.'

And they do love it. Most weekends, sometimes Saturday *and* Sunday. The walk across Millfields Park with a football, Lizzie on her little starter bike, Jon and Jackie laughing, playing with the kids, the kids playing with each other, the fresh air, the greenery, the trees and the pylons, and down the canal to the pub for a drink, well we've earned it, Jackie! I know, Jon!

'What I don't love,' Jackie said, 'is the idea that this is *routine* for any of us, an obligation, that we're settling for it, rather than doing something else that we'd rather be doing, that there's anywhere else we'd rather be.'

Jon shook his head, quickly. 'There is nowhere else I'd rather be. Nowhere.'

'I know, love,' Jackie said. 'But the more you make that sort of remark, the fake smile, the spirit of the blitz of it all, *parenthood*, the here we are again then, the more likely it is you'll start to believe it.'

'Not sure I follow, love.'

'I know there's nowhere else you'd rather be, but maybe say *that*. Maybe say, there's nowhere else I'd rather be. Instead of that British, stiff upper lip thing that you don't even feel.'

Jon thinks she's got a point.

'Maybe you *should* take old Chick with you next week,' Jackie said. 'Maybe that's exactly what you should do.'

'Well, yeah, we had agreed—'

'Not what I mean, Jon.' Jackie smiling now, showing him she's not got the hump or anything. 'I mean, doing something different, it's good for us.'

'You've got a point.'

'I know I have.'

Jon likes their routine, he really does, he thrives on it a little, if he's honest, the solidity of it, the certainty, the knowledge of what he likes about it, what he's not so keen on, the management of the two, balancing them, the expectations –

The kids need it, is his reasoning; his excuse: he needs it just as much as they do.

Of course, Jackie's right. She always is.

The seconds tick by and West Ham lead by two goals to one away at Newcastle United. McAvennie and Cottee have scored the West Ham goals, again, and, according to Jon's rough calculations, this means that Frank McAvennie has now scored ten goals in the First Division this season, and Tony Cottee five.

At least Jon assumes that West Ham lead by two goals to one away at

Newcastle United. That was the score the last time the radio reported from St James' Park. Commentary updates are looping around ten First Division fixtures, and a number of significant lower league matches, too, so you never really know what the score is until you're told, and it does change, the score, whether you know about it or not.

It's a very fatalist exercise listening on the radio like this, Jon thinks.

And it's impossible not to think about what the three points would mean, league table-wise, up to about eleventh, Jon thinks, any higher than that? Those three early defeats, at Birmingham, and then at home to Luton, then away at Old Trafford, really hurt us.

Then, suddenly, we're back at St James' Park and a narrow victory for John Lyall's West Ham, who sit in eleventh place, and after a mixed opening few weeks of the season will be looking to build on the three wins they've achieved in their last four games, Lyall especially pleased with the goalscoring exploits of McAvennie and Cottee, and a lot more to come, they're saying, 26,709 in attendance.

Phew.

Jon thinks now's a very good time then to give Big Chick a ring, invite him, as the going is very good.

He turns the key in the ignition. The radio crackles and fades. He removes the key. He places a black cover over the stereo, disguising it.

He opens the driver's-side door and heaves himself out.

He locks the driver's door. He does a careful circuit of the car, checking each door, making sure they're all closed and locked. He sticks his fingers in the tops of each window and sees, yes, they're wound up, no one's getting in tonight.

Inside, the boy's mooching about with his Subbuteo set, lying with his bum up in the air, arranging the players, his claret and blues versus Jon's green hoops on white, God knows why, flicking the ball at the goal and playing keeper at the same time with his other hand.

'Two-one, Dad!' the boy yells, not even looking up.

'How do you know?'

He points across the room. 'Telly, of course.'

Jon nods, of course. The younger generation can handle television coverage. Under his breath, he says, 'I didn't know your mother let you.'

Down the stairs and into the kitchen, Lizzie in her high chair flinging rice and peas about, bits of salmon, some of it going in.

Jackie with a glass of wine, stirring what smells like a curry on the stove, telephone jammed under her ear.

Jon ducks under the cord, makes a face at Lizzie who widens her eyes in joke-surprise, shows Jon what's in her mouth.

Jackie's saying, 'We're all fine, Mum, I'm just saying hello.'

Jon's into the fridge.

He pulls a bottle of brown ale. He opens it, pours into a pint mug, smacks his lips at his daughter. She laughs and drops rice on the floor.

Jackie hangs up, sighs.

Jon says, 'There is nowhere else I'd rather be, love.'

'Better,' Jackie says, smiling. 'Better.'


They've been in the pub for a few hours now, and Suzi's feeling a lot better, but also a sort of woozy guilt, which she knows is like a sticking plaster over something deeper, and, let's face it, hangover related.

There's a giddiness, too, to her drunkenness now, and it's the sort of temporary euphoria which will only stop her thinking about Keith for so long.

She's not doing anything wrong, as such, except everything she's ever done with Noble and that's not a conversation she ever needs to have with Keith. The thought of it shoots up through her, slides down her back. It induces intense panic. She breathes, she sips her drink, she half-smiles at Noble, Noble gives her a little look – you OK, love?

'Do we really need to keep drinking?' Suzi asks.

Noble shakes his head. 'Not really. I thought you were enjoying yourself.'

'I've had better afternoons.'

'Hang about, yeah,' Noble says. 'I need to use the phone again, then you can go.'

'I didn't realise I was under restraint, officer.'

Noble winks. 'Sus laws were repealed long ago, sweetheart.'

'Don't call me that.'

'Just hang about a second, will you?'

Suzi nods.

She watches Noble chat up the barmaid, buy her a drink, slide the phone across the bar and turn slightly away from her, winking as he does. Class act, she thinks.

She watches Noble dial, say a few words, nod once, hang up.

She watches Noble pick up the now ringing phone.

She watches Noble as he doesn't say much, watches him nod, speak in monosyllables.

She watches Noble nod, hang up, dial again, say a few words, hang up.

Then the phone rings again, and Noble collars and speaks in what looks like an urgent whisper.

She watches Noble hang up.

She watches Noble march back across the pub. He gathers his coat, he finishes his drink, he doesn't sit down –

'What is it?' Suzi asks.

'Something happening up in Tottenham. You want a story? You should come.'

'What is it?'

'Trust me.' Noble nods at Suzi's pint, Suzi's things. 'Drink up.'

'Wait, what about— I need to call my fella.'

Noble digs in his pocket for a ten-pence piece. 'Be quick, I'll be outside.'

Suzi nods, gathers her things.


Parker's into the Turkish cafe across from The New Country Off-Licence and Foodstore for a beer and there's Trevor in the corner –

'You want an Efes?' Parker says from the counter. 'They're fucking delicious.'

Trevor's nursing a brandy and lifts his glass.

'Stick another one in there for him, would you, darling?' Parker says to the young bird doing the serving.

Parker sits down and gets straight to it. 'There's something kicking off in Tottenham and it sounds like some of your local brethren have been back and forth a bit for a little while now. What do you know about that?'

Trevor shakes his head, his eyes red, his lips purple –

'You all right, Trev?'

Trevor shakes his head, tries a smile –

'You're sure you need another one?'

His eyes bloodshot, his nose purple, he slurs –

'I been keeping my nose clean, like you told me.'

'Your nose isn't looking too clever today, son, I might tell you that, too.'

Trevor laughs, flicks his fingers with a snap –

'It's been a long week, what can I say.'

Parker drinks his beer, sniffs, looks left, right, he ain't really got time for this –

'You can't tell me anything about why a bunch of Hackney boys are holidaying up in sunny Tottenham?'

Trevor, grinning, shakes his head, pours his new brandy into his mouth, lets it sit there, slopping about, lips wet and full –

'Then why the fuck am I here?' Parker says.

He pushes back in his chair, gives Trevor the look.

'Marlon,' Trevor says. Trevor points down the road, enigmatic. 'Marlon,' he says again.

'What about Marlon?'

Trevor grinning, shaking his head –

'On a bus, top deck, he was going that way –' pointing again – 'I seen the man.'

'What you saying, Trevor?'

Still grinning. 'Well, Tottenham *that* way –' swivelling in his chair, pointing again – 'so you tell me, yeah?'

Parker shakes his head. 'When you've sobered up, we're having a word, you understand.' Parker stands up. 'Keep away from Tottenham, right? Go home.'

'Yeah man,' Trevor says.

Parker's disappointed, to be fair. But what can you do?

He leaves a note on the table, gives the bird a wink, a nod, shows her, he's out the door –

Then back on the bus, back up the road, back into Tottenham, back onto the fringes of the Farm, into a phone box, leaving word for Noble, waiting, picking up and Noble telling him: 'Stay close. I'm coming up. Steer clear.'

At the nick, a discreet enquiry at the front desk, the dropping of a name and rank and the confusion of a young plod, and Parker gets the specifics.

Parker heads up to 25 Thorpe Road and gets there a little before five p.m. He loiters, perched on a garden wall. At five p.m., a touch earlier, an unmarked car arrives and parks outside the address. Four officers climb out. Moments later, an area car and DSU pull up. No one gets out. Parker hears dogs scratch and whine inside the van. Big white boy like Parker and no one's bothering him.

Parker watches one of the officers pull keys from his pocket and open the door to 25 Thorpe Road.

Now where did you get those from, Parker thinks. That lad languishing in holding, his keys taken a walk, have they?

There's a bit of noise from the house, as you'd expect, Parker thinks, when four coppers have just let themselves in.

Parker wanders towards the area car. There are two uniforms inside. Parker gestures at them. A window is wound down.

Parker says, 'Neighbourhood Watch, is it?'

One of the uniforms laughs. In an accent, he says, 'Darkies, mate, you know how it is.'

Parker nods. 'Where you from?'

'Sheffield.'

'I know it. Feel good to be down here, teaching us a thing or two, does it?'

'It does, yeah.'

Parker thinks: they haven't changed the recruitment policy then.

He says, 'Keys, weren't it, they just used?'

'I didn't see nothing.'

Parker goes, 'Yeah, me either.'

The plod turns. 'Look, lad, you can stay and watch, you seem all right, just do it over there, OK?'

Parker nods. 'Much obliged.'

Parker stands back. He hears shouting. A young man running down the road, yelling, 'Mum, Patricia don't do nothing!'

He tears up the steps. He tears through the open door. There is further noise and the sounds of a struggle of sorts. The crack and clatter of a glass smashing. The squeak and thud of furniture falling.

Two of the four officers are backing out of the front door now, and the young man is telling them that his brother, Floyd Jarrett, does not live at this address, where is their warrant, and you leave my mum the fuck alone.

All four officers now leave the premises, loiter. There is the sound of crying. Floyd Jarrett's brother on his front step shouting. Floyd Jarrett's sister crying, shouting, 'Mum, Mum!'

One of the officers gets on his radio.

The commotion inside does not appear to be dying down at all.

The officers look confused, sheepish.

Another area car, and out jumps another officer, an inspector, Parker notes.

The inspector negotiates with Floyd Jarrett's sister and two of the officers head back inside.

Then: quiet.

A few people knocking about now, and Parker plays the concerned rubberneck.

Nodding away, shaping up, showing anyone who needs to see it that he's about the place.

Time, which Parker is very aware of, its speed, the way the last twenty minutes have hurtled past, slows now. Parker hears cars and distant main-road chatter, birds even, sound system music, Saturday night not far off.

Then Floyd Jarrett's brother comes running out the house and down the road and into a neighbour's, number twelve, Parker thinks. He's in there a few minutes, then he's back out and down the road and back inside number twenty-five.

A pause. The shouting has stopped. There is still the sound of activity, of movement, of a search being carried out.

Serial numbers on the telly, the video, the stereo, that kind of thing, Parker thinks, if Floyd Jarrett is receiving and stashing the stuff at home with his old dear, then plain sight's as good as anywhere. It's a fiddly business, though, and in Parker's experience, the Old Bill won't worry too much about upending and damaging a bit of equipment so's to get an easier look at the serials.

Next: a siren.

Parker watches the plods in the area cars look lively, all out and across the road, a barrier around the front door.

Ambulance.

Paramedics in through the door, officers out again –

A woman on a stretcher, an airway device clamped on her mouth, her body still –

Behind her, Floyd Jarrett's brother and Floyd Jarrett's sister are shouting, shouting about police, shouting about unnecessary force and violence, shouting about intimidation –

Parker thinks: what just happened?

Floyd Jarrett's brother and Floyd Jarrett's sister follow the stretcher into the ambulance. The ambulance pops its siren and off it tears –

Parker watches the officers get into a huddle, a little powwow.

One of them steps up to the front door, pulls it closed, locks it. He posts the keys through the letter box. He turns, smirk on his face, practically whistling, hands in his pockets.

Parker thinks: *hello.*

166

*In the factory out the back you're watching three lads from Canning Town strip out the inside of a van that looks very much like a East London Logistics van, though it isn't a East London Logistics van, it's what you're calling a mock-up of a East London Logistics van. The lads are replacing original parts of this mock-up with parts that are, essentially, more hollow.*

*'Imagine,' you hear one of them say, 'you were looking for something that was hidden, right?'*

*Terry raises his eyebrows. You nod. 'I am imagining that. Go on.'*

*'Well, where would you look?'*

*'I do hope that's a rhetorical question.'*

*'A what?'*

*'I hope you can answer that, is what I mean.'*

*The lad who's doing the talking shoots the brothers a look. They shrug: you're on your own here, son.*

*'Rhetorical question,' the lad says quietly.*

*You smile – thinly. 'We learn something new every day. And I'd like to be next. Where would I look?'*

*'Well –' the lad moves around the van, pointing – 'you'd likely start here and here, areas in the chassis that most obviously have space within. Would you say that's fair?'*

*'I would.'*

*'Good.'*

*The lad is visibly growing in confidence, you think.*

*'So what we do here is replace the interior parts that cover these more spacious areas within the chassis, allowing storage space.'*

*'Which is where you'd look first.'*

*'Exactly.'*

*You give Terry a nod. 'I feel like I'm missing something.'*

*'Well, we don't put anything in these places, that's the point. We set it up so that they look there and nowhere else, you get my drift?'*

*'I do, yes.'*

'Instead, what we do is, we stick the stuff in the roof. No one ever looks in the roof.'

'Why's that then?'

'Well, it's the roof, there ain't room.'

You give this lad another thin smile. 'I think I'm still waiting to learn something today,' you tell him.

One of the brothers chooses this moment to participate. 'It's clever this, guv, straight up.' He points at the lad. 'Show him.'

The lad nods.

On the roof of the van is a ladder that is fixed to it in the manner, you think, of the American fire trucks that pop up in films from over there, almost in the old cherry-picker style. The lad runs his hand over a particular part in the middle of the ladder, demonstrating as he does so that there is no discernible feature that would enable someone who didn't know it was there to find it. He appears to gently squeeze this particular part of the ladder, about halfway down, and the end of the ladder, the square end of the ladder, pops open. The lad beckons you to look: an empty tube, circumference minimal, length exceptional, which is the optimal equation for avoidance of the law, in which is stashed an awful lot of product.

You point at the other leg of the ladder. 'Same there?'

The lad looks at the older of the brothers, who nods. Emboldened, he says, 'Why don't you see if you can open it, guv?'

You nod. 'Terry,' you say.

Terry smiles. Terry looks at the lad, the brothers. 'Flutter, anyone?'

The brothers grinning now, shaping up. 'I'll give you five to one,' says the older brother.

Terry nods. 'A score.'

'Done.'

They shake hands, and Terry steps up.

Logically, you think, Terry locates the equivalent area of the ladder. He runs his hands over and around it, caresses it really, and you wonder about Terry and the more sensual aspects of his character, except you don't

*really, you know exactly what it is that Terry likes to do and there ain't*
*much caressing going on.*

*He strokes and he rubs, he squeezes and he prods –*

*Nothing.*

*He looks over at the brothers. 'This on the level, is it?'*

*'Course.'*

*You smile. 'I expect what we're doing here, Terrence, is a sort of simula-*
*tion exercise, so if the driver of this van was felt, then the long arm of the*
*law might well be doing pretty much what you're doing with your own*
*arm.'*

*'Thanks for the support, guv.'*

*'My loyalty knows no bounds, as you know,' you say, drily.*

*The brothers exchange a look at that, which you notice and enjoy.*

*'All right,' Terry says.*

*He moves up and down the ladder leg, stroking and rubbing, squeezing*
*and prodding –*

*Nothing.*

*He does a second pass, a third, examining every centimetre of it, shaking*
*his head, thinking, no doubt, about that score at 5-1.*

*After a time of this you decide you've had enough. 'I think, for the sake*
*of the simulation,' you say, 'this challenge is over. No plod would last this*
*long if they didn't know about the other one,' – meaning the leg stuffed*
*with product – 'so I think we'll call this, Terry, if you please.'*

*Terry nods and with an exaggerated gesture indicates for the lad to*
*reveal all.*

*He's smiling, this lad, and he's straight over to the ladder, straight over*
*to a rung about a third of the way down – or up, you suppose, depending*
*on how you view these things – and the same gentle squeeze, and, hey*
*presto, the square end pops open.*

*You smile. 'Very good. Pay him, Terry.'*

*Terry pays him.*

*One of the brothers explains that each of the vehicles will have this*
*feature, and in each of the vehicles it will be installed in a different place,*

*and that it'll be enough, no bother, the best system they've ever worked with, and that, combined with the company name on the side, and the work going on across the concrete over there – meaning the prep work for Wapping, of course, and the local constabulary being well versed in what's going on there, i.e., not this – well, it's pretty fail proof, wouldn't you say, guv?*

*You listen to this speech and you appreciate the use of the phrase 'fail proof', most would have gone for 'foolproof' and you reckon that says something and besides, he's right on all counts, and you didn't tell him all of it, so he's clever too, and there is mutual benefit pouring out of this, so you* do *tell him:*

*'Congratulations. You've got the job.'*


Kids in bed, Jackie reading with her legs tucked under her on the sofa by the fire, Jon in his corner of the living room, sitting at his little desk, surrounded by numbered cassettes, headphones on.

Above him on the shelf sits the stereo system – Marantz separates.

Below the desk, beyond his feet, a stack of LPs, his own and Jackie's. To his right, a catalogue of 'Singles' tapes, recordings from 45s, almost a hundred of these 90-minute tapes now, a system of Jon's own, so that, if you wanted, say, to listen to 'Leader of the Pack' by The Shangri-Las, then you'd locate under 'S' the name of the band, find the song – one of several – and learn that it can be found on cassette number 38, side B.

Jon, multitasking.

For his 'Recording Club' – Jon and three friends from school – Jon is making four copies of The Style Council album *Our Favourite Shop*.

It's been on Jon's radar since it came out in June – Jon enjoyed very much their performance at Live Aid – but they have a rota system, so Jon's had to wait.

The rota system is simple: once a month, a member buys four recently released LPs, one chosen by each member, and then records each of these LPs four times.

The member either keeps some, or all, of these LPs, or sometimes sells them on to a second-hand record shop like Reckless Records, which, conveniently for Jon, opened a branch not long ago in Islington.

It means, they reason, you really have to like what you choose to keep. An attempt to be a little more discerning is the idea.

At the same time, Jon's reading, work-related, more reports on the development of the Docklands area.

This from the minutes of a meeting of interested parties connected to the LDDG:

'. . .the Thatcher government [is] already lubricating public and private partnerships to invest in a new business airport and a railway system connecting the City to a new financial district – Canary Wharf.'

Jon's cross-referencing these official documents against broader commentary:

'These infrastructure projects [the business airport, railway system and so on] [are] some years off completion, but there [are] any number of old pubs, clubs and shop fronts that could be picked up cheaply to launder criminal activity and service the sexual urges of, initially, traditional East Enders, the growing immigrant community from the Asian subcontinent, and later, young professionals.'

And, again cross-referenced, this time against police reports, including this from a Detective Chief Inspector at Plaistow police station writing to his superiors with a request for assistance on 18 September 1984:

'This report concerns a group of people operating in the East End of London, particularly in the area of Plaistow and Canning Town, whose influence on crime in London and the Home Counties has grown steadily over a period of eight to ten years. In proportion to this growth has been the development of fear that they engender in the local population until a point has now been reached where the indigenous population would rather tolerate the outrageous behaviour of these people than become involved as witnesses.'

For the third time in the evening, 'Walls Come Tumbling Down' by The Style Council comes on.

It's definitely got a political message to it, he thinks.

It's positive, though, in its way, rather than a protest record.

That energy; like a call to arms if that's not too fanciful a cliché.

For the second time in the evening, Jon examines the sleeve notes:

THE STYLE COUNCIL WOULD LIKE TO TRAIN THE
YOUTH – IN THE ART OF REVOLUTION

It's playful but it's serious; it's not the Weller we knew in the Jam, Jon thinks, more mischievous.

He *does* want to do something or at least says he does, which might not be the same thing, but if he says it and someone else …

AND PLEASE NO MORE TALK OF THE 'BUT WHAT CAN I DO
ABOUT IT' VARIETY. TRACK THE LAST TRACK AND CLEAR
AWAY ANY CONFUSION – UNITY IS POWERFUL!!

The line from the chorus of the song to which Jon now listens.

It's a powerful line, a very strong chorus.

Maybe what Jon needs to do, he thinks, is check on the progress of one of Chick's syndicate's premises.

Suzi eyes Noble. 'Are you sure you should be driving?'

'The driving's easy,' he tells her, crunching the car into a low gear. 'It's parking that's the problem.'

Suzi, despite herself, smiles at this.

They're close, now, to Tottenham police station.

Backstreets and terraced houses, street lights and families shuffling home.

Windows open, the fresh air sobering.

The October night arriving quickly; the dark and the cold, the click of women's heels on pavement ringing out, cutting through the air –

The smell of petrol and damp, bonfires in back gardens.

It all wafts about.

Radio crackle, heating dry, engine throaty, parched.

Noble with a scowl, a look of something Suzi hasn't seen in him before: Concern.

'Where are we going exactly?' Suzi asks.

'Twenty-five Thorpe Road.'

'What's there then?'

'Well,' Noble says, 'a woman was carted off from inside on a stretcher and straight into an ambulance.'

'And?'

'This was just after four police officers turned up uninvited.'

'Right.'

Noble nods. 'What we're hearing is that the old dear has passed, dead on arrival, no less.'

'Jesus.'

'That's what I said.'

'What were they doing there, the four coppers?'

'Looking for stolen goods.'

'She a suspect then?'

'No. Her son.'

'And where was he?'

'Tottenham nick, still is.'

'How did—'

Noble shakes his head. 'It is unclear, Suzi, as to what has happened.' He shoots her a look, makes an ironic face. 'I believe that there may be officers out at this moment offering condolences as an attempt to defuse any community anger, which may or may not be displaced.'

In the backstreets, flashing by the terraced houses, the engine catching –

'I—' Noble begins.

'What is it?'

'Someone you know is there, or he's close by, someone you'll remember. I need to find him, find out what he knows, what he's doing.'

'The big boy?'

'Bingo.'

Suzi, again, smiles. 'You're funny.'

'Should be just up here on the right.'

Flashing by the terraced houses, families and street lights, the damp air and the smell of petrol, the snap and hiss of burning leaves –

Noble pulls over. 'Wait in the car.'

Suzi does as he says.

She watches Noble duck and dive his way through a line of police, push past a gathering crowd hostile to this line of police, a crowd yelling insults and questions, then past the door to what Suzi thinks must be number twenty-five, and now down Thorpe Road to a phone box.

He's in and out and waits.

Suzi watches as the big boy bounds down the road.

He and Noble exchange words.

They nod and they whisper, they shake hands and slap shoulders –

Noble back down the road.

Suzi thinking: *This is something.* Thinking: I know all about Paul Weller and Billy Bragg and Annajoy David and it won't hurt, it really won't –

Noble climbs in, pulls the door behind him. 'We should get out of here. Come on, I'll drop you home. I'll come back tomorrow.'

In the backstreets, the terraced houses, the crowd emotional, angry, vocal.

Suzi turns. 'If I do what you want me to, and I can, you help me get access –' gesturing at the road – 'to all this.'

Noble nods. He starts the engine. 'Deal.'

At home, Keith lounges, flicking through the *NME* again. The heating's on, it's cosy and warm, they're drinking red wine, picking at leftover curry –

'Sounds like you've had quite a day, love,' Keith says.

Suzi nods.

'I'm pleased you're energised by it, a story like this, I mean. It's good, it'll do you good.'

'I know.'

Keith adjusts himself. 'You'll be wanting to get back up there tomorrow, then.'

'I think so, yes.' Suzi smiles. 'After lunch, I expect. Nothing likely to happen before then.'

'Makes sense.'

Keith's right, it will do her good. He'll remember how she was when she volunteered for the Roach Family Support Committee, how involved she got.

She remembers it, too.

She's happy to have Keith's blessing, but she wishes he'd care more about where she's been all day.

It's a trade-off, she thinks, an info swap, quid pro quo is what Noble called it all those years ago –

And it's the same with Keith: he's happy she's happy, and it's as simple as that.

Count your blessings, girl, is how he'd put it.


A shade before midnight and Parker slips out of Carolyn's grandmother's flat on the Broadwater Farm Estate.

He's left Carolyn sleeping, Shaun watching telly, telling him he's nipping out for some air, and, collar up, hat pulled down, he arrows out the estate and over to Tottenham nick.

There, at Tottenham nick, not long after midnight, the Jarrett family – Parker recognises Floyd Jarrett's brother, Floyd Jarrett's sister, he thinks there must be some cousins, too – along with, Parker thinks, at least thirty others.

The family go inside, and Parker hears talk of further representation about the death of Cynthia Jarrett. The death of Cynthia Jarrett during a police visit to her home. Cynthia Jarrett dying, at home, in police custody.

The thirty or so others engage in a noisy protest.

Parker joins in, gets his face seen by a few faces, making it clear whose side he's on.

He doesn't know any of this crowd.

The Jarrett family come back outside; they address the crowd; they thank the crowd. They leave.

As they do, Parker feels the crowd pulse –

Missiles launched at the police station, hands in pockets, hands on bricks and rocks, bottles and cans, windows smash –

The duty officer comes out, appeals for calm.

He is flanked by uniforms. They are not tooled up, which, Parker thinks, is very sensible.

The duty officer is pleading for calm, demonstrating his understanding –

The uniforms will not respond, that becomes clear.

Parker eyes the crowd: there's no appetite for an off.

They don't look ready for it, too emotional, too angry, too raw –

He thinks: back to the flat, back to Carolyn and Shaun, back to their grandmother.

There's no way he's leaving them alone now.

# 4

## *Insurrection*

6 October 1985

Mrs Thatcher has had her four hours and is at her desk with a small cup of black coffee, a relatively new habit, and one that, apparently, complements the health regime of boiled eggs and whiskey that she's decided to resurrect for a fortnight.

In the doorway, Denis stands in vest and boxers with his own cup.

'Like drinking grit,' he says, shaking his head, sadly. 'Get up and go, they say, this coffee. Energising. A yuppie stimulant. Get up and go to the toilet is more like it.'

'Off you go for a sit then, dear,' Mrs Thatcher encourages.

'Earlier and earlier, it's happening,' Denis grumbles. He takes a newspaper from her desk. 'Something to read,' he says, shuffling off towards the 'boardroom', as he calls it.

She's looking over a report that came in the early hours from her favourite senior officer regarding a developing situation in Tottenham. He has prefaced this report, her favourite senior officer, with the remark that some of the details gathered by the police on the ground have not been corroborated exactly. Alongside this preface, however, is a further remark that, given the potential for escalation, this does not mean the details should be disregarded in any workflow decision-making.

She casts her eye over these uncorroborated details, assesses their pertinence.

A milk float, complete with a very large number of bottles likely to be used in petrol bomb-making, has been abducted in the last fortnight.

It has been confirmed that a chemist in north London reported someone buying small quantities of the rare ingredients that make napalm.

Briefings from the police who suggested that the riots in Handsworth, Birmingham were orchestrated by drug dealers.

She, Mrs Thatcher, picks up her telephone and dials, is put through to her favourite senior officer.

She gets straight to the point.

'This is most disturbing,' she tells him. 'Is everything possible being done to assist the police in their duties?'

'It can be, ma'am, yes,' she's told.

'We should stand up for the police force,' she says. 'How about some extra searchlights as a start, and then later perhaps, the possibility of demolishing homes in the more difficult estates?'

'Plastic bullets, I think, ma'am, in the short term.'

'Those too,' she says, and hangs up.

She wonders what Douglas would make of this.

'A number of our cities,' he told her privately only this week, 'now contain a pool of several hundred young people who we have not educated, whom it may not be possible to employ, and who are antagonistic to all authority. We need to think hard to prevent the pool being constantly replenished.'

She, Mrs Thatcher, might even be inclined to agree with his view that alienated black communities represent 'a grave threat to the social fabric of Britain'.

A mealy liberal, really, Douglas, always harping on about how Her Majesty's Prison Service doesn't work and arguing for more rehabilitation and alternative sentencing, whatever that is. He's talked before about bringing in a Public Order Act for the crime of what he calls 'hate speech', anything that is 'threatening, abusive or insulting', spoken in public, with intent or likely to 'stir up' racial hatred.

Half my backbenchers will be in trouble for that, she thinks.

Denis shuffles back in – finished then – tosses the newspaper to her.

As he turns to leave, he says, chuckling, 'I've a new phrase for you, Margaret, cockney rhyming slang, just made it up. Going for a Douglas.'

It'll catch on, she thinks.

*Sunday morning and you're at church.*
*You're actually at several, most Sundays:*

St Anne's Church, Limehouse
London Baptist Church
Stepney Greencoat Church of England
Tower Hamlets Community Church
Our Lady Immaculate & Saint Frederick Catholic Church, Limehouse

*Doing the rounds.*
*Making hefty-looking contributions to the donation trays.*
*Pressing the flesh with the various community leaders.*
*It's no coincidence that they stagger the services – you can be in some*
*sort of communion or prayer between nine and one if you play it right, and*
*a fair number of community figures do.*
*Including you.*
*Outside Tower Hamlets Community Church, you spot local politician*
*Mervyn 'Merv the Swerve' Michaels, Chair of the Tower Hamlets Council*
*Planning Committee.*
*'Bonjour,' says Merv.*
*'Mervyn.'*
*'Lovely service.'*
*'Wasn't it?'*
*'It was. You'll be at our Roman Catholic brethren's celebration in a*
*short while?'*
*'I will.'*
*Merv nods. 'Good. Busier there, so—'*
*He hands you a folded piece of paper, which you pocket.*
*'See you at the altar for a snifter and a biscuit,' he says.*
*You step towards the car where Terry waits.*
*In the back seat, you examine the piece of paper. On it, a list of council*
*estates in the borough:*

Avalon Estate
Coventry Cross Estate
Cranbrook Estate
Lansbury Estate
Robin Hood Gardens
Samuda Estate


*Outside Our Lady Immaculate & Saint Frederick Catholic Church, Limehouse, you clock Merv and walk over to him, smiling.*

*'When, is my question,' you say.*

*Merv nodding, says, 'I can't be any more specific than it could be any of them, it could be a year, it could be five, it could be ten, but it will happen.'*

*'All of them?'*

*'They're all on the list.'*

*'And when will you know the batting order?'*

*'That's the point, my friend, there is no priority with private investment. The cards will fall where they do, depending on who fancies what.'*

*'And you'll facilitate it when it happens.'*

*'That's my job, after all.'*

*'And it's the estates or the surrounding?'*

*'Either or both.'*

*'You're not, then, at this point, at any sort of liberty to disclose certain information.'*

*'You can't disclose what you don't have.'*

*'Fair.'*

*'I'd say estates is a given. Surroundings, take your pick.'*

*'I'll send out a few scouting parties.'*

*'There are a large number of units across the list I suspect you won't have trouble acquiring.'*

*'Cheque's in the post.'*

*'It better not be a fucking cheque,' Merv says.*

Jackie's taken the kids round to a friend who has two more or less the same age, and so Jon gets a rare few hours to himself on a Sunday.

Course, whenever Jon does get a rare few hours to himself, he's so keyed up for them, he doesn't know what to do for the first hour or so.

He cleans the bathroom, half-heartedly, to be fair. He sweeps the kitchen floor. He puts on a record. He opens a beer around midday. He puts on the television for the sport.

He flutters about his desk, he paces and he sits, he sits and he fidgets –

Then he flips to Chick's number in the family phone book and dials.

Chick answers after the third ring.

'Chick,' he says.

'Chick!' Jon says. 'What are you saying?'

'Who's this then?'

'It's Jon, Chick.'

'Jon who?'

'Jackie's Jon, Chick. You know, family.'

Chick snorts. 'Well, *she* is.'

'I mean—' Jon begins.

Chick roars, 'Turn it in, Jon, I'm joking! What can I do for you?'

'Saturday, Chick, Arsenal at home. You game?'

'Where are the seats?'

'Main stand. The boy's coming.'

Chick considers this. 'I'm game. We'll do the players' lounge after and all.'

'That's very generous, Chick.'

'I know it is.'

'We'll meet at the ground?'

'Makes sense with the boy coming.'

'Half hour or so before kick-off?'

'Sweet.'

Chick hangs up.

Jon thinks: that's the easy bit done then.

Noble comes through, and Suzi finds herself at a meeting in Tottenham police station a little before one called by the Deputy Assistant Commissioner.

The Deputy Assistant Commissioner has invited a number of key community figures to this meeting.

Suzi sits in the corner on a plastic chair with her notepad and pen.

Suzi scopes faces and writes down titles and writes down names:

The deputy mayor of Haringey, Councillor Andreas Mikkedes

Eric Clark, Haringey Community and Police Consultative Committee

Chris Kavallares, Police Sub-Committee of the Haringey Community Relations Council

Councillor Ernie Large

Jeff Crawford, Senior Community Relations Officer

Council Chief Executive Roy Limb

Dolly Kiffin, Broadwater Farm Youth Association

Floyd Jarrett

Michael Jarrett

They are given tea in plastic cups. There is milk and there is sugar. They sip their tea. A plate of biscuits is handed round –

Suzi shakes her head. Suzi is concentrating, thinking –

Noble's come through and here I am:

*Official observer.* Protocol. Independent, all cleared and here she is –

*This is a story.*

The meeting starts.

Nobody, Suzi notes, has taken off their coat or their scarf –

The room is hot, prickly –

Strip-lit and a sticky vinyl floor –

The Deputy Assistant Commissioner explains that he has called the extraordinary meeting as there is currently no procedure in place for police and council cooperation or consultation on matters such as this in front of them today.

'Matters such as what?' he is asked.

The Deputy Assistant Commissioner says the possibility of a sharp and significant escalation of trouble in the neighbourhood, specifically on the Broadwater Farm Estate and surrounding streets, and the police desire to work with community leaders to ensure peace and safety in that community.

And he is asked, 'And why would there be trouble?'

The Deputy Assistant Commissioner suggests that certain members of the community may be upset and sensitive due to certain police matters that were carried out the day before, yesterday afternoon, 5 October.

'Police matters,' someone says. 'I'm not sure that anyone thinks that the police matters.'

The Deputy Assistant Commissioner says that's not quite what he meant.

There is a refrain that Suzi picks up, a refrain that emanates from the non-police presence in the room.

'The officers who searched the home of Cynthia Jarrett should be immediately suspended from duty.'

The Deputy Assistant Commissioner responds to this suggestion saying, 'It's out of my hands. The investigation is being undertaken by the Police Complaints Authority.'

This is not a satisfactory answer, it becomes clear.

Plastic cups are squeezed and crack –

Feet scrape and squeak on the vinyl floor –

'The policemen who ransacked my mother's home, who caused my mother's death, should be immediately suspended from duty.'

To this, the Deputy Assistant Commissioner repeats, 'It's out of my hands. The investigation is being undertaken by the Police Complaints Authority.'

Somebody says, 'The investigation might well be being undertaken by the Police Complaints Authority, but that doesn't mean you don't have the power to suspend your own officers, that is surely only a matter for the Metropolitan Police.'

The Deputy Assistant Commissioner says, 'The investigation is being undertaken by the Police Complaints Authority.'

Suzi scribbles down the two key courses of action that are agreed upon:

1. All parties will appeal for calm within the community.
2. The enquiry into Mrs Jarrett's death will be completed as expeditiously as possible.

The Deputy Assistant Commissioner promises that he will request that the investigation being undertaken by the Police Complaints Authority into Mrs Cynthia Jarrett's death will be made public when their conclusions are reached.

There is some unhappiness as the meeting draws to a close –

Chairs are pushed back, coats are pulled closer, scarves are wrapped tighter –

Councillor Large points out that 'if you want to defuse a situation, you have to defuse it by being open'.

Council Chief Executive Roy Limb says that he is very concerned because 'we have heard nothing that could help defuse the tension that is there in the community'.

The Deputy Assistant Commissioner says that there is a plan, he would like to reassure them that there is a plan –

As the invited participants file out, Suzi thinks she notes some optimism on the part of the Deputy Assistant Commissioner.

She says to him, 'What if there's trouble?'

The Deputy Assistant Commissioner shakes his head. 'Who are you?'

'Impartial witness to protocol.'

'From?'

'Sent from Scotland Yard.'

He checks his notes, shakes his head. 'Oh yes, of course.'

The Deputy Assistant Commissioner gathers papers. He hands a sheet to Suzi.

The Deputy Assistant Commissioner says, 'There's a plan. Here.'
Suzi reads the document:

**PLAN TO DEAL WITH DISORDER AT BROADWATER FARM**

It is essential that in order to consolidate and isolate disorder, police should quickly gain control of the walkways connecting the blocks of flats on the estate. Unless this is carried out effectively, units at ground level may be subjected to missiles thrown from above and roaming crowds could move about the estate, thus rendering police mobility in vehicles ineffective.

Once the walkways have been secured, pockets of disorder may be contained and dealt with. In the event of disorder involving numbers of persons, efforts will be directed towards moving the participants towards the empty spaces to the west of the estate for dispersal.

A 'forward control' is to be set up in the Car Park adjacent to the Lordship Lane Swimming Pool and for a local officer, equipped with a radio on the local frequency, to be assigned to all units not from Y District.

Suzi reads, Suzi nods –
The Deputy Assistant Commissioner says, his hand out, his smile thin, 'I'm going to need that back now, love.'

Just before two and Parker is in a crowd of about a hundred blocking off Tottenham High Road outside Tottenham nick and there are banners and there are placards and there is chanting and the gist of it all is –
You, the police, have murdered Cynthia Jarrett.
Carolyn is with Parker and Shaun is with Parker and about a hundred other people are with Parker, in the street, in the middle of Tottenham High Road, blocking Tottenham High Road and announcing, loudly, to the world that the police have murdered Cynthia Jarrett.

There are placards that state:

MURDERERS

There are banners that state:

MURDERERS

There are placards and there are banners that ask:

HOW MANY DEATHS IN POLICE CUSTODY? MURDERERS

Parker wonders about the technicality of these particular banners, these particular placards. Some of the chanting is asking the same question, repeatedly.

Parker wonders if a house visit, the forced search of someone's home, is quite the same thing as police custody.

He imagines that the principle amounts to the same thing –

That the police are responsible for what is happening regardless of the premises. That the police are responsible for the safety of any people within said premises, people that the police protect and serve, and it is exactly that responsibility, exactly that implied custodian nature that makes an unannounced and forced house visit a true example of the term police custody.

It's funny, Parker thinks, what you think about at times like this.

Point being that some of these banners, some of these placards, are recycled and have seen other crowds, other protests.

And the point of that answers the fucking question they're asking in the first place.

We've been here before and we'll be there again.

How Many More?

is the sentiment.

Parker thinks of Michael Ferreira and Colin Roach, of Cherry Groce and now Cynthia Jarrett.

Parker notes the lines of worry, he notes the lines of anguish on Carolyn's face.

He notes the confusion, he notes the anger on Shaun's face, his body sprung, his body loaded, his body tense.

Parker knows that this is in part due to fear, not fear of what's happening now, no, not fear of this, but fear of what might happen next and where it might happen.

Parker keeps a close eye on the line of policemen, the line of policemen that protects the station, protects the station from this hundred-strong mob, this angry and anguished mob of about one hundred worried and confused people.

We're going to kill you –

This crowd tells this line of policemen.

We're going to rape your families –

This crowd informs this line of policemen.

Later, this crowd tell this line of policemen, later, this crowd informs this line of policemen, later, later there will be trouble.

An eye for an eye, Parker thinks –

An eye for an eye and a tooth for a tooth, a head for a head, a body for a body –

But it is not this *crowd* that voices these sentiments, these threats, these promises.

It is not this crowd, but a few members *in* this crowd.

Parker knows this.

Parker has been in crowds.

Parker has been in crowds swearing vengeance, crowds swearing murder –

It is not this crowd.

But to this line of policemen from Bedfordshire and Hertfordshire and Worcestershire and Lancashire and Northamptonshire and Merseyside and every bloody place except north London, to this line of policemen protecting Tottenham nick from a confused, angry, anguished and worried hundred-strong mob –

It *is* this crowd.

One crowd, one message –

Eric Clark, leader of the newly formed Haringey Community and Police Consultative Group, comes out of the police station and appeals for calm.

The placards are lifted higher –

The banners are lifted higher –

The chanting is louder, stronger, louder.

Eric Clark shakes his head. Eric Clark grimaces. Eric Clark goes back inside the police station.

Hyacinth Moody, chair of the Haringey Police Sub-Committee, comes out of the police station and appeals for calm.

Hyacinth Moody, a black woman, appeals for calm, attempts to pacify the crowd.

The placards are lifted higher –

The banners are lifted higher –

The chanting is louder, louder.

Carolyn, her arms crossed, her face lined with worry, her face lined with anguish, Carolyn elbows Parker in the ribs.

She says, 'Too late.'

Parker nods.

The sound of breaking glass. The sound of a car alarm. The sound of a police station window smashing –

Parker's jaw set, his teeth tense –

In time, he thinks, the crowd will disperse.

It is not this crowd.

*You're in the office looking at the books. You're always in the office looking at the books. It doesn't matter that it's Sunday –*

*You're always in the office looking at the books.*

*Columns, figures, sums, additions, subtractions, numbers and names, names and numbers –*

*Numbers that don't surprise you, names that sometimes do.*

*When you have such a diverse portfolio of interests as you do, well, there are a lot of numbers and a lot of names.*

*You consider what old Merv the Swerve told you earlier. You finger the piece of paper on which is written a list of the borough's housing estates.*

*A gambling man might say it's a toss-up as to which of these housing estates will be the first to receive the holy grail – it is Sunday after all – of private investment alongside council green-lighting, plus, and this is the important part of the trinity, a purchase of property in tandem to satisfy both the private investment as well as council social housing quotas.*

*But you're not a gambling man, you're not a betting man, so you want to know the housing estate on which to focus first, and which next, and which after that, and so on, and in what order exactly.*

*It occurs to you that there is one singular organ that controls – or at least is aware of – the money that is flooding into Tower Hamlets, Newham and parts of Hackney –*

The London Docklands Development Group.

*And that information ought to be worth some information in return, you think.*

*You're pondering names and numbers, numbers and names, when Terry knocks and pokes his head around the door.*

'He *wants a word,' Terry tells you.*

*You nod.*

'At *your convenience,' Terry adds.* 'Car's *ready when you are.'*

*You think: good timing.*

*In the car, peace.*

*Terry takes the scenic route.*

*Sunday-quiet on the roads from Canning Town and Limehouse up to Fleet Street. Wapping, St Katharine Docks, Tower Bridge, across into Bermondsey and Southwark, London Bridge and into the city –*

*The river, when you see it, is swollen and grey, dirty brown and thick.*

*Pleasure boats potter about towards Greenwich and Kew –*

*Gulls screaming at the wind –*

*Buses and taxis, white vans and permission plans –*

*Red lorry, yellow lorry.*

'*It suggests a sense of humour, Terry, don't you think,* his *insistence we always meet near the scene of the crime.'*

'*It does suggest that.'*

'*Nothing to see here yet, of course,' you add. 'But it does endear me to* him *somewhat, I'll say that about it.'*

*Terry parks on Gray's Inn Road, the presses quiet, the streets quiet, the inns closed on a weekend, riff-raff excluded, beggars and chancers slinking around the alleyways, sniffing and pissing against the walls in the dirty, piss-stinking alleyways round Holborn way –*

*Bloomsbury, spitting distance. Pissing distance.*

*Literary London –*

*No doubt old J.G. Ballard would enjoy the occasional soiree or salon gathering at both the private and public establishments of the environs –*

*Writing about his tower block from his ivory tower.*

*You've no idea if that's true, of course, but it feels right.*

*Doesn't make the book any less true, neither.*

*A knock on the window –*

*You step out of the car, take a few steps down the Gray's Inn Road, step inside another car, a bigger, roomier interior, a mini-television showing sport with the sound off, looks like indoor bowls, you think, no doubt Allcock and Bryant, that mob.*

*Funny what people watch.*

'*He's not here then?' you ask.*

*Your contact shakes his head, hands you a newspaper:*

Socialist Worker

*You raise an eyebrow. 'Branching out a bit then, are you?'*

'*Read the front page,' your contact instructs.*

*You read the front page, dated just a few weeks ago, mid-September.*

*The front page contains details of the electricians who wired the Facility at Wapping. The front page – and pages three, four, five and six – contains details about Portsmouth, how the EPU's Branch Chair for the Portsmouth area discovered that the branch office was being used as a 'recruiting centre' for employment at Wapping. The front page, and certain inside pages, contains the key job-interview question:*

'Are you prepared to cross picket lines?'

*'Right,' you say. 'Why you showing me this now?'*

*He jabs his finger at the name of the journalist that wrote the story: Geraint Thomas.*

*'Those sparkies you sorted out,' you're told, 'promised us they'd keep their mouths shut – there's a leak, it turns out.'*

*You consider your contact, mealy-mouthed and posh-faced, snide entitlement, daddy's little helper-type, you're not keen on his tone, on the implication –*

*You look at him –*

Up and down.

Up, and down –

*You look at him.*

*'I'd say it's likely a union leak, son,' you say.*

*'You would, would you?'*

Up and down.

Up, and down –

*You look at him and you say, 'We'll have a word with the journalist, find the leak for you, seal it.'*

*'Much obliged.'*

*You nod at that.*

Up and down.

Up, and down –

*'And you do something for me.'*

*He nods at this –*

*You hand him a piece of paper on which are written the words –*

London Docklands Development Group

*'A name,' you say. 'For turning.'*

*Another nod.*

Up and down.

Up, and down –

*Your contact says, smiling, 'You show me yours and I'll show you mine.'*

*'I think it might well turn out to be the other way round,' you tell him.*

Jackie and the kids are still out, but Jon knows it can't be much longer and this doesn't help him relax into the last of the rare few hours he has to himself. He is in the kitchen, dithering, when the telephone rings and it's Geraint Thomas from the *Socialist Worker*, and Jon is both surprised and also somewhat relieved –

You have to answer the telephone, after all.

'I'm both surprised and relieved to hear from you, Geraint,' Jon says.

'Likewise, Jon,' is Geraint's reply.

'You're surprised to hear from me?' Jon pauses, confused. 'You called me, Geraint.'

'You know what I mean, Jon.'

Jon nods, examines the kitchen wall where the telephone is mounted. He picks at a flaky bit of plaster.

'I do know what you mean. What's the news, Geraint?'

'Can we meet this week?'

'You flirt, Geraint.'

'You might be aware that the five print unions have decided not to take any action over the Wapping facility situation.'

'I didn't know that,' Jon says.

'Well, there it is. They all still think it's installation work, I hear, and that *The London Herald* is still on. The unions have been told Christmas to get themselves on the same page.'

'Same page, very good.'

'Excuse the pun.'

'Forgiven.'

'Anyway, this is buying a considerable amount of time. A suspiciously long period of time. So we've been digging—'

'And you've found a mole.'

'There's a document I want to show you, due to go to the unions first of November.'

'What is it?'

'Terms and conditions for work at *The London Herald*.'

'What are the headlines?'

'Where should I start? One, no recognition of chapels or union branches and no negotiations with them. Two, no closed shop, so anyone can leave, any time, union or otherwise. Three, union representatives to be elected by members, but the power to remove them is given to management, per a written warning for disciplinary reasons. Four, no union recognition at all for supervisors and managers, despite the fact that the majority are clerical branch members. Five, complete flexibility of working. Six, the adoption of new technology that may result in job cuts to happen at any time. Six, no minimum staffing levels. Seven, the company has the exclusive rights to select workers for jobs, or deselect them. Eight, and it's all legally binding.'

'Well,' Jon says, 'that's punchy.'

'It's a provocation, is what it is, to action.'

Jon nods. 'How's tomorrow morning?'

'I'll come to your office.'

Jon hangs up and thinks –

If you knew all this, imagine what you might do with the land, the property, knowing newspapers are heading east –

And what does that particular knowledge do for the people that live there now, the people whose interests you're supposed to be looking out for.


Two o'clock and Suzi is now in a meeting at the West Indian Centre on Clarendon Road.

There are about forty people at this meeting of black community leaders. The meeting is chaired by Martha Osamor, Chair of the Haringey Police Sub-Committee. The attendees include William Trant, who, Suzi has learned, is an officer of the West Indian Standing Conference, and two councillors, Bernie Grant and Steve Banerji, who was once chair of the Haringey Police Sub-Committee.

A resolution is passed in which five demands are expressed:

i.   A full public inquiry into the death of Cynthia Jarrett
ii.  The resignation of the Deputy Assistant Commissioner
iii. The payment of the Metropolitan Police precept to be withheld by the council
iv.  The account given by the Jarrett family of how their mother died to be accepted
v.   The four police officers involved in the search to be suspended from duty

As Suzi leaves, she hears someone say, 'All very well the elders saying all this, but where are the youth?'

Suzi writes this down, thinks it's a good point.

Four o'clock and Suzi is now at a meeting at the Broadwater Farm Youth Association.

The atmosphere at this meeting is a lot more charged, Suzi thinks.

It appears that many of the people at this meeting were only moments ago outside Tottenham police station with banners and placards and chants, making their feelings known –

*How many more?*

*How many –*

Suzi notes the anger, the calls for an eye for an eye –

Suzi knows that Martha Osamor and Bernie Grant intend to deliver to this meeting the demands that were made at the previous meeting at the West Indian Centre on Clarendon Road.

Martha Osamor tries to introduce Bernie Grant to the meeting. Suzi sees this, and Suzi sees Martha Osamor unable to introduce Bernie Grant – the *noise*.

The anger and the shouting, the shaking of fists and the calling for vengeance, the calling for revenge, an eye for an eye –

The meeting is being led by a man dressed in army gear –

There are voices talking about this man, a man not long out of prison –

Voices talking about how, not one hour earlier, two police officers, investigating reports of airguns fired on the estate, were attacked by estate youths with bricks and bottles –

Suzi writes this down, notes the anger, thinks – it's too late now.

Suzi sees Dolly Kiffin leave the meeting, climb the stairs to her office.

The meeting goes on, the shouting goes on, the calling for retribution goes on –

Bernie Grant spots Suzi and approaches her, knows what Suzi is doing there, and Bernie Grant says, 'Write this down.'

Suzi nods.

Bernie Grant says, 'The fact they don't allow me to speak seems to indicate to me that if I do speak it won't make any difference at all. People are really hyped up. I have never seen anything like it. People are very, very threatening. They are very aggressive.'

Suzi thinks of Colin Roach, the protests, the anger, the frustration, the helplessness, the powerlessness –

Suzi looks around the room, thinks – there is anger and there is frustration but there is not helplessness here, this is not a powerless group, here in these Youth Association premises.

Suzi listens, takes notes, sketches details of the room, the plastic chairs, the peeling wallpaper, the faux-wood floor, the smoke and the sweat, the chill and the damp from the open windows.

Right at the back of the room, tall and white in bomber jacket and boots, Suzi sees him –

The big boy, Noble's stooge.

She sees him and she looks away, looks back.

He's there with a young black woman, a younger black man –

Suzi sees him see her, that flash of recognition, here we go again –

Suzi gives a faint nod, a sly gesture of the notepad, flexes her fingers –

She sees him nod back, ever so slightly. She wonders if he knew she'd be here, if Noble had told him, if it made any odds either way –

At six o'clock, Suzi slips out of the Youth Association and leaves the estate and walks quickly back towards Tottenham High Road, Tottenham Police Station.

The streets are quiet, eerie.

At Tottenham police station front desk, Suzi is recognised, and she is shown to a room with a telephone –

She dials and on the third ring Noble picks up.

She tells Noble what she's seen, tells him what she's heard –

'Stay where you are,' Noble says. 'I'm coming for you. Both of you.'

Suzi breathes –

Parker leaves the Youth Association, leaves Carolyn and Shaun, leaves the Broadwater Farm Estate, crosses the road to a telephone box, pulls the rusting door towards him, recoils from the smell of piss and booze, feeds coins into the telephone and dials –

On the third ring, Noble picks up.

'Son?'

'This is a fucking nightmare.'

'I'll be there soon, have a word.'

'No.'

'What do you mean no?'

'I can't be seen, I need to stay inside, it's closing up.'

'What are you saying?'

Parker sniffs. 'I don't know, but it feels like something, like they're getting ready.'

'For what?'

'The Old Bill, guv, what else?'

Noble coughs.

'Sorry,' Parker says. 'I'm in a bit of a two and eight, to be fair.'

'Understandably.'

Parker breathes. 'Look, I ain't leaving. And you do need me, remember what you said?'

'She doesn't know who you really are, son, don't forget that.'

Parker says nothing. She meaning Carolyn meaning *nothing.*

Noble says, 'That redhead, you see her then?'

'I did. What's all that about?'

'A bit of information exchange, that's all.'

'She hanging about?'

'I'm on my way to pick her up.'

Parker shaking his head. 'Not me though.'

'You said that.'

'So what are we doing, guv?'

The airless telephone box, the cigarette ends and tart cards, the urine-soaked glass, the dog shit and empty cans of Special Brew –

'Stay, you're right. But keep your head down.'

'There's youth here that ain't from here, guv.'

'Yeah, you've said that too.'

'They've been gathering. Hackney boys, Islington, mainly Hackney.'

'For how long?'

'A month or so, shotting, you know, business.'

Noble saying, 'Keep your head down but keep your eyes open and this could be a good thing for us both.'

'What's that supposed to mean?'

Noble sighs. 'It means, son, that we're both doing a job here and any insight you might have into what might happen might be useful when it comes to the debrief, you understand?'

'So I risk my neck so you can get promoted?'

'Easy on, Parker.'

Parker breathes.

He looks through the dirty glass of the telephone box and he sees a patrol car moving slowly down the road, in between the low-rise houses of the estate on the one side and the two-ups and two-downs on the other.

He checks his watch. It is six twenty-five.

The siren on the patrol car flashes, a single yelp, then –

'Fuck me,' says Parker.

'What is it?'

The sound of smashed glass, shouting, the siren on, more shouting –

'Two kids in crash helmets just put a bottle through a squad car window.'

'You best get back, son.'

'I best.'

'Listen, wait,' Noble says. 'Keep safe, observe, we'll talk, that's all. No heroics.'

Parker thinks: if only Noble knew my nickname.

He hangs up.

He leaves the telephone box and watches as the driver of the patrol car reverses down the road, not bothering to inspect the damage. The two lads in the crash helmets long gone.

Parker heads back towards the estate.

On Griffin Road, he sees a young black woman walking slowly, alone, down the middle of the road, in between the parked cars, in between the low-rise houses of the estate and the two-ups and two-downs, walking slowly towards a DSU, a small number of uniformed officers.

This woman is chanting, Parker hears, as she walks.

'Babylon,' she's chanting, 'you're going to burn.'

Babylon, you're going to burn –

Parker arrows back into the estate, braving the looks of one or two of the local brethren, he nods, keeps on, spots Carolyn close to the Youth Association, keeps his head down, he's been seen, but you never know, keeps on, sees that Carolyn is upset, sees that Carolyn doesn't look quite right –

'What is it, darling, tell me?' Parker says.

'It's Shaun.' Carolyn wiping her eyes, wiping her nose.

'What about him?'

Carolyn sniffs. 'I don't know where he is.'

Parker nodding.

Parker scanning the estate, the exits and the entrances, the youths quiet for now, the odd siren, the crunch of traffic –

'Let's go back to your grandma's and you'll stay there and if he's not, I'll go back out and find him,' Parker says.

Carolyn nodding now. 'I love you,' she tells Parker who –

'I love you, too.'

And they're off across the concrete car park, across the concrete play-ground, up and up the stairs, down the walkway, into the flat –

Shaun not there.

Parker looks at Carolyn, nods. Carolyn nods and Parker's out the door and down the walkway, and down, down the stairs and back into the centre of the estate –

Parker hears sirens, Parker hears shouting, Parker hears truncheons on shields, boots on gravel –

At the centre of the estate Parker sees about two hundred people.

Parker pulls his hat down, his collar up –

He doesn't see Shaun.

He sees about two hundred youths in combat jackets, in balaclavas, in headscarves and in crash helmets. He sees milk bottle crates. He sees machetes and swords. He sees sticks and bats. He sees shopping trolleys full of bricks and stones. He sees petrol bombs.

He doesn't see Shaun.

It's quiet.

And then it's not –

Parker scoots round the inside edges of the estate, his eyes peeled, looking for Shaun, taking mental notes.

First thing he works out: how quickly the police have blocked the entrances, blocked the exits, blocked everyone in, trapped like a siege –

The entrance to Willan Road has a burning barricade between it and the estate, Parker thinks five or six cars have been set on fire.

Cars have been set on fire on Gloucester Road and The Avenue.

At Griffin Road, Parker spots the DSUs, sees the vans and uniforms and gear of the Special Patrol Group, around fifty of the heavy, head-breaking bastards, he thinks.

He doesn't see Shaun.

There is the sound of missiles thrown and glass smashing.

It's nearly half-seven and Parker sees groups of up to fifty attacking the police lines, retreating, peeling off down the alleys and the nooks of the Farm, trying to tempt the police in, splitting into smaller groups, then ambush, then out and attacking again.

It's getting late, early.

Parker keeps moving.

Parker pulls his hat down, his collar up –

Seven forty-five now and Griffin Road has an eight-or-nine-car burning barricade. Missiles are thrown from balconies and the raised walkways. Parker sees a shopping trolley filled with broken paving slabs.

Parker sees the police holding their positions around the estate in five-man shield units, packed tight, several rows deep, which means the front five get a hammering from all sides, and little the units behind can do about it.

Where do any of them want to go? Parker thinks.

The police want to contain the violence to the estate; the violence is directed at the police.

He doesn't see Shaun.

At some time after eight o'clock, a house on Adams Street catches fire. Sirens.

In the confusion, some kid climbs into a Royal Variety Sunshine minibus and drives it at the police line.

The minibus crashes into a wall, the engine running, the youth jumps out and scarpers, a copper calmly getting in and driving it away from the burning barricades, away from the burning house.

Parker pulls his hat down, his collar up –

On Adams Road, Parker sees a pitched battle: about one hundred police in three ranks holding out against a barrage of missiles, flames in the dark flashing from the burning cars, missiles raining down on shields, bricks, pieces of paving stones, bottles, petrol bombs, bricks landing on shields, cracking and snapping, thrown from above, the tower blocks as effective cover.

Parker handed rocks and bottles, sticks and stones –

Parker pulls his hat down, his collar up –

Looking out onto Griffin Road, two hundred are under the tower blocks, and there's a rhythm, Parker sees, a pulse to it –

They gather, they arm themselves, they attack the barricaded lines, they withdraw, they rearm, attack again. Parker sees small groups of whites with scarves and hoods, petrol bombs in their hands, their white hands –

He thinks: these groups are keeping to themselves meaning they ain't from round here.

Parker sees a knife strapped to a long pole.

Parker sees a burning barrel thrown from a balcony.

Parker sees petrol poured across the road and lit, a line, a border.

Parker sees canned food thrown, smack into concrete and glass. Tuna fish and baked beans –

Parker sees young men climb up the front rank of shields to smash lumps of concrete and rock down onto the police officers below, the police officers behind.

Cherry Groce and Cynthia Jarrett, Colin Roach and Michael Ferreira –

Just four names in Parker's mind, so many more, how many more –

Parker sees boys and men syphoning fuel from cars, tearing rags from a large white cloth, milk bottles, a car turned over for petrol –

He doesn't see Shaun.

He wonders when they'll call for baton rounds and CS gas. He's surprised, to be fair, that they haven't already.

He ducks and swerves inside the estate, looking for Shaun.

He's been seen, Parker has, his face clocked, so he's all right, and there are white faces about, but they don't look too integrated, ringers in from somewhere, well up for it, and he's very well aware of that, Parker is, and he can't be seen to be ducking and swerving duty, seen or not, so every now and then he joins one of the raiding parties and hurls a few rocks, aiming wide, and then straight back to squirreling around for Shaun –

Who he still hasn't seen.

He's wondering if Shaun is even *on* the estate.

He sees the anger and the hate, the methodical attack and retreat, the uprising, the insurrection –

Is what it feels like.

Cherry Groce and Cynthia Jarrett, Colin Roach and Michael Ferreira –

Parker knows there are many more names, but how many more –

Parker thinks of Blair Peach, wonders how long until the Special Patrol Group break out their weapons, break some heads –

Parker hears: Fuck off, pigs.

Parker hears: This is the Farm.

Parker hears: No pigs here.

Parker hears: You'll never get out alive.

Parker hears: Kill, kill, kill the pigs.

Parker hears: Burn the bacon.

Babylon, you're going to burn –

he thinks.

Closer to the police lines, Parker hears –

Monkey noises.

Parker hears: Fuck off, niggers.

Parker hears: Go and live in the zoo.

Parker hears: You can burn that down.

Parker hears: Get back in your rat hole, vermin.

Parker hears: You wogs, you vermin.

Parker hears: We'll be in to get you soon enough.

Babylon, you're going to burn –

he thinks.

There's a lull, of sorts.

The smell of petrol, the smell of burning.

Shouting, chanting –

But still a lull, a breather.

Parker finds himself in the Tangmere block of the estate. The smell of burning, the smell of petrol is stronger, earthier. The shouting more pointed, specific –

Fire, fire.

He sees that the supermarket on the mezzanine level of the block is smoking, smoking and burning. He watches as men and boys scuttle around, either side, assessing the damage, it looks like, assessing the danger –

He sees kids and adults, black and white, in and out with plastic bags full of goodies.

He sees a white kid with two plastic bags saying to his mum –

What shall I do with this?

A white boy runs past Parker, his bag aloft in triumph, saying –

I haven't had this much food in six months

In an Irish accent –

I'm unemployed!

Parker sees three white youths with burning rags, in they go with their rags, in they go into the supermarket and the tobacconist next door, in and out with their burning rags –

Fire, fire.

The men and boys gather and consult. There is shouting at the police lines –

Fire, fire.

These men and these boys shouting for the police to come and put this fire out.

Parker waits and watches. It doesn't look like a trap, it doesn't look like an ambush.

The supermarket on the mezzanine floor is at the bottom of a tower block. At the bottom of a tower block below a large number of flats.

Above the supermarket entrance, Parker sees graffiti:

TANDOORI SHIT GET OUT. NIGGERS RULE.

If the supermarket fire is not put out, well, Parker thinks, then we've got something quite different on our hands –

He's at the lower level, close to the parking zone beneath the concrete stairways. He sees the police line. He sees he is alone. He looks left and right, thinks –

He moves closer to the police line and he lifts his hat and he pulls down his collar and he shows his face and he looks the police line in the eyes, in the eyes of the young lads at its front, young lads from Bedfordshire and Hertfordshire and Worcestershire and Merseyside, and fuck knows where else, and he shouts:

Get the fucking fire brigade in here now.

And then Parker pulls down his hat and pulls up his collar and he ducks and he swerves back into the estate, back under the towers of the Tangmere block.

Then it does go quiet, in the immediate area where Parker now skulks, skulks and lurks, watching.

Parker sees two firemen move in, steady, hands raised, quickly up the stairs, left alone, to the mezzanine floor, the floor above, and he sees them have a look at the supermarket, he watches them open the door, check the windows, watches them powwow and nod, and then watches them leave – quickly, steadily – back the way they came.

Parker sees movement in the shadows above, groups circling the walkways that go up, either side, up to the mezzanine floor of the burning supermarket, groups twisting up the stairways, either side, above and below, the mezzanine floor.

Back come the firemen, five of them this time, a hose and an axe and there are eight policemen with them –

They're shouting:

Stand back, we're coming in, we're here only to protect the firemen, help them to do their job, we'll leave when the fire is out.

Over a loudhailer, a policeman says:

We'll leave when the fire is out.

Parker watches the group cross the parking zone and snake up the concrete stairway, unopposed, left alone.

As they drag the hose, as they pull the hose, as they twist and bend the hose up the concrete stairway, Parker hears whistles and bells, and thinks –

Ambush.

Parker skulks and Parker lurks, he stays where he is as men and boys in balaclavas and in hoods, in crash helmets and in scarves, men and boys carrying sticks and carrying knives, men and boys wearing gloves and wearing hats, hats pulled low and collars up high, men and boys float past him, float noiselessly past him, noiselessly on their way up the stairways, above and below the mezzanine floor, either side of the burning supermarket, and as they do, Parker sees box-fresh trainers and a leather flying jacket, and he looks carefully, he looks up and down, and he sees a red scarf across a face, a fat gold watch –

Marlon –

Parker says –

And Marlon turns, his face covered –

And Marlon –

Nothing.

His eyes lock with Parker's eyes, a shake of the head, a nod, pointing across the courtyard, and Parker sees –

Shaun.

And it all happens quickly now, the sound of water, the chugging sound of the hose, the sound of policemen, the sound of the men and the boys, the sound of sirens and fire, of breaking glass and licking flames, and then policemen are running past Parker, policemen and firemen are running down the walkways either side of the burning supermarket, across the courtyard, aiming for the road, out the estate and across the road, but they're being chased, chased by a group of men and boys, armed men and armed boys and then –

Parker sees Shaun, Parker calls his name –

Shaun –

Shaun who turns and sees Parker and stops –

Shaun stops.

The policemen and the fireman keep running, chased, they keep running –

Shaun stops and Parker reaches him, and they stand, they don't move –

Marlon is behind them; he is not moving –

And one of the policemen slips, one of the policemen –

Falls –

Down, onto the ground –

He falls.

And this policeman is quickly surrounded and attacked, attacked from all sides.

And Parker and Shaun watch as this policeman is attacked from all sides, attacked from above, attacked from below –

Parker hears:

Kill, brothers, kill. We've got a beast.

And Parker thinks eye for an eye –

And Parker thinks tooth for a tooth –

And Marlon is next to Parker, next to Shaun, and Marlon says –

Time to go, time to go home.

And they turn, turn to go home, and as they walk away from the noise, away from the beast, away from the vengeance, away from the anger and the hurt, Parker turns back and Parker sees –

A bread knife sticking out the policeman's neck –

And Parker sees –

Policemen dragging a heavy body, a dead weight, dragging it across the courtyard, out the estate, across the road.

There's a crack and an explosion, a smell of smouldering, damp wood –

Petrol and flames, autumn nights and penny for the guy, bonfires and fireworks, and Parker has his arm round Shaun, and Shaun is sobbing, sobbing at the anger, sobbing at the hurt, and Parker wraps his arm further round Shaun and leads him towards his grandmother's flat, and Marlon says:

Stay in now, yeah?

And Parker nods –

What about you?

Don't worry about me.

And Parker nods –

And Marlon turns, nods, noiselessly floating back the way he came.

*Later, Terry pokes his head round the door. 'It's done,' he tells you.*

*You nod, raise an eyebrow: and?*

*'Put it this way, the cunt won't be writing any articles for a while and nor will he be telling anyone why.'*

*'Triffic. Clean, was it?' you ask.*

*'The Canning Town boys took the contract, used a couple of young 'uns, a mugging, could happen to anyone at night in London, terrible business, a real shame.'*

*Terry hands you an envelope.*

*Inside, a couple of Polaroids of a miserable-looking bloke in a hospital bed, jaw wired shut, arms in casts –*

*'Get word to our contact that our part of this quid pro quo has happened and we want our name and sharpish.'*

*Terry nods.*

*'First thing, Terry, all right? Tell him we'll have the kettle on, in a manner of speaking.'*

*In the envelope, a scrap of paper, on which a name, a date, a place and a time:*

**JON DAVIES, OCTOBER 7, OFFICE, NINE O'CLOCK.**

*Tomorrow.*

*'What's this?'*

*'It was in his wallet, just that and some cash, which we let the youths keep.'*

*'Very generous of you, but do we know who this is?'*

*Terry shakes his head.*

*'And he won't be telling anyone neither.'*

*Terry shakes his head.*

*You think: could be anyone, some lefty, some other journo, could be anything.*

*'Remind me of his name, Terry?'*

*'Geraint Thomas.'*

*You think: some Welsh bloke or other.*

*'Ask around, just in case, but nothing heavy. Very likely it's not of inter-est, I'd say, Terry.'*

*Terry nods. 'Will there be—'*

*You shake your head. It's Sunday evening and you've earned yourself a whiskey or three and a bit of kip.*

*'Let's go home, Terry. It's been a long day, all told.'*

*'I'll get the car.'*

*You close your books, your ledger. You fasten the top back onto your fountain pen, place it in the top drawer of your desk. You put on your coat, turn off the lights, step out into the forecourt and look up at the night sky, a black night, streaked with blue, that quiet London rumble somewhere just out of reach.*

*Shaun*: I'm in bed, my clothes on, my hands over my ears, but I can still hear the shouting and I can still hear the chanting, and I can still smell the smoke and I can still smell the petrol, I can still taste the foul burnt air and I can still taste the blood and I can still taste the dirt, I can still taste the blood and I can still taste the dirt –

I toss and I turn and I sob and I sob –

I can hear Parker downstairs, I can hear Parker whispering to Carolyn, whispering about what he saw, but he's not telling her everything he saw, I can hear that he's not telling her, and I can hear my granny snoring, just lightly, but she's asleep and I hope she stays asleep for a long time.

It all happened too fast, and Anton leaving and Anton saying, 'Come on, Shaun, man, get out of here, come on, man, this is not us,' Anton shouting at me to come on, but I stayed, and it all happened too fast and then –

And then that big man Marlon and he's telling me, 'This way, young 'un, this way, yeah,' and I'm following and I'm running, and there's the smell of the smoke, the smell of the petrol, the feeling of bricks and rocks and stones in my hands, and I throw them, but I don't see where they go, where they fall, and Marlon telling me, 'This way, come on, all of you, yeah, heads down—'

I remember Marlon and I remember faces I don't know, white and black, new faces, and I see Marlon looking and nodding, and pointing at me, and that's when I go, and that's when I see Parker and that's when he sorts me out for the second time.

Now, in bed, I see Marlon pointing, I see Marlon nodding and I don't know what it means.

I toss and I turn, I sweat and I shake.

That taste –

Blood and dirt, smoke and fuel –

Fear and hate –

I retch and I sleep.

I sleep –

Sleep

*Daily Star*: RED BUTCHERS: TROTS BLAMED FOR RIOT TERROR.

The *Star* has known for some time of the Trotskyists' involvement in whipping up race hatred among under-privileged communities. The fact that Sunday's violence was planned is borne out by evidence of petrol bomb factories being set up. A van and lorry loaded with dustbins full of bricks and rubble were also seen entering Tottenham's Broadwater Farm Estate.

*Daily Express*: STREET-FIGHTING EXPERTS TRAINED IN MOSCOW AND LIBYA RESPONSIBLE FOR THE TOTTENHAM RIOTS.

The chilling plot emerged as detectives hunted a handpicked death squad believed to have been sent into north London hell-bent on bloodshed.

*Daily Mail*: A daily war being waged against White families by the younger members of a burgeoning Black community who occupy virtually all the flats in the 12 blocks of grey, stained concrete that make up the divided zone.

*Daily Mail*: The local name for the 12 blocks of flats there is Alcatraz, and if you are poor and White, old and ill, it's a vicious and frightening prison.

*Guardian*: THE MIX OF LETHARGY AND CONFLICT

This is irredeemably bleak. Within a handful of weeks, Brixton follows Handsworth and Tottenham follows Brixton. Worse, there is a feeling of momentum, of gathering violence. Now, at Tottenham, the rioters have guns and knives as well as a hail of petrol bombs. One policeman is dead, and others lie direly wounded. The Metropolitan Commissioner talks of plastic bullets, tear gas and water cannons whilst the Home Secretary holds hard to his seemingly unshakeable conviction that these are gangs of criminals, to be cowed and caught and locked away.

Mrs Thatcher turns to a draft memo written by Oliver Letwin and Hartley Booth, the former considered something of a rising star in her party. It's only a draft, she's been assured, it's not oven-ready, but it does suggest some form of response to the problems that are rife on our major inner-city council estates. He's slick, Letwin, she thinks, reptilian, the sort of Eton man who has no concern regarding his standing – or his charms, all that thick hair and fang-toothed grinning.

The root of social malaise is not poor housing, or youth 'alienation', or the lack of a middle class. Lower-class, unemployed white people lived for years in appalling slums without a breakdown of public order on anything like the present scale; in the midst of the depression, people in Brixton went out, leaving their grocery money in a bag at the front door, and expecting to see groceries there when they got back. Riots, criminality and social disintegration are caused solely by individual characters and attitudes. So long as bad moral attitudes remain, all efforts to improve the inner cities will founder.

New black middle-class entrepreneurs will not be a 'force for stability' but will set up in the disco and drug trade; refurbished council blocks will decay through vandalism combined with neglect; and people will graduate from temporary training or employment programmes into unemployment or crime.

Setting up a £10m communities programme to tackle inner-city problems would do little more than 'subsidise Rastafarian arts and crafts workshops'.

Well, she thinks, that's a distinctly controversial position to take, but it's also one that a lot of voters will appreciate.

# PART THREE
# *Homebreakers*

23 June–28 June 1986

# 1

## *Manic Monday*

23 June 1986

Mrs Thatcher reads her newspaper. She's grateful for it, her newspaper, grateful that it's here, every day, first thing – on time.

There was a moment, not long ago, when receiving her newspaper every day, first thing, on time, wasn't necessarily guaranteed.

Well, she thinks, let's not be disingenuous: she wouldn't have allowed that to happen.

It was all a pretence, the closeness of it, really, the whole sense of *it was a close-run thing*.

Well, it wasn't close at all.

It's been nearly six months now, and she receives her newspaper every day, first thing, on time despite the pickets and the threats, the violence and the scabs.

She thinks about the political emphasis Ferdinand Mount, her former Head of Policy Unit, gave it: 'We must neglect no opportunity to erode trade union membership wherever this corresponds to the wishes of the workforce. We must see to it our new legal structure discourages trade union membership of the new industries.'

In a Cabinet meeting in the middle of last month there were discussions on exactly this, how we don't take sides, ma'am, nudge-nudge, wink-wink –

The text, which she turns to now, the *minutes*, doesn't indicate any partiality.

Not that it'd matter, as Denis always tells her, chuckling, 'No one'll read it before you're dead, Margaret. Thirty years is a long time when you're our age.'

Meaning the thirty-year rule and declassification.

What Denis doesn't know about is the escape clause under section 3(4) of the 1958 Public Records Act, and that files can be withheld 'if, in the opinion of the person who is responsible for them, they are required for administrative purposes or ought to be retained for any other special reason'.

There are always plenty of reasons, Mrs Thatcher thinks.

She takes a black pen, draws a line through a name, crosses over letters, reads:

**Cabinet paper, 16 May 1986:**

THE HOME SECRETARY said that demonstrations against [xxxxxxx]'s printing enterprise in Wapping continued every few days. The violence of the demonstrations, and their demands on police resources, were rising, and the situation appeared to be getting beyond the control of the Society of Graphical and Allied Trades (SOGAT). It would not be right for the Government to seek to influence the dispute that underlay the demonstrations, but there was a need to bring SOGAT and the police into closer liaison. At a meeting the previous week with SOGAT representatives and Labour members of Parliament, the Minister of State, Home Office, had asked SOGAT to recognise that violence was the inevitable outcome of these continued demonstrations, but SOGAT's response was that they had no other way to promote their cause within the law.

She turns the pages of her ink-fresh newspaper.
*Will they never learn*, she thinks.

*Bethnal Green Town Hall.*
It's been a funny old year so far, 1986, all told, Jon thinks, Monday morning 23 June, sat at his desk. There was a moment, a definite moment, when West Ham might've actually won the First Division title.
That would've been nice.
Instead, they blew it.
Handed the momentum – and then the title – to Liverpool. Even Everton tripping over themselves to make that happen, to help Liverpool help themselves to the First Division title.
Third, for West Ham then, a club record, snatching an each-way place from the jaws of a win –

The West Ham way.

The boy went into decline for a couple of weeks before Jackie shook him out of it, told him what it was like to be mother, daughter, sister, cousin, *wife* to a West Ham supporter, the reality of it.

To be fair to the boy, he stopped moping.

That draw with Arsenal when they went with Big Chick didn't help matters. And the visit didn't help Jon neither, what with Chick telling him that the syndicate was being dissolved, the portfolio divvied up and sold off.

'Who to?' Jon asked.

'Names-wise, there's a few,' Chick told him. 'But every road leads to Rome, you know what I mean?'

Jon said that he did know what Chick meant.

Problem was Jon didn't want to ask anything in any more depth, and if Chick was no longer in the business, well, there wasn't any point either way.

'You didn't fancy it, then,' Jon asked. 'The property game?'

Chick looked away, thin smile, a nod. 'Seller's market,' was his only comment, offered with a confident, face-saving shrug.

He hasn't seen Chick since. And he hasn't seen Chick's name anywhere either.

That seller's market line Jon had down as Chick bluster, figuring the syndicate was never as well-positioned as he'd made out. The fact he referred to it as the syndicate at all suggested delusions of something or other. Jon assumed it'd been a financial arse-over-elbow scenario and left it.

A few days before the Arsenal game, Jon was visited by someone from the council, representing Mervyn Michaels, Chair of the Tower Hamlets Council Planning Committee. The point of the meeting seemed to be an imminent strike regarding the building in Wapping, and Jon had said to his visitor:

'Funnily enough I was supposed to meet a bloke on Monday about that, a journalist.'

'But you didn't?'

'A no-show, and no word since.'

'What's the world coming to. You been in touch?'

'Number rings and rings,' Jon said.

After that, the meeting didn't last long at all, and the representative of Chair of the Tower Hamlets Council Planning Committee went on his merry way.

Jon tries Geraint from time to time, but never gets through, disconnected now, the number.

He was right about the strike though, Geraint, which doesn't look like being over for a while. What Jon's been doing is trying to figure out the impact of it on land transfer and property dealings, but, like Chick said, the list of names feels endless sometimes, like it might be a seller's market, but there do seem to be a lot of buyers, and without much really happening, visibly.

Jon sighs, leans back on his chair, hands behind his head, he's tired, Jon is.

Over the weekend, the football season safely finished for another year, there'd been the festival up on Hackney Downs, the Hackney Show. Fairground games and food, Jean Breeze and Dennis Bovell, the London All Stars Steels and the Perpetual Beauty Carnival Club, stunts, stalls and sideshows –

Across the park, on the north side, a little bit away from the festivities, a tent emitting pounding reggae, really dirty, pulsating dub.

He and the boy had wandered over towards it, the towers of the Nightingale Estate to their right, Hackney Downs School to their left –

The tent shook with the sound system, the sides flapping, the roof lifting and falling, one or two men dancing on their own just outside it, shirts off and bare feet, eyes red, eyes wild –

Stoic-looking Rastas at the entrance.

Jon felt the bass tearing through him. The boy slowed down a touch as they approached.

He nudged Jon. 'I'm not sure this is for us, Dad,' he said quietly.

Jon shook his head and put a hand on his shoulder. The boy close, like when he was a shy toddler, wrapping himself around Jon's leg, pouting.

The Rastas nodding them in, the tent about half-full –

The volume and depth of the music made the lights shake and flash. What lights there were.

Air thick with smoke –

Jon seeing the boy's eyes start to water, not a great deal else.

They stayed about fifteen minutes, Jon recognising a Steel Pulse track, 'Babylon the Bandit', that had been stripped right down and then powered right up, an MC over the top of it, that was enough.

On the way out, one of the Rastas winked at the boy, grinned.

'Welcome to Jamaica,' he said.

Back over at the main event, Jackie chatting with Doc and Sandra, Lizzie sitting in a circle with her playgroup friends, GLC and I Love I.L.E.A. T-shirts, parents close by in dungarees and sandals.

Doc slapped Jon's hand, snapped his fingers.

'Man like it heavy manners!' he laughed. 'Too deep for me those Dalston boys.'

Jon smiled. 'I'm a discerning man, Doc, you know that.'

Doc leaned in. 'They that side of the park for a reason, yeah. They being nice 'cos a him –'

Thumb out at the boy.

'Right,' Jon said. 'Noted.'

'Let me get you a beer, Jon.'

'Good man.'

Jon wonders now what Doc meant by that, wonders was the boy right, that it wasn't for them. Wonders what he meant and how he knew.

He didn't ask, assumed it was the state of the bassline, pretty elemental as it was, a nausea-inducing rumble –

Still, the boy had felt something that Jon hadn't.

Which is happening more and more, Jon thinks.

Passage of time and whatnot –

Monday blues.

Too much Red Stripe and Doc's rum, fried chicken and hot sun –

No one in the office, though, checking up on him, telling him what to do.

That hasn't changed.

*Shaun*: Anton ain't been around much, and more and more he don't want to come back from school with me, so I'm walking around a lot on my own, and I know why he don't, but I don't know how to fix it, neither, which is vexing me, but it ain't his fault, he's doing that after-school ting and working hard, and he's keeping his head down, fair play, but it makes me sad.

'Homework club, innit.' He shrugs. Or: 'Extra maths, yeah.'

Once he even said, 'Debating practice.'

What even is that, though of course he'll be good at it. He's keeping away from the Farm as much as he can, is what it seems, just using the place to sleep at, I think, and someone told me his mum is trying to move but the neighbourhood office is chocka for fam wanting to get away, but he's on a list, Anton, I heard, so there it is.

See what happened was a couple months after the riot there's coppers all over the place and they're stopping most all the boys at some point, and they're dragging some in and leaving others and it's hard to know which and why and wherefore, yeah, and it's just a matter of time before it's us, and it's coming, we know it is, and we know what you're supposed to say, how you're supposed to be with them, respectful and firm and know your rights and then –

And then when it *is* us, they let Anton jog on, and it's just me.

What they tell Anton is, 'You, you can fuck off, it's him we want a word with,' meaning me.

And that throws me, and I panic a little and I see the look in Anton's eyes and I can't miss it, you know, it's there, he's saying, a little bit, with his eyes, he's saying –

You should of left when I did, you should of run when I did. You wally, his eyes telling me, you fucking wally.

And he's right. But he still jogs on. Course he does, he ain't any choice, has he.

'So we know who you are and what you done,' they tell me. 'And if you know what's good for you, you'll do whatever it is we tell you.'

I shake my head and say nothing more than I don't know what you mean, I don't know what you're talking about.

They've got me just on the edge of the estate, under the walkway as you come in, the fringe, which means no one can see what's happening from the street or from the flats above neither.

There's four of them, two uniforms, two plain clothes. One of the plain clothes is chatting shit to me, right in my face, spitting.

'We'll come to your gran's flat and search every fucking nook and cranny, every nook and granny, get it, you little cunt?'

I nod, the other three laughing, though this one ain't laughing, I can feel the hate and the anger pouring off of him.

'Every little corner, we'll get every-fucking-where, we'll have the clothes off your fucking back, the food out your fucking cupboards and they'll prove what you did, you murdering black cunt, it's serious, murdering an officer of the law, what you lot did, you savage fucking monkeys.'

I say nothing but I bite my lip and I try not to cry and I try to remember what we were told, that if they don't nick you straight off the bat then hold tight, they ain't going to, they just about scaring you and putting the wind up for another time, hold tight, I tell myself, but it's so hard not to cry, my lips wobbling –

'We'll be round, we'll be round soon, and you better be in if you want to protect that old gran of yours, 'cos if you ain't in then who's to say, you know what I mean, all's fair in love and fucking war, you murdering little black bastard, you got that?'

'Give me that –' meaning my bag – 'we'll start with that, and don't fucking move in the meantime.'

And he nods at the uniforms, who move a little closer, and he's pulling gym shoes and sports vest, a pair of dirty white shorts, a biro and my history notebook, socks that have seen better days, bit crusty –

'The state of it,' he's saying, 'the fucking state of it, fucking animals, don't know how to use a washing machine, fucking stinks in here.'

But I hold tight and I watch as he drops my things one by one onto the ground, stepping on each one of them and grinding it into the ground with the heel of his dirty white trainers.

I feel tears come now, hot and salty, *shame*, shame –

Then he's finished and the bag's on the ground too –

And I'm nodding, nodding and blubbing a bit now, and one of the uniforms steps in and he goes:

'You can stop crying, lad, you're all right for now, go and tidy yourself up and get yourself home.'

So I bend down and pick up my things, stuff them into my bag, and I reach for my history book and just as I do the other uniform kicks it out of my hands, picks it up, rips it into pieces as he walks away, chucking the pieces onto the bit of yellow grass out front where people take their dogs to do their business, right on top of a big pile of shit.

So it's on my way home walking quickly past the Youth Association that I bump into Marlon – walk *into* him, big man that he is – and he sees I've been crying and tells me come back here tomorrow, same time, and we'll have a chat and that he can help.

And I do go back the next day, there's no reason not to, it feels like my best friend wants nothing to do with me, and I don't tell my gran or my cousin or anyone else about the coppers, how can I?

Marlon goes, 'Let's get some grub somewhere else.'

And we walk to the caff, where I ain't been for a good while, and Marlon slaps hands with the old proprietor and orders us the works.

'On me, yeah,' Marlon says, nodding at the counter.

He pulls a hefty purple pack of cigarettes from inside his flying jacket and lights one. He takes a loooong drag and blows smoke out for what feels like ages.

'You want?'

I shake my head.

'Clever cookie.' He grins. 'We eat and then we talk.'

226

I nod. The waitress brings over a pot of tea. Marlon asks, 'You warmed it first, yeah?'

The waitress shrugs like she doesn't understand, she doesn't know much English that's for sure, and the proprietor yells, 'Course she did! She my daughter!'

And Marlon goes, 'Yeah man,' and pours a splash of milk, then tea, into both our mugs.

'Sugar?'

'Yeah, three.'

He shakes his head. 'Not long for this world then, those teeth of yours.'

'Yeah?'

'How much tea do you drink, daily basis?'

'Maybe two, three cups.'

'That's nine sugars a day. Know what that means?'

It's my turn to shake my head.

'Two things gonna happen.'

'Yeah?'

'First, your teeth will rot.'

I shrug.

'Second, you get fat. That skinny frame of yours won't last forever, mate, you want to look after yourself.'

'Like smoking, you mean?'

Marlon winks. 'No flies on you, son. This' – gesturing at the smoke, wafting it about – 'is an affliction, granted, but also a habit I very much enjoy. You need to enjoy parts of your life, you hear?'

'OK.'

'Good man.'

Marlon's version of the works appears:

Chips and mushrooms and eggs and beans –

'What, no bacon?' I ask.

Marlon makes a face, gives me the look. 'Pork,' he says, shaking his head, 'ain't right.'

'Meat is murder, you mean?'

Marlon thins his lips, gives this some thought. 'It pays to ask yourself why you eat what you do, is what I'd tell you. That's all.'

I nod fair enough.

'Now eat up and think about it in silence, bruv?'

Which I do.

What happens after that is we leave the caff and there are the two plain-clothes plods from the day before, and Marlon looks at them, nods towards me, nods at them, and they nod back, and as we head back into the estate he goes, 'Done.'

That quick, that simple –

Class.

And a few days after *that*, he introduces me to some of the Hackney youth and tells me what I need to do in return for his squaring of my predicament, as he put it, stylish as ever.

True, I didn't see those plods again.

It seems easy enough what he wants me to do, the Hackney lot are all right, so I tell him no problem, I can help.

Suzi's in Solid Bond.

Paul Weller, fag on in the kitchen, pot of tea, talking into her tape recorder –

'I don't believe that a human being's responsibility is to keep up his payments on his television, or that he cleans his car once a week. I'm sure that there's got to be more to it than that. I'm not saying everyone should come to a concert and attend it like it was a political rally. But there's no reason why you can't do both things at the same time. I can't see the dichotomy between entertainment and serious messages. Look at Billy, probably eighty per cent of his material, love songs. But his actions and example.'

The Style Council are spending most of the month holed up in the studio, recording new material. Paul Weller's having a bit of a break from quote unquote party politics. A bit of a break from old Billy Bragg.

'There was a blinkered view of socialism from the right wing that says that socialism is going to drag everyone down to the same level. But the idea of socialism to me is to raise people up to a comfortable level, where the necessities are provided for. I wanted to do something about it.'

This all for a piece Suzi's writing about Red Wedge and The Style Council, what's next for Paul Weller.

An easy pitch for Suzi, a bit of favourable coverage for the band, a teaser-trailer for the new material –

The old day job, as Keith enjoys calling it.

'Not exactly the coalface, is it, love?'

Gist Suzi's going for is the Red Wedge tour in January was a success, absolutely, sold-out gigs and day events raising awareness, surprise guests and ensemble jams, the whole thing run slick thanks to Paul Weller's manager –

Big John Weller, Paul's old man.

He didn't seem an obvious Red Wedge devotee, Big John, Suzi thought, but the commitment to it, the commitment to helping his son achieve something of what he set out to achieve, was something else.

'Proper staunch, Big John,' Keith said, on pretty much a daily basis.

But the gist Suzi's going for is also what did we really achieve?

There's that well-worn cultural protest movement idea that if we turned one kid on to the benefits of socialism or the horrors of Thatcher then it's been worth it, but Suzi's wondering if the bill for all those gigs and all that travel is really needed to turn one kid on.

Paul Weller paid for the Red Wedge tour and is too nice to mention this himself, so Suzi doesn't push the angle, the was-it-worth-it question.

He'd no doubt say it was if Suzi *did* ask.

Billy's fault is the other thing he'd no doubt say about it, what got him involved.

That meeting Suzi helped to broker last year, and there they all were, 11.30 in the morning on the terrace of the House of Commons, 21 November 1985, the official launch of Red Wedge, not six weeks after the riots in Tottenham.

Neil Kinnock making a bad joke that Red Wedge wasn't the name of his hairstyle.

Someone saying, 'The system promises young people paradise but gives them hell.'

Suzi thinking now about the line she jotted down about the Prime Minister and led with in her own piece:

'If we shed a tear for all the sorrow she's caused, we'd drown.'

That was Sade saying that, in a telegram from the States, where she was touring.

Sade and meeting Kirsty MacColl were the highlights of Suzi's experience on the House of Commons terrace.

Suzi's role then and on tour was journalist-photographer.

She didn't get involved in the organising; she didn't get involved in the activism –

She's been burnt, in the past, in more ways than one and she wasn't going to do any more than a bit of reportage –

And sending her little reports to Detective Constable Patrick Noble as per their little quid pro quo, not that it's been going hugely well.

Noble knows Suzi's been feeding him stories that a day or two later turn up in *NME* or *Melody Maker*, and she's not getting the help from him that she needs to really work on a Tottenham story. But she's been there, Tottenham, and she's written about what happened, and she's been welcomed, now, thanks to what she's written –

'There was a great camaraderie among the musicians,' Paul Weller is saying now. 'But meeting the politicians reinforced what I already believed: that they were just out for themselves. There were so many careerists among them. Once we started meeting these MPs it was just like "Oh God, we don't want to be a part of this." They were more showbiz than the groups. It was an eye-opener, it brought me full circle in how I feel about organised politics. It's a game.'

Suzi smiling sweetly, thinking Paul Weller spent most of the time he wasn't on stage kissing Dee, the pair of them like teenagers, back of the bus, it was lovely to witness, though Suzi kept it out of her articles.

She and Keith didn't do a great deal of kissing.

How it goes, the natural arc of the long-term relationship, Keith says.

But it's about time, love, isn't it, time is how you spend it.

This is what Suzi's been telling herself, but you've got to put in the time with the person actually present, not ships in the night in a shared flat.

'If I was an author,' Paul Weller goes on, 'I wouldn't get questioned so much about, "Is this the right thing to do; should politics be in music?"'

Suzi thinks this question might be a good headline. She's got the pedigree to try and answer it. Her Rock Against Racism experience counts for a lot.

She often remembers what David Widgery wrote about how they 'didn't stop racist attacks, far less racism', and Suzi wonders if that alliance of RAR and the Anti-Nazi League is being replicated now in a more mainstream way with Red Wedge and the Labour Party. In 1978, it was DIY in Victoria Park, now Live Aid at Wembley and sell-out tours –

What is activism and what is posturing is a question that Suzi is asking herself a fair bit these days.

Paul Weller nods at the rehearsal room and Suzi follows him in.

Paul Weller tells Suzi that what's next for Paul Weller is The Style Council performing at the Artists Against Apartheid concert on Clapham Common, end of the month, and he's not thinking a great deal beyond that.

Free concert, free as in Free Nelson Mandela.

Paul Weller tells Suzi he'll get her a few lanyards.

Mick Talbot and Steve White are gassing in the rehearsal room, Camelle Hinds tuning his bass guitar, Dee fiddling with her earrings, smiling and winking as Suzi sits down.

Paul Weller picks up a chunky, sunburst cutaway Gibson guitar as Mick Talbot and Camelle Hinds blend a couple of snaking, bass-heavy lead-in lines. Dee stands and, happy with her earrings, adjusts her microphone –

With Paul Weller, as the song reaches its hook, she sings:

*Move on up*

Suzi grinning, tapping her feet, her fingers.

Wait until you hear this with percussion, the band tell her.

Suzi says, 'I can't.'

Parker's reflecting on what got him involved in this bloody mess.

Last November and Noble on the other end of the blower and Noble saying –

'I am right in thinking, son, that your old man and his brothers are printworkers?'

'You are right, guv, yes. Chapel out of Gray's Inn, lifers, you know the sort.'

'I do. You didn't fancy it then?'

Parker sniffed. 'I did not. And it wasn't an uncontroversial position to take, let's say that.'

'You on good terms?'

'Swings and roundabouts.'

'Fathers and sons.'

'And brothers and uncles. Why?'

'They said anything, your family, about Wapping?'

Parker thought: Wapping, that's the second time you've said that word to me.

'We don't really talk business, what with the controversial position and so on.'

'Any chance you'll be round there for Sunday lunch any time soon?'

'I'll see what I can do, guv.'

'Sweet.'

Parker's more of a Christmas and birthdays sort of man, but he gives his mum a bell and pops round, and the word is that the family's professional position is 'uncertain', and Parker passes that back on to Noble and thinks nothing much more of it until Noble rings him again and tells him that after Tottenham and Parker's unfortunate proximity to *that* tragedy, he's going to have a little part-time redeployment, and it appears very likely, January-February, that Parker's old man and his uncles might soon be looking for new jobs.

Parker isn't too upset about a bit of time away from the north-east, that business on the Farm was something else, something like he'd never seen, thought he never would, far worse than anything back in the summer of hate, 1978, when he was with the Front and poor old Alan got clobbered by an SPG unit with a cosh, and though he'd never say anything to anyone, the word trauma isn't far off.

Very ugly business.

He hasn't seen Shaun much since.

Couple of times only, he thinks, and the lad wasn't as friendly as you might hope even then.

Parker gives him the benefit, though, who wouldn't?

Carolyn says Shaun's been quiet for a while, friends of his questioned, the estate on edge, the estate under siege, it feels like, surrounded by police –

Parker thinks: give him time.

And the thing with Trevor was stalling, Parker feeding Noble a few odds and sods, but nothing concrete, so a little less time on that doesn't hurt, especially given young Trevor's developing a brandy and rum habit, so Parker's put that on ice, as it were, just like young Trevor does.

Carolyn's switched her attention a little from Rectory Road and the Roach Family Support Committee and is now helping on the Farm at the Youth Association, trying to get legal advice for the teenagers who've been wrongly collared, keeping a record of what exactly the boys in blue are up to.

'Pigs,' is their running joke. 'Fucking pigs.'

Course, Parker's keeping shtum about how it came about that Carolyn is now working with that redhead bird of Noble's, Suzi, up at the Youth Association.

'You remember she was at Rectory Road, boy,' Noble said.

'I do remember.'

'Well then, get them onside, all right?'

Reluctantly, Parker gets them onside.

What he says to Carolyn is pretty much what Noble said to him.

And when he's had the talk, he's relayed it up, and a couple of days later and Carolyn's on about this lovely white woman who's writing about the inquest into Cynthia Jarrett's death, but in the right way, and does Parker remember her from Rectory Road, she thinks she does –

'I think I do too,' Parker says and leaves it at that for now.

Carolyn's making their little joke a lot at the moment, *pigs, fucking pigs*, of an evening.

The stories she comes home with.

Doors battered down, no warrants.

Kids with no idea what's what taken in and no solicitor.

They're pulling all the 'sub-normal' youths first, to use the state's delectable phrase for the undereducated.

Carolyn says it's a clear tactic: confuse and divide.

Parker knows better: easier to groom a grass if the kid's got a bit missing upstairs. In a close community like this, even the most gormless know something worth knowing.

'There's now been,' Carolyn tells him one evening after dinner, sitting together on her sofa, 'three hundred and fifty-nine arrests since the riots.'

'To now?'

'End of May. That's six months. Which is around sixty a month, meaning an average of two a day.'

'Fuck me,' Parker admits.

'Two hundred and seventy-one homes on the estate have been searched. Eighteen of them had their front doors opened with sledgehammers.'

Parker sniffs. 'I know what you're going to tell me.'

Carolyn twists in her seat, narrows her eyes. 'Do you?'

'Police claim the doors were fortified, barricaded by the residents.'

She nods.

'Whereas in fact this fortification was a council-led response to crime, protection against burglary.'

Carolyn sits back. 'Clever boy,' she sighs.

The window's open and there's that dappled summer light that turns up around eight o'clock, bothering the trees, flickering about among the branches and leaves, all dazzle and shadow.

A little breeze drifting in, and Parker takes a big old sniff of the window box, the gentle smoke from allotment fires, the air –

Feels good.

'How many of that three hundred and fifty-nine are black?' he asks.

'About three-quarters.'

'And what about charges?'

'I think it's up to a hundred and sixty now.'

Parker nodding. 'Grey area, yeah, the new law, makes it easier to hold suspects, extended powers, fewer safeguards—'

'If any.'

The new law is the Police and Criminal Evidence Act of 1984 which only came into force in January 1986, meaning it hadn't at the time of the riot.

But Tottenham nick were trialling it, so there was a fair amount of uncertainty regarding the right to a solicitor, searching of premises, seizure of property –

All the exact things the Old Bill were up to.

State-sanctioned powers and no one knows the official safeguards, so no one asks.

'I'm tired of hearing stories, hero,' Carolyn says. She rests her head on Parker's shoulder. 'You can never find out where anyone is, where they've been taken, which station, they're using them all over.'

'I heard as far as Chingford.'

'Sometimes. There was a kid at the nursery, took them a day to find out where the mum was, and that's just the Residents' Association phoning round. They're holding people for two or three days with no charge.'

Parker knows all about this tactic –

Nick someone on a minor, apply to the Magistrates Court for a three-day remand into custody for continued questioning regarding 'more serious offences', hope that they give something up, and if they don't, kick 'em back blinking out onto the street and wait until next time.

He says, his arm around Carolyn, lips brushing her hair, 'You're doing what you can, darling, don't forget that.'

She sinks into the crook of his neck, kisses him, murmurs something about you make it all OK, kisses him again, and Parker slides down in his seat, faces her –

Sometimes, Parker thinks, he wouldn't mind talking about something else.

His mouth finds hers, his hands on her face, her hands under his shirt, his mouth on her neck, under her bra, her tongue in his ear, she wriggles out of her jeans, her knickers, her arms up, her top off –

Sometimes, it's best not to talk about anything at all.

What he hasn't told Noble: he's moved in with Carolyn now, cosying up, all his clothes and records there, his domestic appliances –

It's nice. It's really very nice.

He's kept his pokey Stoke Newington studio, course he has: Special Branch pays the rent.

And Carolyn doesn't know *that*.

Yeah, sometimes, it's best not to talk about anything at all.

So, end of the day, he isn't hugely unhappy to spend a little time away from Tottenham, from Stoke Newington, have a bit of a change of scene.

'You're an activist, hero, you're doing the right thing,' Carolyn tells him. 'This is what we do, we help out.'

So Parker's a sympathetic ear as the union negotiations get under way, and he's on standby, telling his family it's appalling and we can't let them do to you what they did to the miners, but he worries about his dad and what this is going to do to him, and he hears the word Wapping a lot and he wonders about that, too.

Fait accompli is another thing he hears –

It's announced in December that *The London Herald* is happening with or without trade union agreement.

And when Parker learns in January that the Commissioner of Police for the Metropolitan Area has used legislation from 1839 to impose restrictions on pedestrian and vehicular movement in Tower Hamlets, he thinks:

Uh-oh.

When the strike itself kicks off, Parker's old man is so delighted that his wayward son wants to get involved that very quickly Parker is helping out as a sort of picket ringer, behind the scenes, organising, that kind of thing.

And it feels good to Parker to stand alongside his old man and his uncles and the other pickets, and he squares what he's doing by reasoning that there's no other way at this point in his life that he ever *could* stand alongside family.

'Your father's proud of you,' Parker's mum tells him, more than once.

'It's about time,' is Parker's reply to that.

'Never too late, my boy, it's never too late.'

Doesn't stop him writing the reports for Special Branch, of course.

It's been an eventful few months.

What Parker does is a bit of observation, effectively, relaying what's happened from the picket side of things, not so much revealing any seditious plans, but all past tense, like a match report.

First couple of months and it was generally civil – generally – not too much aggro, the feeling being if not quite it'll be over by Christmas, then the sense that this is London, we ain't northerners down a hole in the ground, it can't last too long, they'll see sense.

When they don't see sense is when it gets a bit livelier.

Parker had been wondering for a while if they weren't on to a hiding to nothing.

If the newspapers don't need the printworkers anymore to get printed, then how the fuck are they ever going to win?

Target distribution. Target journo-scabs. Weaponise the unions –

You know you're on to a hiding to nothing when there are more lefties knocking about in hoods and scarves than workers, and there's fighting –

Parker's been there, got stuck in, course he has, he knows the score.

And it got heavier, the violence, at the beginning of May.

First Saturday was the worst of it, Parker thinks.

In his report, Parker noted the key statistics:

One hundred and seventy-five police officers injured with nine detained in hospital and 81 persons arrested. Ten of the prisoners were injured and 38 other demonstrators required treatment.

What Parker discovered pretty quickly was that by this point in the protests, there was considerable coordination between the multiple marches that were happening simultaneously. And it happened that night as the marchers convened around ten o'clock at the junction of the Highway with Virginia Street. When they did, smoke bombs, thunderflashes and other missiles were thrown at police lines. The police response was immediate, sustained and it worked, too. Mounted officers riding deep into Wellclose Square where they were met with more missiles. Parker watched them regroup on the Highway, followed by demonstrators hurling wood, bricks and other heavy miscellany.

His second key discovery was confirmed yet again: the violence was not perpetuated by the middle-aged printworkers like Parker's old man and uncles.

It was younger hooligans, all sorts, Trotskyites, anarchists –

Parker reckons, though, that there was no particular extremist organisation orchestrating the violence, no one pulling the strings, no grand plan, really, no *insurrection.*

No, Parker reckons it's troublemakers taking advantage of the situation to have a row with the police.

Parker heard: TUC get off your knees, call a general strike.

Parker heard: I'd rather be a cowpat than a cop.

Parker heard: The Mets are the biggest scabs of all.

Among other things.

Parker heard a story about a woman, a new mother she was, kids at home, doing her bit for the union, leading the hokey-cokey down the Highway at two in the morning, nicked for the pleasure, her arm broken on the way to the station by an overenthusiastic uniform.

Week after, FA Cup Final day and another march to the Wapping facility from Tower Hill.

This time some coordination between brass and the union leaders on the basis that the violence of the previous week was caused by extremist elements, not printworkers.

Parker observed the usual rabble: Socialist Workers Party, Workers Revolutionary Party, Young Socialists, Labour Party Young Socialists –

Anarchists, too, but hardly mobbed up.

A quiet afternoon with radios bringing in news of Liverpool's defeat of Everton by three goals to one at Wembley –

King Kenny Dalglish and a league and cup double –

Some wag saying something about Heysel and what Liverpool would've done in Europe the last year or so had they not been banned, bloody shame, better off a tear-up with the Old bill, and a few West Ham types laughing along at that, but, yes, a fairly quiet afternoon really.

Bit before midnight, and Parker spots movement from a line of mounted police.

He sees them form a barrier across the Highway.

He sees that this line of mounted police intends to create a shield for the safe departure of a number of distribution vehicles.

He sees the 400 or so demonstrators surge forward and a small number of thunderflashes and smoke bombs thrown.

Parker thinking, here we go again –

Too much of my life in violent crowds –

Ringleaders, Parker sees, are half a dozen men in donkey jackets, aged between twenty-odd and forty –

There are looks shared, hand signals made, nods given –

They appeared at the exact same time as the Old Bill, Parker notes.

More thunderflashes, more smoke bombs –

The donkey jackets directing, pushing the crowd into what look like the weaker points in the police line.

Police in helmets and with shields –

Snarling dogs on short leads –

Horses.

Fucking come on, come on –

There's a football violence feel to it –

It's going to go off –

Parker swirling near the front, eyeing the Old Bill, shoulders up, head down –

In his report, later that night, Parker writes:

Although the use of thunderflashes and smoke bombs caused some inevitable alarm, the only impact they made on the lines of police was to singe three inches from the tail of one of the horses. However (perhaps appropriately on Cup Final day) two demonstrators scored spectacular 'own goals' and had to be removed to hospital to receive treatment for burns.

Noble enjoyed that one.

'You're a heartbreaker, son,' he told him. 'I'll give you that. That doesn't change.'

'I'm starting to think I'm neglecting what we're about up in Stoke Newington, guv.'

Noble sniffed. 'Yeah, well, needs must.'

'For now, yeah?'

'Temporary deployment, you know that.'

Parker nodded, cradled the telephone in his neck. 'One thing, guv.'

'Go on.'

'First sign of the flash bang wallop, there were union men on the blower.'

'Who to?'

'Word is the peaceful accord that has been parlayed with the Old Bill might not be that peaceful.'

'OK.'

What is now clearer than ever – and it was pretty clear in Parker's eyes from the off – is that the police are there to make sure the newspapers printed in Wapping make it out onto the streets and all over the country.

And any pickets that try and stop them are nicked and criminalised.

'Way of the world, son,' is Noble's take. 'Unions are dinosaurs.'

The rest of May is pretty quiet.

Noble tells Parker that with the violence having reached its peak at the beginning of the month and the 'secret talks' that have been ongoing, with the last offer of 50 million in compensation rejected early June by the unions, Special Branch have decided that they don't need a daily presence and that Parker's only required there on Wednesdays and Saturdays now.

'So you can spend a little more time with that bird of yours.'

Parker nods, says nothing.

'Two jobs when you *are* about on your temporary deployment on Wednesdays and Saturdays,' Noble says. 'One, word is there's a council flat being used in the vicinity by some of the lefties, organising and so on. Sedition, you know, fomentation.'

'Brewing beer?'

'Very good, son, I suspect your vocabulary stretches to my meaning.'

'Which lefties?'

'Does it make any odds?'

'It does, guv.'

'Hang on.'

Parker hangs on. Parker hears the rustle of paper, the thumbing of pages of paper.

'SWP.'

'Roger that, guv.'

'Yeah, and the rest of the week, we're back where we were, you understand?'

'Yes, guv, I do understand.'

'Sweet,' Noble says.

'You said there were two jobs, guv.'

'Silly me,' Noble says. 'Yeah, that fire, they're saying arson over here. See what you can find out about that.'

'They're saying this side that the fire helped discredit the cause.'

'Either way.'

Parker nods. 'Yeah.'

'Like I said, sweet.'

The fire was at a warehouse in Deptford, suppliers to Wapping, 9,000 tons of paper and seven million quid's worth of transportation all damaged –

Fire at a paper warehouse: insert joke about piss-ups and breweries, Parker thinks.

Thing is, Parker's old man and his uncles won't be too chuffed to hear golden bollocks is going to be a part-time picket, so Parker keeps coming down and here he is again, Monday 23 June, drinking bitter in a pub in Limehouse before opening time, surrounded by men with buzz cuts and lined faces, donkey jackets, awaiting instruction, and he might as well try and figure out about this flat while he's at it.

Another thing Noble doesn't know is that Parker's bird is proud of him, helping out his family and whatnot, and has accepted the temporary deployment on the basis that he goes home to their Hackney nest at the end of every day.

Carolyn knows exactly what it is Parker did for her cousin Shaun back in October.

The nickname Hero is well-entrenched in the family now, as is the man who wears it with a certain degree of modesty.

Other thing is, when he has been back up north in his old capacity, he's been hearing the word Wapping again and he's not sure it's got anything to do with union politics.

Parker's learning to accept what he is exactly: a small piece in a jigsaw.

Though it only takes one to go astray for the whole puzzle to get fucked.

*You're in your favourite Chinese on Mandarin Street, the Old Friends Restaurant, Limehouse.*

*Dim sum late breakfast, Monday tonic –*

*'You see, Terry,' you say, 'we are in fact sitting on the site of the original Chinatown.'*

'Not up west then, guv?'

'Not originally, Terry, no.'

'Nothing's what it used to be.'

'That's very profound.'

'I have my moments, guv.'

You smile and nod, encouragingly. 'And, Terry, if you were to hazard a guess as to why this place, in fact, is the site of the original Chinatown, what might that guess look like?'

Terry sniffs. 'The docks, guv. Sailors.'

You applaud, clap generously.

The Chink comes over with your starters, your pot of herbal tea, and you thank him.

He scurries off, bowing –

'They called it the Yellow Peril, Terry, in the old British press, back in the 1920s, interwar years.'

Terry nods. You watch him push a gelatinous dumpling around his bowl with a single chopstick, spear it.

'Fear of the other, Terry, interracial breeding, all that. You should see the state of the lurid paperbacks written in the service of this myth.'

Terry helps himself to a spring roll.

'Yes, there were brothels and there was gambling and there were opium dens, but they weren't exactly confined to the area.'

'That why you always choose this particular restaurant, guv? Authenticity?'

'We are but what we choose, Terry.' You fasten napkin into shirt collar. 'Well, that and other reasons,' you say.

The Chink comes back with a folded piece of paper which he hands over, smiling. He waits, head down.

You open it. On the piece of paper is written –


21 July


You refold the piece of paper and slip it into your shirt pocket.

'Cheers, John,' you say to the Chink. 'Pass on our thanks.'

The Chink bows.

'Here, John,' you say. 'What did the Chinese bootlegger say to his girlfriend?'

'I don't know, sir, what did he say?'

You smile. 'It pays well, darling, but it's a whiskey business!'

'Ha ha, very funny.'

Terry chuckles through a mouthful of food –

'They call it doing a Billy Chang, Terry, you know what that is?'

Politely, Terry shakes his head, doesn't risk opening his mouth –

'Billy Chang, Brilliant Chang, Chan Nan, Canton drug dealer who came over in 1913, I believe. That right, John?'

The Chink nods. 'This' – he points at the floor – 'his restaurant, originally.'

You nod. 'Birmingham, then down here,' you say.

You tug the napkin from your collar and wipe your fingers, wipe your mouth.

'Doing a Billy Chang, Terry,' you go on, 'has two meanings. The first is about your flash foreign crook putting it about with the white woman.' You pause. 'The second is what you might call obfuscation.'

Terry nods, mumbles something into his plate.

'Old Billy was deported after the death of a couple of white women in his employ, or service, you know, chorus girls, dance instructresses, those sorts of sorts, right. And for old Billy to enjoy his autumn years, he needed a distraction, get the Old Bill off of old Billy.'

'And how did he do that, guv?'

'Here, Terry, are a few of the stories of what Chan Nan did next.'

You rub your hands together. John smiles and bows. Terry sits, mouth open, noodles slippery between his teeth –

'One, that he had returned to Blighty to continue his ungodly trade. Two, that he was working out of France or Belgium or Switzerland. Three, that he was managing a dance club in Nice. Four, that he was the Dope Emperor of Europe, whereabouts unknown. This would have been 1927.

*Five, in 1928, French police found him in Hong Kong in exile, blind from*
*his heroic levels of drug consumption.'*
*'And the truth, guv?'*
*'Unknown.'*
*Terry chews thoughtfully.*
*'Point is, you've enough stories, you've enough endings, you know what*
*I mean?'*
*Terry nods. 'I think so, guv.'*
*You raise a finger. John hands over his pad and pencil –*
*You lick the pencil, write neatly, quickly:*

Diversion of services to enable demolition of old warehouses to the
    west of Limehouse Studios and general site clearance
Fencing and site security
Site investigations and test borings
Setting up of temporary site office cabins
Provision of temporary site services and project signs
The protection of existing services and features

*You tear the piece of paper you've written on from John's pad. You fold*
*the piece of paper, run your thumbnail over the fold, define the crease,*
*hand it over to John –*
*Who bows.*
*'You'll see to it, John?'*
*John grins his toothless smile, smacks his gums –*
*'Stories,' he winks.*

Jon's been doing a little digging into the Chief Executive of the London
Docklands Development Group, Ron Bishop.

In 1980, for nine months, Ron Bishop was the only member of staff
at the LDDG.

Apparently, Jon reads, he spent that time walking the area and sketching out possibilities for redevelopment.

Literally sketching them out.

According to a source, he had a bucket for a seat and an upturned tea chest as his easel.

He was reactive, had something of the market trader about him, despite being the son of a miner. There was no plan, only, his words, a 'market-driven approach, responding pragmatically to each situation'.

Bishop invited the Yank banks over for a shufty and it was them that thought the area would work, trading floors, a financial hub, all that.

Bishop thought: bingo and helped sell the idea to the government.

Jon reads: Bishop's greatest achievement was to persuade hard-nosed City and property investors that a Docklands revival was going to work. By 1986, the LDDG had spent around £300m of public money, but had succeeded in attracting £1.4 billion in private investment.

That's not a bad offset, Jon thinks, in a balancing-the-books sort of scenario.

The question is where the private investment has come from exactly.

Jon examines an application by something called The Canary Wharf Development Co. Ltd for a licence to carry out preliminary work on Canary Wharf.

Thing is the application is being made to the London Docklands Development Group.

Jon thinks there might be a blurred line here somewhere.

If Ron Bishop is in charge of the LDDG and also the one putting together the Canary Wharf consortium, then he's giving himself the licence, isn't he?

If he approves his own application.

Jon leafs back through his file. He's looking for a specific press release and he remembers the date of it as it was the boy's birthday last year, 18 October 1985 –

GROUP BOARD COMMITTED TO ACHIEVING CANARY
WHARF FINANCIAL CENTRE DEVELOPMENT

Jon reads:

The Board of the London Docklands Development Group today (October 18) agreed to the American Consortium's masterplan concept for the development of a 10 million square feet financial centre at Canary Wharf on the Isle of Dogs, thus allowing it to proceed to the next stage, which is the negotiation of a Master Building Agreement [...]
The board welcomed the scale and content of the scheme as a remarkable opportunity to extend the activities of the financial centre of London eastwards, providing many thousands of much-needed jobs in Docklands in the near future and fulfilling the employment needs of generations of East Enders for years to come [...]
The Group will retain control over the content, phasing and quality of the scheme through the terms and specifications of the Master Building Agreement [...]
The Board was unanimous in resolving that a fundamental part of the process in reaching the Master Building Agreement will be continuing discussions with the London Borough of Tower Hamlets, local people and those statutory bodies whose interests are affected.

Jon thinks: maybe I need the names of the board members of The Canary Wharf Development Co. Ltd.
Then: what's the name again of that snake that eats its own tail?

Suzi leaves Solid Bond and heads north-east towards Tottenham.
She bounces up Edgware Road, dancing onto the bus, top deck –
In her bag:

**THE BROADWATER FARM DISTURBANCES AND THE PRESS –**
A REPORT BY DOROTHY KUYA

She is on her way to meet the author of this report, to interview her and find out more about what she's been doing.

Immediately after the uprising, Broadwater Farm was overrun with journalists and TV crews looking for news. But the stories and the pieces that were coming out in the weeks after were almost without exception painting the estate and the community in a very negative light. Combine this with the constant police harassment and presence in the weeks and months after the uprising, and a siege mentality is very much how residents would describe the mindset of the place.

Suzi's in with Noble meant she had a little currency and she quickly established herself as a journalist sympathetic to the estate and started taking down the stories of residents, working mainly out of the Youth Association.

She listened, is the point, when not many people were listening.

One man told her: 'When the newspapers interviewed me the next day, they wanted me to say it was black against white. When I said it wasn't, they didn't really want to know anything. It didn't make headlines.'

Cliff Ford, 'estate sweeper and active Tenants' Association member', told Suzi he'd tried to add a bit of balance to all the press coverage: 'I wrote to the *Daily Mail* myself and said, "What about the Christmas dinners, the social things that the Youth Association does?" They didn't want to know about that, they never published that at all.'

Suzi remembers one piece in *The Times* that offered the opposing view: that the estate was a hellhole war zone tragedy in the waiting, a structural problem, not about the people that lived there:

THE ESTATE THAT DOLLY KIFFIN RESCUED FROM NIGHTMARE

That was about it though, she thinks now, her bus dragging itself across the Euston Road and up to the west of Camden, traffic thinning, air thick with exhaust hanging above a baking Somers Town –

Suzi and Keith were here a lot, back end of the 70s, squat parties mainly, a real centre for them, squats springing up seconds after, it felt, some municipal building or other, hospitals sometimes, closed down. Well, right to buy is putting paid to that scene, she thinks. Tenants get their flats at a significant discount, sell them to yuppies and hightail it out to Essex or Hertfordshire or wherever.

'You watch,' Keith has said more than once, 'one day London will be only yuppies and second-generation immigrants living cheek by jowl, transients all.'

'That doesn't sound very right on, Keith.'

'Dystopia, darling, that's all I'm saying.'

Looking down at Somers Town from the bus –

Bengali restaurants and derelict terraced housing, for-sale signs at half mast, windows blackened, the Phoenix Cafe and Snack Bar, closed up and past caring, sloppy black NF graffiti scrawled on rotting, white-washed boards, on a low white wall:

G DAVIS IS INNOCENT OK

Video shop with English and Indian titles, Architectural Ironmongers, Neasden Electronics, JP Whippet Supplies –

Crawling north, up, up the hill, shunting and gas, seat scratchy on the backs of Suzi's thighs –

Kentish Town Road, Archway, Seven Sisters, Bruce Grove –

Keith saying things like that a little more than she'd like, joking not joking, that odd little line.

She shakes her head, reaches into her bag. Down the stairs, pulling the cord, bell ringing, jumping off as the bus slows, off the High Road and left towards the Farm.

On the telephone, Dorothy Kuya told Suzi:

'It is instructive to compare the way the press handled the news of the deaths of Mrs Cynthia Jarrett and of PC Keith Blakelock.'

Suzi said that she'd heard Dorothy Kuya was doing just that.

'I monitored twenty-five newspapers,' Dorothy Kuya said. 'Seventeen of them were national papers, five were local, one was a London-wide paper.'

'Which ones?' Suzi asked.

'The local papers were the *Haringey Advertiser, Haringey Independent, Weekly Herald, Yorkshire Post, Wolverhampton Express and Star*,' Dorothy Kuya said. 'The London-wide paper was the *London Standard*. The minority ethnic papers were *New Life, Asian Times, Caribbean Times* and the *Voice*. The national papers were the *Daily Mail, Morning Star, Sun, Express, Mirror, Daily Telegraph, Financial Times, Guardian* and *The Times*. The Sunday papers were the *Sunday Mirror, Observer, Sunday Times, Mail on Sunday, Sunday Express* and the *Star*.'

Suzi said that she thought that was pretty comprehensive.

Suzi also said that she'd like to talk to Dorothy Kuya some more if that was OK, and Dorothy Kuya told her that it was.

The Youth Association is quiet, no sign yet of anyone who might be Dorothy Kuya, a couple of teenagers playing pool.

Suzi helps herself to a cup of tea, puts her fifty pence in the honesty box –

She leafs back through the report, rereads headlines:

'London riots kill a PC' 'PC murdered in riot fury' 'Rioters kill policeman' 'KILL, KILL, KILL' 'Police officer knifed to death' 'Hacked to death' 'Red butchers' 'Name the killers' '150 pounce to slice him up' 'Police left woman who died on the hallway floor' 'Tottenham riot after black woman's death' 'Mother dies in police raid' 'One mother is like all our mothers'

When Suzi looks up, a woman is standing over her.

'Dorothy?' Suzi asks.

The woman nods, sits down.

'Let me get you a cup of tea.' Suzi smiles.

Five minutes later, Dorothy Kuya is speaking candidly and quickly and Suzi is struggling to keep up.

'In nineteen seventy-five,' Dorothy Kuya says, 'the National Union of Journalists laid down its first set of guidelines for journalists. Two of these were: only mention someone's race or nationality if strictly relevant. Resist the temptation to sensationalise issues which would harm race relations.'

'Guidelines that don't seem to have been followed here, then,' Suzi says.

'Sir Kenneth Newman,' Dorothy Kuya goes on, 'Commissioner of the Metropolitan Police, might have made the same thoughtful comments about Mrs Jarrett as he did about PC Blakelock.'

'But he didn't.'

'In most of the reports I've seen there's been an attempt to suggest that Mrs Jarrett might be responsible for her own death – after all, she was overweight, she already had certain medical conditions.'

'Still.'

Dorothy Kuya leans forward, her tea untouched. 'I'll put it in simple terms, if I may, Ms Scialfa. The media is helping British society to wash its hands of the death of Mrs Jarrett and to not take responsibility for it whatsoever. We have seen that Mrs Jarrett's colour had conferred on her a "differential status" and a differential treatment which reveals the extent of racism and sexism which is still prevalent in the British press and which is a reflection of what is going on in the wider society.'

Suzi, chastened.

# 2

## *Trevor*

October 1985–June 1986

What happens to Trevor is he leaves the Turkish gaff after Parker heads off up to Tottenham, but not before he has another brandy. And then a bottle of Efes. Yeah, Parker was right, they *are* fucking delicious. So Trevor knocks a rum down after the beer. It's a good combo. Cold, then hot. Teeth chill and belly fire. Great stuff.

He sometimes wonders: what came first, the drinking or the fear?

He pays the girl. The other girl judging him. He doesn't care. His eyes red. His hair matted at the forehead. Booze-sweat. He shivers. He shakes. Feels good. Where next? he thinks.

He turns south towards Dalston. He misses a step and stumbles. He catches himself on a lamp post. He thinks: people about, shoppers, it's only the afternoon. Chill, Trev, easy on.

He heads south, swaying a bit, swinging a bit. Lean into it, he thinks. Calypso.

You got to *own* these streets. A black man in a racist country. A man says to Trevor, Jamaicans are brainwashed before coming to this country that England is a marvellous place. When you're in Jamaica, this man tells him, you don't see the bird shit on the Houses of Parliament, nothing like that.

This man's a deep thinker. Yeah, that's for sure. He tells Trevor something Trevor knows is true. He tells him, 'In Jamaica we were taught to respect strangers, we were taught to look after them because they didn't know their way around. When we came to England it was the opposite.'

So, yeah, own *these* streets. You got to. But not too much, is the point. Don't draw too much attention. So you can sway, but don't bump. You can swing, but don't thump.

As this man tells Trevor, 'In England, black people are treated like shit. Never mind if you have a trade or you are educated, it doesn't make a whole heap of difference.'

So keep your head down. Keep your chin up. You style it out, brother.

Trevor walking slowly now. Trevor smiling at the passers-by. Trevor thinking to himself that he ain't going home just yet. Why? Trevor thinking on about this man, this deep thinker.

This man telling Trevor, 'When I first came to England, black people couldn't get council houses, and then we ended up in all the shitty houses and the tower blocks, all the homes white people were not prepared to live in.'

Trevor thinking amen to that. His own one-room shithole in Clapton. A burnt carpet and mould in the kitchen sink. Mould in the bathroom sink. Mould in the toilet. Eighteenth floor. Moved in from a nice low-rise as he's only one man, Trevor, families' needs come first.

This man telling Trevor, 'It is a conspiracy, and black people are forever being used. We cannot get jobs unless somebody employs us, and racism prevents us from setting up our own businesses. We will always be in the situation where we pay the same electricity bills, the same gas bills, and everything else, but we do not get the same wages. Black people are almost forced to do things to compensate. Those of us who do not, live in poverty.'

Trevor thinking, yeah, this is the truth. Trevor thinking Trevor's drunk now –

What happens to Trevor is he's swaying and swinging down the road. He's thinking these thoughts. He's thinking about this man, this deep thinker. It's making him feel hopped up. Making him feel goooood. The drink does that to Trevor, some days. It makes him feel like he's top of the world –

Invincible.

Own the streets. Head down. Chin up. Invincible.

But what happens is Trevor sways and swings and then –

His face pushed against a wall. His arm bent back around him. A hand on his neck. A hand in his eyes, fingers round his throat, fingers in his eyes –

Trevor hearing

Don't fucking struggle you keep still calm yourself you know what you did if you fucking move you black bastard keep your hands down don't move don't move don't move

Trevor coughing and spitting

What what what what *what*?

What did I do what did I do what did I do

Trevor's ears pop and the street rushes in.

He feels himself pulled round. He faces the street. His cheek is slapped. His cheek is slapped again. 'Right, listen,' he hears –

'Right, listen, you—'

Trevor listening, spit and blood –

'Who was that geezer in the Turkish place?'

Trevor scanning. Leather and jeans, white trainers: Regional Crime Squad.

Those same faces. Last year. Trevor's scared now. Those same new faces.

'Who was that geezer in the Turkish place?'

Trevor shaking his head.

His cheek is slapped. His cheek is slapped again. Listen, he hears –

'Who was that geezer in the Turkish place?'

'I'm fucking warning you, son, you speak.'

Trevor shaking his head. Trevor groans –

'I—'

'You fucking what?'

Trevor shaking his head. Trevor groans –

'I—'

'You want me to do you for drunk and disorderly?'

Trevor shaking his head. Trevor groans –

'I—'

'You put those hands down, son. You want me to do you for assaulting an officer?'

Trevor hears that. Trevor knows what that means.

Trevor thinking about what this man told him, this deep thinker's voice in his head, the street quiet now, a small crowd tutting –

Trevor with his man's voice in his head, going:

'Justice. That is a dream.'

The voice in Trevor's head, going:

'It seemed that things were going to change at one time. There was Martin Luther King on the one hand, who was a Christian, and there was Malcolm X, who was a rebel.'

Trevor nodding now, the voice still on at him:

'One was saying, "If they kick you, don't fight back, they can't kick you forever, allow them to, they will have to have mercy at some stage." And the other man was saying, "If they kick you, kick his arse back."'

'You going to talk or what? Fucking nig-nog.'

Trevor's man's voice still going. 'They killed both of them, they shot them dead.'

'Yeah,' Trevor says, 'I'll talk.'

'Car. Now.'

And Trevor marched to the car. Arms on his neck. Hands on his back. Head pushed down. Car smell. Air freshener and stale fags. Dog shit and blood on the back seat.

Trevor –

Remembers the name of this wise man: Rennie Kingsley.


*Stoke Newington nick.*

Trevor's man's voice still going. Trevor thinking. Trevor has no idea why –

'These drugs do not come from Africa or the West Indies, they come from Europe and the United States, and organised crime is responsible. Black people are not bringing these drugs into the country, we do not have the contacts to do that. Whether it is the police who are organising it, or not, black people are at the bottom. Black people are the users and the street-level dealer.'

No idea why he's in here.

One of the leather jackets comes in with a coffee and a smile.

'Here.'

He says, 'You all right, Trevor? Feeling all right?'

Trevor's thinking about all the stories he's heard about planting, the times it happened to him, what's this one about –

'We've got a job for you, Trevor.'

'OK.'

'If you're not going to tell us who that fella in the Turkish is – and it seems you're insisting it was just some man, some chatter about the gee-gees over a beer – then we've got a job for you, Trevor. Coffee, all right?'

'Bit cold.'

'You've been in before.'

'I never dealt drugs.'

'Not what I said. We've had an eye on you. It's time, Trevor.'

'I don't know who you are.'

'You remember Rice and Cole, what you did for them?'

Trevor thinks: say nothing, do nothing.

'Who's the white fella, Trev?'

Trevor shakes his head.

'All right, let me show you something.'

The leather jacket stands up. He bangs on the door. The door opens. A hand offers a bag. The leather jacket takes the bag. The door closes. The leather jacket puts the bag on the table in front of Trevor. The leather jacket sits down. He unzips the bag. He points with his finger.

'Have a gander, why don't you, Trevor.'

Trevor has a peer inside. Trevor whistles.

'That's right, Trev. You're right to express surprise, even admiration. There's an awful lot of product in there. We might say nearly fifty grand, road value.'

Trevor sips his cold coffee.

The leather jacket digs in his back pocket.

'There's a community leaflet going around. Here. Have a read.'

Trevor looks at a crumpled flyer. On it:

In the early days of black settlement in Hackney, Afro-Caribbean migrants lived in privately rented accommodation in Stoke Newington, Clapton and Dalston. The reason for this was the blatant discrimination against early black migrants. More recently black people have moved into the dilapidated housing estates dotted around the borough.

It is in the large estates of Stoke Newington, Clapton and Dalston where crack cocaine has emerged as a problem. The south of the borough, on the other hand, is recognised to have more of a heroin problem.

In 1982 a report by the Commission for Racial Equality found that black applicants and tenants received poorer housing than white people. This led to the Commission serving a Non-Discrimination Notice on Hackney Council in 1983.


'Your lot ruining the old East End community, is the way I read that. They never think of it that way, do they? Do *you*, Trevor?'

Trevor shakes his head. He sips his coffee. His head is pounding. His throat is dry. All he can think: drink.

He says, 'That's a bigger bag than you normally put on us, I'd wager.'

The leather jacket grins. 'Let me tell you what's going to happen next.'

Trevor sniffs.

'Who's the white fella, Trev?'

Trevor shakes his head.

'Right, listen, you—'

Trevor sits tight. His head light.

He listens. He nods. Yes, he'll do it, yes –

He stands. He takes the bag. He is led to a side door. He is led out of the side door. Across the road, a car. A blue Ford. Trevor walks to the car. Opens the boot. Places the bag in the boot. Closes the boot. He about-turns. He opens the driver's door. He climbs in. He waits.

Five minutes later, his hands on the dashboard. His head on the wheel. Uniforms swarm the car. Trevor out the car. Handcuffs. The bag pulled from the boot.

Trevor waits. Trevor listens. The uniforms deliver the bag. They point at Trevor, handcuffed. Trevor in custody. The custody sergeant takes the bag. He goes. The leather jackets are back. Three of them. They arrange police bail for Trevor. All this takes two hours. Trevor escorted outside.

They give Trevor a lift home in an unmarked car.

'You're staying in tonight, son,' they tell Trevor.

He doesn't argue the toss.

Brandy bottle and warm wine –

Next day, the same unmarked car. Trevor climbs in. His head banging. They drive Trevor to the station. They drop him off nearby. Trevor goes in.

The custody sergeant tells Trevor that there are no charges and that Trevor is free to go.

Later, they tell Trevor it's called recycling, this line of work. Now it's a word that's going round Trevor's head. Something the big man said. *Recycling.* Keeping the police acquirement of drugs *off the books*, was how he described it. *Re-up.*

They give Trevor an envelope with a grand in it. They tell Trevor: say nothing, act normal. Trevor thinks: what does that mean? They tell Trevor: monthly salary. Don't spend it all at once.

Trevor counts out 1,000 pounds in dirty notes. He does some maths. He stashes 970 pounds in dirty notes in his dirty mattress. Thirty pounds in his pocket. Trevor thinks: per diem. Pay yourself a daily rate. It's a decent screw, all told.

Say nothing, act normal. Down the Line and into the bookies. Don't overdo it. Two thirty at Chepstow. Pound each way. Ticket in his fist, Trevor's eyes red, mouth dry.

Place. That's a result, couple of quid. Two each way this time at Doncaster. Next door and into the corner shop. Red Stripe for lunch in a paper bag. Hold on, hold on. Place. Another few quid. Trevor's eyes red. They flicker. Trevor thinks: move on.

Say nothing, act normal.

Outside the bookies, a man Trevor knows.

'Trev-or!' this man yells. He flicks his fingers with a snap. They slap hands. He gives Trevor a leaflet. 'Frontline Sound at the Four Aces tonight.'

Trevor nods. Trevor thinks: why not? Trevor says, 'Crucial. I'll be there.'

'Bring the flyer.' The man nods. 'Discount entry. Friends and family.'

Trevor grins. 'Red Stripe's on me.'

The man laughs. 'Members only, Trev. They'll let you in.'

Say nothing, act normal.

They slap hands. The man leaves. 'Off to play pool in the dumplings cafe,' he says. Trevor appreciates the pastime. He's in there a lot.

Say nothing, act normal.

But Trevor thinks: Turkish caff. Let them clock me there alone, should they be looking.

Up onto the high street, past the mosque, and –

Smile at the lickle girl and her mate. Brandy and a kebab. Efes, too, go on.

'Big man, now, are you, *food*?' the blonde bird tells him, winking.

Trevor goes, 'Yeah man.'

Clock says gone three and Trevor decides to while away the afternoon. Racing pages under his arm. Unfolds them, ink on his fingers.

Hand in his pocket, fingering his dirty notes. More ink.

Counting his dirty notes in his pocket. Trevor thinking, what am I doing here exactly? Not meaning the cafe, no, the scenario in which he finds himself, into which he has, if he's honest, delivered himself.

Thinking they see me in here, that's a good thing. The nick only steps down the road. Chances might be good. So long as Parker ain't coming in.

And Parker ain't, they ain't got a meet, but does he come in on his own?

'The geezer I meet here,' he asks the blonde. 'He ever come in on his tod?'

She shakes her head. 'No, just with you.' She points at the paper. 'You really must like the racing then, speaking like that, that cockney slang, I mean.'

Trevor grins. Tod Sloane, on your own. Yank jockey. 'Yeah man,' he says. 'They're kind to me today, the nags.'

'You fancy a dessert then?'

'I do. Another brandy.'

She's laughing, Trevor sees, which pleases Trevor. 'Coming right up,' she tells him.

Trevor sits. Trevor smiles. The door opens. In comes a leather jacket, him with the coffee. Trevor thinks: yeah man.

'Here you are, young Trev. This is your local then? Here.'

He pushes a piece of paper across the table. 'I won't sit down.'

Trevor studies the piece of paper. A phone number on a betting slip.

'What you do, right, is you call that number every morning at exactly ten thirty, right?'

Trevor nods.

'That's your job. Instructions await. Or not. It's a flexible gig.'

He laughs at this.

Trevor nods. Trevor says, 'What they call you then?'

'Never you mind. Need-to-know basis, I think, is the phrase them Yanks use in the pictures.'

'But—'

'No buts. For now, I'm your friend, that's all you need to know.'

Trevor shrugs.

'That white fella not in with you today then?'

'I told you I don't know him.'

'Yeah, you said that.'

The waitress back with Trevor's brandy –

She looks at the leather jacket. 'Help you?'

'Just off, darling. Be lucky, Trev.'

Trevor raises a finger, slouches in his seat. Trevor thinking: whatever it is Parker done to me, I need to keep him and me a secret –

'He a friend of yours, is he?' the waitress asks.

Trevor shakes his head. 'Business contact, we'll call it that, shall we?'

'Here's your brandy.'

Trevor raises his drink, pauses. He winks, smiles. 'To world peace,' he decides.

The waitress laughs at that. Trevor feels a twinkle in his little eye.

'What's that?' she asks, pointing at the flyer.

'Sound system, tonight. Four Aces club.'

'You going?'

Trevor shrugs.

'They any good?'

Trevor grins. 'Frontline Sound the best! Such named as they're currently based on Sandringham Road. The Frontline.'

'I know Sandringham Road. Very clever.'

Trevor says, with a touch of performance. 'And not to be confused with Brixton's famous Frontline International featuring Natty at the control, Chuckle and General Saint at the microphone. Original rockers.'

'Noted.'

'You wanna come?'

'Do you know how old I am?'

'Do I want to?'

'I'll ask my mum, shall I?' She smiles. 'If I can come.'

Trevor laughs. 'I'll take you after your exams.'

'You better.'

Trevor actually prefers Phebes, the club up in Stoke Newington, used to be The Regency, a villain's club. Jack the Hat and all that. A machete and a sawn-off. Trevor likes it now as it's Dominoes and Jah Shaka Sound System, lovers rock upstairs, selector Danny Casanova, Roy Shirley –

Jah Shaka: the spiritual dub warrior.

But Trevor thinks it might be a lickle heavy for a white girl, however old she claims she is.

Trevor thinking about another wise man.

This other wise man telling him: 'There are no rights for black people, and if you are poor it is worse; as far as the law is concerned you have no place in society.'

Trevor drinking his drink, nodding.

'You are a dog; when they kick you, you move.'

This wise man's name is Hugh Prince.

Say nothing, act normal.

Finish your brandy, Trevor. Four o'clock. One for the road. Pushing five o'clock. Trevor tips his imaginary hat.

'You have a good night, yeah,' the waitress says.

'What's your name?'

'Lauren.'

'Lauren, thank you, I will endeavour to do so, just for you.'

'What a gentleman.'

Trevor laughs. Trevor ducks out the door –

Down the high street and left. Amhurst Road. Hackney Downs. Trees making shapes in the gloom. Trevor's breath in the air. Downs Park Road.

Say nothing, act normal.

Clarence Road. Cricketfield Road. Past the pub, across to Granny's.

Gonna be a late night, so Trevor goes in.

'Chicken box,' he says.

He points at a table for one. He pays with a dirty note. He sits down.

Say nothing, act normal.

Trevor eats. Trevor wipes his mouth. Trevor leaves.

Clapton Pond. Lower Clapton Road. Salvation Army –

Regal Records.

Downstairs: record shop. Upstairs: HQ of Unity Sounds, record label. Producer: Ribs, Trevor's old mate, Robert Fearon, one time selector for Fatman Sound.

Another wise man.

The shop is throbbing. Bass heavy. Trevor feels the door rattle as he goes in. Couple of elders rack-flicking. Nodding their heads. 'True Rasta', Trevor thinks. Misty.

The record squeaks to a stop. New one cued up and on. Trevor recognises the vocal. 'Pick a Sound'. Trevor thinks Selah Collins. Feels different. Electronic edge, bass softer, jumpy, bouncy –

The windows shake.

Trevor nods at the man behind the counter. What's his name? Trevor thinks Errol. 'All right, Errol?' Trevor asks.

Errol nods in time to the music. 'You like this, you should hear what we done with Kenny Knots.'

Trevor points at the speakers. 'Baby-sized,' he laughs.

Trevor points to the stairs. Errol nods and Trevor goes up, two at a time.

In the label's main room, Ribs is talking on the telephone. He smiles and gestures Trevor should sit down. Trevor sits down on the purple leather sofa.

Ribs saying, 'The more DJs you have on your sound and the better they are the more popular your sound is. Jack Reuben, Yabby You, Charjan, Roy Ranking, Demon Rocker, Raymond Napthali, Flinty Badman, Speccy Navigator, the Riddler, there was a few more. At that time whosoever a DJ in Jamaica, Admiral Bailey, Chakademus, Peter Metro, Lieutenant Stitchie, they all had to pass through, come to the dance where we were. Sugar Minott, he was living in the area when he created his Black Roots label. Speccy Navigator brought Selah Collins in, Ruddy Ranks knew Mickey Murka, Kenny Knots was going out with one of Ruddy's family, Peter Bouncer and Jack Wilson lived in the area, Jack Reuben brought in Demon, and Demon brought his brother Flinty.'

Trevor zones out, settles himself.

Trevor hears Ribs saying, 'Watch how the people dancing.' Laughing. 'Watch all the man dem dancing.'

Say nothing, act normal.

Ribs hangs up the telephone. 'Interview, yeah. Regional press, but it's something, you know? Got to talk up the label.'

'Kenny Knots?'

Ribs grins. 'Gonna be a hit, mate.'

'Here.' Trevor pushes dirty notes across the desk. 'What I owe you.'

Ribs raises an eyebrow –

Say nothing, act normal.

'You got yourself a job, Trevor?'

'Gee-gees very kind to me today.'

'OK.' Ribs picks up the cash, pockets it.

Trevor stands. 'Four Aces later?'

Ribs nodding –

'Unity's not playing, but we'll slip them the Kenny Knots.'

Trevor smiles. They slap hands. 'Crucial,' Trevor says.

Down the stairs. 'See you, Errol.' Out the door. Pushing six o'clock.

Lower Clapton Road. Clapton Pond. Cricketfield Road –

Say nothing, act normal.

Into The Cricketers, the pub quiet. Pool balls kissing. Radio on. News all about Tottenham, some dead copper. Trevor zones out, settles himself.

Say nothing, act normal.

UB40 on the speakers, 'I Got You Babe'. The elders laughing about reggae and the pop charts.

Trevor feels like a Guinness. He takes it to a table. Thinking about Parker. Who *is* the white fella, Trevor? Trevor doesn't know. Trevor knows who it is Parker knows. Trevor knows that Parker was his friend, then he turned. Other hand, Parker got Trevor out of it all, guaranteed immunity is what Parker's associate told Trevor. That copper, what was his name? That copper Noble.

So, what, Parker works for Noble in some capacity. Trevor works for Parker in some capacity. Now Trevor works for Stoke Newington again, in some capacity.

What does Trevor tell Parker?

Say nothing, act normal.

Trevor thinks: Parker's unhappy with Trevor's drunkenness and perceived incompetence. Parker told Trevor to give Parker a bell when Trevor's sober. Trevor turns Parker over, that guaranteed immunity is likely no more. Short end of the stick is Parker's Trevor's insurance, Trevor thinks.

*That's* who the white fella is.

Best keep him arm's length from Stoke Newington then.

Say nothing, act normal.

Have another Guinness.

Keep your head down, Trevor. Tell Parker nothing. Give him a swerve for a little while. It's what he wants himself, Trevor thinks. He told you, after all.

Say nothing, act normal.

Have another Guinness.

The elders giving Trevor quizzical looks.

Past eight, time for some fresh air. Out the pub. Cricketfield Road. Clarence Road. Pembury Road. Estate settling for the night. Kids yelling. Balls against walls. Cars with their black windows up, shaking with bass. Dalston Lane. Labour Club. Trevor thinking, ain't been in there since he was a kid. Booze buzzing. Settle yourself, Trevor. Too early yet for the Four Aces.

Say nothing, act normal.

Have another Guinness.

Over to the pub across the roundabout. Queensbridge Road. The Victoria. Heavy manners on the benches out front. Friendly enough looks, though. Trevor knows one or two of these fellas. A nod, a smile. Killer systems inside on a weekend. Bit quieter today, but not much.

Inside, Trevor sees a woman he knows. She's waving at him to come over. Trevor sits down on a plastic chair. His friend is called Lynne. And she's telling a story. Everyone listening, as close as they can listen, what with the boom-boom-thump-thump of the speakers.

Her fella Dennis was picked up, Trevor knows this. Trevor listens.

'He told me that he had been standing in Sandringham Road outside Ladbrokes betting shop talking to a few of the blokes. He had put a bet on, and the bet was about to run. No sooner had he walked back inside when it seemed like the whole shop just caved in. They dived in, pulled him out and threw him against a car. One of the coppers then came out holding a small bag and said, "This is yours."'

The bass thudding, she goes on, her voice cracking.

'They just put him in the car and drove off with him. They told him to keep his hands on the seat in front of him where they could see them. As they were going along he felt one of them rubbing against him. Dennis turned round to see what they were doing and one of them said, "Face the front and keep your hands there." There wasn't anything he could do about it. When they reached the station and searched him again in front of the sergeant, they found another one, whatever it is they use, in his jacket top.'

Trevor pours rum into plastic cups. Thanked, Trevor smiles. Trevor nods.

Another woman at the table, Ida, is telling her story now.

Her story: how she accidentally witnessed two Stoke Newington detectives supplying her friend with crack cocaine. Later, police at her own house. Trevor listens.

'One of them walked back in with an ordinary carrier bag in his hand, behind him was the other one. We all knew the carrier bag did not belong in my house. My mind went at that moment; I was in a daze. I came back to reality when I heard my babysitter ask where did he get it from, and he said in the old freezer where we kept our house keys. She called him a liar.'

What now, what *now*? What is all this? Trevor thinks.

'He opened the carrier bag and produced four self-sealing bags, three of which were empty and one was full to bursting. They asked me what it was and I told them I did not know, it was not mine, it was their own and they had planted it, wherever they had got it from.'

Say nothing, act normal.

'At Stoke Newington police station, in the charge room, the sergeant was sitting in his chair behind his desk, typewriter in front of him and loads of papers on one side of him. On the other side of the desk were scales, cling film and a roll of foil which they had taken from my kitchen. There was also their bag with their drugs in it.'

Say nothing, say nothing –

'The sergeant took the self-sealing bag out of the carrier bag and placed it on my own scales in front of me. It weighed twenty-eight grammes. But, by the time we got to court, they said it was twelve grammes.'

Act normal.

The story ends. Everyone rocking back in their seats, shaking their heads, saying, all together, like a pre-written chorus, 'Nooooo!'

Trevor nods goodbye to his friend. Trevor's up the road to the Four Aces. 'Evening, Mr Dunbar,' he says to Newton, the owner, on the door. 'Rocksteady, yeah.'

Newton Dunbar tells Trevor he better behave himself. Trevor waves the flyer. 'Friends and family,' he says. 'Sir Collins in tonight?' Meaning Charlie Collins, the producer and co-founder.

'Don't be cheeky, Trevor,' is all Newton Dunbar will say. Trevor grins and ducks under the brown arch of the door.

Inside, Trevor goes down into the Hideaway for a rum and a Red Stripe. Waves to the friendly face who runs this part of the club. His lickle boy helping behind the counter, drinking a Britvic Orange. Must be ten, eleven years old.

Trevor settles himself.


*January.*

Trevor gets an envelope. It's got the usual grand in there and another monkey on top. 'Annual bonus,' Trevor's told. 'Five hundred quid. A monkey. Apt, I'd say.' Laughing at this.

Trevor eats the insult and nods. Winter months. Trevor out and about in the cold. Hairy jacket and fur-lined boots. Trevor uses a bit of his salary to buy an electric fire for his shithole. He sits next to it in the dark, watching the box.

Every couple of weeks, the morning phone call leads to work. It's varied, the work. Varied to a point.

Trevor picking up a bag full of product dropped by a leather jacket and delivered by some kid. Trevor getting arrested by uniforms as he walks around with the bag. Trevor hauled into Stoke Newington nick.

Trevor released on bail by the custody sergeant. Back in the next day but there's never any charges.

Each time, Trevor's told to use a different name. A name they give him. Trevor's been quite a few different men, quite a few different drug mules. *Recycling.*

*March.*

Trevor's line of work changes a little. Bit more variety. Trevor taken to flats and garages and warehouses and empty terraced houses –

Trevor knocking at the door, looking to buy. Trevor getting the door open and the leather jackets kicking it in after him.

Trevor put on the floor with the dealers and the buyers, wrong place wrong time, not Trevor's fault, just wanting a little taste.

The jackets clearing out the place and no arrests made.

Straight after one of these jobs and Trevor's nicked by uniforms with the same bag. New name Trevor, that is.

Clever Trevor, they've started calling him, the leather jackets.

Trevor doesn't feel too clever.

Alias. That's their other nickname for him.

Some days it's AKA.

Trevor prefers that one. It's a bit punchier, a touch more glamour about it.

After he's been on the sauce, if they see him then, it's Trev the bev.

Which is fine, really. Normal.

*June.*

Trevor makes his morning call and they tell him he's in line for promotion. Trevor says that it's about time.

They tell Trevor to get himself over to a garage behind Green Lanes, east side, between Springdale Road and Aden Grove. Trevor decides he needs to take his hangover for a walk. Some fresh air. He sets out with plenty of time.

It's a bit of a stroll. Trevor stops in a caff on Amhurst Road. He treats himself to a fry-up and a cup of tea. When he's finished, he says to the waitress, 'While I'm aware these premises are unlicensed—'

Leaves the sentence hanging there.

The waitress rolls her eyes but she nods, too. A few minutes later, she deposits a tea pot on Trevor's table, a new mug.

Trevor treats himself to a pour. Trevor knocks down the lager and feels better. Trevor checks the clock on the caff wall. Pushing eleven.

He walks up to the corner of Stoke Newington High Street and Church Street and goes into the Three Crowns. Straight up to the bar. Place is empty. No one serving. With a flourish, Trevor raps three times on the counter.

A man appears. 'We're not open.'

Trevor points at the door. 'You sure?'

The man looks at his watch. 'Not eleven yet. We open at eleven.'

Trevor nodding. 'I'll wait over there, shall I?' Pointing at a table by the window.

The man shakes his head. 'We're not open. Not to you. Not this morning.'

Trevor gets it. 'All right. You have a good day, sir.'

Trevor leaves. Trevor crosses the road. Waits. A white pensioner shuffles into the pub, doesn't come out. Trevor thinks: wankers. Trevor looks around. Trevor sees a cement mixer and a skip not far down the road, no one there, probably eating their own fry-up somewhere close by. Trevor sways down the road. Casual look to his left and right –

Hand into the skip. Hand round a broken brick.

Trevor crosses the road. Past the Three Crowns on the Church Street side. As he passes the pub's last window, Trevor casually throws the half-brick through it.

Crosses Church Street and down into the residential grid that inches towards Green Lanes. No shouts. No one follows.

Say nothing, act normal.

Head down, chin up.

Trevor stops at a corner shop. He buys a small bottle of rum. Swallows half of it down. Holsters it in his inside pocket. Warm belly on a hot day.

He finds the garage. A big, unmarked door. No view of inside from the street. Trevor knocks. He's been told the magic word.

'What's the magic word?' someone calls out.

'Abracadabra,' Trevor says. 'Open sesame.'

The door opens. Inside, two vans, marked up with logos, painted nice. Trevor thinks: flash.

A leather jacket is talking to a bloke in overalls the same colours as the vans. Behind, two other leather jackets are unloading bricks of product. Sitting in the garage office, separated from the shop floor by glass, three men Trevor's seen before. The bricks are being parcelled out and divided between these three men that Trevor's seen before.

'This way, Trevor,' a leather jacket informs him.

Trevor follows.

Round the back of the office, a closed space, dark, a lock on the door. The leather jacket opens the lock. Inside, among the garage detritus, the rope and the oil, the old tools and the new rubbish, the fast-food boxes and empty bottles, bags, about a dozen sports bags.

The leather jacket says, 'These bags are going all over. The three lads out front there are in charge, but it's not right that they do the couriering themselves, OK?'

Trevor nods.

'Once that job in the vans is cushty, then the three lads will have a word with you. Tell you where and when, each load. You got that?'

Trevor nods.

'This is a summer-long project, Trev, hence the promotion.'

'I get a raise then, do I?'

The leather jacket laughs. Gives Trevor's cheek a friendly little slap. 'Do me a favour,' he says.

Trevor stares.

'You get nicked with one of these, you know the drill. Same as always, but might not be the advanced warning, all right?'

Trevor nods.

'And keep off the bev, Trev, before work, there's a good fellow.'

There's a chair lying among the crap. Trevor picks it up. Trevor dusts it off. Trevor sits down and waits.

It's dark inside and Trevor is grateful for the little sit-down, the peace and quiet.

He can just about see through a grease-stained window into the office. Comings and goings, Trevor breathes in deep, Trevor breathes out –

Trevor sees Marlon in the office, a couple of youths with him. Laughing with the leather jackets, Marlon. The youths' eyes to the ground, kicking their heels and Marlon nodding and Marlon laughing.

Trevor moves back further into the murk of the space, further back in among the garage detritus, closer to the dozen or so sports bags.

He thinks whatever Marlon's doing here, it won't pay for Marlon to see Trevor.

Say nothing, act normal.

# 3

## *Freedom beat*

23 June–28 June 1986

The first thing Parker thinks looking round the pub is: donkey jackets? It's fucking June.

There's a pre-match feel to the place, everyone standing, crowding into the space in the public bar.

There's eighteen of them here, ages ranging from late-teen to early middle-age. Parker's with his cousin Jimmy, who's a couple of years younger but been in the union for a few himself, and he and Parker are taking up the family crest for the day, what they're here for is not really on the radar of their old men, it promises to be a bit livelier, a bit more active than older limbs might care for –

Parker notes the younger contingent are, in fact, in lighter coats than your traditional workman's jacket, some even making do with a polo shirt, one or two in shorts, thinking it's the bloody Riviera or some such, the older guard giving them gyp for their wardrobe choices.

Parker's in a light rain jacket over T-shirt, jeans and white pumps. He's two pints down and it's not yet eleven. One of the older fixers is mates with the landlord and there's a kitty running for the drinks. Off the books, it looks like, jugs of best poured straight from the barrel –

Well, to be fair, jugs poured off the top of a number of barrels, Parker reckons, meaning this round is on the brewery.

Jimmy nods left and right, says, 'These all know you now, right? You're not the only out-of-towner neither, know what I mean?'

Parker nods. Jimmy meaning they all know Parker's a ringer but also that he's family, can be relied on.

Parker says, 'Why today exactly?'

'Mondays is women's day, right?' Jimmy says. 'Should be quieter round the way. Therefore, yeah?'

Parker nods.

Last few Mondays in June it's been mainly women, a few hundred here, a few hundred there, a sort of family vibe to the protest, to the picket lines. Up at Gray's Inn, or doing the Tower Hill Wapping shuffle, trying to keep face with whatever plod are out and about, demonstrate this is a cause that ain't yet lost.

'What are the timings?' Parker asks.

Jimmy says, 'Midday they set off, bit of a waltz down the Highway and up to Fortress Wapping. We'll move out just after.'

Parker checks his watch. That's over an hour. He'll have to pace himself on the beer, he thinks.

Parker sees Jimmy see Parker's eyes flit from pint mug to watch and back again.

'We had to get in before it opens,' Jimmy reasons. 'Otherwise, we'd have been clocked, wouldn't we, yeah?' He nods. 'Drink up,' he says, 'I'll get us another.'

Parker bends his knees, stretches.

He needs a piss but if he goes too soon he'll only have to go again when they're out on the street. He sees some of the elders shuttling back and forth to the gents and thinks that he doesn't much fancy being boxed in at the urinal by a couple of them and decides to wait, jump in as everyone's out the door, catch them up –

'Get your laughing gear round this, big boy.' Jimmy handing Parker another pint.

'Cheers.'

'Your good health.'

They touch glasses and nod, purse their lips, bob their heads, bounce a little from foot to foot, roll their necks, roll their shoulders, try to ease out some pre-match nerves –

There's a lowish murmur of chatter from the groups of twos and threes and fours, much of it about West Ham's chances next season.

Parker hears a couple of the youth comparing notes on their weekend conquests, bloody loved it, and no means yes and yes means up the arsehole kind of thing, two holes and a heartbeat and the heartbeat's a bonus, and Parker's wondering if any of these know anything at all about a lefty council flat and who and how many might have lit a match or thrown a petrol bomb at the paper factory, and what are most of these blokes doing here anyway?

It's frustration and it's powerlessness and it's helplessness, Parker thinks, overall.

That's why they're here *now*.

They've run out of ideas. The point of a strike, if it goes on, and it's been going on now for six months, is that it's a game of attrition, at the troops-level, at least.

You place yourselves in a line and try to persuade people going to work not to go to work. It's not a complicated exchange.

There are two problems with the game that is currently being played.

The first is that the rules of the game have changed and there's nothing that the pickets can do about that.

If British Rail workers strike, there's nobody to drive the trains, to sell tickets, to work the signals, all that. In other words, a strike means no functioning rail network, no trains, no travel.

In this case, something Parker's not exactly been voicing aloud when his old man is in earshot: the papers are being printed and delivered every day, the strike is not affecting that at all, there is a functioning printing press, there are papers, there is news.

Which tells you what?

The workers are striking about jobs that are no longer actually needed.

They are, Parker thinks now, looking around at these East End faces, these several generations of printers, literally redundant in every sense.

If a strike doesn't affect the daily business of the company against which it strikes, well, it's not so much a strike as a security issue.

Which comes to problem number two.

If it's a security issue, then anything the police are doing is in service to the protection of both the company and the public from this perceived and actual threat to security.

In other words, make sure the papers are printed and distributed; criminalise those standing in the way of that happening.

If pickets are merely a criminal irritant they're no longer *really* striking.

So what's it all about then? Parker thinks.

Someone claps their hands, Jimmy gives Parker a nudge and goes, 'Here,' nodding to the side of the bar, where one of the elders has hoisted himself up onto a table, and not without a little effort, huffing and puffing, a cheer when he manages it, quickly hushed –

'Why are we here?' he says to some muttering and nodding. 'I don't mean here in this pub, I mean here in this situation, in this state.'

Parker's seen this bloke's face around but he can't put a name to it.

'We're here because of mistreatment, end of. We're here because working-class men like yourselves are once again getting shafted by the people in power.'

A couple of hear-hears and the odd whistle –

Parker thinking, I'm pissed –

'We're here because of duplicity and intrigue, because, as is proving abundantly clear, we're here because it turns out we're expendable and no one gives a toss, no one gives a monkeys.'

A cheer at that, swearing and the shaking of heads –

'Our employers have chosen this path, this strike. They have forced our hand and in the process they are showing us that we are no longer needed, that we no longer have jobs, no longer have livelihoods. They have taken our jobs, our livelihoods, by underhand, duplicitous means.'

Parker thinking finally some geezer's getting to the rub –

'And while our union does what it can to secure something for our futures – and we all surely now know that there won't be a fucking job in our futures – then let's at least make the lives of our employers and their' – and he spits the word here – 'scabs, as miserable as we can.'

Men sniffing, men cheering, men saying too fucking right –

Parker breathes deeply, steadies himself, thinks there can't be too much more of this –

'So today, chums, we're trying something new.' A pause. 'Some bright cunt had the idea of calling it, wait for it' – another pause, men stamp their feet, a little low-level ooh-oohing starts up, ironic – 'calling this something new, calling it: walkabout.'

And the room erupts in laughter and cheers, though Parker doesn't really understand what's funny.

Jimmy digs him in the ribs. 'It's Australian, innit, walkabout. Fucking apt, wouldn't you say so, cuz?'

And Parker gets it and grins and goes, 'But where are we fucking going walkabout anyway?'

And where they're fucking going is straight out the pub side door and into the warren of backstreets around Wapping and Shadwell and Limehouse, and while the women are picketing at Gray's Inn Road and Bouvier Street and turning out down the Highway from Tower Hill to Wapping for the police-sanctioned 'official protest', Parker and this little firm in which he's found himself, are going off-piste looking for ELL vehicles to turn over –

A hunting party.

*You're sitting in the office watching* Top of the Pops *on the portable.*

*Tears for Fears with a new version of their hit special for Sports Aid or some other soppy nonsense. The video's best avoided, you think.*

*Here's Bob Geldof pratting about with a starter's flag, there's Duncan Goodhew stripping off, Midge Ure in headphones and socks and sandals on a bike, big Frank Bruno's glistening muscles, tight red shorts and boxer's boots, Jimmy White and Alex Higgins, hardly 'Snooker Loopy', is it?*

*Here's Sharron Davies and Tessa Sanderson, always had a soft spot for Tessa, never hurt her being pitted against Fatima Whitbread, did it, in the old sexpot athlete stakes, you think, Sharron's barnet looking hair-band-ready, big earrings and long-legged, the lot of them bending and stretching, poor old Geldof feeling his age and experience –*

*There's Goodhew doing his butterfly stroke through the chlorine-heavy water of your local municipal, Viv Anderson and a bit of head tennis with Geldof, who's acting chops need a little refinement, to be fair, Steve Hodge – is that Steve Hodge? – kicking a ball into Midge Ure's goolies, Chris Waddle's hair bigger than Sharron's demi-wave, Peter Reid saying something hilarious no doubt –*

*Back to big Frank and he isn't half monumental in those trunks, he's got Tim Witherspoon in a couple of weeks for the WBA Heavyweight Title and you hope he's looking like this when he gets in the ring, Witherspoon's no mug after all, and speaking of no mugs, Carl Lewis with a couple of children in the woods, mouthing good tidings, and then here's Geldof again, this time not managing to do the pole vault, is there nothing this man can't do, then Kirk Stevens and Jimmy and Alex again, they'll be running all over the gaff if Kirk's got anything to do with it, you think, Just Say No, lads, is what Carl Lewis is likely saying to them and the adorable children holding his hands –*

*Then lovely Tessa leading a gang of kids on a jog round the old track and field, lapping Midge and Geldof, what a laugh, eh?*

*Terry comes in, nods.*

*'Nicked this off of Weller,' he says.*

*You feign horror. 'That's a serious allegation, Terry.'*

*'In the chorus, there's the line about walls come tumbling down, which is a song by The Style Council.'*

*'Which they played at Live Aid. And now here's Sport Aid. What's the world coming to, eh?'*

*'Not sure there's enough aid to go round, guv.'*

*'Now there's a sentiment I can get behind.'*

*'Nice to see Tessa Sanderson in there.'*

*'Reigning Olympic champion, Terry, first black Briton to win an Olympic gold medal.'*

*'Legend.'*

*'She is.' You turn off the portable. 'What do you need, Terry?'*

*'Ron Bishop wants a word.'*

*'He knows where to find me. What's it about?'*

*'Compulsory purchase orders on land for the new highway schemes.'*

*'Right.'*

*'There's a press release due end of the month. Here.'*

*Terry hands you a piece of paper. On it:*

(i)    Westferry Circus and roundabout

(ii)   Shed 35 Link

(iii)  Billingsgate/Prestons Road Link

(iv)   Heron Quays/Prestons Road Link

(v)    Prestons Road Widening

(vi)   Limehouse Link

(vii)  Poplar Bypass

(viii) East India Dock Link

(ix)   Blackwall Tunnel Junction Improvements

(x)    Lower Lea Crossing

(xi)   Connaught Crossing

(xii)  Royal Albert Dock Spine Road


*You indicate the telephone and Terry dials, says a few words quietly,
then hands you the receiver.*

*'Wotcha Ron,' you say.*

*Then:*

*'Say this: we should be able to acquire land and relocate businesses by
mutual agreement in advance of the completion of compulsory purchase,
in accordance with our normal procedures.'*

*Then:*

*'You got that?'*

*Then:*

*'That's right, you heard,* should *be able to.'*

*You hang up, hand the receiver back to Terry –*

*'Put the kettle on,' you tell him.*


Jon Davies in Lincoln's Inn Fields first thing knocking on the door of
the Land Registry Head Office. Reason being he wants to know a little
more about how purchases of council housing under the Right to Buy
scheme are registered. Reason for this is the day before, round at Jackie's
parents for Sunday lunch, Chick tells Jon how he's fronting the cash so
that Grandad Ray can buy his council flat at a terrific discount.

'Small change, Jon, they've lived here so long,' Chick said. 'It's a favour. The discount is fifty per cent.'

'And you're just giving them the money, are you?' Jon asked. 'Just like that?'

'Just like that,' Chick grinned, running the words together, quickly, juslikedat –

'How does that work exactly, in terms of ownership?'

Chick made a face, semi-ironic. 'Who is it you work for again, Jon?'

'Council. You know, Chick, planning.'

'So, what, this line of questioning is something of a busman's holiday?'

Jon nodded. 'I'm not well versed in the Right to Buy process, Chick, that's all.'

Chick roared. 'Pulling your leg, old son, not like you're fucking Inland Revenue now, is it?'

Jon, sweating slightly, noticed the family looking at them. 'I certainly am not, Chick,' he laughed. 'Humour me, though, how is it registered?' Jon gestured around them. 'The flat, I mean. You doing this as a loan or a gift?'

Here Chick winked. 'A loan agreement that means they default and it's all mine, in name, anyway.'

'Likely to default, are they?'

Again, Chick roared. 'Interest rates I've given them, fucking right they are.'

Jon knows Chick's bluster serves a rhetorical purpose, but he also knows old Chick is not about to fleece Grandad Ray. Family, for Chick, is golden, what he always says, thicker than water, is the claret running through the family's veins, the claret in common, their *blood*.

No, what Jon really wants to know is who else might be doing it if Chick is.

Chick said, 'I might come down your gaff this week, if I may? Office hours. Planning questions is the purpose, all right?'

'Any time, Chick,' Jon said. 'Mi casa and all that.'

Chick grinned. 'That dago talk will get you precisely nowhere, old son, only come in handy on the Costa, as in, it'll cost her!'

Chick laughed long and loud and Jon didn't exactly get the joke and later told Jackie all about it and she told him that Chick's lump sum was a loan in name only and that everyone was happy.

Jon wondered exactly what Chick might get out of it, which is why he's now in Lincoln's Inn Fields.

And, of course, there is his separate, professional interest given his council role.

The Right to Buy proposal is ostensibly council-run and therefore to an extent he should be looking out for the interests of council residents including Grandad Ray. Point is, if Chick can buy Grandad Ray's council flat as a favour, who else – more unscrupulous even than Chick – might be profiting from similar arrangements.

Jon presents his cross-council legal credentials, which is enough to get him five minutes with a registrar who tells him:

'This is our head office, Mr Davies, I won't be able to look up records, not specific records, but I can give some sense of what we do here.'

Jon chooses his words carefully. 'What I'm interested in is the obligation to register property and who exactly is obliged to do what.' He pauses and smiles. 'If you know what I mean?'

The registrar smiles back, kindly, *forgivingly*, Jon thinks.

He says, 'Nineteen twenty-five, Mr Davies, feels like a long time ago, wouldn't you say?'

Jon nods. 'Sixty-one years, give or take.'

'Exactly sixty-one years, Mr Davies.'

'I mean, rounding to the year, of course.'

'Either way, Mr Davies, in our business it's not as long a time as it might be in other businesses.'

'That feels a little cryptic, if I may.'

The registrar's eyes twinkle.

Jon feels as if he's about to be let into some clubbable secret or other.

There's something about the office – location for a start – that feels *very* 1925.

Clerks pottering, double-barrelling about with their fountain pens and tie clips, a grey sheen of bureaucracy, a light, chewy mist of pipe smoke, all very beige and a touch itchy –

The carpet's got a definite whiff about it.

'Nineteen twenty-five, Mr Davies, is when compulsory registration became enshrined in law.'

'Compulsory registration.'

'Compulsory registration, exactly.'

'Which means,' Jon asks, 'that since nineteen twenty-five all property transactions and land purchases and acquisitions have been registered with you here at the land registry?'

'Let's not get ahead of ourselves, Mr Davies.'

'It's something of a misleading phrase then,' Jon smiles.

'In nineteen twenty-five, compulsory registration was established as the principle to achieve what we call here total coverage.'

'Total coverage in terms of the registration of all property and land ownership, I hope?'

'Exactly.'

'And how's that coming along?'

'Slowly, Mr Davies, a lot more slowly than you might suppose.'

Jon smiles. 'It feels like any assumption I might have had before coming in,' he says, 'has been – or is about to be – turned on its head.'

'I hope it's not a disagreeable experience.'

'Not at all,' Jon says. 'As John Maynard Keynes put it, once or twice, when I'm wrong, I change my mind – what do you do?'

'A noble sentiment.'

'If you're ever wrong,' Jon winks.

'Compulsory registration has been phased in across the counties in a piecemeal fashion, which means that we are still in the process of trying to work out exactly which bits of this country of ours are owned by whom.'

'Church and the queen, then?' Jon offers.

'Once upon a time, yes.'

'What about now?'

'Ongoing.'

'Alongside one helpful development.'

Jon raises his eyebrows.

The registrar, seeing this, smiles. '*Voluntary* registration.'

'Meaning?'

'One voluntarily registers one's purchases of land and property.'

'Voluntarily. Interesting.' Jon shifts in his seat, sniffs at the coarsening air, the animal scent of sweat and smoke –

'And what's the advantage of going through all that red tape, voluntarily?'

'There are several advantages, Mr Davies, you might be surprised to learn.'

Jon winks. 'I was ready for that one.'

'Principally, Mr Davies, if your *holding*, your land, is registered as yours, registered as *owned by you* according to land registry records, then, Mr Davies, it's much easier to dispose of it, easier to disperse of your holding—'

'Easier to sell it.'

'Easier to sell it, Mr Davies.'

Jon thinks: that was a bit of a mouthful.

He says, 'What about in the case of council-housing tenants and the government Right to Buy scheme?'

'Same principle.'

'Compulsory or voluntary?'

'Depends on the county, Mr Davies. Not all counties are acting compulsorily at this time.'

Jon thinks: you got a list?

He says, 'But if a council property is bought up privately and the sale is registered, future sales are simpler as a result?'

The registrar beams. 'You've been paying attention.'

'But you don't have to, depending on the county?'

The registrar, smiling, is nodding away now –

'And subsequent sales same thing, just that first subsequent one'd be easier, that fair enough?'

'It is.'

Jon thinks: how many council residents will have the energy to do all that after the headache of the purchase in the first place?

Not many.

'I represent the housing interests of the people of Tower Hamlets, Hackney and Newham –' true to a point – 'so where can I see records of registered Right to Buy purchases? General right of access to records held by public authorities, surely?'

The registrar opens his arms. 'The Land Registry holds these records, Mr Davies. And I can arrange an appointment.'

'Cushty,' Jon says.


Suzi's bright idea is to take a few of the estate's youngers down to Clapham Common for the anti-apartheid event on Saturday and use her insider status to swing a few passes and show them a good time.

'They deserve it, don't they?' she says to Carolyn, her new friend at the Youth Association, courtesy of Detective Constable Patrick Noble.

What he hasn't done for her isn't worth doing, she sometimes thinks, bitterly.

It's not always clear to her what she wants from all this, but she got involved at Rectory Road for the right reasons, and there is, she thinks, an atonement angle to it –

Carolyn remembers her, she says, from back then, only a couple of years ago, of course, and Suzi knows Carolyn's new live-in boyfriend, but they're keeping quiet about quite how well, and he's not around much, it seems, which suits.

Carolyn tells her it'll be hard to choose who comes.

'Then again,' she laughs, 'how many boys round here want to watch Peter Gabriel?'

Suzi hoots, reads from the poster she's brought with her. 'Hugh Masekela, Maxi Priest, David Grant, Gil Scott-Heron, Sade, Princess – they'll know Princess, *surely*? – Lorna Gee, Billy Bragg, The Communards, Boy George, Elvis Costello, Sting, Big Audio Dynamite, Roddy Frame, Gary Kemp – him from Spandau Ballet – Jerry Dammers—'

'Who's Jerry Dammers?'

'The Specials, "Free Nelson Mandela", that single, that was him.'

'I should know that,' Carolyn mutters.

'He's organised the whole thing.' Suzi winks. 'I'll introduce you backstage.'

'You can do that?'

'I can. Though I suspect he might be a little busy.'

Carolyn laughs. 'Something for everyone, then. It's the day out as much as anything, isn't it?'

'We could have a record-playing session in the Youth Association, day before, what do you think? I'll bring stuff by all the bands, get everyone in the mood.'

'Another good idea, Suzi.' Carolyn nodding. 'Which is the band your man is a part of?'

'The Style Council. He's not actually *in* the band. He does the sound.'

'And they're not on the poster?'

'Special guests, doing a Curtis Mayfield number as a surprise, first on, I think. Don't tell anyone!'

Carolyn laughs. 'Who am *I* going to tell, exactly?'

'I think you might have more influence than you think.'

'If I had more influence,' Carolyn says, solemnly, 'then we wouldn't have to take people to a free concert just to cheer them up.'

Suzi nods. 'I think I can get half a dozen passes, and anyone else who wants to come with us—'

'Share them around?'

'Yeah, why not,' Suzi says, knowing this is a bit of a no-go, in fact, not the done thing at all. Who cares, it's a bunch of kids. 'There won't be any names on them, so that'll work.'

'I'll let you know tomorrow?'

'Great. And we'll do the march, too? We need to be prompt if we're going to make the opening act—'

'That I don't know about!'

'Exactly,' Suzi grins. 'And, besides, it's important, the march. Good for them all to see it.'

'It's not something they'll have seen before, not on this scale.'

'The privilege of the white middle class—'

'I wasn't going to say it—'

'No, it's true,' Suzi says. 'And more and more so. When I was working with Rock Against Racism, it was a mixed crowd, black, white and brown faces at the gigs, at the marches. Live Aid was a bit different, and that's the danger, it becomes too removed.'

'You mean why support a cause abroad when there's so much wrong at home?'

'Exactly that, yes. I think Junior Giscombe said exactly that, in fact, about Live Aid, a man committed to anti-racism, to equality, distanced and closed out by what was an *event*, not a reality, not by any stretch.'

Carolyn nodding –

Suzi says, 'And this is a cause that needs to resonate here, *here* –' meaning the estate, meaning Tottenham, meaning inner London – 'because this is a place built on inequality, because people here are living a form of apartheid, so we need to show the people here that there is a future, that there is hope and that there are people in this country who do care.'

'And that's why you're here, is it?'

'I'm here,' Suzi says.

'But you're not here every day, you won't be here tonight, next month, next year – who knows. You were there for Colin Roach but you didn't stay. Not many of us stayed. Is that fair?'

Suzi thinks she's right but –

'I can help make a more positive story about this place. I can do that.'

'You think that's what we need here?'

'It can't hurt, surely, can it?'

Carolyn nodding –

'No,' Carolyn says. 'It can't hurt, no.'

Back home, Suzi drafts her Red Wedge / Paul Weller piece, thinks what she'll say to Noble at their next meeting, what bit of insider info she can give him, what detail she can dress up as *intelligence*, thinks: all this thanks to a conscience eight years ago now.

Keith's out, she's not sure where, likely rehearsals for Saturday –

She's covering the anti-apartheid event on assignment, photographs and text, and she thinks, here's a chance, let's get the story in here, too, talk a bit about these youngsters who you're showing a good time.

It can't hurt.


They pile out the side door of the pub and Parker says to Jimmy –

'What about that fire, then? Any word?'

And Jimmy hisses, 'I'd keep your trap shut about that if I were you. Especially round here.'

'Explain.'

'Hang on.'

They're in a Wapping side street, eighteen big blokes looking for trouble.

Well, looking for East London Logistics delivery vehicles. Aside from that, there ain't much of a plan, Parker's realising.

'We need to give the OB the slip is what this is about,' someone's saying. 'Let's split up. Two groups of four and two groups of five. We need a local in each, which should work.'

They shuffle about, the blokes, like being back at school, sticking close to your pals, and Parker and Jimmy end up in a group of five with three blokes who clearly know each other and one of them says, 'We're all Silvertown, know this neck of the woods like the back of our hands,' and Jimmy jokes, 'Take your gloves off then, mate,' and the bloke gives Jimmy a look that means Jimmy won't be opening his mouth again any time soon.

The bloke who was giving the speech in the pub says, 'Meet back here in ninety minutes, we'll debrief, then go out again. In theory, the Old Bill should be looking after the women's march down from Tower Hill.'

'In theory,' someone mutters.

'On your bikes then,' the bloke says.

The Silvertown bloke who gave Jimmy the look takes charge, and they head east, towards Limehouse, Parker thinks, this is not exactly his manor, and they keep to the side streets that flank the bigger roads they expect the East London Logistics vehicles to be using.

Parker and Jimmy hang back a touch.

'Not too quick,' the Silvertown bloke's saying. 'We're just on our lunch break, off for a pint, yeah? Not too urgent.'

But it's difficult to keep to a lunchtime stroll, there's that anticipation of *something* in the air, adrenalin, and they have to stop a couple of times and recalibrate.

'How hard can it be,' the Silvertown bloke says, 'to *walk*?'

It's a fair point, Parker thinks.

He puts his hand out and slows Jimmy right down –

'What about that fire then?'

Jimmy stops. He gives Parker a look, *turn it in*.

'Why you so keen to know about that?' he says,

'Curious, that's all. Can't have been an accident, can it?'

'I wouldn't know about that.'

Jimmy moves off, ups his pace a touch to get nearer to their teammates.

Parker joking –

'You're not a suspect, Jimmy, I'm only asking.'

'And curiosity did what to the cat?'

'Actual bodily harm.'

'A lucky cat, maybe.'

Parker's hand's out again, he stops, he says –

'Why are you being so cagey?'

Jimmy makes a face: OK, you've twisted my arm, but after I tell you what I've got to tell you, you shut up about all this and we'll be rosy. All right?

Jimmy says, 'Our Silvertown chums just up ahead. *That's* the word.'

'You should have said.' Parker being ironic.

'You'll understand my reticence.'

'I do.'

Parker's wondering who exactly these Silvertown lads are but keeps shtum.

They're doing what feels like a series of figures-of-eight, circling and looping, checking on the bigger roads, doubling back against the one-way systems –

Nothing. For about an hour, nothing.

Half-time:

Parker nips into a greasy spoon for a piss and a bacon sandwich –

He thinks: arson, then, but how to get confirmation –

He thinks: maybe leave off the council flat today, one line of questioning probably enough even for Jimmy, who's family after all –

The bacon sandwich goes down a treat, great slabs of fatty pork and brown sauce, which he's wiping off his chin when he exits the caff and the Silvertown top bloke says:

'Let's head down the river. Then west back to the meet.'

Meaning the pub where they started –

More drinking then.

They arrow down to the Shadwell Basin, a disused dock, so their Silvertown friends are telling Parker and Jimmy, closed down in the sixties when the docks became uneconomic, tell that to my old man, and bought by the council after that and guess what fucking well happened when those jokers took over, yeah, that's right, it fell into dereliction and disrepair, open and disused land and water –

Parker says, 'Building site now, though.'

'Docklands, innit, regeneration, all that game. They're doing round here, too.'

'Worth a few quid, I expect,' Parker suggests.

He notes the brief looks shared among his Silvertown associates –

'Yeah, I s'pose,' top bloke says. 'If you had a pub or shop or something, what with the area all yuppified, it'd be an earner.'

'What they doing here then?'

'Residential, flats, you know? A waterside development, very aspirational. Quote unquote *apartment complex*, that sort of thing.'

Parker thinking: if the place is going to be some sort of hub –

This strike really is a lost cause.

He says, 'Looks like they're only building on around about half of it.'

He notes another furtive shared look –

'Wouldn't know about that, mate—'

Then:

'Hang about. Over there.'

They've spotted the top of a van doing a three-point turn not far from what Parker knows is the Prospect of Whitby pub.

'You two, straight line that way, we'll go round—'

Things move fast.

The Silvertown lads are off to the right, they're quick, Parker will give them that, and he and Jimmy hustle down the Thames Path and back towards Wapping High Street, jogging now, not speaking, Parker thinking –

Now what?

A bang, smashing glass –

They hear brakes scream, tyres screech –

They hear shouting.

They round the corner and see the three Silvertown blokes pulling the driver out the window of a East London Logistics van –

They're about fifty yards away now and they see the driver with his hands up and he's remonstrating, saying something, saying it again and again it sounds like, though Parker can't make out what, and they let him down, slowly, let him go, let him gather himself, and as Parker and Jimmy arrive, Parker hears –

'Yeah, yeah, on you go then, no harm no foul—'

And Jimmy says, '*What?*'

And the Silvertown blokes look at Jimmy, all three of them, and they give Jimmy a snide sort of a smile, each of them gives Jimmy the same snide smile, and they tell Jimmy:

'Don't worry about it. Our mistake. Let's head back to the boozer.'

And Jimmy's sharp enough not to argue the toss.

The Silvertown blokes get a round in, and they're all pals, and then the speech-maker tells everyone that that's enough for the day and they can all go home – ·

Jimmy says cheerio and does one almost immediately.

Parker gets himself and his Silvertown chums another pint.

He drinks it quickly and drifts off, waits –

From across the road, in an alley, in the shadows, he watches the three Silvertown lads leave and he follows –

He follows them down backstreets and across estates, past the old power station, through Milk Yard –

He's careful, Parker, and he keeps his distance.

Through Wapping Woods and Maynard's Quay –

And Parker watches the three men approach a warehouse, a warehouse complex, it's big, he thinks, no signage, nothing to indicate what it is, but a barrier goes up, a gate opens, and the three men are swallowed into this complex, and Parker catches a glimpse of what's inside, shipping containers and open space, gravel and machinery, and, he's sure of it, the colours of East London Logistics on the side of a lorry, and he thinks –

What the fuck's all this then?


*You're in with one of the lower-downs from the LDDG, a snotty-nosed brat who doesn't accept your generous offer of a cup of tea.*

*'You're sure,' Terry insists. 'It's the morning, we're in England, aren't we? It's only polite.'*

*'I'll have a coffee? If there's one going.'*

*Terry smiles. 'We don't drink coffee in this office.'*

*'We do not,' you add.*

*'I'm fine, thank you, really,' the kid says. He busies himself settling into his chair.*

*'Sparkling water?' Terry says.*

*'Oh—'*

*'We don't have any of that either. I can do you tap?'*

*'Terry,' you say. 'Stop torturing the poor lamb.'*

*The kid smiles –*

*You smile at the kid.*

*'So why don't you tell me why you're here at my place of business.'*

*'I—'*

*'And what I mean by that is, why it is that you're here and not Ron Bishop?'*

*'Mr Bishop, um, Ron, he feels, well, he feels that—'*

*'He feels what?'*

*'I'm quite senior now, and he wanted me to, you know, take some responsibility.'*

*'How very empowering of him.'*

*'Right.'*

*The kid shuffles some papers, glances nervously at Terry behind –*

*'I'll have a cup of tea, I think,' you say. 'Terry, you'll do the honours?'*

*Terry nods and slips out the door. The kid looks a little easier already, you think.*

*'So I'm assuming,' you say, 'that this is what you will likely call a delicate situation.'*

*The kid nods. 'It's a little delicate, yes.'*

*'Pray tell.'*

*'Shadwell Basin,' the kid says. 'The contractors are in and beginning the first stages in the development. They've run into a snag, however.'*

*'Have they?'*

*The kid nods. 'They've been able to start the initial excavation work on the north and west sides of the basin.'*

*'Sounds positive.'*

*'But they are so far unable to begin work on the east and south sides.'*

*You smile at this, say nothing.*

*'So, what Mr Bishop wants to know is when they can start the excavation work on the east and south sides of the basin, in a nutshell, is why I'm here.'*

*'When you say unable, what do you mean exactly?'*

*'The contractors have been denied access to the land.'*

'Denied access by who?'

'By a guardian company acting on behalf of the owner of the property, the land.'

'Right, so there is a security company currently guarding the land on behalf of the owner, meaning the contractors are unable to start work. Is that a fair appraisal?'

'Yes, very fair.'

'Well, I don't see the problem. Surely your contractor – or your contractor's employer – need only talk to the owner of the land to clear up this misunderstanding.'

'It is our opinion that the land was acquired by us in 1981. From Tower Hamlets Council.'

You smile. 'Ah, well, I now understand your predicament.'

The kid smiles. Terry comes in with a teapot and three cups and saucers –

'In case you've changed your mind,' he says to the kid.

'This land that's being guarded,' you say. 'You got any idea what's going on there?'

'It's wasteland,' the kid says. 'There's been nothing going on there since nineteen sixty-nine.'

'Now that's just not true, sunshine,' you say, losing the smile.

Terry pours the tea. The kid accepts a cup.

It rattles on the saucer as he takes it from Terry's steady hand –

You sip at your tea. 'Delicious, Terry.'

You sit back in your leather office chair, swivel –

'The land you're talking about, son, has been in use since the end of nineteen seventy-three, just after Christmas to be precise, which is more than twelve years. Do you know what that means?'

The kid shakes his head.

'There are records of possession of this land, records of intent, too.'

'But the land is unoccupied.'

You smile. 'Possession is not the same as occupation, young man.'

Terry says, 'It's not so much what you know—'

'As what you can prove,' you finish.

'I'm not sure I understand,' the kid says, looking, you think, genuinely bewildered.

'I'm pretty sure that you don't.'

There is silence now, for a moment.

'What should I tell Mr Bishop?' the kid asks.

Sensibly, you think, he's ready to leave and defer to a senior party –

'You tell him exactly what I've just told you.'

'I'm not sure what it is you have just told me.'

'Now, on that one,' you say, 'I'm pretty sure that you are.'

The kid's nodding now, confused.

He shuffles his papers, squares them off, puts them back in his briefcase, stands –

'I'll tell Mr Bishop what it is you've just told me,' he says.

'Good man,' you tell him. 'Terry will see you out.'


*Shaun*: My cousin tells me there's some trip planned end of June, on the Saturday, some pop concert down south and that we've all got backstage passes from that white woman, Suzi, who's been around the Youth Association a fair bit, and that I should come.

Saturdays I don't do anything for Marlon, but I run it by him anyway.

He shrugs and tells me my weekend is my own. 'Worker's rights, you know. You don't have a union, after all.' He laughs at that.

Fact is, I wanna go as this Suzi keeps turning up with a camera whenever she's around, and it's interesting what she does with it, like taking pictures as a *job*? And of what? The estate? The kids? Like, it must mean someone gives a fuck to pay her to do that, even if it is some middle-class crusade, playing politics, which is what Anton said when he saw her at it.

'Safari is what it is, Shaun's cousin,' he told Carolyn, though he was joking, I think, trying to make her laugh. 'Come and have a look at the poor people in their cages.'

'That'd be the zoo, Anton,' my cousin said, sarcastically. 'A safari is the *natural habitat* experience.'

'Either way, it ain't real. When did you ever see a lion on top of a small car in the jungle, yeah?'

Then someone tells Anton that lions live in Africa, desert plains, all that, not the jungle, that's a myth.

'Looking at the animals from afar as you can't cohabit with them, is what I'm saying. End of.'

One or two nodding at that, Carolyn with thin lips and a funny look on her face, like what's all this then, like she's sad, not about what Anton is saying, but about Anton.

I'm not sure I agree with him, anyway, and I'm not sure how much is him and how much is Mr Gibbs, our history teacher, who has opinions on pretty much everything. All those photos after the riot that we seeing in the newspapers show one side of a story and maybe this Suzi is showing another. That's what I think.

Anton hasn't been back to the Youth Association since that day, it's been a while now, and he tells me there's more to learn elsewhere.

He's tougher, since the riot, more ruthless, especially with me, more ruthless with his time, you know. Tougher in a way that no one else is seeing. They're just seeing a kid working hard at school, that's it, a brown-nose, a swot. What they don't get is that it's harder to do *that* and not care what no one thinks than it is to fuck about. It takes a bit of steel, in my mind, what Anton is doing, and maybe his mum gets that transfer out the Farm, and maybe it pays off, but whatever does happen, I wanna hang with him, and I told him that and he just shrugged, nodded at some of the Hackney boys on the corners, said, 'Sure.'

There's no point me pretending I don't know what's in them bags I bring over from Stoke Newington, but I don't look, and it's not every day, and what Marlon always says is that I'm perfect, I've got family over there, an address, what he calls a 'justification for loitering', and no one's bothered me anyway, I do that trip all the time on the bus, it's normal, enough Hackney knew me before, and now they nod and wink when they see me, whistle, jog on, you know, all that.

Marlon says there's just one trip to do, week before the concert, a quiet week for whatever reason, but I ain't complaining, though the girls in the Turkish cafe are well nice and every time I'm in there they smile and give me a drink of something, always got some little Turkish delicacy, they call it, for me to try, like a syrupy cake.

The white one, Lauren, I think, is mouthy and funny, but it's her friend I like, Leenie, Lauren calls her, and if they know what I'm doing there picking up every week or so, then they don't say nothing, they don't seem to mind, or judge me, which is pretty nice.

*Bethnal Green Town Hall.*

Chick says, 'It's a good job you ain't got a cat, Jon.'

'Why's that, Chick?'

Chick looks left and right, opens his palms –

'Because where the fuck are you going to swing it, am I right?'

Jon smiles while Chick slaps his own thigh, hooting.

'You wanted to see me, Chick,' Jon says.

'And here I am.'

'And here you are.'

Chick looking around the room. 'They've kept the place nice, then, I appreciate that.'

'You been here before, have you?'

'Not *here* here –' meaning the office – 'this is where I got married, old son, weren't you there?'

'No, Chick, I wasn't there.'

Chick mock-thoughtful, rubbing his chin. 'That's right, it was before Jacks had the misfortune to hitch her wagon to your donkey!'

'In a manner of speaking.'

'Plans for the weekend?' Chick asks.

'Me and the boy are off to Clapham Common for the concert on Saturday.'

'Free Nelson Mandela, all that?'

Jon nods, all that, yes, thinks:

Get to the point, Chick, there's a good chap.

'I'll get to the point,' Chick says.

Jon thinks: he always does that, makes it feel like it's me that's arsing around –

'Remember I told you all about my syndicate and how we sold it on, the portfolio, I mean?'

Jon nods.

'Well, I said that as I wasn't exactly sure what was what. Truth is, we're still in the game, it's just that we've got a new partner.'

'OK.'

'What I mean, really, is that the new partner bought us out, but has cut us in, too.'

'Right.'

'So what I mean is that my syndicate's share of any portfolio is considerably lower than it was.'

'Because you sold it, though, Chick.'

'That's right.'

'It was your choice—'

'You're right, Jon, to say that. It's a fair point and I appreciate it.'

Jon thinks: where's this going?'

'What I'm here for,' Chick says, 'is a technical question. Well, to be fair, I'm here for the answer, but you see what I mean.'

'Fire away.'

Jon's got a few questions himself for Chick, on the whole Right to Buy business, his purchase of Grandad Ray's flat, or at least his loan to secure that purchase. Jon's not got his appointment at the Land Registry for a few weeks and he wouldn't mind knowing a little bit more about the process, the actual procedure –

He's signed off on the principle of the thing enough times these last twelve months but he wouldn't mind hearing a bit more nitty-gritty about it all.

Chick moves uncomfortably in his seat.

It's a warm day, and all there is to relieve the heat is Jon's electric fan, which is turned off, as it's too noisy to use when there's more than Jon in the room.

Jon thinks it might not be the heat that is making Chick uncomfortable.

'What if our partner,' Chick begins. 'What if he presented us with no other option than to sell?'

'You'll have to be more specific, Chick,' Jon says. 'What does no other option mean?'

'This is a somewhat delicate question, Jon,' Chick admits. 'I'm struggling, to be honest, asking it at all, but it did occur to me the other day that you might be able to help.'

'How is it delicate?'

'The partner I'm talking about. He's, well, he's serious.'

'OK.'

'We had a number of properties in our portfolio. I believe I told you all about it round your gaff Live Aid day, which was a cracker, and I must thank you again for your generosity and hospitality.'

Jon nods, bats away Chick's thanks. 'You did, yes. Everything was going to change, except the pub, which was going to be a better pub. Right?'

'You're not wrong, Jon, that's exactly what we intended.'

'But—'

'Yeah, well, but.'

Chick looks down, twiddles his thumbs.

Jon thinks: he's shrinking, Chick, perhaps to fit the office, perhaps some other reason, but he looks flat, Chick does, he looks *deflated* –

Chick says, 'It became clear, after a couple of conversations, that the land these premises was on, was in fact owned by someone else.'

'Your partner?'

Chick makes a face, moves his hand from side to side, like it's shaking.

'Mas or menos, you know. His companies, his associates, you'll remember I told you there were a lot of names.'

'I do remember.'

'Anyway, we're told that something called adverse possession means it's his and our best bet is to take the terms he's offered, and we decided, all told, that was sensible.'

'I'm assuming your partner doesn't know you're here.'

'He doesn't, and I'd appreciate it if you kept my visit to yourself.'

Jon draws his thumb and forefinger across his lips like a zip.

'Appreciate that, too, Jon.'

'So, what, you want to know what you can do about it?'

Chick shakes his head. 'No, we're not stupid, it is what it is now, and we're happy enough with the terms, and, regardless, we don't have a choice.'

'So why are you here?'

Chick grimaces. 'I'm a bit embarrassed, to be fair. It's a bit embarrassing.'

'Think nothing of it, I'll keep quiet—'

'You bloody better.'

Palms up, Jon nods. 'Abso-fucking-lutely, Chick.'

'Well, we don't *want* anything, as such, I just want to know if we've been had, if we've been mugged off, if anyone's laughing at us, yeah?'

'If you can hold your head high sort of thing—'

'Nail on the head.'

'All right,' Jon says. 'If you can get me a copy of the paperwork, I'll have a shufty, and we'll talk.'

'I was hoping you'd say that.'

Chick pulls a zip-up leather portfolio case from his Adidas sports bag, unzips it, and slaps a hefty sheaf of paper onto Jon's desk.

'That's all of it,' Chick says, 'but I'd reckon you only need to look at an example or two for the picture.'

'Why's that?'

'Because it's the same story for the lot.'

'That's helpful, Chick.'

'Yeah, well.'

Chick stands, extends a hand –

'Give me a few weeks, all right?' Jon says.

Jon shakes Chick's hand – firmly.

Chick says, 'Sweet.'

*

*Clapham Common, 28 June, Anti-Apartheid Movement March and Festival for Freedom in Namibia and South Africa.*

Suzi's standing at the side of the stage next to a handful of kids from Broadwater Farm as Keith finishes setting up for The Style Council's surprise guest performance, and she looks out over what must be close to two hundred thousand people, and she thinks –

I thought Live Aid was big.

She's snapping away.

The empty stage fringed by black, red and green flags held by people squashed in down at the front.

At the back and spaced out evenly across it, huge drapes in black, yellow, green, red, blue hang down like ships' sails buffeting in the wind.

Below and stretching out and away, the crowd thickening, more and more people streaming through the gates at the back, arriving from the march hopped up and excited, into the space lined by white refreshment tents and beyond that:

Vast oak trees in the faintest of breezes, branches swaying gently, leaves whispering, light flickering and mottled, offering only a little shade on what she's thinking must be the hottest day of the year –

Snap, snap.

She's aware of one of the kids taking an interest in what she's doing.

He's sidling towards her, shuffling past the others, name's Shaun, she thinks, might be a cousin of Carolyn's –

Given the feet-dragging nature of teenagers and the need to get there nice and prompt, they decided to skip the march itself.

The session at the Youth Association got them all listening to the bands, and Suzi and Carolyn told them about Nelson Mandela.

'Isn't he a terrorist?' one of the kids asked. 'That's what my dad says anyway.'

So Suzi explained who the ANC is, and what they can get up to, and how Mrs Thatcher isn't a fan of action of any sort and doesn't agree with sanctions or boycotts, and that might be why this young lad's old man has the opinion he does.

'So why's he in jail if he's not a terrorist?' another asked.

Carolyn fielded that one and the kids quickly began to understand what wrongful imprisonment means in an apartheid country, given their own context, and Carolyn showed them photos of white police using clubs on black crowds and they were outraged and righteous, Suzi saw it descend and take, this feeling, and the cause became theirs, and really part of the reason for that was they didn't know police violence existed outside their own world, and that was shocking and that was what politicised them, unity, solidarity –

All of them know someone who has been nicked or harassed or stopped and searched or had their front door smashed in or been pinned up against a wall or seen their mum or dad in handcuffs or a friend carted off in the back of a jam sandwich since the uprising in October.

They liked the song, too, '(Free) Nelson Mandela', easy to sing along to, pretty simple message, nice little details in the lyrics like the shoes that are too small –

Suzi zooms in on placards –

Snap, snap:

SOLIDARITY

WITH

**ANC**

SOLIDARITY

WITH

**SWAPO**

Nelson Mandela's face on a thousand chipboard signs.

She turns her lens on the kids –

Snap, snap.

They seem remarkably unbothered by the enormous crowd just to their right, giggling and tossing their hair, decked out in bright green and pink and orange T-shirts.

The kid Shaun points at her camera as the band bounce onto the stage –

Suzi leans over to him, mimes adjusting the focus, taking the picture, lifts her camera to her face –

She arrows in on Paul Weller, yellow Fred Perry polo shirt and tiny, checked shorts, white socks and black penny loafers and he's saying –

'Big round of applause for all the marchers coming in now, please … I would like to dedicate this one to all the people that were on the march. This is called … "Move on Up".'

She hears one of the kids saying, 'Why's he wearing shorts?'

'Because it's hot!'

'But he looks like a wally!'

Suzi laughs, tells them that Paul Weller's too cool to care.

Dee looks more relaxed than at Live Aid, Suzi thinks, beautiful in long white top and cinched black belt, shorts, New York Yankees cap on back to front, hooped pearl earrings, dancing as the band change gear and then up to the mic –

Suzi hands her camera to Shaun, puts the strap over his head, round his neck, says, 'Go on, you have a go then.'

She steps back and watches as Shaun delicately turns the lens, hesitates, lifts the camera, weighing it in his hands, checking the strap is secure, closing an eye, opening it again, bringing the camera up –

He snaps once, twice, looks at Suzi, who smiles, makes a gesture encouraging him, and he nods, considers the heft of the machine, turns back to the band –

Who are now driving through the frantic percussion-only section of the song, Dee dancing wildly, back into the riff –

Shaun grinning at Suzi, hands back her camera, smiles shyly, says, 'Thank you.'

Then Paul Weller's leading the band into the home straight, another little drum flourish, and he's saying –

'Thank you! See ya.'

And they're off the stage, Paul Weller winking at Suzi, the kids oohing and ahhing at that, Dee, who kisses Suzi quickly on the cheek, Steve White in black vest and sunglasses grinning and sweating, Mick Talbot looking pleased with it all in short-sleeved white shirt and grey slacks, calmly delivering himself to his next appointment, Camelle Hinds topless again, Steve Sidelnyk in a white vest –

Keith twiddling, then he's up and his hand now on the small of Suzi's back guiding her down the steps and into the lush grass of backstage, the kids in front screeching, it's all got a bit more lively, and Keith says –

'That was magic, love, what did you think?'

'Magic, it really was, love, really was.'

And then Suzi spots Carolyn and waves, and look, there's that boyfriend of hers after all.


Parker wasn't going to come.

He was keen to follow up on what he saw in that warehouse in Wapping but he needed to tread carefully and to check in with Noble –

'A car? It's going to be tricky, son?'

They sat in a caff on Chatsworth Road, same one they used to meet at back in 1978, Noble's missus Lea no longer working there.

'Well, I can hardly just stand around the place, can I?'

Noble nods at that. 'Point is, you're getting involved if you're in a car, you're actively investigating, you're not simply observing, you see?'

'I realise that.'

'Also, you'd be looking out for something that's not strictly your remit. We're not trying to catch baddies, you're just an onlooker.'

'Like up in Stoke Newington, you mean?'

'Yeah, well, I'm trying, aren't I?'

Noble a bit sniffy after that and Parker softens –

'Point is, guv, there's the arson angle, you asked for that, specifically. Can't you square it that way?'

Noble nods. 'I can try,' he says. 'I guess we've got your word, what you've heard, I mean, we've got fuck all else any other time.'

'There is that.'

'It does all sound very fishy.'

'It's just an unmarked car, guv, so I can follow up on a lead.'

Noble nodding, says –

'I reckon our mob will want to know if it *is* arson, it helps with the crowd control element of it all.'

'What do you mean?'

'Papers are out and delivered every fucking day, son. The Metropolitan Police have basically guaranteed that. Any excuse to break heads for an actual crime and the policy, the position, *unofficially*, of course, justifies itself, know what I mean? Circular.'

'I do know what you mean.'

One day, Parker thinks, this News Inc. is really going to owe the Met –

'I'll see what I can swing, all right?'

'Thanks, guv.'

Parker considers Noble. He looks well, he thinks. Happy, relaxed, *content.*

No doubt this has a lot to do with his domestic situation, shacked up with the former head waitress of the dining establishment in which they now sit.

Other than no Lea, it hasn't changed much. New owners, apparently, didn't fancy forking out for a facelift so did the opposite – stripped the walls of all adornments of the previous regime (Turkish) and turned it back into a proper old-school English caff, which is, in fact, what it's called:

PROPER OLD SCHOOL CAFF

Run by two young blokes, yuppies, Parker thinks, or used to be.

The bacon sandwiches and the cups of tea taste exactly the same.

What Parker's really wondering about Noble is what it is exactly that he really *does* anymore. Couple of years ago, he was *involved*, he was on the street. Yes, he ran Parker, but he was also on the sniff for the iffy mob in Stoke Newington.

Now, that 'case' seems to be on the back burner. Every time Parker seems to be making any progress – Trevor, for one – Noble tells him his – Parker's – priorities now lie elsewhere.

Parker doesn't know exactly how the SDS structure works – which is entirely the point.

Looking at Noble now – smartly cut jacket, pressed white shirt, *chinos* – he thinks what's happened is Noble's gone admin –

Desk jockey.

Noble says, 'This in you've got, your bird –' Parker bridles at that, shuts the feeling down, kyboshes it – 'she'll be able to tell you all about the Roach Family Support Committee inquiry, I expect.'

Parker's thinking quite likely, yes.

After the official coroner's inquest into Colin Roach's death delivered an 8–2 verdict of suicide, the family decided to pursue their own independent investigation into Colin's death and Hackney policing more generally.

'What exactly do you need, guv?'

'Match report, state of play, that sort of thing.'

Parker nods. What he doesn't say:

We could use what they're using to help incriminate Stoke Newington's finest –

He does say, 'I gather some of the stuff they've been turning up is not dissimilar to some of the stuff we already have.'

'Yeah, sweet, makes sense,' Noble says vaguely. 'A sense of where they are is what we want, yeah, maybe a timeline.'

Parker nods. He trusts Noble, he knows Noble has Parker's best interests at heart, yet –

That trust can only get you so far given a hefty part of it is keeping yourself in the dark. Accepting that you're very much in a best-foot-forward, one-step-at-a-time type scenario.

Parker's essential dilemma:

Does Noble want this intelligence to further their cause together, the *unofficial* one, to expose corruption and malpractice in the Stoke

Newington police, or does he want it 'cos his senior officer wants it for his senior officer?

Parker's problem, of course, is that he'll never know.

'Otherwise?' Noble asks.

'We're golden.'

Noble nods. 'Keep everything quiet for a little while, *everything*, know what I mean? Like carry on as per for a few weeks, at least.'

Parker nods.

'Sweet,' Noble says. 'I'll get this –' meaning the cups of tea and the bacon sandwiches – 'have a good weekend. Take a couple of days off.'

So Parker decides he will go to the concert and Carolyn tells him about their 'laminates' and here he is with a cold lager in a plastic cup, Carolyn's arms around his neck, the pair of them about to be introduced to Paul Weller.

'Cracking number,' Parker tells Paul Weller.

'I know, mate,' Paul Weller winks.

Parker nods, raises his plastic. 'Cheers,' he says.

He's got his sunglasses on and he's keeping an eye on the redhead, his *colleague*, if he's on the square about it, not that they'll be talking shop any time soon.

She's got Shaun in her ear about the camera, it looks like, and Parker lets *his* ear drift, and he hears, 'I'll bring the ones you took up to you in a few days, after they're developed.'

'Developed?'

And then she's into a technical description that he chooses not to follow.

He flinches a little at the intimacy.

What she does for Noble has nothing to do with Parker, but still, it feels a little off, a little close.

Shaun is Carolyn's cousin, so that's that, in Parker's eyes, he's family.

And, yes, Suzi was around in Stoke Newington, but any connection with his world, this world he hides, this world he buries every day, has to bury to get through it, to be *in* it, makes his blood freeze, his stomach hollow –

Carolyn whispers in his ear, 'Don't be too jealous with all these pop stars running around.'

She points as Maxi Priest saunters by, whistling.

Parker grins. 'I got any reason to be, darling?'

Carolyn gives him a soppy look, a sloppy kiss. 'You're my hero, I don't need anyone else.'

Parker examines his watch. 'I do want to see Roddy Frame, maybe out front?'

Then Suzi's standing next to them, introducing her bloke, Keith, and she says, 'So you two are *living* together now, I hear.'

Parker smiles – thin. He thinks *I should have bloody known* –

And Carolyn says something, and they all laugh, and Keith goes, 'Living in sin, eh, can't beat it.'

'She's one in a million,' Parker says. 'Most days, I can't believe my luck.'

But he sees Suzi weighing this and he sees her thinking, thinking *something*, something working away up there, and he can see, too, how friendly she's got with Carolyn, and he wonders if she might have said something to Noble that maybe Parker should have said, pre-empt, explain why –

So he does what he always does when this happens, when he feels empty and tight, his blood cold, his head light –

'How long you been with The Style Council, Keith?'


*A rare weekend at home.*

*It's a relief, the time you do get at home, a respite –*

*So rare are they, these weekends, they're an actual pleasure, tangible, you can really feel it, this pleasure, touch it, let it wrap you up and wear it –*

*Somewhat the opposite of what you hear other husbands and fathers harping on about her indoors and the ball and chain, the childcare and the money, always on about the bloody money, as if that's what family is, simply, a drain on one's resources.*

*It's safe, too, calming.*

*Your house is entirely legit, bought with legitimate income from the garages and showrooms you own in Dagenham, all above board, your two sons privately educated at a decent spot, not too uppity, fees paid thanks to a number of legitimate business interests, all traceable, you've made sure of that.*

*Very little that isn't legit, now.*

*Nothing at all that's* purely *illegal in the proper sense of the term, legally speaking –*

*You can't run away from your past, but out here in a village near Colchester you can pretend for a couple of days.*

*Then Terry calls and tells you that journalist, Geraint something, Welsh bloke, is sniffing around again and they think he and a few others are sniffing out a council flat on the manor and what to do.*

*What to do?*

*'For now,' you tell Terry. 'Nothing. Keep an eye, that's all.'*

*You're not having your weekend ruined, no way, not this one.*

Jon drives home in the purple light of the early night-time, north, over the river on Battersea Bridge, up the King's Road, through the Knightsbridge lights, Hyde Park corner and Piccadilly, Clerkenwell and Shoreditch, Dalston and Clapton, the boy asleep in the back, clutching his programme, thrilled by the day out, The Style Council's surprise appearance, David Grant and Sade, Sting and Elvis Costello, didn't stay for Big Audio Dynamite, which Jon wasn't chuffed about, but it was a bit late, and the boy was looking woozy from the sun and the excitement of it all, and Jon's flushed and worn out, dog-tired in the right way, never happier, and he parks outside their home on Mildenhall Road and carries the boy inside, he still can, up the stairs and into his bedroom, and Jackie's waiting, and she kisses them both, eases off the boy's shoes and socks, strokes his head as he murmurs and smiles, Jon watching from the doorway, never happier, into Lizzie's room to kiss her softly on the cheek, and downstairs he says to Jackie, 'I hope your day was half as good as ours,' and she smiles and tells him he's a silly bugger and she's glad he's home.

Midnight and Suzi and Keith's is in, if not full, then semi-swing.

Backstage at the festival was the usual liveliness, but the Sting / Peter Gabriel crowd meant it was never in any danger of descending into all-out, riotous hedonism.

They left at nine-ish with a small crew – usual suspects – chasing a good time, a stop-off in a Battersea dive bar for a few and provisions, then taxis back to theirs –

The living room is basically eight or nine people hovering over the coffee table as Keith chops out lines and holds court –

Suzi in the doorway, watching, thinking –

*Again?*

She reckons she knows about half the crowd, scenesters and hangers-on, at least one other sound man, at least one other journo –

'Oh, have a listen here,' Keith is saying, 'the *growl* of the opening riff is something else!'

'Growl!' someone yells. 'Turn it in.'

'Turn it up?'

'Turn it in, Keith, you goon!'

Keith, when 'partying' back at theirs, is wont to put on music that he himself has some professional connection with, and to point out – with words like growl, or dirt, or bottom – certain aspects of the production.

Given the day's work, they're in a Style Council mood.

Suzi listens as the intro to 'Homebreakers' – growl and all – comes on. Mick Talbot singing if you can't get work where you're from, then look somewhere else –

'It's that Tebbit line,' Keith's explaining. 'You can't find a job then get on your bike and find one—'

Someone on about Wapping down the road, the dismantling of unions, Mick Talbot's old man might be a printworker –

Suzi wondering where *her* home town might be, if it's *here* –

Love never put dinner on the table.

Someone saying something about the Tories and how the turnout today will show them –

Suzi slips into the kitchen, glass of water from the tap, thinks –

When has it ever before?

She did a good thing today, Suzi reflects. The kids had a ball, really felt part of something, *loved* the whole access-all-areas element –

Felt recognised, *seen*.

Suzi's proud of what she did, of what Carolyn said to her, told her what she's doing is right, is *good* –

She's resolved, Suzi, to do more.

She'll start by taking those photos up for that kid Shaun.

She watches her living room talking to itself, house prices and designer drugs, and she withdraws to her bedroom with her camera, starts prepping the film.

*Home.*

And Parker thinks this really is home and Carolyn puts on a record.

It's been something, parlaying with the in-crowd –

'Really living it up today, eh, darling?' Parker says.

Carolyn in the kitchen making them a nightcap, laughing –

'Sting seemed really pleased to see me!'

'What about Sade, eh? Killer.'

Carolyn hands Parker his drink –

'She was *very* nice, I must say.'

'She *was* very nice.' Parker points at the speakers. 'What's this then?'

'Style Council, you wally!'

'It's not Weller singing though, is it?'

'It is not. It's the other one.'

Parker, thoughtful, nods. He listens to the words –

Carolyn says, 'Suzi told me it's about union politics.'

'Oh, very sexy, these pop stars.'

Thinking, this friendship is not something I'm wild about, not something I want to encourage any further, though the redhead might well be thinking the same thing, and maybe that's Noble's talent, everyone's got everything to lose –

Though he doesn't yet know where I now live, Parker thinks.

Carolyn flicks her eyebrows at the stereo. Parker hears something about thirty years on just the one firm, now it's thirteen months redundant –

'Could be about your dad,' Carolyn says.

Parker says nothing. Instead, he smiles, says, 'How about a quick role play?'

Carolyn grins. 'You be Sting and I'll be Sade.'

'I'm your man, Roxanne,' he says. He indicates his lap. 'All aboard.'

'Your love is king, hero.'

And as Carolyn knots her thighs around his waist, Parker smiles at the obvious joke that Sting used to be in The Police.


Mrs Thatcher reads a note about the concert on Clapham Common.

Numbers, estimates, how many were there –

Between 150,00 and 250,000, it seems.

She thinks not many then.

It's interesting timing, of course, to stand up for Namibia and South Africa, to call for the freeing of Nelson Mandela, to oppose apartheid.

The European Council Meeting in The Hague on Thursday and Friday was somewhat dominated – and divided – by the question of possible sanctions against South Africa. West Germany and Portugal stand with Great Britain opposed to their use.

She reflects on the to and fro of it, the statement; it is somewhat ambiguous, she thinks now, plenty of wriggle room:

In the next three months the Community will enter into consultations with the other industrialised countries on further measures which might be needed. These would include the possible ban on new investments, the import of coal, iron, steel and gold coins from South Africa.

Sir Geoffrey making it clear that a visit to Africa is on the menu 'in a further effort to establish conditions in which the necessary dialogue can commence', nicely put, if fairly meaningless, she says out loud.

Shuffling past on his way for a sit, at Sir Geoffrey's name, Denis mutters something about Sir Geoffrey Howe on earth did he get a job –

'A fair question, Margaret,' he adds, but she ignores him, as she tends to, at night-time, anyway, when he's at his most blocked up and acerbic, poor Denis.

In her own press conference, Mrs Thatcher clarified that any failure of this dialogue with South Africa did not automatically mean sanctions were to follow.

In *The Times*, bloody Mitterrand is quoted, saying, unhelpfully, that 'no member state will block the package of measures if the peace mission is considered a failure'.

Will today's events have any traction? Did Live Aid?

She's been reading intelligence on this Red Wedge, and it doesn't sound too threatening, kids will always go to pop concerts and politicians will always put them off voting for them if they try to be a part of that scene.

Never fails to fail, that routine.

Kinnock and the rest, they're hardly an ad man's dream.

Tainted by union backing yet trying to shrug that association will only send more voters my way, she thinks.

Miners, now a deregulated press not far behind.

Fortress Wapping, they're saying.

She's impartial, of course, except she's not, and the police have been very helpful, and here she sits with her copy of *The Times* –

*He* said to her, not long ago, that the unions have a noose round the neck of the industry and they've pulled it very tight.

Well, the noose has been well and truly slipped, she thinks.

It can't go on much longer, this strike, surely, given its utter lack of success.

An election will have to wait. Let the strike collapse, prey on the disillusionment.


*Shaun*: To be fair, I never knew who Nelson Mandela was before and I never knew that all these people cared about what was happening over there in South Africa, and I never knew what apartheid was, not properly, and I definitely never stood on a stage before, and I never took a photo of some brother called Paul Weller before neither.

It was a really good day.

There was a voice in my head saying what Anton would be saying, but you hear the music and it sort of went away, that voice, floated off, yeah, that's exactly what happened.

I mean, you do something or you do nothing, I suppose.

# PART FOUR
# *Red menace*

September 1986–January 1987

# 1

## Firm in a firm

September–October 1986

*Ayeleen*: It's a quiet afternoon at the cafe, which is good as I've got home-work, and already the new school year feels like it might be, well, I don't know yet, but it's a bit more grown-up, and that on its own is weird.

Lauren's at the corner table using my maths homework as a guide, she says, I'm not copying the *answers*, just checking your *working*.

'Oh, look, Leen,' she keeps saying, 'we've got another one right.'

It's called teamwork, we're *collaborating*, to use a new word they're saying a lot at school. She's better at English and history, things like that, and I'm better at maths and science. We help each other.

It makes the workload a bit easier when you can help each other. A bit more fun, too.

'You want that general studies essay, Leenie? I did it at lunch.'

'Yeah, thanks.'

'All right, I'll leave it on the table.'

I look at the New Country Off-Licence and Foodstore, trying to work out what's going on over there. They never closed after that shooting or nothing like that, which was a funny one, and even Mesut's stopped pretending he knows what's happened.

All I can tell is that it's still there, the same owner is in and out, the same boys doing the deliveries, the same girls working inside, but it's weird, there never seems to be any customers at all, at least never when I'm looking.

'Will you leave off that place over the road, Leenie, I mean, give it a rest, really.'

I shake my head. 'I'm just staring out the window.'

'Well stare the other way then.'

'How am I supposed to do that?'

'You can see your new mosque, can't you? Focus on that. It'll be good for you, too. Get your prayers in early and whatnot.'

'You're so funny.'

'I'm just looking out for your soul and that, you know.'

'So funny. I mean look at that girl –' I'm pointing – 'she's in there all day, trotting about, rearranging the shelves, never does anything else.'

'Tell you what,' Lauren says, 'I'll mind the cafe and you go over there and ask her. She looks nice.'

'I don't know her.'

'Like I said, she looks friendly.'

'It'd be weird.'

'You're weird.'

'I'm not going to.'

'Well then.'

I turn away from the window, face Lauren.

'Here,' she says. She pushes my maths book across the table. 'Ta.'

I pick up her essay with a little flourish. 'And thank you.'

The bell rings as the door opens, and I smile and look up expecting a customer, but it's my uncle.

'Ladies,' he grins, arms open. 'A lovely surprise.'

'Leenie always works this shift, Mr Ahmet.'

'And once again your humour, Lauren. Lovely it is, yes, but *never* a surprise.'

'Shall I get you something to drink, Uncle?'

'You know,' he says, 'I'll try that new water we've just got in stock.' His own little flourish, where I get it from, Lauren says. 'Sparkling.'

'You mean Perrier?'

'The green bottle, heavy.'

Lauren says, 'You becoming a yuppie, Mr Ahmet?'

'In business, Lauren, it's important to know what it is that the customer wants.' He jabs at the air. 'And why!'

'Makes sense.' Lauren sniffs. 'That why you have a lamb kebab every time I'm here then?'

'Never a surprise, Lauren, never a surprise!'

I hand him his drink. 'Ice in the glass and a slice of lemon, just like you told me.'

He opens the bottle, which makes a fizzing sound, but doesn't spill over. He pours, weighs the bottle in his hand.

'These are well built,' he says. 'It's a satisfying product, feels very sophisticated. You can really taste it, too. Water! Who knew!'

'Well, the French did for a start,' Lauren mutters.

Uncle ignores her.

Outside, I see a car park right in front of the New Country and two men in leather jackets and jeans get out and go in.

Uncle sees it, too, and joins me at the window. He smiles at me, sips his drink.

'How's school?'

'You know, all right.'

'We're very proud of you, Ayeleen.'

Lauren coughs.

'You too, Lauren.'

The two men come back out the shop, both of them carrying sports bags.

Looking out at them, Uncle says to himself, 'Must be the new people then.'

As they get in the car, they stop and nod over at us, point, one of them says something and the other one laughs. They give Uncle the thumbs up and a sort of salute, like a wave, and they're off.

Uncle raises a hand, but they don't see it and he pulls it down again, a bit embarrassed, I think.

'Who was that?' I ask.

Uncle shakes his head quietly, makes a gesture with his hand like, it's nothing.

'Locals, you know,' is all he'll say. 'Look at the books with me?'

I nod. 'You all right if we go in the back for a bit?' I ask Lauren.

'I reckon I can manage.'

We leave her to it and go through to the office, look at the stocklist, compare it with sales, spend about half an hour on it, all pretty simple and easy, and he doesn't say anything else about the men across the road, and I think about how I never gave a bag again to no one after that one time a couple of years ago, except for that nice black boy who comes, but he's picking up from his cousin or something – anyway, it's not the same thing, is it – and is that because Uncle won't let me or is there maybe another reason, but I don't say anything, course I don't.

*You've got where you are thanks to an understanding of how to adapt and develop an existing model for the greater good of the business, looking beyond the usual preoccupation in the game for short-term dividend.*

*The model began as your basic protection package as offered by hardmen for decades, perhaps centuries. You did the rounds like any other up-and-comer, but you were fair to those you were collecting off of and noticed something: kindness buys loyalty.*

*This led to the first iteration of your adjustments to the model.*

*One thing the firm never lacked was cash, ready money. A decent lump sum – but not eye-watering by any means – gets you a mortgage from any number of providers. If that sum is substantial enough, then the monthly payments can remain relatively low.*

*So, with the firm's cash, a mortgage is secured on a pub, say, or a shop, a gym, a garage, a business premises, and on this premises you install a willing worker: what you're saying is, here, have a pub.*

*The willing worker takes on the business, from which mortgage payments are made, as well as a fixed amount to the firm. Any other profit stays with a willing worker. Given this chap hasn't had to fork out a deposit, this is a fanciable and incentivising opportunity.*

*And it's legit, basically.*

*One key alteration to existing practices was the use of offshore shell companies in the acquisition of the mortgage, thereby hiding the provenance of the cash used to make that acquisition.*

*Buying mortgages with laundered money.*

*That was the key principle: we own the mortgage, it doesn't matter if the business is a restaurant or a dirty bookshop, that's our loyal proprietor's problem.*

*Regular money and lots of it and everyone happy. And, of course, the more of it that's made legitimately, the more goes back in, and in a few years the ratio of legal to questionable earnings has changed significantly.*

*And the fail-safe element: a proprietor defaults, and he is replaced, simple as that. And if anyone tries any funny business, well, there are plenty of hardmen more than happy to keep their hands in, as it were.*

*Which connects to your second innovation.*

*The narrative generally runs one of two ways: hard men trying to go straight by using the ill-gotten gains of their colourful past; hard men as career criminals who have no intention of going straight and, in fact, enjoy robbery and extortion and tearing about the place in flash clobber and flasher cars.*

*Career criminals, though, much like civilians, do also enjoy their job security.*

*So, what you do is you manage, from a distance, using the firm's infra-structure, those career criminals, as well as providing a home for those hard men looking to go straight.*

*The logic is this:*

*Heavy crime, serious crime – your armed robbery, drugs, porn, extor-tion, racketeering and so on – is never going to go away, and if you don't manage it, indeed actively participate in it (at a distance) then someone else will, and that threatens the property and business element on which your legitimacy and position of civic influence are based.*

*And this is how you rose: an understanding of how to balance and coordinate these seemingly disparate interests and priorities.*

*Man management.*

*And the timing was perfect for these innovations:*

*The docks.*

*Or, more pertinently, the end of the docks as a commercial enterprise, both legally speaking and otherwise.*

*The firm needed a new focus. And, carefully, subtly, you brought it:*

*Man management.*

*Terry comes in with news, disturbing your nostalgic reverie, your taking of stock, brought on by the time of year, beginning of school, you think, a new year always does it, September is how you've always measured the beginnings of your life, your lives.*

*'That journo I mentioned again a few months back.'*

*You nod. 'Welsh bloke.'*

*'We've found him.'*

*'OK. Where?'*

*'He and a few others holed up in one of the flats we're looking at.'*

*'Doing what?'*

*'Something political. Looks like unions.'*

*You nod. 'Which estate?'*

*'Cable Street.'*

*Very close to the action. This is interesting.*

*'Keep an eye on it, do nothing, leave it with me,' you say.*

*Terry nods.*

*As he always does.*

*And he does leave it with you, course he does.*

*And a little while later, out you go, all alone, breathing in the air –*

*Wapping stinks –*

*That was your first thought, twenty or so years ago, early sixties, down near the docks, a Canning Town teenager on the make, the day you estab-lished yourself with the firm, your credentials, just a big kid with a knife –*

*Another time, it was. Innocent, a sort of dirty glamour.*

*Some days you leave your office, your yard, and you walk the streets, you smell the air, you look at the area with fresh eyes, you think about the past, too, that autumnal reverie, the end of summer, all that.*

*You arrange to meet your contact, your contact for him, and you do this outside, on the same streets, and you do this with no one else in attend-ance, not even Terry.*

*Why?*

*Because you think you know what your contact will do with the infor-mation you are set to give him, information about that journo and, spe-cifically, where he's now holed up.*

*An understanding of how to balance and coordinate seemingly dispar-*
*ate interests and priorities.*

*What you think will happen is that your contact will tell* him *this, and*
*then* he *will inform the police in order to have the journo arrested. You*
*think that'd be the cleanest way to handle it. But it's not in your business*
*remit to grass, regardless of the whys and wherefores, so, here you are,*
*alone.*

*Man management.*

*Here you are alone, on the streets, the streets where you first made your*
*name.*

*You look now out at the river, its murk and throb, its sludge and heft –*

*Your contact appears. 'Make it quick,' he says.*

*'I was just thinking about something,' you tell him.*

*'What?' he says.*

*'The past.'*

*'What's that then?'*

*'How it changes every day.'*

*'Yes, very clever.'*

*'I was thinking about how the punishment should fit the crime.'*

*'All right,' says your contact. 'I won't disagree.'*

*'It usually does,' you say. 'Fit the crime, I mean.'*

*'Oh, I know that.' Your contact rolls his shoulders. 'Are you going to get*
*to the point then?'*

*You nod. You hand him a piece of paper. On it, an address. An estate*
*on Cable Street. A second-floor, low-rise council flat –*

*'That journalist,' you say. 'You'll remember him,* Socialist Worker.*'*

*'We do remember him.'*

*'That's where he is. What I've heard, there's something going on in*
*there, something your lot'll want stopping.'*

*He's nodding, your contact.*

*'That address,' you tell him. 'It's of interest, to us.'*

*'Understood.'*

*'You've got a week,' you tell him.*

'Right.'

'Then we do what we have to do.'

'A week.'

'It's reasonable, given the circumstances. And besides, you owe me.'

'For what?'

'The name for turning, LDDG. You never provided one.'

'We didn't need to.'

'You reckon?'

'You've got everything you need already.'

'Not quite.'

'What do you give the man who has everything?' He's laughing, your contact.

'A week.'

There's no argument there.


*Bethnal Green Town Hall.*

About a week after he dropped off his file and asked Jon for that favour, Chick rang Jon and said, 'Second thoughts, don't bother. Put the file somewhere safe, and we'll pretend we never had the conversation.'

'What conversation?'

'That's the spirit!'

And Jon hasn't thought much about it since.

It crosses his mind today as he's looking at the papers he got back from the Land Registry on council home Right to Buy purchase registrations, and he wonders if they've registered Grandad Ray's place yet, or whether they even intend to.

It took a couple of months to get the appointment, and the copies another few weeks –

As that stuffy clerk explained wittily, winking at Jon: 'If you don't know what you want, we'll give you what we've got!'

Which amounted to a list of council home Right to Buy purchase registrations in the tri-borough area of Hackney, Tower Hamlets and Newham.

Problem is, they're registered by name, not location.

Examining what he has in front of him now, without the name of the purchaser, it's hard to imagine how he'd find a flat registration that he might know about, let alone something he's not sure he's even looking for.

And what *is* he even looking for? A pattern, he thinks, some sort of pattern.

And after a couple of hours looking, he finds one.

Two estates in the Tower Hamlets area have multiple registrations, and by multiple, Jon sees it's in the dozens.

Nowhere else has anything like that sort of uptake.

One of these estates is on Cable Street in Wapping, the other a little further east, just past the Shadwell Basin.

What's interesting is not simply the relatively high number of registrations, but the fact that while most other purchase registrations pertain to houses, in these two instances it is flats that have been bought.

The clerk himself, not one to pass non-objective judgement on anything, Jon remembers, did indicate – his words – that it was council houses rather than flats that were mostly purchased in the initial flurry after the policy went live.

'But if you've got a flat in the right location,' he said, 'the wise move would be to take up Mrs Thatcher's invitation.'

Jon's not sure what the point is about this pattern he's found – it could be entirely coincidental, it could be a domino effect, someone bought and then others in the same situation followed – but the fact of what Chick is doing for Grandad Ray, and the possibilities that are built into that, nag at Jon.

A couple of days after looking through the Land Registry papers, Jon's sitting in a planning committee meeting that involves an application in the Shadwell Basin from a development conglomerate including the London Docklands Development Group, an American bank, and an unnamed third-party syndicate.

It's when Merv Michaels says, 'Land previously believed to have been acquired by the LDDG is now understood to have in fact been under the ownership of this unnamed third-party syndicate via the well-established principle of adverse possession, and as a result the planning application involves this three-way engagement,' that Jon's ears prick up.

He says, 'Legally, the adverse possessor only becomes the property's new owner if the property's previous owner does not exercise their right to recover their property.'

Merv nods. 'There has been no attempt to exercise that right.'

Jon nods. 'If I may. Adverse possession is defined by the ability to prove occupation of land. To have occupied land *without permission*.'

'Exactly,' Merv says.

'But the previous owner is the LDDG—'

'The land is *believed* to have been acquired by—'

'But they're collaborating in the planning application—'

'A key idea in adverse possession, Jon, as I'm sure you know,' Merv smiles, 'is that it doesn't matter *why* the original owner does not exercise their right to recovery.' Merv opens his palms, makes a gesture as balancing scales, raises an eyebrow. 'Hence and therefore,' he says.

'The company name,' Jon says, 'this third party?'

'Is protected by a standard confidentiality agreement, details in the application.'

Jon thinks, very few details.

Not long after this, Jon gets hold of planning applications that are in some way reliant on the principle of adverse possession and finds that the assumption of adverse possession as a right to ownership in the Docklands area exists in a higher than average number of instances.

Company names protected by standard confidentiality agreements.

Besides, as Jon digs around in these planning applications, he finds a good deal of investment in the Docklands development – or associated land projects – by multiple companies acting as syndicates in which the actual spread of interest and ownership is complicated by the number of individual or collective holdings within each company, or syndicate.

Jon understands that the green lighting of all this practice is, too, explicitly stated within the establishment of the London Docklands Development Group, and in part *green-lit* by Jon's council role.

And the rub here, Jon thinks, is that the London Docklands Development Group's financing is maintained, in large part, by the proceeds of land disposal, regardless of the identity – or, indeed, the anonymity – of the company or companies that have paid for the land.

It's a very circular situation.

Then there's the right-wing media's favourable analysis of the regeneration of the area, which helps public opinion. And, of course, the LDDG's founder is the Secretary of State for the Environment, so, by extension, has the explicit support of Mrs Thatcher's government.

What tickles Jon is that Labour-controlled councils are technically sidestepped, but owing to their actual control of certain land, complicit in its sale to outside interests, undermining those of their residents.

What Jon isn't clear on, is why. What's the councils' motivation?

And this question drives Jon to dig deeper, into council records and then at Companies House and then again at the Land Registry, and he finds that a company called Excalibur has issued bearer instruments, via offshore nominee directors, to enable the anonymous investment of approximately £10 million in buildings in the Docklands area. Jon smiles grimly at the inevitability of *that* name, and it being a subsidiary of Compliance Ltd.

Ten million is a lot of anonymous money to come from *somewhere*.

Jon goes back through his own files to have another look at Compliance Ltd licensed buildings, and that's when the pattern he's found in the Right to Buy records clicks –

It's the same area, the same area where the printing press has moved to, the same area that is being flooded with money from anonymous investors, and he thinks:

Can that really be a coincidence?

The first time Suzi goes up to Broadwater Farm to give Shaun the photographs he took, he's not at the Youth Association, Carolyn hasn't seen him and neither has anyone else, and Suzi shrugs and thinks nothing of it.

A couple of weeks later she tries again. Same result.

A week or so after *that*, same thing.

Suzi's always enjoyed that Freudian maxim that madness is doing the same thing again and again and expecting a different outcome, so she places the developed photographs – colour versions, black-and-white – alongside the negatives in a padded envelope and decides to simply keep them in her bag and wait patiently for the next opportunity.

'I can drop them off with my gran if you like,' Carolyn offers.

But Suzi tells her thanks all the same, but I'd like to do it personally, have a word with him, tell him why he's done a good job, make sense?

Carolyn nods. 'It does. I haven't seen him for a while, come to think of it,' she says.

Though she doesn't look especially perplexed by the comment and Suzi just assumes family, you know.

Another month passes and Suzi begins to notice looks among some of the other kids who were backstage at Clapham Common whenever she asks after Shaun.

You'd have to be looking to spot it, but they close ranks, consider the question, present a united front of oh he's fine, O levels, you know, all that, lot of homework, that sort of thing, I'll tell him you're looking for him.

Suzi's up there almost every week and that's largely thanks to Carolyn, so she wants to keep her onside and not thinking about where's your cousin then, eh, so Suzi doesn't push it, aware that it's by Carolyn's grace she's where she is, that's that, really.

She starts to arrive at the Youth Association first thing in the morning, and then at around four in the afternoon to try and catch Shaun either side of his apparently very full days at school.

It's by now several days a week and Carolyn, for one, notices.

'Your bed on fire, is it?' Carolyn says. 'You up here this early so often.'

Suzi smiles, indicates the paperwork on the table she always uses as

a desk. 'There's a lot to document, to type up,' she says. 'You know that.'
To be fair, it is true.

They're gathering documents and paperwork to publish a report of the independent inquiry into the disturbances of 1985 at the Broadwater Farm Estate, to give it its full title, and it's all hands on deck, Lord Gifford QC, leading the panel, Suzi's acquaintance Dorothy Kuya involved, a couple of religious leaders and a couple of academics, too –

Suzi is about the only person connected to the Youth Association who can type, let alone who has a typewriter, and she's brought her fancy electronic machine up from home and is banging out pages of notes, pages of testimonies, pages of statements, all about how residents of the estate have been treated – mistreated – by the police.

All about what the police have been taking from people's homes when inside them on search warrants:

6.25 Bagfuls of personal possessions were removed from many homes: including complete wardrobes of clothes, contents of food cupboards, or kitchen knives, television and stereo equipment, personal diaries and photographs. People needed emergency assistance from Social Security because they were literally without anything to wear ... Were the searches and seizures normal for a serious inquiry, or were they also part of a process of intimidation?

The way in which the rights of juveniles have been breached, ignored, you name it:

6.35 The case was of a 15-year-old boy arrested as a suspect for murder and held in the police station for two-and-a-half days. He was finally released at a police station miles away from Tottenham without any shoes on.

Suzi transcribes the story of Howard Kerr, which was reported in the *Daily Mirror* on 20 March 1986. Seventeen years old, in custody for three days. Forbidden to see a solicitor. Forbidden to talk to family. Howard Kerr who claimed that on the night of the riots, he was in Windsor.

And yet, he signed:

6.38 A 50 page 'confession' to taking part in the riots, naming 20 other 'participants', describing a 'factory' of petrol bombs, and claiming to have seen the murder of the police officer. But later it was established from independent evidence that he was in Windsor that evening, and the prosecution dropped all charges against him.

'I was frightened, so I told them what I thought they wanted to know.'

Suzi types this up quickly and Carolyn takes the pages and files them, and Suzi's started noticing that whenever some of the younger lot are in Carolyn is furtively seeking them out and asking questions. She can't hear what's being said, Suzi, and that's because Carolyn doesn't want her to.

And each time Suzi gets a minute alone with one of these kids and is about to ask after Shaun, Carolyn appears holding something else for Suzi to type up, saying something like, 'Here's the statement from that social worker I promised.'

And Suzi nods and Suzi types –

In general terms, the situation that many people are living in is so extreme and severe that the overall effect is to make people feel intimidated, fearful and very frightened.

And as Suzi types, Suzi thinks about Shaun.

Suzi thinks about where he is exactly, what he's doing, and she's not sure why it bothers her, him not being around, but those photos and those negatives, those photos and negatives are burning a hole in her bag, and it's been nearly a year now since the uprising, but the estate isn't any more settled, and every evening Suzi's there, around five, just as it's starting to get a little darker, Carolyn offers to walk her to the bus stop, Carolyn's hand gentle on Suzi's back, and Suzi knows she can't say no to that offer, to that instruction, so she doesn't.

'You sure you don't want me to take those photos over to my gran's?' Carolyn asks, most evenings.

And Suzi shakes her head and smiles and says, 'Goodnight.'

Keith's either at home, or he's not –

And either way, Suzi's reading, reading and taking notes, reading and taking notes about transfer requests at the Neighbourhood Office, 90 to 100 new tenants making applications to leave, a list that grows and grows, grows and grows as outside perception of the estate worsens and worsens, as outside perception of the estate means you can't secure financial credit, means the postbox is sealed up, means mail-order firms won't deliver, means TV hire companies won't come, means companies trading on hire purchases refuse outright to deal with people from the estate –

And Suzi types and Suzi types –

Even when I go for a job, and they say where do you live, and I say Broadwater Farm, they look at you totally different.

It was considered unreasonable to ask our teleclub meter collectors to make calls on the estate as this could well lead to possible injuries to our staff who were known to be carrying reasonably large sums of money.

And every few weeks, Suzi tells Noble something about Red Wedge, and most of the time she doesn't even have to make it up it's so prosaic, so *obvious*, and every time Noble tells her the same thing:

'You're doing great, darling.'

And she thinks, it's quid pro quo, and yeah –

Maybe I am doing something right.

Parker got his car.

What he did, in the end, to get it, wasn't strictly by the book –

'You're sure about this?' was all Noble said.

Parker nodding. 'Premeditated down to the brand of matches used to set fire to the place, guv.'

'And you know how exactly?'

'Walkabouts.'

'Remind me about those, would you, Parker, what they are?'

Parker thinks he doesn't sound entirely convinced, Noble, but it's not him that needs convincing.

Parker's not convinced himself about the walkabouts, but he's been on a few more. The pattern is pretty familiar by now: they march about, twenty-odd strong, on prearranged routes, through the alleys and narrow streets of Wapping and Shadwell and Whitechapel, looking for lorries.

Funny thing to be looking for, a lorry: it's either there or it's not. Can't exactly hide, now, can it, Parker thinks as they march about, trudging along those narrow streets and dirty alleys.

Couple of times, towards the end of the afternoon it's happened, they've chanced upon an articulated lorry – and it really was just that, pure chance – and a couple of the heavier lads have thrown stones and bricks, figuring the cunts driving are mercenaries and any danger is theirs, this is war, and all's fair in it –

Thing was the wire-mesh screens covering the windows: no pasarán.

Your stones, your rocks, your bricks: they shall not pass.

They bounced straight back, and Parker and one or two others had to take cover that first time. On subsequent occasions, Parker drifted as far from the action as he could: he didn't want to throw stones and he didn't want to get hit by any, neither.

One result was that the police delayed the departure of the lorries. After that happened, there wasn't much to do, except keep doing it: the threat of violence, of stone-throwing, being as effective as the actual throwing of stones. Which was ineffective, anyway, really, what with the wire-mesh screens. But stones being stones (and rocks being rocks and bricks being bricks) there is a perceived threat: they do hurt if they hit you, they can smash things. As Parker put it one walkabout: it's concrete, our threat, after all.

Another result was increased attention from the Old Bill. Busloads of head-breakers in formation, splitting up the walkabout groups or escorting them on their routes. Though, Parker quickly realised, the police might have been flanking the walkabout but they were also following: only a few days before, Parker and his mob took them on a four-hour tour of those narrow streets and dirty alleys, finishing up back at the plant at Wapping, cheered on by the main striking protest of the day, pushing two o'clock in the morning and the Old Bill knackered and feeling stupid –

Not sure much more than that was achieved.

Something he did find out, spending more time with the same crew: they weren't all looking for trouble, they didn't all have an agenda, political or otherwise. A good number were ordinary men and women, ordinary men and women with kids at home, elders with dodgy knees and dodgy hips and tired feet, ordinary people trying to do something to protect their ordinary jobs and ordinary lives because no other cunt was doing nothing about it.

Parker tells Noble all this and Noble chews it over.

'Sounds like a stalemate,' he says.

'Yeah,' Parker says. 'All quiet on the eastern front.'

Noble snorts. He stirs his tea, looks off into the middle distance, or somewhere else, anyway. He says, 'You wonder what we're doing really.'

'Tell me about it.'

'I mean, you're observing an event unfold to an inevitable ending, an ending we already know.'

'You mean you know the score, so why bother.'

'Something like that.'

'Just like watching *Match of the Day*.'

Noble laughs.

'So let's do something about it, guv.'

Noble nodding –

'I *know* who we can do for that arson.'

'We can't do anyone with your evidence, son, you know that too?'

'Course I do, guv. You know what I mean.' Parker presses his point. 'And it's not just the arson, it's the political side. You give me the car and I give you the address of that flat.'

Noble smiles at this, shakes his head –

'Something I said, guv?'

'I think we'll stick to the arson, son. We've got an address for that flat.'

'You what?'

'Word from above.'

Parker says nothing. What he hasn't told Noble –

He hasn't seen another van anywhere near that warehouse again.

Parker's quite aware that he hasn't mentioned this –

Noble says, 'How many times you seen them then? What's the count?'

Meaning, of course: vans and that warehouse.

Parker lies. 'Half a dozen. Likely different vans, of course.'

Noble nodding –

'Listen,' he says. 'I think I can swing the car if you do one thing for me.'

'Course.'

'Here's the address of that flat. You get over there and find out exactly what's what. All we need is to know if there's someone there and the lay of the land. Nothing too detailed, right? Don't get *involved* if you get my drift.'

'Right-oh.'

'You've got a few days, son, that's all. A week, tops.'

'It's a deal.'

'Yeah,' Noble says. 'You could say that.'

So next chance he gets, Parker gets over to this council flat.

Cable Street address: a low-rise, double-level, horseshoe-shaped affair, the flats spread over two floors, and his flat in one corner at the very top.

It's quiet, he thinks, the estate. He hasn't exactly thought it through.

He checks the map on the edge of it.

He scoots the stairs, floats down the walkway –

It really is very quiet.

All he can hear is the shudder and crunch of the works going on over the back, the Shadwell Basin development. The flats on this side, at this height, will have a cracking view of it, he thinks.

It's very *empty*, too.

Parker's experience of council estates – which is extensive, given he grew up on one – is all the crap left outside the front doors, rusting bikes and dead pot plants, garden furniture and buckets of sand as ashtrays, all that game.

But there's nothing here at all.

No lights in the windows.

He presses his face up to a few of them, and they do appear to be entirely empty.

He knocks on a few doors. No answer.

There's a bit of movement on the floor below and Parker goes down for a shufty.

A couple, pensioners, tugging a pair of shopping caddies, shuffling.

'Need a hand, do you?' he asks.

'Much obliged,' says the bloke.

He points at his wife. Parker takes her caddy, then his.

'You're a nice young man,' says the wife.

'It's a dirty job,' Parker grins. 'Where to?'

The bloke points. Parker nods. As they walk, he gestures above.

'What's the story up there then?' he asks.

'Oh, we don't know about that, son.'

'No?'

The bloke shakes his head. His wife says, 'There were some nice families up there. Lovely people.'

'What happened?'

The bloke shakes his head. 'They left. Sold up, we think. But we don't know.' He shakes his head. 'No, we don't know.'

'All of them?' Parker asks.

The wife, nodding. 'Most of them,' she says. 'We've seen a few people, youngsters, you know, on the stairs. Friendly sorts, quiet, too.'

Parker nods. 'You didn't fancy moving on then?'

'This is where we live,' the bloke says. 'We've lived here all our lives. We ain't going anywhere.' He stops. 'Here we are,' he says.

'What about your neighbours?'

'Floor above,' the wife says. 'Not down here.'

Parker nodding. 'Let me help you get these inside.'

'Much obliged. The kitchen's straight through.'

Parker carries the shopping down the corridor, past the living quarters and into the back kitchen. He looks, quickly, outside. The view down here is considerably less impressive, he thinks, than it must be on the next level up, and the walkway factored in, too. You can't see the building works, which means you can't see the water.

'Would you like a cup of tea?' asks the wife.

'Much obliged,' Parker winks. 'But I better be on my way.'

As he closes the door, he hears, 'Very nice young man.'

Back down the walkway, back up the stairs, bending, twisting, along the walkway again –

Still quiet.

Parker slows down, thinks. He stops outside the flat. It's quiet, but there's light, faint thought it is, coming from inside.

He knocks on the door. He waits. He knocks again –

The door opens a crack, chain on. 'Yeah?' A man's voice, gruff.

'I got a delivery downstairs in my van for you.'

'Yeah?'

'Just checking it's the right address, that's all.'

'We didn't order anything,' the man says.

'Right. You sure?'

Parker thinking: observe, that's all you have to do, look and listen.

Thinking, there's no one else in any of these flats, that's all you need to confirm, that this *is* the address.

'I'm sure. Have a good day, yeah?'

'Bit lonely up here, is it?' he asks. 'Looks like everyone's fucked off.'

The man snorts. 'How we like it. Take care, yeah?'

And he closes the door.

Back downstairs, Parker chooses a wall with a view of the flat, sits on it.

He waits about half an hour. He sees two men arrive, one man leave. A few minutes later, a woman leaves. All of them dressed like lefty trendies dressed like working people. Meaning: that's the flat then.

Job done, Parker thinks.

He needs confirmation, though, and follows the woman at a respectable distance.

She walks past the mural on the side of the town hall, which takes Parker briefly back to his days as a National Front infiltrator, what with its depiction of the Battle of Cable Street, protestors fighting fascists and the police, too, not a new thing that, then, in terms of taking sides –

She turns into Leman Street, goes into the Brown Bear pub –

Parker finds this a little troubling: Leman Street is a CID HQ, and this boozer's got the look of an Old Bill pub about it.

He goes in. At the bar, he sees she's taken a seat in the corner with another woman and a man, papers spread about, *Socialist Worker* –

They look like vendors, Parker thinks, judging by the bags at their feet.

He orders a drink and stays at the bar.

It doesn't take long before a plod comes in. You can spot them a mile off. Another one a moment later, they order their pints and their crisps –

Parker watches them notice his little group, watches them wink –

They don't do nothing, though, and the group don't notice. They haven't realised, he thinks, they haven't worked out this is a police pub.

He finishes his drink, leaves.

He writes Noble a report and files it. Noble says, 'Sweet. That's everything we need, son. You're golden.'

Day or two later and Parker gets his car.

It's not exactly new, his new motor, but it does work.

A brown Ford hatchback with dirty windows.

'Oh good,' Parker says to the bloke who delivers it. 'I ordered camouflage.'

'Just make sure you give it back in the same shit state it's in now.'

Parker says, 'Nice one, Q.'

The bloke grins. 'The ashtray's an ejector seat.'

First thing Parker does is a couple of laps of the Wapping warren, as he's taken to calling it, see how the car handles, cornering and so on.

Radio works, at least. Some joker's left a tape in the stereo:

NOW THAT'S WHAT I CALL MUSIC! 7

Parker pops it in and has to laugh –

Pete Wylie, then Stan Ridgway singing 'Camouflage'.

Chris de Burgh and Genesis, Bowie and Simple Minds.

'When the going gets tough, the tough get going.'

Well, Parker thinks, *quite*. Good old William Ocean, wise man.

He does a couple of drive-bys of the warehouse, thinking this is the tough getting going then.

The tough getting going for Parker is basically all about looking for a parking space.

Pure Hollywood.

He's already scoped the availability: around a dozen spots on one side of the road, opposite the entrance, fifty yards or so upwind, various regulations – resident bays, short-term drop-offs, meters, all that game – and no shortage of traffic wardens.

Nothing at all on the other.

Meaning he can't park it and leave it and there's going to be competition for the few legal places there are.

Thinking Michael Douglas didn't have this issue squiring that blonde all over the place in that film.

Parker knew all this, yet he still reckons the car – the yacht, he's minded to call it, in subtle homage to that film – is worth the favour he's swung from Noble.

Back home, after mooring the yacht then giving his gaff a quick once-over, he waves the cassette at Carolyn.

'Have a listen. Now that's what I call an indictment of our times, is what I call it.'

Carolyn laughs. 'Lie back and think of England.'

Tosses him a tape of her own.

Parker puts it on next morning for the drive south: Anita Baker.

Now that's more like it.

The sleek and sophisticated nature of the music, the effortless soar and swoop of Anita Baker's voice, a neat contrast to the gear-crunching rage it takes to navigate Commercial Road and its surrounding.

Windows down as it's quieter inside. Left leg hard on a sticking clutch. Heater roaring. Dry throat and red eyes. Steam and ice. Choking smog.

He bumps the yacht into a free space after only three laps of the warren. Pulling the handbrake like dropping heavy anchor. Parker fancies another week of this damp weather and the bottom'll rust out and he'll have to be careful not to get his feet wet, as it were. Then he sinks into his seat and he waits and he watches –

He's after a van that matches the description of the one he saw go in but he reckons he'll follow anything that comes out, on balance.

He watches and he waits –

Waits and watches.

Not much goes in and nothing comes out, and Parker spends a few days on the mooring before he thinks he might as well go and knock on the door himself.

But Noble made it clear that ain't an option, he's observing is the condition, so Parker stares out the window and thinks of England.

*You remember:*

*A pimp, cutting an insult into the skin of one of his tarts.*

*His accomplice at knifepoint, a beating, leaving him black and blue in the face, enough for the world to see that he's a liar, a cheat and a no-good whore-botherer –*

*A snide.*

*They were very happy with the result, the firm.*

*You didn't chop him, you made your point, and with some subtlety –*

*They appreciated that. The message was communicated: loud and crystal clear –*

*Things worked out; they always do.*

*That's what they do, things, they work out.*

*Punishment usually fits the crime.*

*All that.*

*Bethnal Green Town Hall.*

Jon's that tired he's fished out Chick's file and is thumbing through it before he realises what he's doing.

Tired enough the words and numbers blur –

He shakes his head. His back teeth feel *loose.* He stands and he stretches, shakes his head again, sure he feels the rattle of something troubling –

Chick's file:

He studies it through a fog –

But when the fog clears and Jon sees quite what's happened to Chick's property development scheme, he thinks, you really must not have had any choice at all, old son.

Jon picks up the phone and gives Merv the Swerve a buzz on the internal line.

He's not there, Merv – he's never there – but Jon leaves a message asking about a couple of commercial properties fringing the Shadwell Basin and backing onto the Cable Street Estate. Mentions, pointedly, the planning application records.

If Jon's hunch is correct, these applications will have Chick's syndicate's name all over them –

But they won't yet have been updated to include the name of the new majority stakeholder in the now restructured ownership consortium:

*Compliance.*

The message might jiggle something free, Jon thinks, just as long as it's not my molars.

She's at it again, Mrs Thatcher, with the *writing*.

Another conference, another speech. They write themselves, these days, she thinks. Well, she writes them herself, which is the same thing.

She considers the fact that the Labour conference of the week before does somewhat leave her with an open goal, as Denis put it.

'They'll never leave you on the ropes, gasping, when you always have the last word, Margaret,' he said.

She told him not to mix his metaphors.

'Another rule to remember,' he grumbled at that.

He's right, though, she thinks. Every week at PMQs it's the same: he who laughs last, laughs loudest.

He meaning she, of course.

Pen in hand, she dithers for a moment. It's the shape of the speech that's the thing, the narrative, as much as the words. Its rhythm, its ebb and flow.

Cadence is what it is. *Arc*.

She writes:

We are a Party which knows what it stands for and what it seeks to achieve.

We are a Party which honours the past that we may build for the future.

Last week, at Blackpool, the Labour Party made the bogus claim that it was 'putting people first'.

Putting people first?

Last week, Labour

– voted to remove the right to a secret ballot before a strike

– voted to remove the precious right we gave to trade union members to take their union to a Court of Law.

Putting people first?

Last week Labour voted for the State to renationalise British Telecom and British Gas, regardless of the millions of people who have been able to own shares for the first time in their lives.

Putting people first?

They voted to stop the existing right to buy council houses, a policy which would kill the hopes and dreams of so many families.

Labour may say they put people first; but their Conference voted to put Government first and that means putting people last.

What the Labour Party of today wants is:

– housing – municipalised

– industry – nationalised

– the police service – politicised

– the judiciary – radicalised

– union membership – tyrannised

– and above all – and most serious of all – our defences neutralised.

Never!

Not in Britain.


She thinks, the rhetoric is all well and good at the outset, but then, detail.

Not many are as good at detail as Mrs Thatcher.


Why are we Conservatives so opposed to inflation?

Only because it puts up prices?

No, because it destroys the value of people's savings.

Because it destroys jobs, and with it people's hopes.

That's what the fight against inflation is all about.

Why have we limited the power of trade unions?

Only to improve productivity?

No, because trade union members want to be protected from intimidation and to go about their daily lives in peace – like everyone else in the land.

Why have we allowed people to buy shares in nationalised industries?

Only to improve efficiency?

No.

To spread the nation's wealth among as many people as possible.

Why are we setting up new kinds of schools in our towns and cities? To create privilege?

No.

To give families in some of our inner cities greater choice in the education of their children.

A choice denied them by their Labour Councils.

Enlarging choice is rooted in our Conservative tradition.

Without choice, talk of morality is an idle and an empty thing.

One rhetorical sleight of hand, she thinks, not sophistry exactly but certainly using the perceived strength of your opponent to *your own* advantage – something, she gathers from Denis, that Big Daddy and Giant Haystacks do every Saturday in some regional fairground wrestling.

What is it that Labour claim to want to do, above all else? What is it that Labour *really* want?

What you want and what you want people to believe you want is, of course, two different things.

She, Mrs Thatcher, writes down four words:

POWER TO THE PEOPLE

Now there's a section heading, she thinks.

POWER TO THE PEOPLE

The right to buy, to *own*, to control your capital –

The great political reform of the last century was to enable more and more people to have a vote.

Now the great Tory reform of this century is to enable more and more people to own property.

Popular capitalism is nothing less than a crusade to enfranchise the many in the economic life of the nation.

We Conservatives are returning power to the people.

That is the way to one nation, one people.

Yes, she thinks, there's rather a lot to be proud of, given the circumstances. It's not been an unproductive time in office, that's certainly true.

'You could hardly have a more favourable opposition, though, Margaret, don't forget that.'

Denis's words.

'That lot on the other side are about as much use as a chocolate watch.'

Yes, there is much to be proud of, she thinks.

She engages her pen –

Inflation at its lowest level for twenty years.

The basic rate of tax at its lowest level for forty years.

The number of strikes at their lowest level for fifty years.

# 2

## *The cost of loving*

November 1986

Suzi's in Hackney on the set of the new Style Council project.

A film called *Jerusalem*, the 'U', 'S', and 'A' kitted out in stars and stripes, which, she thinks, isn't subtle. Then again, neither is the line about being the best pop group ever, included in the voice-over in scene 1, the band released on bail on that particular charge, tearing down the stairs of a municipal building in Hackney, long coats and sunglasses.

There's a lot of laughter on set, but Suzi's a bit tired of irony.

They're looking at the storyboards and hooting.

It *is* quite funny, to be fair, and Paul Weller as a vicar preaching about how if America were a pair of jeans, then Britain would be its back pocket is a nice idea. Two song promos planned, 'Angel' and 'It Didn't Matter', from the forthcoming album, *The Cost of Loving*, out next year.

Suzi thinks: it's a good question, as in what is the cost?

They're taking the piss a bit with some of the archness. A journalist – absolutely *not* based on Suzi, she's been helpfully informed more than once – asking repeatedly why the band is called The Style Council, Paul Weller eventually telling this journalist, 'Enough is enough, oh my children, away back we must go to face the music, press, and drippy inkies.'

But here Suzi is, the fourth estate, taking photographs, all four of them looking pretty gorgeous, haircuts and smiles, Paul and Dee young and in love, Mick and Steve clowning about –

He's certainly having fun, Paul Weller, and they seem to be pretty aware of the folly of the pop group making a pretentious film motif, they seem to be enjoying this particular banana skin, in fact.

Fetching scarves though, and Suzi nabs one, black and orange, in the merch for next year's tour, she gathers.

It's only a couple of miles away, but it feels a long way from Tottenham, Suzi thinks.

It's a funny thing being an outsider on set, and it's not her first time. There's a distance to it, and while the thing's playing out in front of you, it still feels like you're looking on through a screen.

She quite likes the anonymity, today, Suzi does.

Left alone. No one's asking what she's photographing, leaning in over her notepad –

She's got that from The Style Council, trust.

Paul Weller's mate Paolo Hewitt wrote the screenplay, although Suzi thinks 'is writing' it might be fairer, at this stage, given the advice that's pouring in his ears.

She overhears something about a conference in Budapest and the relationship between free jazz and socks, which feels about right.

There was a whisper that Suzi herself might have been engaged to do the job, and she wonders if all this time she's spending in Tottenham might have influenced the outcome.

Well, she's here now, anyway.

It takes a while to shoot, this opening scene.

Down the corridors they run, the municipal building doubling nicely for a prison, or institution, which says something about Hackney Council, Suzi thinks.

Down the stairs they run, out the front door, skipping the steps, into a waiting car, a 1957 black Wolseley, apparently, special request of Mr Weller.

It's a good-looking car, very *mod*.

And whisked off, though Suzi's not sure where yet, as they keep coming back to film the same scene again and again –

Dorset, she thinks, is where they're headed next. Might have been nicer, Dorset.

Nicer than down the road, at least, Keith might even have come, they might have made a holiday out of it, such as they have holidays.

It can sometimes feel like Style Council business has become a de facto replacement for an actual holiday. She can't remember when she and Keith *didn't* use a Council trip as an excuse for a getaway.

It's funny, working for yourself: you're always at work. There's no one telling you to have any time off.

The day wears on.

Mid-afternoon, and Suzi thinks she needs only one more thing from Paul Weller, and then whatever piece this visit becomes will work.

A word on next year.

'General election tour,' Paul Weller tells her, winking.

On the bus to Tottenham, Suzi writes:

Maybe he knows something we don't.

At the Youth Association, she scouts for Shaun. He's not there. Neither is Carolyn. Neither are any of the youngsters Suzi took to Clapham.

She takes off her coat. She sits down. She looks at her watch.

She wonders what time Keith will be home, whether she might as well head there now –

And then she sees Shaun arrowing past, head down.

Suzi's up quick, grabbing her coat and bag –

Her notepad falls out. Fuck –

She scoops it up, dumps it in her bag, out the door –

She turns left. She's jogging, almost, trying not to run –

Along the path, under the walkway, concrete-panelled blocks flanking her, rising up, and she thinks, I've never been here before and it's already dark, and here's a group of young men, and there's another one, and where is he –

She can't see Shaun. She hesitates, thinks –

Did he turn down one of these side alleys?

Then –

If he did, what am *I* going to do about it?

Trying not to run, her coat in her arms, her bag slipping off her shoulder –

She can't see Shaun.

End of the path, exit to the left, estate to the right, Suzi stops, realises she's out of breath, bends over, breathes –

She feels something on her back, straightens, her heart thumping –

'Who you looking for, bitch?'

Three men around her. Her eyes dart –

One man and two kids, in fact.

'I—'

'Who you looking for?'

Suzi's eyes wide, heart thumping –

The two kids have backed up a bit, and she sees they've done so to stop anyone coming round the corner, she thinks –

Run.

Then two more at the exit –

Then Shaun –

'You're looking for me, yeah?' he says.

Suzi's mouth open, no words –

'Why?'

'I—'

'I don't want them, yeah? Leave me alone.'

'I—'

'Leave me alone.'

Shaun turns, walks away –

The man comes closer to Suzi, leans closer to Suzi, she can smell cigarettes and fried food, she can see red in his eyes –

'You don't come here again, understood?'

He sniffs. Suzi nodding –

From inside his flying jacket, he takes a packet of cigarettes, a gold Zippo lighter. He sniffs again. His fingers thick, his thumb flips –

A cigarette into his mouth, he snaps the lighter open, a click, he lights his cigarette, leaves the flame burning –

He waves the flame under Suzi's nose. She smells fuel, tar –

The heat tickles then singes –

It's sharp, this pain, insistent –

'Understood?'

Suzi nodding –

'Just because you're a white woman doesn't mean you're privileged.'

'I—'

'Nothing to say. Nothing more to say.'

He snaps the lighter shut. He pockets it. He nods at the boys –

He nods at the exit. Suzi leaves.

Parker is starting to think he's set himself up on a fool's errand –

The sheer lack of activity inside this warehouse – at least when he's watching it – is certainly notable.

Occasional deliveries, men in and out, a couple of faces from the walkabouts –

Not much else.

And then a van comes out, the sort he's looking for, and he follows it.

By this point, Parker's local knowledge is Hackney Carriage-level proficient. The one-way systems, for a start, mean it's almost impossible *not* to follow the van at a discreet distance.

Regardless, he doesn't have to follow it very far as, before he knows it, he's pulling into a space slap bang next to that estate on Cable Street.

Well, *well.*

He watches as two blokes carrying toolboxes climb the stairs to the second level.

He watches them open the door of the first flat they come to.

He positions himself so that he can see them go in and out.

They're in this first flat for about five minutes, before one of the blokes comes out and goes in next door.

Soon enough, bloke number one comes out the first flat and lets himself into flat number three.

Bloke number two is out the second flat and into number four.

Parker concedes that it's almost balletic, the synchronicity of the timings, the loop and overlap, reminds him of Torvill and Dean, in its way.

And so on. Until the final flat. They don't go in there. They don't even acknowledge it. Parker watches very carefully: it's like the place don't exist, even.

The whole thing takes about an hour and a half.

He watches the men descend and then do one. He follows them back to the Wapping warehouse.

Then Parker carries on with sitting in his car.

Later, on an evening walkabout, Parker has a clear and obvious thought: the only time he's seeing any of these ELL vehicles is at night. Course he is. That's the only time *anyone's* seeing them.

Well then.

Next few nights, he gives the walkabouts the swerve and camps out in the yacht. Bigger vehicles come out, ghost slowly to the Wapping facility, past the strikers, the protestors, swallowed up by the gates, disgorged later, full, Parker thinks, of newspapers. And off they go around the country –

Depots and whatnot. Parker does not follow.

Instead, back to the warehouse, waiting for another smaller van –

And a few more nights of this and bingo, he gets one. And instead of turning left it turns right, and Parker thinks, here we go.

West along Commercial Road, right onto the B108, which Parker knows heads *waaay* north. Up they go, across Mile End Road, Whitechapel and the Blind Beggar to the right, past Vallance Gardens, it's quiet, pushing two in the morning now, just the neon of kebab shops, though it looks like slim pickings in the windows, those sweating hunks somewhat depleted, Parker thinks, hate to think how long the dregs have been on that spit, fuck me.

It's good to keep an eye on the surrounding, Parker reckons, means you're not on top of the mark.

Here we go, Weavers Fields then across Bethnal Green Road, through Pollard Square with its bit of greenery either side, all shadows and branches at this hour, shapes slumbering behind the bins, a right onto Gossett Street, then a quick left north, past Warner Green, then Ion Square Gardens, scenic route, Parker's thinking, then left onto Hackney Road.

Happy days, Ye Olde Axe, just up on the right. Parker smiles.

It's the class of the place, he remembers, the 'strip pub': terminology that doesn't exactly reek of glamour.

That bird undressing to Bonnie Tyler.

Turn around, darling, and all that. Bright eyes.

She was lovely.

A right and north up Queensbridge Road, Haggerston Park looking a bit shabby, Parker thinking we're not going to the Holly Street Estate, for God's sake, not there again.

No.

A left before the canal, and west on Whiston Road for a bit, then right onto Kingsland Road and north, and now Parker is getting very interested.

Heading to the manor.

Past the mosque and keep going, then a left turn, a slight surprise given where Parker thought they might be headed, though based only on his instinct this was, no evidence.

Downham Road then right onto Southgate Road and De Beauvoir, then Newington Green, terraced semis and nice cars, mostly. Through the Green and up Winston Road. Christ, Parker thinks, we're only round the corner from my gaff, the one paid for by Special Branch.

Wiggle round Albion Parade, double back, Springdale Road, a left, and Parker sees the van go into a garage before Aden Grove, back of Green Lanes.

What the fuck are they doing up here?

Parker doesn't dawdle, pulls back round, heads east to Carolyn's –

Thinking: might be time to engage young Trevor.


*You've got Merv the Swerve on the dog and bone and he's telling you something quite interesting.*

*Something about some colleague of his asking about quote unquote a couple of commercial properties fringing the Shadwell Basin and backing onto the Cable Street Estate. Asking, in no uncertain terms, Merv emphasises, about the planning application records.*

*'Right,' you say. 'Cheers, Merv.'*

*'Yeah, well,' Merv says.*

*'What's the name of your colleague, Merv?'*

'His name is Jon Davies.'

*Another fucking Welshman, you think. They're everywhere. Then: that was the name in that* other *Welshman's wallet.*

*Merv sniffs. He's waiting for something, reassurance, perhaps.*

'Speaking to you, Merv,' *you say,* 'you might as well bring your own eggshells.'

'Yeah, well,' *Merv says.*

'Don't worry, Merv, your secret's safe with me.' *You laugh, loudly.*

'I just thought you'd like to know.'

'I do like to know, as a rule. See you, Merv.'

*You hang up. You stand. You open your office door. You whistle. Terry's over sharpish.*

'That lug, Terry,' *you say.* 'The wally with the portfolio, syndicate, for Christ's sake, you remember him?'

*Terry nods.*

'I want a word with him.'

*Terry nods.*


First thing Jon realises when he gets down to the Shadwell Basin is that his geography isn't quite right. He can't see anything that fringes the Basin and backs onto the Cable Street Estate, let alone anything that looks like Chick's syndicate's commercial properties.

That said, it'd be hard to know quite the right words to do justice to the place: there's nothing there.

Well, there *is* something there, it's just it's very bleak and very derelict. Or it's a construction site.

About a third of it – *it* being the Basin and the surroundings – appears to be under construction, though it's hard to see exactly what they might be doing.

Further east, the *Limehouse* Basin, a useful comparison, formerly the Regent's Canal Dock, as Grandad Ray has informed Jon more than once:

'The actual Limehouse Basin, old son, was about a half mile to the east and filled in in the twenties, good it did anyone.' So goes Grandad Ray's history lesson. 'It connected the West India Import and Export docks and it connected them both to the Thames.'

Looking that way now, Jon can see a couple of tower blocks, the Oast Court Estate, he thinks, and a single, three-storey building – might be an old pub – that's been sliced from its neighbours, it looks like, on the side of it, the words:

THE

HOUSE

THEY

LEFT

BEHIND

Painted in thick black script.

Jon's been reading up, and the Limehouse Basin is not an easy development project, or one with an obvious solution. He wonders if Shadwell is at all similar.

Planners wanted to fill it with concrete a few years ago, worried children might drown in it. A reasonable fear, it looked pretty sketchy. Terrible traffic problems, too. Talk of demolishing the viaduct and building a four-lane dual carriageway, which came to nothing. An architectural competition run by the British Waterways Board and a £70 million winner involving half the Basin to be filled in, creating 100,000 square feet for offices and a few hundred luxury homes. The locals didn't fancy that, strangely enough, and nor did the planning inspector agree, but he was overruled by the then Secretary of State for the Environment, Patrick Jenkin, who gave it the green light in August last year, during his final week in office, which is interesting.

Prince Charles came down and gave a speech on behalf of the locals and their petition to stop the British Waterways Board's foolhardy scheme.

Jon is impressed by this fact.

He said, Prince Charles:

'Apart from any other considerations, private, public and nationalised businesses should all have a vested interest in building up socially and financially stable communities who will eventually become customers. Otherwise the potential long-term problems of social unrest, if companies continue to avoid the fundamental issues of inner-city areas, will be to their detriment.'

Yeah, Jon thinks, one way of ensuring the inner city is developed responsibly is to appeal to capitalism.

But fair play to Prince Charles, he got stuck in and they got a result, of sorts, in the end.

Kenneth Baker, the subsequent Secretary of State for the Environment said:

'What we are trying to do is involve the people in the inner cities in a positive way.'

Which is hardly very specific.

Kenneth Baker is now in charge of Education, Jon notes, which isn't promising given that statement.

Anyway, what a palaver.

The sensible, capitalist approach seems to have prevailed:

'Development in phases when the financial climate permits.'

And at the Shadwell Basin, the financial climate permits, or at least permits a phase or two.

That Limehouse petition uses words like panoramic views and unique location and character and gateway and canal structures and leisure and pleasure and opportunity and irreplaceable asset.

It also uses words like dilapidated and demolished and shortage and council staff cuts and permanently padlocked public toilets and tennis courts and rape and racial assault and muggings and glue-sniffing and alcoholism and heroin addiction and truancy and depression and out of work and sink estate.

Money isn't mentioned, though, apart from in the context of the poverty levels.

Jon checks his notebook and wanders back to the end of Cable Street, where he intends to have a look at an estate with a surprisingly high number of Right to Buy purchases.

It seems to Jon that Chick's commercial properties are part of the area under construction.

It would tally with the addresses, he thinks, but it's hard to be sure.

At the edge of the estate, he consults the map and heads for the stairs.

Up a flight, another, onto the second level –

He checks his notebook: it must be *all* of these units, Jon thinks.

A door opens and closes, opens and closes.

A head pops out. A bloke in overalls, fixing the hinges, it looks like.

'You here for the viewing then?'

'I am,' Jon says quickly. Nodding.

'Bit early.'

'Catches the worm, you know.'

The bloke snorts. 'Yeah, nice one. Hang about.'

He pulls a master key from his pocket. 'This does the lot,' he says, gesturing at the row of flats. 'You can have a look at an empty one after the show.'

'The show?' Jon says.

'Show flat, mate, the *viewing.*'

'Course, sorry.'

'That's all right.'

The bloke closes the door, nods. He opens the first flat along the walkway. 'Come in,' he says. 'The estate agent told me there might be one or two before he got here.'

'Yeah, he told *me* there'd be someone who could let me in.'

'Muggins here.' Smiling.

'Indeed.'

'Look, I've got to finish up. Have a gander and I'll be back in ten minutes.' He points at the living room table. 'There's some, er, *literature* over there, to *peruse.*' Laughing.

'Cheers,' Jon says. 'Appreciate it.'

'Yeah, triffic,' the bloke says and leaves Jon to it.

The flat looks like what it is: a very smart council home redecorated and opened out, all light and wood. The kitchen – now open-plan – has views across the Basin and beyond.

Jon thinks you can't change where the front door is on an estate though they'd probably try – to get the views the better way round.

Though the upstairs balcony does afford something pretty spectacular.

Three bedrooms into two, lots of light –

Jon examines the literature. Most of it guff about opportunity and vibrancy, community and regeneration.

At the very bottom, in very small print, are the listed partners.

One word screams:

COMPLIANCE

The bloke lets himself back in. 'All right?'

Jon nods. 'You say you can do the lot with that key?'

'All except the last one.'

'Who's in there then?'

'Fuck knows.' Laughing again.

'You mind if I wander down?'

'I'd say the one next door to it might be the best spot. Treat yourself, I've left them all open.'

'Cheers.'

Jon wanders down. He nudges the door to the last but one, trying to get a look into the window of the flat next to it. Curtains closed, darkness.

Jon goes in. Dust and plaster, plastic sheets hanging. He jumps the stairs to the second floor. He goes through what will become the master en suite and out onto the balcony –

He looks out across the Basin. The bloke was right: the angle is smashing from here.

He thinks, easy does it –

He moves to the far left of the balcony. There are plants at around head height on the other side. No way of getting a proper look without prising them apart. On his side, there is an upturned pot, about a foot high, which he stands on, peers over –

He thinks: why am I doing this?

What he wants, Jon, is to understand why the occupants of this particular flat haven't sold up. Well, haven't *bought* then sold up.

He thinks: just have a look, you're a potential buyer, that's all –

He sticks his head between the plants, has a proper look –

He sees, through the French windows, three figures, smoking, moving around a table, papers spread out all over it.

He sees one of these figures turn.

The figure, he sees, does a double take –

The window is pulled across and in the clarity of the light, Jon sees that the figure is Geraint, that journalist who never turned up to Jon's office all that time ago –

And Jon is gobsmacked.

But, judging from the state of Geraint's boat race, not as gobsmacked as Geraint is.


Suzi's with Noble again in the Royal Oak pub.

Noble saying, 'I need something on what's happening in Stoke Newington and you've got an in with this young woman Carolyn.'

'That wasn't the arrangement.'

'All best-laid plans, darling, you know that.'

'I'm not doing it.'

'Listen.' Noble shifts in his seat, points. 'This is what I've heard.'

He takes a piece of paper from his pocket.

'Following the death of Colin Roach in the foyer of Stoke Newington police station on January twelfth, nineteen eighty-three,' Noble reads, 'the Roach Family Support Committee commissioned an independent report "Policing in Hackney Nineteen forty-five to Nineteen eighty-four".'

Suzi shakes her head. 'So what?'

'So I need a bit more than that.'

'And?'

'That's where you come in.'

'I've already given you what you need,' she says. 'General election tour? Red Wedge January plans? Isn't that what you wanted?'

Noble nods. 'You're doing it.'

'I thought your big boy—'

'You don't worry about him, all right?'

They sit in silence for a moment. The clinking glasses, the coughing –

'Hardly a coffee morning vibe in here, is it?' Noble says. 'The clientele look like they've barely left this week. The early shift.'

Suzi sniffs. 'I'm not doing it.'

Noble nods, stands. He drains his glass, takes it to the bar.

'You are,' he tells Suzi as he leaves.


Parker outlines his plan to young Trevor, who's looking a bit better, Parker thinks, than the last time he saw him.

'You're looking a bit better, Trev, if I may,' Parker says.

'You know.'

Parker nods. 'Yeah, course. Anyway,' he says, 'for the foreseeable, I need you to keep an eye on that garage I told you about. And this is why I am affording you the use of a lovely little flat just around the corner.' Parker digs in his pocket. 'Address,' he says, 'and keys.'

Trevor takes both.

'Good lad,' Parker says. 'You give me a bell on the usual, twice a day with a report. Lunch, close of play. If I don't pick up the first time, I will the second.'

'Got a phone then, this flat?'

'All mod cons, Trevor, my son.'

'Good.' Trevor smiles.

'Yeah, magic,' Parker says, winking. 'You be clever, Trevor.'

# 3

## *The sweetest girl in town*

December 1986

*You're listening to Jackie Wilson yelling 'Reet Petite' on the radio.*

*One of the Canning Town lads says, 'I'm going to make a pile when this is Christmas number one.'*

*You laugh. 'It's the glamour and the challenge of gambling, the sport of it.'*

*You sniff. The lug's sitting on a chair in the back room of your office.*

*Well, you think, more like lolling on it, the condition of him.*

*'What happened to him?' you ask.*

*The other lad smirks. 'Slipped in the shower.'*

*'Wake him up, will you?' you instruct.*

*The lads fill a bucket with cold water and throws it over him.*

*He's a sorry state, and it's troubling that this still has to happen, time to time, the queasiness you feel is about that, that need to act in a way you don't want to, rather than the blood and the bruises, the ropes round his wrists, the cigarette burns on his chest.*

*He groans and comes to. He sees you, and there's something there in his swollen eyes – understanding.*

*'Listen,' you say. 'It's really quite simple.'*

*He vomits and spits into sawdust. Enterprising, you think, preparing the floor like that.*

*He breathes heavily.*

*'It's all right,' you say. 'It's over.'*

*He nods.*

*'I mean,' you clarify. 'This' – indicating the violence – 'is over.'*

*He tries to speak, but his lips are chafed and thick.*

*Jackie Wilson's still at it, caterwauling.*

*'To the naked eye,' you say, 'you've been beaten up attempting to rescue a young fella from a mugging. These two know the young fella and he's been briefed. A vicious assault is what happened to you. My boys will find you and this young fella, witness members of our coloured brethren engaged in this malevolent act, a sickening reminder of urban decay,*

our social climate. I believe the suspects are likely already known to the police.'

The lug nods.

One of the lads mutters, 'There's enough of them about.'

'But while in hospital, a recovering hero, a working-class white man standing alone against a sea of filth, all that, you'll mention to your cousin's husband, the brief at the council, that all might not be quite what it seems.'

The lug nods.

'You'll tell him to leave off sniffing around council flats and planning applications if he knows what's good for him. Choose your words carefully, if I were you.'

The lug coughs, tries to speak –

'What was that?'

Tries again –

'He's a – civilian.'

'So are you, son,' you say.

The lug moans.

'Other than that, you keep this to yourself. It's win-win. You get some coverage in the local papers, we get a bit of leverage with the Old Bill, and the Old Bill gets to lock up a few blacks on a cast-iron fit-up.'

The lug spits.

'We clear?' you say.

The lug nods.

You gesture at the lads. 'Go on, look lively, don't be shy.'

And then: 'Now find me the Welsh bloke, the journalist.'

Your friends over at Scotland Yard have confirmed it's him.


Bethnal Green Town Hall.

Shortly after the Cable Street Estate visit, Geraint visits Jon at his office and joins the dots.

'Whose flat is it exactly?'

Geraint says a name that Jon doesn't recognise.

'Who's she?'

'Just an ageing lady with a conscience.'

'That feels a bit enigmatic.'

'Her son is one of the *Socialist Worker* staff. She let us use it.'

'What for?'

'Trying to get inside knowledge on the strike, you know, behind-the-scenes stuff. The flat's the HQ.'

'Very covert, Geraint.'

'You need somewhere to do God's work.'

Jon laughs.

Geraint smiles. 'She was approached, you see.'

'To sell it?'

'Exactly.'

'But she didn't.'

'No.'

'Why not?'

'She didn't like the sound of the financial arrangements. Also, she's lived there most of her life. She likes it, the area.'

'I'd say that's a surprise.'

'Up and coming.'

'Up and left, more like.'

'Well.'

Jon smiles. 'What do you know about the financial arrangements?'

Geraint clears his throat. 'She didn't have the means, first of all, so she wasn't interested. She was then approached by a representative of some company. This representative said they'd loan her the money so she'd be able to buy her flat, and at a very reasonable price too, given how long she'd lived there, register it in her name, then buy it off her, and *then* write off the loan.'

'That sounds a bit too good to be true.'

'That's what she thought.'

'Her neighbours didn't think that then?'

'I can't be sure,' Geraint says, 'as we keep our heads down a bit, but it looks that way.'

'You know the company name?'

'I thought you'd ask that.'

Geraint hands Jon a card.

EXCALIBUR FINANCIAL SOLUTIONS

It says on it.

Jon nodding –

'Ring a bell, does it?' Geraint asks.

'It does, yeah.'

Geraint stands. 'Well, nice to catch up.'

'What about the strike then?' Jon asks.

'It's dead in the water.'

'Which bit, Shadwell Basin?'

Geraint laughs. 'Very funny.'

'What's the story then?'

Geraint winks. 'The people involved in the violence, the protests. Not just agitators and anarchists up for a scrap, bit more organised, if you know what I mean?'

'I think I do, Geraint. Good luck with it.'

'Cheers, Jon. Give me a ring if you think of anything else.'

Later, it occurs to Jon that he should speak to the woman, the owner of the flat. But no one appears to want to answer the phone whenever he does ring.

A week after Geraint's visit, he decides to go back down there himself.

When he arrives, that bloke again, playing with the door –

'You here to see this one now, are you, early bird?' Laughing like an engine.

Jon nods. 'Same literature and all that, is it?'

The bloke nods. 'Not much gets past you, mate.'

'The estate agent's all over this estate.'

'Yeah, good one. Go on in. Age before beauty.' Cackling.

Inside, nothing –

Plaster and dust.

Geraint and his friends must have evacuated, pulled the handle on the old ejector seat.

Back to the town hall and he consults what he *does* have on the Basin development.

Adverse possession, land acquired from the unnamed syndicate by the LDDG and the American bank, a condition being unlimited investment potential in the development by this unnamed syndicate.

Jon notes that anonymous £10 million investment in the Docklands development project, bearer instruments and offshore nominee directors, and thinks:

Same thing.

The question is where exactly Compliance and Excalibur are getting their money.

Why their investments and acquisitions – and sales – need this anonymity.

Chick might know.


Suzi hasn't been to Tottenham for a while. She doesn't know how she feels about that. She doesn't want to do what Noble's telling her she must.

So she doesn't do it. She stays in her lane.

'You seem a bit down, girl,' Keith decides one weekend. 'Let's have a day out.'

Outside the Leopold Buildings, words in fresh paint across the houses over the road, daubed thick above the doorways, state, boldly:

WE WANT DECENT HOUSING IN THE E1 AREA

'Not so much graffiti, then, as it is advertising,' Keith declares, all ironic.

Suzi smiles, grips his arm.

For a change, for the first time in a long time, Suzi thinks, Friday night wasn't a 'big one', so they're fresh-faced and bushy-tailed and walk down the Hackney Road and past the city farm and along to the canal towards Islington.

It's full of rubbish, the canal. Floating plastic bottles and crisp packets, empty cans. That murk.

'I learned something the other day,' Keith says.

'Special day, then?'

'Don't be cheeky, girl.'

Suzi smiles.

Keith says. 'That green stuff, on the canal. What do you reckon it's called?'

'It's a good question.'

'That's what I thought.'

They walk on. Gas holders and derelict wharves, men fishing – Advertising in faded ink on the sides of blocks of flats:

BLACK CAT CIGARETTES

EXTRA LARGE

10 FOR 6d

'You going to tell me then, professor?' Suzi asks.

'Well,' Keith begins, 'you'd think it was something to do with all the crap in there, wouldn't you?'

'I suppose you might, yes.'

'Well,' Keith says. 'It's not.'

Suzi's laughing now.

'I ain't being funny,' Keith says.

'You are though, love.'

'Well, yeah. Anyway, it's duckweed, that's what it is.'

'Duckweed.'

'Indeed, love. And you know what?'

'Surprise me.'

'They're individual, tiny plants. They *join up* to form the blanket we now see before us. Isn't that amazing?'

'What do they do?'

'Well, that's interesting. Food for ducks, for one thing.'

'As the name suggests.'

'And shelter and protection for spawning frogs and toads, for another.'

'That's very considerate.'

'Isn't it?'

'I love you, Keith.'

Keith winks. 'We're very lucky, love, in love.'

'Spawning frogs.'

'Now there's a thought—'

'Yeah,' Suzi says. 'I *am* thinking about it.'

'Me too, love.' Keith's arm around her shoulders –

More paint and letters:

NF FUCKED

When they reach Angel, they come off the canal and head through Finsbury up and over the hill towards Bloomsbury.

Down they go, arm in arm, almost skipping –

'Thirsty, love?' Keith asks. 'I know a place.'

'You always do.'

'Come on then.'

Across Gray's Inn road and west along Guildford Street –

Left into Lamb's Conduit Street –

And into a pub, The Lamb, which is very cosy indeed, given the time of year. Leather seats and wood. A horseshoe bar. Pillars and lamps, frosted-glass panels, pint mugs in rows above and below.

On a thin crossbeam over the pumps, a fat, proud-looking lamb painted in a black circle on a red crest.

Suzi takes out her camera, snaps –

'Two pints of Special, mate,' Keith says.

The barman obliges.

They find a table and sit.

Snug is the right word for it, Suzi thinks, and the pub's at that perfect winter level of business – enough people to feel like you might be in a country retreat by the fire; not so many you can't get quick service or a seat.

They say little at first, warm up, let the beer do its work, smile.

Suzi says, 'So you've been thinking about it too, then?'

Keith nods. 'I have been.'

'And?'

'If it's what you want, then I'm in.'

Suzi laughs. 'That sounds very committed.'

'Straight up!' Keith grins. 'I mean it. I'm up for it.'

'It's something you want then?'

'Everyone wants that, don't they? Something you should do.'

Suzi bites her lip. She thinks: it's Keith, it's his way with words.

She says, 'I'm not sure that's quite what I asked, love.'

Then: 'I'm not really talking about everyone. I'm talking about you.'

'Fair enough.' Keith nodding. 'Why is it that you want children, Suzi? I mean, what's the reason, 'cos for me it's just something to want, right?'

'I—'

'I mean there's no other reason, surely, than the simple desire to do it, yeah.'

'It's a bit more complicated than that, love.'

'Is it though?'

'It is for me.'

'What do you mean?'

'I mean' – Suzi pats her stomach, points at the clock on the wall above the bar at the back – 'tick-tock, you know? You know about that?'

'Course.'

Keith offers a hand. Suzi takes it.

She says, 'This isn't quite how I imagined this conversation going.'

Keith sighs. 'I'm sorry, I'm—'

'I know.' Suzi squeezes his hand. 'Maybe think about how you say things, that's all.'

Keith nods. 'Yeah.'

He smiles at Suzi, thanks her.

She says, 'So you do have this simple desire then? You do want it?'

'I want you.'

'That's not the same thing.'

'It is, love, really.'

'You can just say it, either way, I won't mind.'

'I want it, with you.'

Suzi nods, quickly, insistently –

'I'll get us another drink.' She makes a face. 'We can celebrate.'

'Absolutely,' Keith says. 'Then I've got a surprise for you.'

'Time for another, though?'

'Tick-tock,' Keith winks.

They drink their pints. There's a high turnover, lot of tourists, Keith says, out-of-towners, not far from Kings Cross, on the way up west –

Suzi almost tells Keith about what happened up in Tottenham but doesn't.

The moment is there, she opens her mouth, but it doesn't feel right, she thinks –

What good comes from him knowing?

She thinks –

I don't tell him, I don't go back.

The logic of this sentiment feels faulty, yet right, she's not sure why.

Then Keith swallows down the last of his Special, says, 'Drink up, love,' and he's ushering her out the door, into the darkening afternoon, Christmas bunting hanging in the trees, lights and decorations –

He guides her next door and quickly seats her at an outside table under fierce heating.

'What all this, love?'

'This,' Keith declaims, arms wide, 'is rapidly becoming an institution.'

'Trust me,' he adds.

'Warm under here.'

'Seasonal charm, my love.'

A waiter approaches, bald and tough-looking, like an Italian dock worker, Suzi thinks, perhaps uncharitably, though he's grinning.

'Keith!' He points and gives Keith a thumbs up. 'Wotcha,' he says, like he's practising.

'Giuseppe,' Keith nods. 'This is my bella Suzi.'

'Ciao, bella,' Giuseppe declares with a bow.

'Which, of course,' Keith indicates, 'is the name of this restaurant.'

They order wine, some olives.

Suzi thinks he's very good, Keith, at befriending *men* in *establishments*. It's helpful, of course.

'They seem to know you here, love.'

'I've only been the once, not long ago. Weller brought us after a session. Very reasonable, is the point. Friendly, big portions.' He gestures at the menu. 'What will you have, do you think?'

Afterwards, they sashay up Lamb's Conduit Street, some sort of Christmas fair going on, the smell of mulled wine, stalls outside the shops and restaurants, kids crowding round a makeshift pen on Rugby Street, two reindeer poking about inside, their handlers taking the fun out of it a bit, Suzi thinks, *educating*, but they mean well.

They walk east along Theobalds Road, Clerkenwell Road, groups of drinkers going one way, families the other.

Onto Hackney Road, Suzi tucked under Keith's arm, her face in his neck, smiling and happy.

They cross and turn –

And Suzi sees him. Noble. Waiting outside their front door –

She swallows hard, her stomach flips, she feels faint –

Keith eases his arm away, digs in his pocket for his keys.

Suzi thinking: they've met before, years ago in the old Turkish drinking club on Kingsland Road, but how is that going to –

'Can I help you, mate?' Keith asks Noble, friendly enough.

'You're all right, thanks, mate,' Noble says. 'Just waiting for someone.'

'Bit parky, out here, isn't it?' Keith grins.

Noble laughs. 'Good for the constitution.'

'Have a nice evening,' Keith says.

Suzi gives Noble a tight smile as they squeeze past into the building.

Noble says nothing, his expression, Suzi thinks, inscrutable.

The rhythm of the thing is Parker watching the vans leaving Wapping and Trevor clocking them up by Green Lanes. They keep track, and it's not every night, and there isn't a weekly system exactly, but over the course of a month, it averages out to a few times a week.

Parker making the obvious point that you vary delivery when you've got something that isn't supposed to be being delivered, element of surprise and so on.

Though the official-looking nature of the vehicles might cushion that somewhat.

Parker meets Trevor at the flat.

It's time to alter the system, Parker thinks.

He brings four cans of Red Stripe and a box of fried chicken. Trevor digs in.

Parker sticks to the lager.

Trevor wipes his hands on his jeans. Parker points at the plastic take-away bag –

'They've got tissues in there, son.'

Trevor licks his fingers. His eyes dart, like a rodent's, Parker thinks. He does look better, it's true, but there's that shifty vibe pouring off of him, as usual.

Perhaps that's only natural, given the circs, the history of the thing.

'What do you reckon then, Trev?'

Trevor chews and swallows.

'Trevor?'

He sniffs, Trevor. His eyes flicker and dart –

He wipes his mouth with the back of his hand.

'The vans go in, yeah?'

Parker nods.

'Some time later, cars leave.'

'Together?'

Trevor shakes his head.

'Who's in these cars?'

'I dunno. It's dark, innit?'

Parker opens his palms. 'Get a fucking head torch.'

'All right. I dunno. Men.'

'Where do these cars go?'

'You never told me to follow them.'

'It's a fair point.' Parker thinking he should tell Trevor to follow one.

'You got a bicycle, Trevor?' he says.

'I ain't following one without a car, boss.'

Parker takes a drink of his Red Stripe.

Trevor opens his second can, slurps at foam.

'You never told me what you've been up to, Trevor.'

'Not a lot.'

'Though you are looking better, more, you know, *secure*.'

Trevor makes a face. His eyes red, narrowing –

'Maybe 'cos I ain't had to do nothing for you for a bit, know what I mean?'

Parker sniffs.

Another fair point, he thinks. He wonders for a moment what more he can do about this whole thing, about Trevor.

When does *observation* become something else?

'Question, Trevor. If a bear shits in the woods and no one's around to witness it, does it make any noise, do you think?'

'No idea what you're on about.'

'It's a philosophical position.'

'Squatting?'

Parker laughs. 'Very good.'

'What you saying?'

Parker shakes his head. 'I'm not sure, Trev, to be honest. I'm not sure.'

Parker eases open another Red Stripe, the click and hiss –

'Just keep doing what you're doing, for now,' he says. 'All right?'

Trevor nods.

'We'll talk more again soon.'

'Here?'

'Why not.'

'Will I be bringing the picnic?' Trevor asks.

Parker grins. 'Nah, mate, it'll be on me.'


*What you're hearing from your drivers has a nice symmetry to it:*

*As the vans are kitted out with all the ELL paraphernalia, and because these vans are driving – in some part – through Wapping and Shadwell on their way north, and because there are groups of pickets wandering around looking to put bricks through the windows of the larger vehicles, the police, by keeping these pickets at bay, are helping make sure your vans have a clear run.*

*It's very considerate, considering.*

*The boys up in Stoke Newington enjoy it, too.*

*The distribution model appears to be working nicely. The Canning Town mob have a handle on the manufacture and now the business side.*

*You're a silent partner. So silent you're non-existent, push comes to shove.*

*You decide, though, that a little insurance is sensible, it generally is.*

*A gift, you think, to your Scotland Yard payroll CID:*

*You will arrange a couple of arrests and a licence-based establishment shutdown, with the cooperation of, and carried out by, Stoke Newington Regional Crime Squad, soon to be Drug Squad, you gather –*

*A rose by any other name.*

*The principle being that attention will be drawn from your operation and kept elsewhere.*

*Word comes back from the Yard and it's a thank you very much and, yes, that'll do nicely, cheers. Usual logistics, you know the drill.*

*So, you get word to the drivers to pass this on to Stoke Newington: that this is approved by you and with the cooperation of their superiors.*

*An arrest or two, the closing down of a troublesome licensed premises – someone, somewhere they feel could do with a sabbatical.*

One of the Canning Town lads feeds this along and a day or two later knocks on your door.

'And?' you ask him.

He's nodding. 'All arranged, guv.'

'But?'

'Not so much a but as an addendum.'

'That's a long word for you. You sure you know what it means?'

'It's aspirational.'

'It certainly is. I'm flattered. Go on.'

'There's a whisper up in Stoke Newington, a feeling is what it is, no evidence or nothing, that there might be someone on the inside.'

You nod.

'So, these arrests,' he says. 'This favour we're doing to balance the books with the Yard. Does it matter if they use the information to flush this someone out?'

'Not from my end of the khazi it doesn't.'

'I'll tell them.'

'Good man.'


*Bethnal Green Town Hall.*

Jon phones Chick's room at the Royal London and Chick tells him when it's visiting hours.

'You might have to queue, though, old son,' Chick says, laughing. 'It's a media feeding frenzy!'

In good spirits then, old Chick, Jon thinks, considering.

Jon has another look at his copy of the *Hackney Gazette*, the 'Chick Special', in which Chick's heroics are relayed in some detail and this report is accompanied by an 'exclusive' with Chick himself alongside a photo of young Chick down the gym, hands up in boxing gloves next to the heavy bag, and then another of him grinning in the hospital, two bandaged thumbs prominent, a couple of councillors presenting him with an award for his bravery.

Jon folds the newspaper and shakes his head, smiling.

He checks his watch. If he walks, he can leave now, then head straight home afterwards on the bus, pick up a Christmas tree outside the Round Chapel, dig out the festive box from the cellar and help the boy decorate it.

Leave the bicycle in the garage and walk in tomorrow, even.

Jon likes to walk in winter, the crispness and tinsel, that pre-holiday buzz in the pubs post-work, everyone aflutter before the break, always so different in January, even though it's exactly the same, really, in terms of the dark and the cold.

He wraps himself up in coat and scarf and thinks:

I should buy Chick some flowers or fruit or something from one of the stalls on Whitechapel Road; he'll like that.

It's a bit strange that old Chick's summoned Jon personally like this, but Jon puts it down to their delicate conversations over the last few months, their visit to West Ham not that long ago, and some sort of effort at a 'continuing relationship', that game, *family*, though this is not quite the phrase Jon expects that Chick would use in the circumstances.

Four o'clock and it's already dark.

As the market winds down, Jon settles on a one-pound box of mixed fruit – leftovers, though looking half-decent – and a bunch of chrysanthemums, the one flower he's heard Chick reference in the dozen or so years, or whatever it is, he's known him, as in, laughing, 'Her indoors and her bloody chrysanths!'

Jon hasn't been in the Royal London in a long time and there's that familiar shudder as he walks in, the institutional muscle memory, he's called it before, that sense of something's going on, coming in here, whether a hospital, a court, a town hall, even –

They've been lucky with the kids, he and Jackie, hospital-wise.

The boy in the Queen Elizabeth's on Hackney Road the once for a scan and a look-see, but all right, and only an afternoon visit, which was a result. Little Lizzie's been pretty robust, *sturdy*, as Grandad Ray has it, bit of a bruiser, rarely without a snotty nose, but rarely any worse than that, really. Maybe they develop some sort of immunity when they're a younger sibling, there's no doubt books on it, the sort Jon tried to read before the boy was born but never got past a few pages, always thinking, it's common sense, isn't it?

After the boy was born, he realised, yeah, it *is* common sense, but try telling that to your *sense*.

Jon's one of those dads who always knows exactly what he's doing wrong exactly as he's doing it.

He's not sure any amount of literature will change that, will change *him*, though it helps remind him of his failures when he does dip in.

As he jumps the stairs, he considers that line about madness and doing the same thing again and again and again and expecting a different result.

That's parenting in a fucking nutshell, he thinks.

He can hear Chick's room when he's half a corridor away.

The noise, it sounds like the snug bar at an after-hours knees-up, Jon laughing at this turn of phrase, it brings it out of him, this kind of word-play, being around Chick.

As he hovers at the door, he listens as Chick winds up one of his 'narratives'.

'So the bloody nurse was trying to feed the old dear soup for a full half hour before she realised,' Chick's saying. 'Kept looking at me, she did. Engaging in conversation. Lost her appetite, she was saying. Poor thing, she's a slip, isn't she? And I'm going, yeah, you're right, love, I can barely see her from over here, don't spill the soup pouring it down her throat, though, will you, darling?'

Everyone laughing now, Jon smiling.

'On and on she goes, the nurse, long life this, good innings that, in the war she was, survived the Blitz, I'm thinking, she's surviving more than that with you in her earhole day in day out, soup dripping down her front, all over the floor, gushing out of her, it was, nursey wiping it up as quick as she's putting it in.'

More laughter.

'So after a time, I'm thinking, she really doesn't fancy this soup, the old bird, how about I help her out with it, seconds, you know, and the nurse is there levering open the poor dear's gullet, but she can't, can she, she can't open her jaw because, well, it's, you know, it's too stiff, isn't it?'

There's some guffawing now.

Jon sees in the window's reflection one or two with hands covering gaping mouths, pulling that 'Oh, Chick, don't, you are awful' look.

'Nursey goes, "Oh, I say, well, I think—" and I go, Christ, girl, it's not soup you need, it's bloody formaldehyde!'

A roar of laughter now –

'Anyway,' Chick says, finishing up, 'that's why I've got a room to myself for now. Death by drowning!'

'What was it, Chick?' someone asks. 'The soup?'

Chick, an open goal in front of him, pulls back his favoured right foot to hammer this one home.

Jon waits, as they all do, with a widening grin.

'Leek!'

And that brings the house down.

Jon shuffles in, there's four in there on plastic seats, two couples, Jon thinks, though he doesn't recognise them. He makes himself known –

'Oh, hello, Jon,' Chick greets him. 'How's tricks?'

'You know, Chick, all right.'

'Magic,' Chick says. 'The boy all right?'

'Golden.'

'The little girl?'

'Triffic, Chick.'

'Last time I saw her,' Chick says to his friends, 'she was having a difficult morning at nursery, crying when my cousin Jacks, his old lady' – pointing at Jon –'dropped her off. Anyway, an hour later and the bird at the nursery rings. Said the girl was fine now. She'd had a cuddle and was having a drink with her friends.' A pause, big grin. 'A cuddle and a drink with your friends, I said? Where do I sign up?'

Jon laughs. Everyone else laughs, too.

Chick's demeanour changes. He grimaces at his friends. 'If you don't mind, Jon and I have a little family business to discuss, yeah?'

The two couples nod and of course and struggle into their oversized winter coats, struggle into their hats and their scarves, ta-ta for now, and all the best then Chick, and Jon shuffles out of the way, then takes a seat.

'How you feeling, Chick?' he asks.

'Not great, to be fair. All this' – gesturing at himself, his bandages and whatnot – 'ain't quite what it seems.'

'Right. What do you mean?'

'What did you do, Jon, with them files I gave you? Because I think you did something.'

'I—'

'It weren't you that done wrong, Jon, it was me. It's *me*, it ain't you. I just need to know, all right? I'm not upset with you. I'm upset with myself.'

'When you say not what it seems—'

'It don't matter. My bit of bravery, the papers, the *coverage*. It don't matter.'

'Right.'

'I just need to know, that's all, what you did.'

'I had a look, Chick, you're right. I had a look at the files and I asked a question about a couple of premises near the Shadwell Basin. Commercial ones.'

'Who did you ask and what was the question?'

'Chair of the council's planning committee. Merv Michaels. I simply asked about planning applications regarding the two properties.'

'And what did he say?'

'Nothing. He never got back to me.'

'Well,' Chick shrugs. He opens his palms to say, have a gander at this. 'He sort of did.'

'I don't know what you mean, Chick.'

'It don't matter, Jon, all right? It don't matter.'

Chick looks over at the door. Jon sees that there's a bloke standing outside. Chick nods at him, this bloke.

'That geezer out there is going to have a word with you, all right? I suggest you listen carefully.'

'OK.'

'I'll say it again: it weren't you that done wrong, it was me. I shouldn't have asked you to have a look at them files. I'm not upset with you, I'm upset with myself. We're all right.'

'I'm pleased to hear that, Chick.'

'Now jog on.' Pointing at the door. 'Thanks for the flowers, they really brighten the place up.'

Jon nods. Jon feels light-headed, faint, sick to the stomach –

He steps outside.

The geezer is smartly dressed, old-school type, Jon sees.

Nice camel-hair coat, briefcase, shiny leather shoes, black with a gold buckle –

'I'll walk you down,' he says.

Jon nods.

They walk in silence, heels clicking, echoing in the corridor.

They take the stairs in silence, too.

Jon decides it's best to follow this bloke's lead –

'We'll talk outside,' the bloke says. He shivers. 'These places give me the heebie-jeebies.'

Outside, the afternoon darkness is thick with cold.

They stand by the road.

'My car's down there. Walk with me.'

They head west and take the first left. The street is well-lit, Jon notes.

The bloke stops by a long black Jaguar, an inside light on, a big chap sitting in the driver's seat. Jon swallows. The big chap stays where he is.

'This is me,' the bloke says.

'Nice motor,' Jon offers.

'Cheers.'

Jon swallows again.

The bloke says, 'Your wife's cousin got a bit confused, that's all.'

'Right.'

'You don't sound surprised.'

'Well, you know.'

'Yeah, he's a bit of a wally.'

Jon says nothing.

'So,' the bloke goes on. 'The confusion pertains to a number of planning applications and development opportunities in the Shadwell Limehouse area and the surrounding.'

'Yeah.'

'They're all legit, is the point. There's nothing to see, nothing to find.'

Jon thinks it best to say nothing to this.

'You're probably wondering why I'm telling *you*.'

Jon nods.

'Your wife's cousin's confusion was unfortunate. You've seen the state of him.'

Jon thinking *what*?

The bloke shaking his head now. 'Interested parties, council and government approved, American investment, money trickling down, social housing provisions, it's a good thing. You should be happy about it all, given your role.'

Jon thinking this might be my cue –

The bloke hands Jon a business card. On it:


COMPLIANCE/EXCALIBUR


'I understand,' Jon says.

The bloke extends a hand. 'Good man.' He nods at the big chap. 'My driver here will give you a lift home.'

His handshake is firm, reassuring, in its way.

'Oh, that's all right, no need for that,' Jon says, quickly. 'Besides, I need to pick up a Christmas tree on the way.'

The bloke makes a face that says: it's no bother, mate, I insist.

'My driver will help you pick one out.'

The bloke opens the door to the back seat. Ushers Jon towards it –

'Cheerio,' he says.

Jon climbs in. The bloke closes the door gently behind him.

Jon says, 'I—'

The big chap interrupts. 'I know where you live, mate.'

'Right.'

The bloke puts his head through the passenger-side window. 'He needs a Christmas tree' – pointing at Jon. 'See to it, will you?'

'No problem, guv.'

'Cheers, Terry,' the bloke says.

They pick out a Christmas tree and Terry pops it in the boot.

At 99 Mildenhall Road, Terry delivers the Christmas tree to the door.

'Who's this, love?' Jackie asks.

Terry, his arms full of tree, wrestling through the narrow space, winks. 'Work associate. Helped me out with something, your fella. Much obliged. Season's greetings and all that.'

Jackie nonplussed, nodding, Terry propping the tree against the wall in the living room, a hello to the boy and off he goes, Jon, bewildered, smiling through his teeth –

As he leaves, Terry hands Jon a piece of paper, a photocopy of a note which reads:

**JON DAVIES, OCTOBER 7, OFFICE, NINE O'CLOCK.**

Jon shakes his head. 'What's this?'

Terry smiles. 'They found it in some journalist's wallet. Geraint something.'

'What do you mean *they* found it?'

'The Old Bill found it. I expect they'll be in touch. Friend of yours, was he?'

'*Was*? Look, I didn't really know him—'

'My condolences. A terrible thing when a man takes his own life.'

'What—'

'Be lucky,' Terry says.

Later, the fire going, a glass of wine, Lizzie gurgling happily away in bed, Jon and the boy hanging baubles and lights, The Style Council LP on the stereo, Jackie on the sofa with her feet under her bum, reading.

Jon thinking, all right, understood, that's that then and stick to what you *can* do –

Because there must be something.

Thinking: what the fuck have I *done*?

*50 Rectory Road, Stoke Newington.*

Suzi is listening as Carolyn explains what's happening next with the Roach Family Support Committee.

She's listening to Carolyn but she's looking at Carolyn's bloke, Parker. He's looking supportive, Suzi thinks, *staunch*. And well he might.

Suzi's wondering if Noble's asked him the same questions he's been asking her.

She's thinking she looks close enough, she'll find that out at least.

Carolyn's running through the timeline, some of which Suzi knows, reading from a pad of paper.

'So, February nineteen eighty-four, and the *Mail on Sunday* reports that the officers in the Colin Roach case will not be disciplined. Then, in April, the Police Complaints Board informs inquest jurors that no further action is to be taken. Then, in April nineteen eighty-five, on the thirteenth, an Independent Committee of Inquiry into Policing in Hackney is launched by the Roach Family Support Committee.'

Suzi nodding, Parker leaning against a table, arms crossed, also nodding.

Carolyn goes on. 'Stuart Hall is writing the foreword. They're hoping to publish next year, nineteen eighty-nine at the latest. The title will be something like Policing in Hackney, nineteen forty-five to nineteen eighty-four, and the RFSC will publish jointly with someone called Karia Press.'

'This is really good,' Suzi says.

Carolyn's nodding now. 'It really is.'

'What can I do to help?'

'Write about it,' Carolyn says. 'Publicity, right?'

Suzi agrees with this, thinks she can easily swing a favour –

'Listen to this,' Carolyn says. 'This is what will be on the cover somewhere: "We believe this document is important. It is certainly unique; to our knowledge, it is the only study to collate so extensively the experience of the policing of one community. Yet, although a specific study in that sense, we also believe it is of much wider significance, touching as it does on the ever more crucial issue of the policing of the inner-city."'

'That's powerful,' Suzi says.

'Yeah,' Parker agrees. 'It is.'

'So that's where we are,' Carolyn says. 'It's in progress, it's going well. It will make a difference.'

Suzi jots down a few details. She closes her notebook. She pops the lid on her pen.

'Get what you need, did you?' Parker asks.

Suzi breathes in and out. She has what she needs, should she need it. Parker eyeing her, she looks away now –

She takes the bus down the High Street.

Sitting on the top deck, she looks out the window to the right, the side streets and backstreets that snake west and north around the old flat where she and Keith lived, their first proper address together after the squat down by the canal in Clapton.

The top deck thickens with smoke and Suzi thinks about asking for one but decides the smell is satisfaction enough. Down past Dalston Kingsland, down past Dalston Junction, through Haggerston, over the bridge, looking down at the murk of the canal, joggers on the towpath where they'd walked not long ago, a lovely day that was, even the moment with Noble couldn't ruin it.

She gets off just before the junction with Hackney Road.

The air is crisp, thin, damp, that sulphurous smell of fireworks, she thinks, the spit and crackle of a bonfire nearby.

Lights strung between trees, plastic reindeer and Santa Claus effigies hanging from the branches, the pavement bustling with after-work drinkers between pubs –

Drunks and kids on the low walls of the estates with their cans and bottles and their plastic bags.

Suzi crosses the road and heads down towards the Leopold Buildings and her flat, her home, *their* home.

She sees:

Noble, again, talking to Keith.

Noble turning from Keith walking towards her.

Keith looking shocked, brow furrowed, mouth open, tongue lolling –

She sees:

Noble approach her, look her in the eye –

She hears:

'Don't worry about it, darling,' as he passes her.

She thinks:

*What?*

Her heart jumps, her stomach flips, her legs *go* –

Keith walking towards her now.

Suzi saying –

It's not what you think

Keith, shaking his head.


Parker's got Noble on the blower and Noble's saying something that resolutely has Parker's ear.

Noble's saying, 'I've been told to tell you to keep your head down.'

'Why?'

'There's something happening.'

'What exactly?'

'Names.'

'And what's that got to do with me?'

'As in they might name you.'

'Who's they?'

'Stoke Newington.'

'Name me how?'

'Nick you.'

'Nick *me*?'

Noble sighs. 'I don't know, son, all I know is there's something and names are being named, so keep your head down.'

'My name ain't come from your end?'

Noble coughs, splutters. 'You having a fucking laugh?'

'That council flat business,' Parker says. 'What I confirmed for you. I thought I had some credit.'

Noble sniffs. 'Yeah, well, one of your lefty journos has gone and turned up dead. Suicide, they reckon.'

'You what?'

'Geraint Thomas. They found him with his head in an oven.'

'*His* oven?'

'You being funny?'

'Makes a difference, don't it?'

'They've closed the book. Suicide.'

'And my name ain't come from *that*? Higher up, I mean, not you, guv.'

'I've been assured that's not the case.'

'So it might well be nothing?'

'It might well be.' A pause. 'I'm cautiously optimistic.' Being ironic. 'Still, you know.'

Parker nods. 'I'll be careful.'

'Yeah.'

Parker thinking: *Trevor.*

He checks his watch. Trevor's 'day shift' should be over now, the garage done for the day. He should be back at the ranch before heading out again later –

Parker hotfoots it across Stoke Newington High Street and down towards Green Lanes.

He's got a bit of time before meeting Carolyn over in Tottenham, dinner planned with her granny, Shaun coming over, making nice –

Parker one of the family, all that game.

He's down quiet residential streets, bulbs flickering weak in the lamps –

He's up quiet residential streets, the odd parked car sparking light as a spliff is activated, low voices and hooded tops –

Parker digging in his pocket for the keys, pulling them out, one of them into the lock, turning to the left, then to the right, once, twice, the door opening, banging against the wall behind, Parker up the stairs, two at a time, calling Trevor's name –

Another key, another lock, left, right, once, twice –

Into the hall, calling Trevor's name –

Into the kitchen, calling Trevor's name –

Into the bedroom, calling Trevor's name –

Into the living room:

Trevor slumped in the armchair. Arms hanging down, topless, trousers open, cuts on his chest, cuts on his arms –

His throat opened, closed, crusted blood and his tongue pulled through –

Trevor's eyes wide, aghast –

A handwritten sign hangs round Trevor's neck, reads:

GRASS

Parker pukes.

Parker scans the room. Parker wipes his mouth. Parker gags.

He sees:

The telephone pulled from its socket, left at Trevor's feet. The cord wrapped around his wrists.

A message.

Parker back down the stairs –

Out and onto Green Lanes. He sees a taxi with its light on. Arm up, waving and shouting –

'Tottenham, mate. Broadwater Farm.'

'You sure?' the cabbie joking.

'Yeah, and don't mess about.'

Parker running it:

Call Noble, empty the flat, disappear –

The cabbie saying, 'I ain't going in there, guv, I'll drop you on the corner. That's as close as anyone will take you, all right? I ain't being funny.'

Parker out the door, throws a tenner through the window –

'Much obliged,' the cabbie yelling. 'Cunt.'

Parker into the estate, the Youth Association surrounded, Parker sees police –

Parker sees:

Shaun in handcuffs, two plods either side of him, his head down, his eyes dazed, empty.

Parker sees:

Carolyn crying and yelling –

Parker sees:

Marlon holding her, holding her back, talking, talking into her ear –

Parker sees:

Carolyn pointing at Parker, pointing and crying, her eyes –

red

Her eyes –

dead


*Ayeleen*: me and Lauren walk up the high street to the cafe for my shift and we're both laughing and smiling, school holidays and we're going to celebrate.

But as we get closer, something looks weird.

Lauren digs me in the ribs. 'Oi, Leenie, what's all this about?'

She sees the police van at the same time I do, Uncle confused and shaking his head, staring at a sheet of paper, a couple of people in yellow vests explaining something to him, slowly, it looks like.

It looks like he's unhappy with whatever they're telling him, too.

'I don't know, no idea,' I say.

I see the detectives from before, the ones that were across the road, leaning against the van in their leather jackets, their jeans and their white trainers.

'What's going on, Leenie?'

I shake my head, tell Lauren I don't know.

Uncle sees me. He sighs, it looks like he's crying –

'Inside, you two, inside now,' he says.

He pushes us through the door into the cafe, which is dark, all the lights are off.

He goes back outside.

The men in yellow vests are saying something, handing Uncle another sheet of paper.

They stick yet another sheet of paper on the front door, which neither me nor Lauren can read, another one on the window, another one –

Uncle opens the door, closes it, locks it.

'They're shutting us down,' he says. 'Licence revoked.'

'Why?' is all I can think of saying. 'What have we done wrong?'

'Nothing, my dear.' He tries to smile but he looks so tired, I think. 'We've done nothing wrong.' He bangs on the window. 'And we'll fight!' he shouts. 'We'll fight this!'

He turns to us, his hands shaking, and he really is crying now.

And then I'm crying, too, and Lauren puts her arm round me and says, 'Come on, Leenie, let's go home.'

So that's what we do, we go home.

# PART FIVE
## *Landslide*

June 1987

# 1

**It's great to be great again!**
*(Conservative Party election campaign slogan)*

13 June 1987

Noble's outside Chief Inspector 'Special' Young's office at the Yard. A review of the year to date, he's calling it.

Noble's early and flicks through a tabloid.

The screaming headlines indicate which one without too much bother.

A 'best of' collection in the run-up to the election:

WHY I'M BACKING KINNOCK BY STALIN

For one.

He tosses the paper onto the plastic chair next to him –

STRIKE! he thinks. It didn't do fuck all, that strike, in the end.

The press over that poor young lad run over near the facility in Wapping, out celebrating something with his friends, hit by one of the strike-affected vehicles –

Well, they turned that on its head, didn't they?

The protestors were to blame. An innocent young man minding his own business, a tragedy.

And not just the press, neither. Parker telling him the episode took the sting out of those walkabouts, that a lot of people simply lost heart.

That final big demonstration towards the end of January, too.

Violence being the key word.

Douglas Hurd using it more than once, applauding the way the police handled the 'thugs', reminding union leaders that the soon-to-be-enshrined-in-law Public Order Act means they'll need to think of alternative methods of demonstration.

Maggie, Maggie, Maggie.

Kinnock wasn't too complimentary of the thugs, himself.

Noble remembers both leaders putting in appearances at the cup final a month ago. Especially sweet Coventry's win after extra time; Spurs thought it would be a cakewalk, the wankers.

Look at the teams, Noble thinks, now.

Ossie Ardiles and Glen Hoddle on one side, Greg Downs and Trevor Peake on the other.

Hardly fair, on paper.

Keith Houchen though: Roy of the Rovers.

It's not often a neutral cup win brings so much pleasure –

He clears his throat, gives the bird on reception a look. She makes a face, suggesting he'll have to wait a little longer.

He pulls his copy of the *New Musical Express* from his inside pocket, something of a prop for the meeting.

Dated with today's: 13 June 1987.

On the front cover:

### LOVELY, LOVELY, LOVELY!
#### NEIL KINNOCK INTERVIEWED

It is a good full-pager of old Neil, hair swept back, sensible-looking suit, red rose, non-threatening tie –

In the top right-hand corner:

#### RED WEDGE ON TOUR

Thirteen: unlucky for some.

One day, Noble thinks, they'll see the folly, *magazines*, of publishing before the date they give to the bloody issue.

I expect Neil's press office might have a quiet word, at least.

Others featured in the issue include:

#### SIMPLE MINDS
#### T LA ROCK
#### POP WILL EAT ITSELF
#### KEN LIVINGSTONE
#### THE REPLACEMENTS

Red Ken. Red Menace.

Fairly low down on the bill now, though, it appears.

He got re-elected to the House, though, Red Ken, Noble thinks.

Despite Thatcher absolutely pissing it, there were one or two gains for the left, one or two significant inroads.

Diane Abbott, Bernie Grant – Hackney, Tottenham – they got in, which can only be a good thing, *progress*.

Red Wedge fizzling out.

The last thing Noble heard from Suzi on that one was when she went to the Commons with Annajoy David, and Bernie Grant took them to the tuck shop to buy cigarettes or something, and there was Maggie leaving with a bag of booze, Bernie joshing, Maggie shrill –

Face to face with the enemy within, for a moment, Maggie was, her handbag tidied over her arm, Denis shooing her away, keen to get stuck into the port.

'Do I know you?' Maggie asked Annajoy David.

'No, but I know exactly who you are,' was the reply.

Noble liked that story.

He checks his watch –

Parker should be here by now.

Cutting it fine, what might be considered making me wait, Noble thinks, will he, won't he, the tease –

There wasn't much anyone could do.

A seditious journalist holed up in a council flat: suicide.

That snout Trevor with his throat cut in a Special Branch address and nobody the wiser on the ground or otherwise.

Parker claiming it was Stoke Newington in cahoots with some Marlon or other, and this didn't sit well with Noble's superiors.

Parker's identity compromised, so he disappeared, and the word was simple: cover it up.

His in with that bird well and truly fucked, though Noble's not sure quite what's happened there.

Trevor had previous, so it wasn't too problematic, in that sense.

Stoke Newington seemed pretty pleased with the result, given the relish with which they covered it up.

*Where is he?* Noble thinks.

The door opens –

There Parker is, sulking, it looks like.

'Good six months off, was it?'

'No.'

Noble shrugs. Parker pulls a piece of paper from his pocket.

Parker reads: '1 January. A young black man, a different Trevor, Trevor Monerville, was arrested and held incommunicado at Stoke Newington police station. On 8 January he had emergency brain surgery to remove a blood clot from the surface of the brain. The Family and Friends of Trevor Monerville was set up to campaign in support of justice for Trevor. In June, Tunay Hassan died in custody at Dalston police station. His family and friends set up the Justice for Tunay Campaign.'

'Dalston?' Noble asks.

'Yeah,' Parker says. 'Stoke Newington was being renovated.'

'You're joking.'

'Couldn't make it up.'

'And since?'

'A new organisation, I've heard. The Hackney Community Defence Association, which will provide support to the victims of police crime. Campaigning, that sort of thing. Self-help, they're calling it.'

'No one else will bloody help.'

The bird indicates that Young's ready to see them –

'Well,' Noble says, standing. 'Let's see what we're doing next then.'

'I got any choice?'

'No,' Noble concedes. 'You ain't.'

**End of Book Two**

# Acknowledgements

*Red Menace* is a work of fiction based on, and woven around, fact. Much of this fact is recognisable in terms of certain names, places, statistics, institutions, events, documents, laws and policy, which have been adapted and, in some cases, changed for dramatic purposes. I grew up in Hackney; this experience accounts for much of the information, and many of the anecdotes, in the novel. Friends, family, colleagues, associates and contemporary media outlets all informed the writing of the novel, both directly and indirectly. Most of all, and as with *White Riot*, I want to thank the people who were there for their accounts of what they did.

Equally, and as per *White Riot*: much has been written about this period; I am grateful to the writers who have gone before. Once again, I made extensive use of the exhaustive online archives of the wonderful *Radical History of Hackney*; the *Hackney Gazette*, too, was an invaluable resource; where documents from these resources are quoted, it is listed in the Notes section that follows. John Eden's illuminating article for *Datacide* magazine remains essential reading and an inspiration. The *Undercover Policing Inquiry* hosts an archive of documents relating to the spycops scandal at ucpi.org.uk that is important, fascinating and terrifying. Internet resources are cited in the Notes section where appropriate. Far less righteous, but no less useful in this context, was the online archive of the Margaret Thatcher Foundation, at margaretthatcher.org, which catalogues everything she ever uttered in public, as well as private papers and declassified documents. I came across this thanks to the author's note in Sandbrook, *Who Dares Wins*. The Special Branch Files Project is an extraordinary resource, 'a live-archive of declassified files focussing on the surveillance of political activists and campaigners.' A useful starting point is 'Wapping strike – story' by Nicola Cutcher, 12 January 2016, at http://specialbranchfiles.uk/wapping-strike-story/ which is an excellent introduction to the archive and its reach. The Bernie Grant archive, https://berniegrantarchive.org.uk/, is an invaluable and important resource and where I first encountered the Gifford Report on the Broadwater Farm uprising, and Dorothy Kuya's insightful and rigorous report on Broadwater Farm and the Press. The National Archives threw up a number of significant documents as they became public under the 'thirty-year' rule, further details in the Bibliography and Notes sections. Where fiction appears listed in the Bibliography, it has informed the novel in a broad sense.

The police officers in the novel and their actions are entirely fictional.

Trevor is a fictional character. Elements of his backstory are based on details from 'Fighting the Lawmen', specifically in terms of the experiences of Hugh Prince, Rennie Kingsley, Lynne, and Ida Oderinde, as detailed in the pamphlet. Where Trevor encounters these real-life figures in the novel, he quotes their words faithfully, but his interactions with them are wholly imagined.

The London Docklands Development Group is a fictional organisation that shares certain powers and structures with the real-life organisation, the London Docklands Development Corporation. References and documents in the novel pertaining to the LDDC are used fictitiously. All storylines involving the LDDG are entirely fictional.

The Broadwater Farm uprising of 1985, sparked by the tragic death of Cynthia Jarrett while police officers attended her home, is a matter of the historical record. The depiction of events leading to, part of, and following the disturbances is fictional, and references and documents pertaining to it used fictitiously.

The industrial action that takes place in the novel is inspired by and based, in part, on the industrial action of 1986 that became known as the Wapping Dispute. The news organisation in the novel and *The London Herald* newspaper are fictional; the scenes of industrial action depicted in the novel use references and documents pertaining to the Wapping Dispute fictitiously.

Jon Davies is a fictional character. All interactions he has with characters in the novel are wholly imagined. The journalist, Geraint Thomas, is a fictional character, and while the newspaper he works for, *Socialist Worker*, is real, the portrayal of his work and his interactions with this real newspaper are wholly imagined.

Parker is a fictional character; the Undercover Policing Inquiry has demonstrated that spycops were placed in activist groups in Hackney.

Whilst the bands, the music and the magazines in the text are real, my characters Suzi and Keith are fictional and therefore the portrayal of their work and their interactions with those real people and groups is wholly imagined. Suzi and Keith's interactions with Paul Weller and members of The Style Council and associates are fictional. The influence of Paul Weller and The Style Council on this novel is far-reaching and I'd like to thank them, sincerely. Suzi's interactions with the inspirational Annajoy David and the Red Wedge movement are also fictional. In the novel, I quote the words of real-life figures in the Red Wedge movement from a number of sources cited in the Bibliography and Notes sections of this Acknowledgements. The situations in which they interact with my fictional characters are wholly imagined. As with *White Riot*, of help here was Daniel Rachel's masterful oral history, *Walls Come Tumbling Down*, and, again, I thank Daniel for the depth and rigour of his research and writing.

*Bibliography*

### Non-fiction books

Beckett, Andy, *Promised You A Miracle: Why 1980–1982 Made Modern Britain*, (Allen Lane, 2015)

Blackman, Rick, *Babylon's Burning: Music, Subcultures and Anti-Fascism in Britain 1958–2020*, (Bookmarks Publications, 2021)

Bloom, Clive, *Violent London: 2000 years of riots, rebels, and revolts*, (Palgrave Macmillan, 2010)

Brindley, Tim; Rydin, Yvonne; Stoker, Gerry, *Remaking Planning: The Politics of Urban Change*, (Routledge, 2005)

Butler, Tim with Robson, Garry, *London Calling: The Middle Classes and the Re-making of Inner London*, (Berg, 2003)

Gifford, Anthony, *Report of the Broadwater Farm Inquiry*, (Karia Press, 1986)

Gillard, Michael, *Legacy: Gangsters, Corruption and the London Olympics*, (Bloomsbury Reader, 2019)

Independent Committee of Inquiry, *Policing in Hackney 1945–1984*, (Karia Press, 1989)

Jones, Dylan, *The Eighties: One Day, One Decade*, (Preface Publishing, 2013)

Lang, John & Dodkins, Graham, *Bad News: The Wapping Dispute*, (Spokesman, 2011)

McLean, Donna, *Small Town Girl*, (Hodder & Stoughton, 2021)

McSmith, Andy, *No Such Thing as Society: Britain in the Turmoil of the 1980s*, (Constable, 2010)

Moore, Tony, *The Killing of Constable Keith Blakelock: The Broadwater Farm Riot*, (Waterside Press, 2015)

Morton, James, *Bent Coppers: A survey of police corruption*, (Warner Books, 1994)

Munn, Iain, *Mr Cool's Dream: A Complete History of The Style Council*, (A Wholepoint Publication, 2011)

Paphides, Pete, *Broken Greek*, (Quercus, 2020)

Rachel, Daniel, *Walls Come Tumbling Down: The Music and Politics of Rock Against Racism, 2 Tone and Red Wedge*, (Picador, 2016)

Sandbrook, Dominic, *Who Dares Wins, Britain, 1979–1982*, (Penguin, 2019)

Sinclair, Iain, *Lights Out for the Territory*, (Penguin, 2003)

Sinclair, Iain, *Hackney, That Rose-Red Empire*, (Penguin, 2009)

Stewart, Graham, *Bang! A History of Britain in 1980s*, (Atlantic Books, 2013)

Thatcher, Margaret, *The Autobiography*, (Harper Press, first published as *The Downing Street Years*, 1993, and *The Path to Power*, 1995)

Thorn, Tracey, *Bedsit Disco Queen*, (Virago, reprint edition, 2013)

Turner, Alwyn W., *Rejoice! Rejoice! Britain in the 1980s*, (Aurum Press, 2008)

Widgery, David, *Beating Time: Riot 'n' Race 'n' Rock and Roll*, (Chatto and Windus, 1986)

### Articles

'The Daniel Morgan Murder, Police Corruption & the Evolution of the "Firm within a Firm"' by Jake Arnott, *Byline Times*, 14 June 2021

'Letwin apologises over 1985 Broadwater Farm riot memo' by uncredited, BBC News Online, 30 December 2015, https://www.bbc.co.uk/news/uk-politics-35192265

'The Right to Buy' by Andy Beckett, *Guardian*, 26 August 2015

'Red Wedge: bringing Labour party politics to young music fans' by Johnny Black, *Guardian*, 22 April 2015

'Thatcher dismissive of Mandela after first phone chat, files reveal' by Owen Bowcott, *Guardian*, 28 December 2018

'How Mossack Fonseca helped hide millions from Britain's biggest gold bullion robbery' by Simon Bowers, *Guardian*, 4 April 2016

'Interview with Paul Weller' by Steve Clarke, *NME*, 7 May 1987

'How a Married Undercover Cop Having Sex with Activists Killed a Climate Movement' by Geoff Dembicki, *Vice*, 18 January 2022

'They Hate Us, We Hate Them – Resisting Police Corruption and Violence in Hackney in the 1980s and 1990s' by John Eden, *Datacide Magazine*

'Special Demonstration Squad: unit which vanished into undercover world' by Rob Evans, *Guardian*, 24 July 2014

'Met deputy too busy for questions on spy officer's relationship with woman' by Rob Evans, *Guardian*, 16 March 2021

'Party Music' by Simon Frith and John Street, *Marxism Today*, June 1986

'Legacy In The Dust: The Four Aces Story: a film by Winstan Whitter – Interview with the Director' by Bryony Hegarty, *Louder than War*, 13 July 2016

'Rupert Murdoch and the battle of Wapping: 25 years on' by Jon Henley, *Guardian*, 27 July 2011

'Did the Police cause the Fatal Fall? Inquest rejected denial' *Institute of Race Relations*, https://irr.org.uk/app/uploads/2015/11/BWF_News_didpolicecausefatalfall_edited.jpg

'Broadwater Farm: a "criminal estate"? An Interview with Dolly Kiffin', *Race & Class*, Volume 29, Issue 1, 30 June 2016

'Secrets and lies: untangling the UK "spy cops" scandal' by Paul Lewis and Rob Evans, *Guardian*, 28 October 2020

'Selector's Choice' by Dave Hucker, via Pete Murder Tone, *The Beat*, November 2002

'Imagery and Reality in the Broadwater Farm Riot' by Martin Loney, *Critical Social Policy*, Volume 6, Issue 17, 29 June 2016

'I was engaged to an undercover police officer' by Donna McLean, *Guardian*, 29 January 2021

'Wapping dispute 30 years on: How Rupert Murdoch changed labour relations – and newspapers – forever' by Donald Macintyre, *Independent*, 21 January 2016

'When Queen took "Bohemian Rhapsody" to Live Aid' by Wesley Morris, *New York Times*, 11 November 2018

'Did Margaret Thatcher really call Nelson Mandela a terrorist?' by
  Martin Plaut, *New Statesman*, 29 August 2018
'Running the Gauntlet: British Trade Unions under Thatcher, 1979–
  1988' by Brian Towers, *ILR Review*, Jan. 1989, Vol. 42, No. 2, pp.
  163–188, Sage Publications, Inc.
'National archives: Margaret Thatcher wanted to crush power of trade
  unions' by Alan Travis, *Guardian*, 1 August 2013
'Oliver Letwin blocked help for black youth after 1985 riots' by Alan
  Travis, *Guardian*, 30 December 2015
'I was abused by an undercover policeman. But how far up did the
  deceit go?' by Kate Wilson, *Guardian*, 21 September 2018
'Redemption Songs' by Lois Wilson, *MOJO*, issue 150, May 2006

### Documents

'A Crime is a Crime a Crime: A Short report on Police Crime
  in Hackney' pamphlet by the Hackney Community Defence
  Association, November 1991
'A Crime is a Crime a Crime: Graham Smith interviewed by Ken
  Fero', transcript, 2001, http://www.uncarved.org/blog/wp-content/
  uploads/2009/03/colin-roach-a-crime-is-a-crime-is-a-crime.pdf
Cabinet Paper, 16 May 1986, National Archives
'Fighting the Lawmen' pamphlet by the Hackney Community Defence
  Association, 8 October 1992
Local Government, Planning and Land Act 1980
National Archives, note to Prime Minister, 'Civil Disturbance Update',
  19 November 1985, signed 'Hartley Booth', document 851120 No.10
  mnt for MT 19-1783 f63
News Release, London Docklands Development Corporation,
  'Preliminary Work to Start on Canary Wharf'
News Release, London Docklands Development Corporation, Friday 18
  October 1985, 'Corporation Board Committed to Achieving Canary
  Wharf Financial Centre Development'
News Release, London Docklands Development Corporation, 30
  June 1986, 'Vital New Roads for Docklands Get Go-Ahead from
  Corporation Board'
News Release, London Docklands Development Corporation, 3

November 1986, 'West Ferry Circus Planning Application to be sent to Secretary of State'

News Release, London Docklands Development Corporation, 17 July 1987, 'LDDC signs Canary Wharf Master Building Agreement'

News Release, London Docklands Development Corporation, 29 September 1987, 'Social and Community Benefits for Newham Docklands Residents'

'On the Border of a Police State' pamphlet by the Hackney Community Defence Association with the Hackney Trade Union Support Unit, September 1993

'Police Out of School' – Hackney Teachers' Association, 1985

SDS Spycop debrief, Undercover Policing Inquiry

SDS Annual report, 1983, Undercover Policing Inquiry

Special Branch report, 14 March 1986, from the Special Branch Files Project

Special Branch report, 27 March 1986, from the Special Branch Files Project

Special Branch report, 6 May 1986, from the Special Branch Files Project

Special Branch demonstration report, 12 May 1986, from the Special Branch Files Project

Special Branch report, 12 May 1986, from the Special Branch Files Project

Special Branch memorandum, 23 May 1985

Special Branch threat assessment, 27 May 1986

'The Broadwater Farm Disturbances and the Press' – a report by Dorothy Kuya

The Broadwater Farm Inquiry by Lord Gifford (Gifford Report)

### Online resources

Isle of Dogs – Past Life, Past Lives, 'Limehouse Basin. No, Not That One' https://islandhistory.wordpress.com/2018/06/08/limehouse-basin-no-not-that-one/

Ransom Note, https://www.theransomnote.com/art-culture/reviews-art-culture/the-four-aces-club/

Wholepoint Publications, Jerusalem Scene by Scene, https://www.wholepoint.co.uk/the-style-council/jerusalem/

*Fiction*

Ballard, J.G., *High-Rise,* (Jonathan Cape, 1975)

Nath, Michael, *The Treatment*, (Riverrun, 2020)

Peace, David, *GB84,* (Faber & Faber, 2004)

Shreeves-Lee, Jac, *Broadwater,* (Fairlight Books, 2020)

*Film/television/media*

*Babylon* by Franco Rossi (1980)

*Bent Coppers: Crossing the Line of Duty (3-part BBC series)* by Todd
    Austin (2021)

*Jerusalem* by Richard Belfield (1986)

*Juvenile Crime Hackney 1985*, News Report, https://www.youtube.com/
    watch?v=odG6095KjLs

Live Aid broadcast, BBC 1 (13 July 1985)

*Live Aid – Rare Backstage Impressions (13 July 1985)* https://www.
    youtube.com/watch?v=O7ae7crjNSg

*Long Hot Summers: The Story of The Style Council* by Lee Cogswell
    (2020)

*People's Account* (1985) by Milton Bryan, Ceddo Film and Video
    Workshop, with support from Channel 4 and the GLC, but never
    shown on British Television: 'the Independent Broadcasting
    Authority (IBA) objected to the description of the police as racist,
    lawless terrorists, and to the description of the riot as a legitimate
    act of self-defence' https://the-lcva.co.uk/videos/
    59787f52e811330af43ebb2a

*Small Axe (5-part BBC series)* by Steve McQueen (2020)

BBC Interview, Live Aid – The Style Council, BBC 1 (13 July 1985),
    https://www.youtube.com/watch?v=HgJT4pEUHq4

Style Council performance, Clapham Common (July 1986) https://
    www.youtube.com/watch?v=aVsMMyzULG8

The Style Council Internationalists Tour Programme, 1985

The Style Council, *Shout to the Top*, record sleeve, Polydor (1984)

*Uprising (3-part BBC series)* by Steve McQueen (2021)

*Violence During the Wapping Dispute*, 1986, Thames News Archive
    Footage https://www.youtube.com/watch?v=VPLQZjSkcZw

*Yardie* by Idris Elba (2019)

*Notes*

2–3    While Trevor is a fictional character, some of his experiences
       are based on certain details from 'Fighting the Lawmen'
       pamphlet by the Hackney Community Defence Association,
       8 October 1992, a pamphlet that documents testimonies of
       victims of the Stoke Newington and Hackney police, https://
       hackneyhistory.wordpress.com/hcda/fighting-the-lawmen/
12     As above, and 'You can go now but we're going to get you' is a
       quote from 'Fighting the Lawmen' pamphlet by the Hackney
       Community Defence Association, 8 October 1992, https://
       hackneyhistory.wordpress.com/hcda/fighting-the-lawmen/
13     Parker quotes from SDS Annual report, 1983, Undercover
       Policing Inquiry, ucpi.org.uk
12&c   It's twelve noon in London, seven a.m. in Philadelphia, and
       around the world it's time for Live Aid. BBC 1, Live Aid
       broadcast, 13 July 1985
15–17  While Suzi is a fictional character and her interactions with
       real participants in Live Aid fictional, certain dialogue that
       she observes is from video footage 'Live Aid – Rare Backstage
       Impressions (13 July 1985)' at https://www.youtube.com/
       watch?v=O7ae7crjNSg
16     Royal line-up based on 'Live Aid – Rare Backstage
       Impressions (13 July 1985) at https://www.youtube.com/
       watch?v=O7ae7crjNSg
17     It's like punk never happened. From Jones, *The Eighties*, loc.
       296–297
17     Don't be a wanker all your life, have a day off. Jones, *The
       Eighties*, loc. 742–743
25     Information on formation of London Docklands Development
       Group adapted: London Docklands Development Corporation
       (Area and Constitution) Order 1980. Hansard. 1 July 1981 and
       The Isle of Dogs Enterprise Zone Designation Order 1982.
       Legislation.gov.uk
26–9   Style Council performance description based on BBC 1, Live
       Aid broadcast, 13 July 1985

27  Mrs Thatcher quoted from 'The Right to Buy' by Andy Beckett, *Guardian*, 26 August 2015

28  Details from the *Shout to the Top* record sleeve. Photo credit: Brian Ward

28  This shows what can happen when people get together, and this song is dedicated to that spirit. Paul Weller, Style Council, BBC 1, Live Aid broadcast, 13 July 1985

29  They might have cornflakes and milk but no sugar. Then the next morning, there'll be milk and sugar but no cornflakes. Something is missing all the time. Rachel, *Walls*, p. 354

29  People always hold up the Eastern Bloc as examples that socialism doesn't work, but it wasn't socialism, so that argument is redundant. Socialism doesn't mean everyone should have nothing, it means everyone should have something. From the Internationalists Tour Programme.

29  *Walls Come Tumbling Down!* has that unashamed message of optimism. *Unity is powerful.* I thought, "Yes!" When we did the demo Paul said, "It's got to be a balls-out soul tune. I want it to be very on-beat like a Motown thing. When you do the drum fills, think of Keith Moon. Rachel, *Walls*, p. 351

29  Bob Geldof quoted from Jones, *The Eighties*, loc. 2123–2124

39–41  Dialogue from footage 'Live Aid – Rare Backstage Impressions (13 July 1985)' at https://www.youtube.com/watch?v=O7ae7crjNSg

40  Bob Geldof quoted from 'When Queen took "Bohemian Rhapsody" to Live Aid', *New York Times*

43–4  Certain details in Marlon's anecdote based on amateur footage archived on The Radical History of Hackney site https://hackneyhistory.wordpress.com/2011/03/28/sandringham-road-e8-1983/

49  Sting played solo only as his band had demanded to be paid before they went on. Sting told them to fuck off and promptly walked on stage with just a guitar and started with 'Roxanne'. From Jones, *The Eighties*, loc. 2966. The insider Suzi references is Midge Ure, who is quoted in Jones, ibid

50  Paul Weller quote from Jones, *The Eighties*, loc. 892. Suzi's interaction with Paul Weller is fictional

58–9    Certain details from footage 'Live Aid – Rare Backstage
        Impressions (13 July 1985), at https://www.youtube.com/
        watch?v=O7ae7crjNSg

59      Details on the Saudi Arabia arms deal from McSmith, *No
        Such Thing*, p. 3

70      Information on formation and purpose of London Docklands
        Development Corporation from London Docklands
        Development Corporation (Area and Constitution) Order
        1980. Hansard. 1 July 1981 and The Isle of Dogs Enterprise
        Zone Designation Order 1982. Legislation.gov.uk

70      Deputy Chief Executive quote from Brindley, Tim; Rydin,
        Yvonne; Stoker, Gerry (2005). *Remaking Planning: The Politics
        of Urban Change*. Routledge.

73–7    Annajoy David and Paul Weller quotes from Rachel, *Walls*, p.
        393, p. 387, p. 398, p. 346

74      Paul Weller quote: It's not a time to be non-partisan. You
        have to care and if you don't you have your head in the sand
        or don't give a fuck about anyone but yourself. You can't sit
        on the fence. It is very black and white. Thatcher is a tyrant, a
        dictator. Adapted from 'Redemption Songs' by Lois Wilson,
        *MOJO*, issue 150, May 2006

74      Paul Weller quote: I think she should be lined up against a
        wall and shot. Adapted from interview with Steve Clarke,
        *NME*, 7 May 1987

82      Quotes from and based on footage in 'Juvenile
        Crime in Hackney 1985' https://www.youtube.com/
        watch?v=odG6095KjLs. LONDON PLUS Programme
        number: D:LCAR519P Date: 09/05/1985

82      In part, the examples of police malpractice are based on
        'Fighting the Lawmen' pamphlet by the Hackney Community
        Defence Association, 8 October 1992, https://hackneyhistory.
        wordpress.com/hcda/fighting-the-lawmen/

97      *NME* advert for The Style Council, 5 October 1985, cited in
        Munn, *Mr Cool's Dream*, section 'October 1985'

101     Quotes from speech to the Conservative Party Conference, 11
        October 1985, margaretthatcher.org

105–6   Dolly Kiffin references from Moore, *The Killing*, loc. 729–736

105–6    Quotes the Gifford Report, op. cit. 8, para. 2.30, via Moore, *The Killing*, loc. 639

111–2    Quotes *High-Rise* by J.G. Ballard

118–9    The scenario here is fictional, though certain details regarding Wapping recruitment are based on Lang & Dodkins, *Bad News*, loc. 393

118–9    While *The London Herald* is a fictional newspaper, certain details here are inspired by *The London Post* from Lang & Dodkins, *Bad News*, loc. 32

138    If this dog do you bite, soon as out of your bed, take a hair of the tail the next day, from Brewer, the *Dictionary of Phrase and Fable* (1898)

144    Certain details from Floyd Jarrett's arrest based on Moore, *The Killing*, loc. 2044–2060, and The Broadwater Farm Inquiry by Lord Gifford (Gifford Report), Chapter 4, 'The Death of Mrs Jarrett'

149    Details and quotes regarding Brink's-Mat robbery, Gillard, *Legacy*, loc. 229–235

150    East London Logistics is a fictional company, though is in part inspired by details and quotes regarding Thomas Nationwide Transport from Lang & Dodkins, *Bad News*, loc. 331–339

154    Eel and Pie shop reference from Sinclair, *Lights Out for the Territory*, Chapter Two, 'Albion Drive E8. To Abney Park Stoke Newington', via https://archive.nytimes.com/www.nytimes.com/books/first/s/sinclair-territory.html

156    Newsagent cards quote from Sinclair, *Lights Out for the Territory*, Chapter Two, 'Albion Drive E8. To Abney Park Stoke Newington', via https://archive.nytimes.com/www.nytimes.com/books/first/s/sinclair-territory.html

165–6    Details and quotes from Moore, *The Killing*, loc. 2060–2081 and The Broadwater Farm Inquiry by Lord Gifford (Gifford Report), Chapter 4, 'The Death of Mrs Jarrett'

171    Jon's documents here are fictional, though are based on Gillard, *Legacy*, loc. 923–943, as follows:

The Thatcher government was already lubricating public and private partnerships to invest in a new business airport and a railway system connecting the City to a new financial district – Canary Wharf.

These infrastructure projects were some years off completion, but there were any number of old pubs, clubs and shop fronts that could be picked up cheaply to launder criminal activity and service the sexual urges of, initially, traditional East Enders, the growing immigrant community from the Asian subcontinent, and later, young professionals.

This report concerns a group of people operating in the East End of London, particularly in the area of Plaistow and Canning Town, whose influence on crime in London and the Home Counties has grown steadily over a period of eight to ten years. In proportion to this growth has been the development of fear that they engender in the local population until a point has now been reached where the indigenous population would rather tolerate the outrageous behaviour of these people than become involved as witnesses.

172    The Style Council would like to train the youth – in the art of revolution And please no more talk of the 'but what can I do about it' variety. Track the last track and clear away any confusion – Unity Is Powerful!! From sleeve notes to *Our Favourite Shop* by The Style Council.

173    Details and quotes from Moore, *The Killing*, loc. 2179–2187 and The Broadwater Farm Inquiry by Lord Gifford (Gifford Report), Chapter 4, 'The Death of Mrs Jarrett'

175–6    Ibid.

179    The senior officer's report here is fictional, though the details in it that my character, Thatcher, peruses, are from the National Archives, note to Prime Minister, 'Civil Disturbance Update', 19 November 1985, signed 'Hartley Booth', document 851120 No.10 mnt for MT 19-1783 f63

180    Douglas Hurd quotes from 'Oliver Letwin blocked help for black youth after 1985 riots', Alan Travis, *Guardian*, 30 December 2015

184–5    While Suzi's attendance at the meeting here is fictional and her interactions with real characters also fictional, details and quotes are from Moore, *The Killing*, loc. 2196–2223, and The

Broadwater Farm Inquiry by Lord Gifford (Gifford Report), Chapter 5, 'October 6 – What happened?'

187 Suzi's reading of the plan to deal with disorder is fictional; the plan itself is from Moore, *The Killing*, loc. 2196–2223

187–90 Parker's experience at this gathering is fictional, though details and quotes are from Moore, *The Killing*, loc. 2230, and on The Broadwater Farm Inquiry by Lord Gifford (Gifford Report), Chapter 5, 'October 6 – What happened?'

192 *Socialist Worker* article details based on Lang & Dodkins, *Bad News*, loc. 386–393

194 As noted above, *The London Herald* is a fictional newspaper, though certain details are inspired by *The London Post* union negotiations, including Geraint's redacted list of conditions, from Lang & Dodkins, *Bad News*, loc. 393–409

195–7 As above, while Suzi's attendance at the meeting here is fictional and her interactions with real characters also fictional, details and quotes are from Moore, *The Killing*, loc. 2256–2263 and The Broadwater Farm Inquiry by Lord Gifford (Gifford Report), Chapter 5, 'October 6 – What happened?' and include lists of those present and resolutions made. Suzi's perceptions of the meeting are fictional, though rooted in readings of these sources.

197 Bernie Grant's statement, while speaking to Suzi in a fictional context, is adapted from Moore, *The Killing*, p. 123

201–8 While his involvement is entirely fictional, the depiction of Parker's experience and perception of the Broadwater Farm riot is based in part on *The Killing*, pp. 130–147, and on The Broadwater Farm Inquiry by Lord Gifford (Gifford Report), Chapter 5, 'October 6 – What happened?'

 Specific details that Parker hears and sees, including dialogue, insults, slurs, graffiti and operational activities are quoted from these sources; the sensory experience of the riot is, in part, imagined, and in part based on these sources and other media outlets reporting on the disorder. There are some contradictions and disagreements between these two sources, though both are thorough, it feels to me, and both attempt a full and balanced examination of what happened, outside any potential bias. This appraisal of the sources is my own.

213 The draft memo Mrs Thatcher reads quotes from Oliver Letwin and Hartley Booth's confidential joint paper, National Archives, and via *'Oliver Letwin blocked help for black youth after 1985 riots'*, Alan Travis, *Guardian*, 30 December 2015

219 Ferdinand Mount quote from National Archives via, 'Margaret Thatcher wanted to crush power of trade unions', Alan Travis, *Guardian*, 1 August 2013

220 From Cabinet Paper, 16 May 1986, National Archives

228 Paul Weller quoted from Rachel, *Walls*, p. 472 & p. 473

229-30 Suzi's involvement in the Red Wedge launch is fictional; her thoughts on it – and Sade's quote, plus the line 'The system promises young people paradise but gives them hell' is in part based on Rachel, *Walls*, p. 407

234-5 Statistics that Carolyn cites are from The Broadwater Farm Inquiry by Lord Gifford (Gifford Report), Chapter 6, 'The Aftermath', p. 130

235 Discussion of Police and Criminal Evidence Act 1984, ibid., pp. 131-2

235 Detention and arrest information based on certain details from The Broadwater Farm Inquiry by Lord Gifford (Gifford Report), Chapter 6, 'The Aftermath'

236 '... the Commissioner of Police for the Metropolitan Area has used legislation from 1839 to impose restrictions on pedestrian and vehicular movement in Tower Hamlets', adapted from Lang & Dodkins, *Bad News*, loc. 1053

237-8 Parker's observations and details on the strikes/protests of 3 May 1986 based on Special Branch report, 6 May 1986, from the Special Branch Files Project, http://specialbranchfiles.uk/wapping-strike-all-files/

238-9 Parker's observations and details on the strikes/protests of 10 May 1986 based on Special Branch report, 12 May 1986, from the Special Branch Files Project, http://specialbranchfiles.uk/wapping-strike-all-files/

241 'Secret talks' details from Lang & Dodkins, *Bad News*, loc.

1722 and Special Branch threat assessment, 27 May 1986, http://
specialbranchfiles.uk/wapping-strike-all-files/

241    Special Branch decision to reduce presence to Wednesdays
and Saturdays only from Special Branch memorandum, 23
May 1985, http://specialbranchfiles.uk/wapping-strike-all-files/

241    Although the council flat to which Noble refers is fictional,
it is in part inspired by a reference in Special Branch report,
14 March 1986, from the Special Branch Files Project, Special
Branch report, 27 March 1986, from the Special Branch
Files Project and Special Branch demonstration report,
12 May 1986, from the Special Branch Files Project http://
specialbranchfiles.uk/wapping-strike-all-files/

242    Details of the Deptford warehouse fire from Lang & Dodkins,
*Bad News*, loc. 1753

243    '21 July' from News Release, London Docklands Development
Corporation, 'Preliminary Work to Start on Canary Wharf'

244    Details on Billy Chang's criminal career from https://
en.wikipedia.org/wiki/Brilliant_Chang

245    List of jobs beginning 'Diversion of service . . .' adapted from
News Release, London Docklands Development Corporation,
'Preliminary Work to Start on Canary Wharf'

245    Ron Bishop is a fictional character who shares certain
biographical details with Reg Ward, adapted from obituary,
*Estates Gazette*, 10 January 2011, and quote on Bishop/Ward's
achievement from obituary, *Daily Telegraph*, 12 January 2011

246–7  Quotes from News Release, London Docklands Development
Corporation, Friday 18 October 1985, 'Corporation Board
Committed to Achieving Canary Wharf Financial Centre
Development'

247    'The Broadwater Farm Disturbances and the Press' – a
report by Dorothy Kuya, via berniegrantarchive.org, http://
berniegrantarchive.org.uk/wp-content/uploads/2014/06/
Dorothy-Kuya-BWF-Riots-and-Media-Report.pdf

248    When the newspapers interviewed me the next day, they
wanted me to say it was Black against White. When I said
it wasn't, they didn't really want to know anything. It didn't

make headlines, from Lord Gifford (Gifford Report), Chapter 6, 'The Aftermath', p. 125

248     Cliff Ford reference, detail and quote, ibid.

248     Suzi's reflection on the *Times* headline, 'The Estate that Dolly Kiffin Rescued from Nightmare', based on, ibid.

249–51  Suzi's interaction with Dorothy Kuya is fictional; Dorothy Kuya's words and Suzi's notes quote 'The Broadwater Farm Disturbances and the Press' – a report by Dorothy Kuya, via berniegrantarchive.org, http://berniegrantarchive.org.uk/wp-content/uploads/2014/06/Dorothy-Kuya-BWF-Riots-and-Media-Report.pdf

258–61  Trevor's interactions with Rennie Kingsley are fictional; Rennie Kingsley's words quote 'Fighting the Lawmen' pamphlet by the Hackney Community Defence Association, 8 October 1992, https://hackneyhistory.wordpress.com/hcda/fighting-the-lawmen/

259–60  The flyer Trevor examines is part of 'Fighting the Lawmen' pamphlet by the Hackney Community Defence Association, 8 October 1992, https://hackneyhistory.wordpress.com/hcda/fighting-the-lawmen/

264     Trevor's interactions with Hugh Prince are fictional; Hugh Prince's words quote 'Fighting the Lawmen' pamphlet by the Hackney Community Defence Association, 8 October 1992, https://hackneyhistory.wordpress.com/hcda/fighting-the-lawmen/

265–7  Regal Records on Lower Clapton Road was the HQ of Unity Sounds. Trevor's interactions with Robert Fearon are fictional. Robert Fearon's words, in his fictional phone conversation, are from *Jahtari* Magazine, as part of the article 'Selector's Choice' that appeared in *The Beat* magazine, November 2002, https://jahtari.org/archive/magazine/reggae/unity.htm

      A Unity compilation – 'Watch how the People Dancing' – which features Kenny Knots' *Watch how the People Dancing* and 'Pick a Sound' by Selah Collins is available on the Honest Jon's record label.

269–70  Trevor's interactions with Ida Oderinde are fictional; Ida Oderinde's words quote 'Fighting the Lawmen' pamphlet by the Hackney Community Defence Association, 8 October 1992, https://hackneyhistory.wordpress.com/hcda/fighting-the-lawmen/

270    Details on the Four Aces club from Winstan Whitter, director of Legacy In The Dust: The Four Aces Story, via https://www.theransomnote.com/art-culture/reviews-art-culture/the-four-aces-club/

280    Although these 'walkabouts' are fictional, they are in part inspired by Lang & Dodkins, *Bad News*, loc.2075

283    Press release and details of compulsory acquisition based on and quotes News Release, London Docklands Development Corporation, 30 June 1986, 'Vital New Roads for Docklands Get Go-Ahead from Corporation Board'

286–70    Details on compulsory and voluntary registration in the Land Registry from Local Government, Planning and Land Act 1980, https://www.legislation.gov.uk/ukpga/1980/65/contents and specifically from Section 142, https://www.legislation.gov.uk/ukpga/1980/65/section/142

290    Junior Giscombe reference from Rachel, *Walls*, p. 370

306–7    While Suzi's interactions with the band and Paul Weller are fictional, details from The Style Council performance, Clapham Common, https://www.youtube.com/watch?v=aVsMMyzULG8

309    'After the official coroner's inquest into Colin Roach's death delivered an 8–2 verdict of suicide, the family decided to pursue their own independent investigation into Colin's death and Hackney policing more generally' which became: Independent Committee of Inquiry, *Policing in Hackney 1945–1984*, (Karia Press, 1989)

310    Parker's interaction with Paul Weller is fictional.

314    Keith's involvement with 'Homebreakers' by The Style Council is fictional. Speculation about Mick Talbot's old man's work is based on *Long Hot Summers: The Story of The Style Council* by Lee Cogswell (2020)

314    Parker and Carolyn's interactions with Sade and Sting are fictional.

315–6    Thatcher on the European Council Meeting in The Hague quotes *The diplomacy of international relations: selected writings* by Johan Kaufmann, Kluwer Law International, p. 63, including identifying and quoting Geoffrey Howe as 'the British Foreign Minister'

316     Mitterrand quote from *The Times*, ibid.

316     'the unions have a noose round the neck of the industry, and they've pulled it very tight' from 'Rupert Murdoch and the battle of Wapping: 25 years on', by Jon Henley, *Guardian*, 27 July 2011

323     Excalibur and Compliance are fictional companies and their interest and investment in the Docklands area also fictional. Suggestions of real-life anonymous money invested in Docklands, and its provenance, in 'How Mossack Fonseca helped hide millions from Britain's biggest gold bullion robbery' by Simon Bowers, *Guardian*, 4 April 2016

335–7   Suzi's involvement in the gathering and typing up of data, etc. for the Gifford Report is fictional. In her typing up, she quotes from (in order), The Broadwater Farm Inquiry by Lord Gifford (Gifford Report), Chapter 6, 'The Aftermath', p. 134, p. 139, p. 140, p. 148, p. 150

338–9   Certain details from fictional 'walkabouts' inspired in part by those documented in Lang & Dodkins, *Bad News*, from loc.2075

347–50  Quotes Speech to Conservative Party Conference, 10 October 1986, https://www.margaretthatcher.org/document/106498

353–5   Although Suzi's observation of the filming is fictional, she records details of 'Jerusalem' directed by Richard Belfield (1986) and starring The Style Council. Further information regarding the shoot – as well as frame-by-frame analysis – here, https://www.wholepoint.co.uk/the-style-council/jerusalem/

353–5   Jon reads, and quotes from, The Limehouse Petition, published by The Limehouse Development Group, ed. Nick Wates, June 1986, via, http://www.nickwates.com/wp-content/uploads/2018/07/Limehouse-Petition-singles-Lo.pdf

365     Following the death of Colin Roach in the foyer of Stoke Newington police station on 12 January 1983, the Roach

Family Support Committee commissioned an independent report "Policing in Hackney 1945–1984." 'Fighting the Lawmen' pamphlet by the Hackney Community Defence Association, 8 October 1992, https://hackneyhistory.wordpress.com/hcda/fighting-the-lawmen/

365    Although Carolyn's involvement is fictional, she references and quotes details, including from Stuart Hall's Foreword, and from the front and inside cover, from the publication *Independent Committee of Inquiry, Policing in Hackney 1945–1984*, (Karia Press, 1989), from 'Policing in Hackney 1945–1984' https://hackneyhistory.wordpress.com/2011/03/12/policing-in-hackney-1945-1984/

401    Noble refers to a tragic incident that occurred on 24 January 1987. A young man, Michael Delaney, was killed by a lorry in Wapping. He was not part of the picket or protesting but celebrating his nineteenth birthday with friends. Lang & Dodkins, *Bad News*, loc. 2394

401    Douglas Hurd reference, Lang & Dodkins, *Bad News*, loc. 2552

403    Annajoy David and Margaret Thatcher meeting and exchange refers to and quotes from Rachel, *Walls*, p. 499

404    Parker reads from 'Fighting the Lawmen' pamphlet by the Hackney Community Defence Association, 8 October 1992, https://hackneyhistory.wordpress.com/hcda/fighting-the-lawmen/

*With thanks to*

Will Francis, and all at Janklow and Nesbit; Paul Engles, Katharina Bielenberg, Corinna Zifko, and all at Arcadia and Quercus; Angeline Rothermundt; Ross Dickinson; Lucy Caldwell; Martha Lecauchois, Lucian Thomas-Lecauchois, and Louise Thomas-Lecauchois